Copyright © 2019 by Nick Bruel

Published by Roaring Brook Press

Roaring Brook Press is a division of Holtzbrinck Publishing Holdings Limited Partnership

120 Broadway, New York, NY 10271

mackids.com

All rights reserved

Library of Congress Control Number: 2019941008

Our books may be purchased in bulk for promotional, educational, or business use. Please contact your local bookseller or the Macmillan Corporate and Premium Sales Department at (800) 221-7945 ext. 5442 or by email at MacmillanSpecialMarkets@macmillan.com.

First edition, 2019

Book design by Cassie Gonzales

Printed in the United States of America by LSC Communications, Harrisonburg, Virginia

1 3 5 7 9 10 8 6 4 2

BAD KITTY

Joins the Team

NICK BRUEL

ROARING BROOK PRESS
NEW YORK

• CONTENTS •

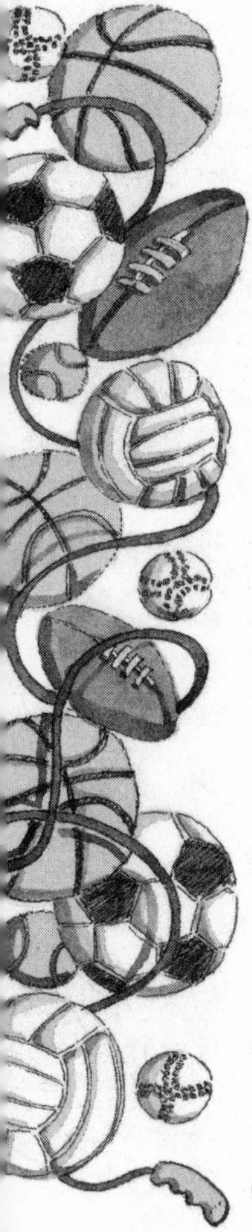

•CHAPTER ONE•

SUCH A CALM, QUIET MORNING

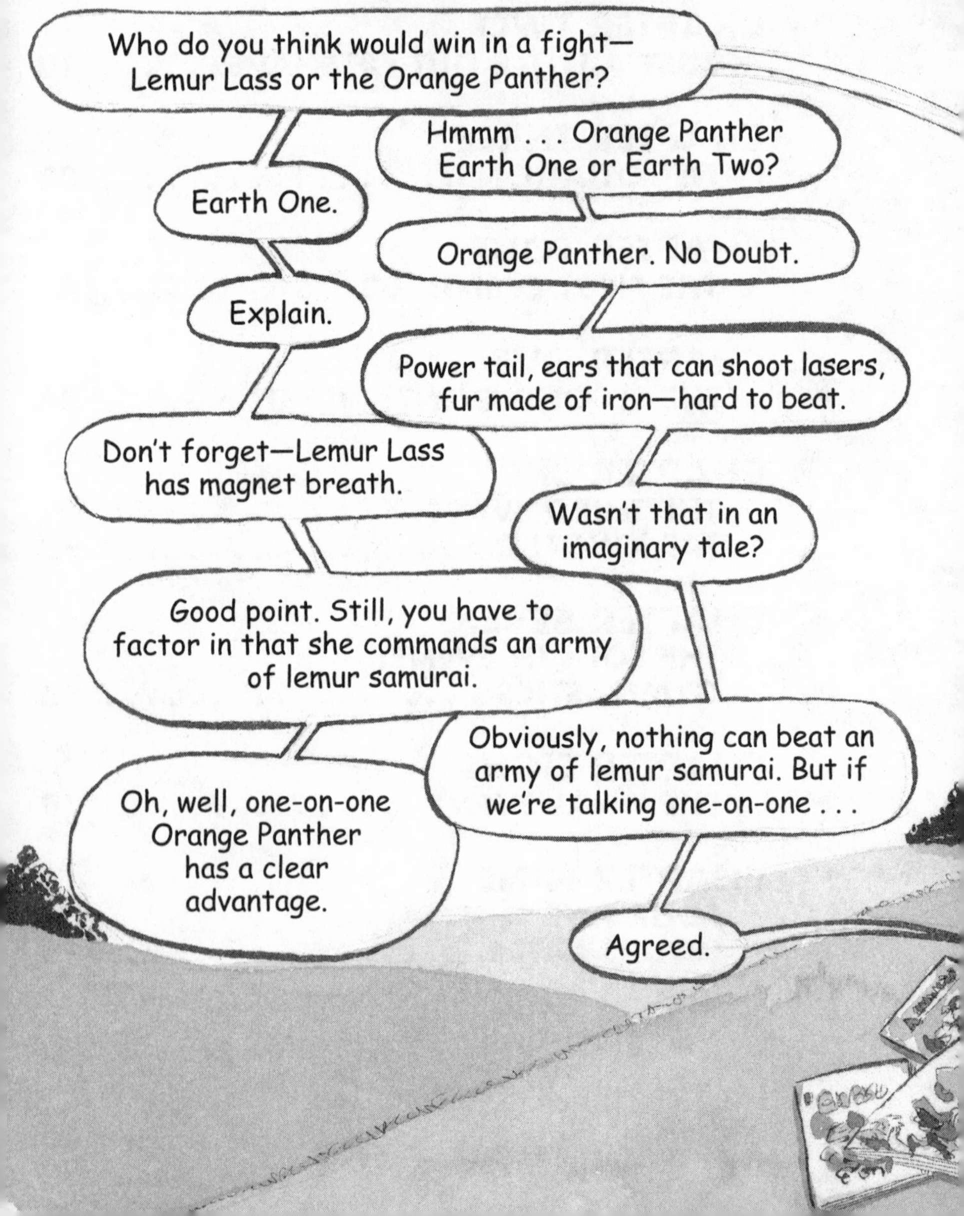
Who do you think would win in a fight—Lemur Lass or the Orange Panther?
Hmmm . . . Orange Panther Earth One or Earth Two?
Earth One.
Orange Panther. No Doubt.
Explain.
Power tail, ears that can shoot lasers, fur made of iron—hard to beat.
Don't forget—Lemur Lass has magnet breath.
Wasn't that in an imaginary tale?
Good point. Still, you have to factor in that she commands an army of lemur samurai.
Obviously, nothing can beat an army of lemur samurai. But if we're talking one-on-one . . .
Oh, well, one-on-one Orange Panther has a clear advantage.
Agreed.

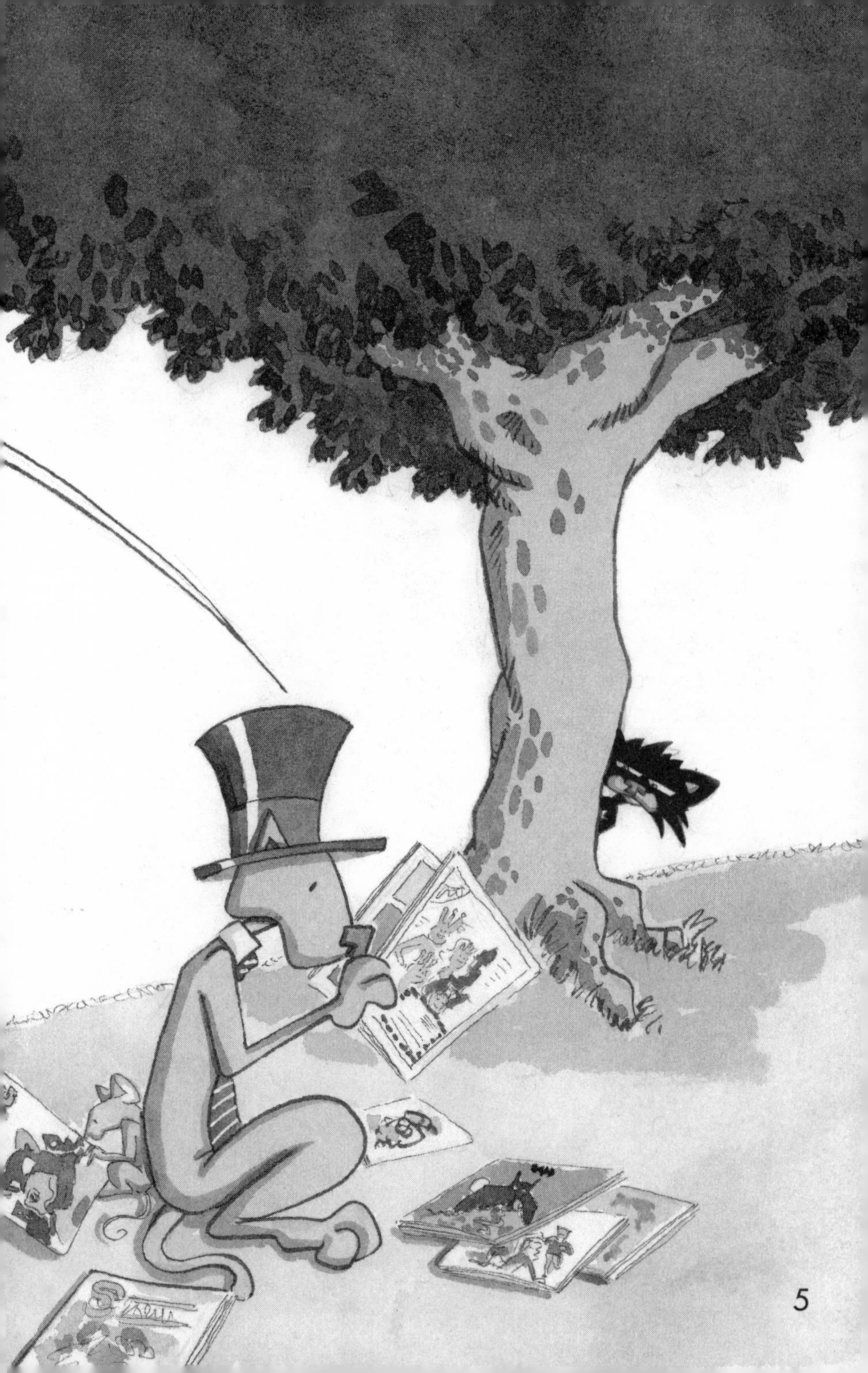

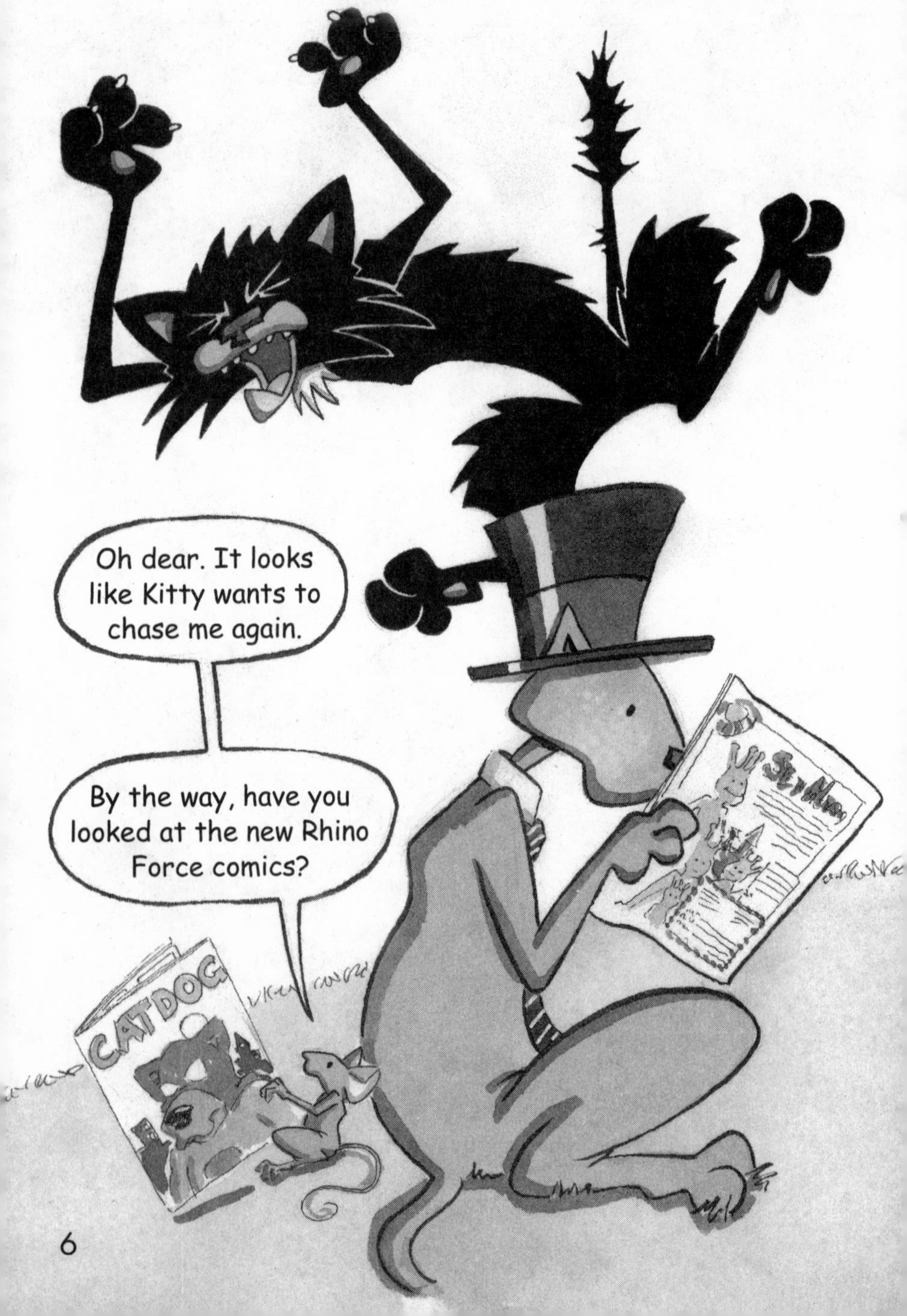
Oh dear. It looks like Kitty wants to chase me again.
By the way, have you looked at the new Rhino Force comics?
CATDOG

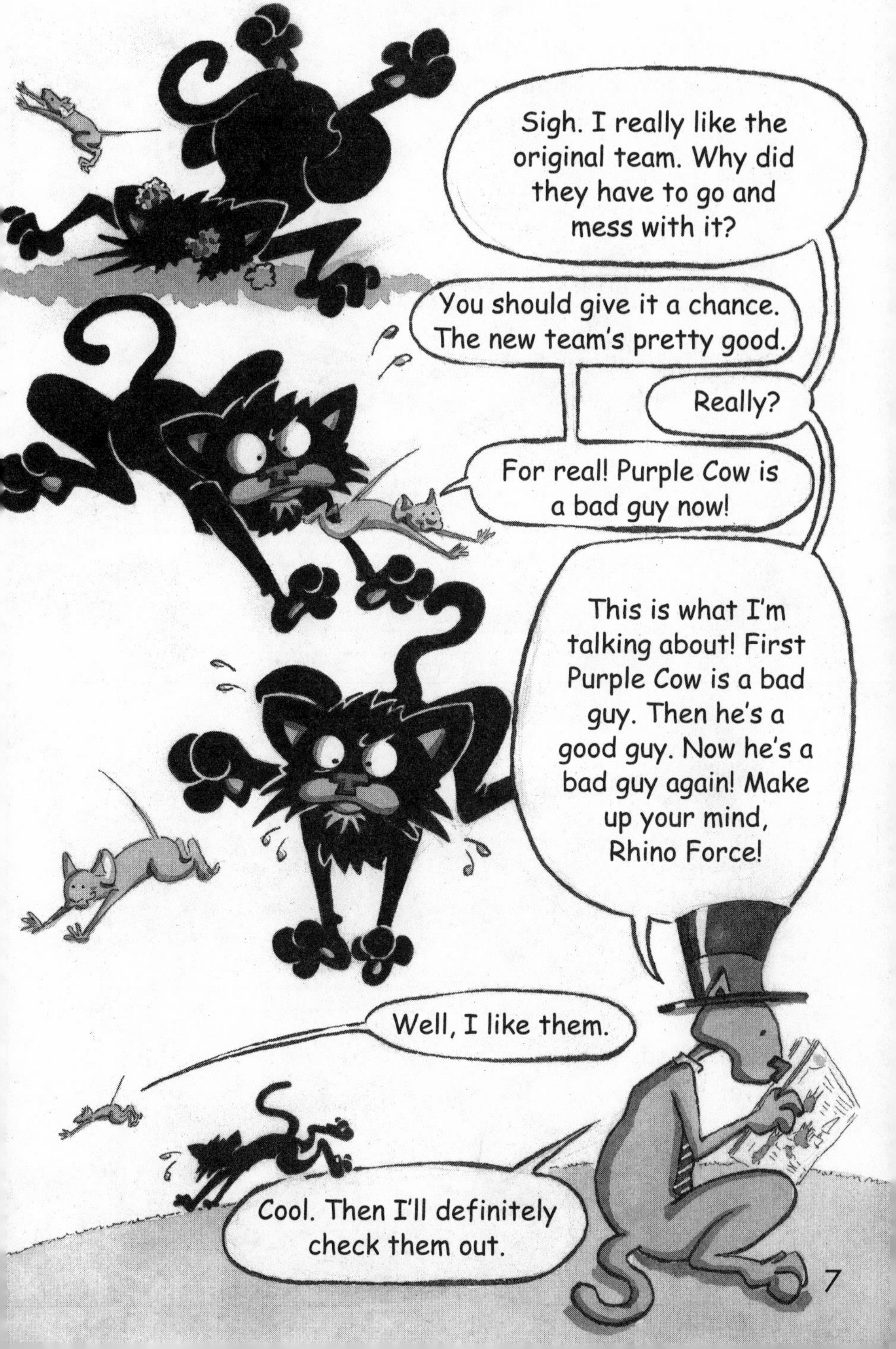
Sigh. I really like the original team. Why did they have to go and mess with it?
You should give it a chance. The new team's pretty good.
Really?
For real! Purple Cow is a bad guy now!
This is what I'm talking about! First Purple Cow is a bad guy. Then he's a good guy. Now he's a bad guy again! Make up your mind, Rhino Force!
Well, I like them.
Cool. Then I'll definitely check them out.

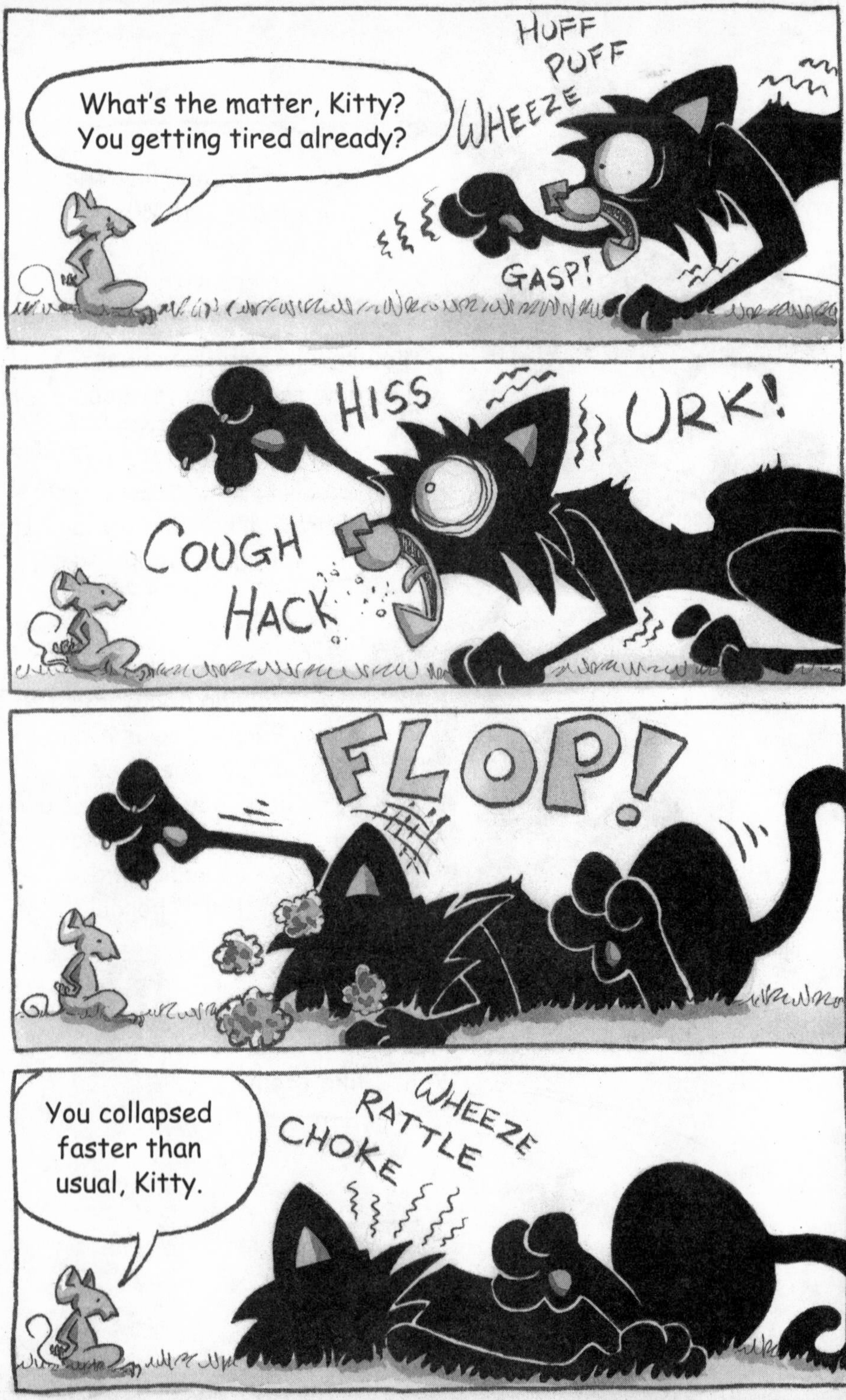
What's the matter, Kitty? You getting tired already?
HUFF
PUFF
WHEEZE
GASP!
HISS
URK!
COUGH
HACK
FLOP!
You collapsed faster than usual, Kitty.
WHEEZE
RATTLE
CHOKE

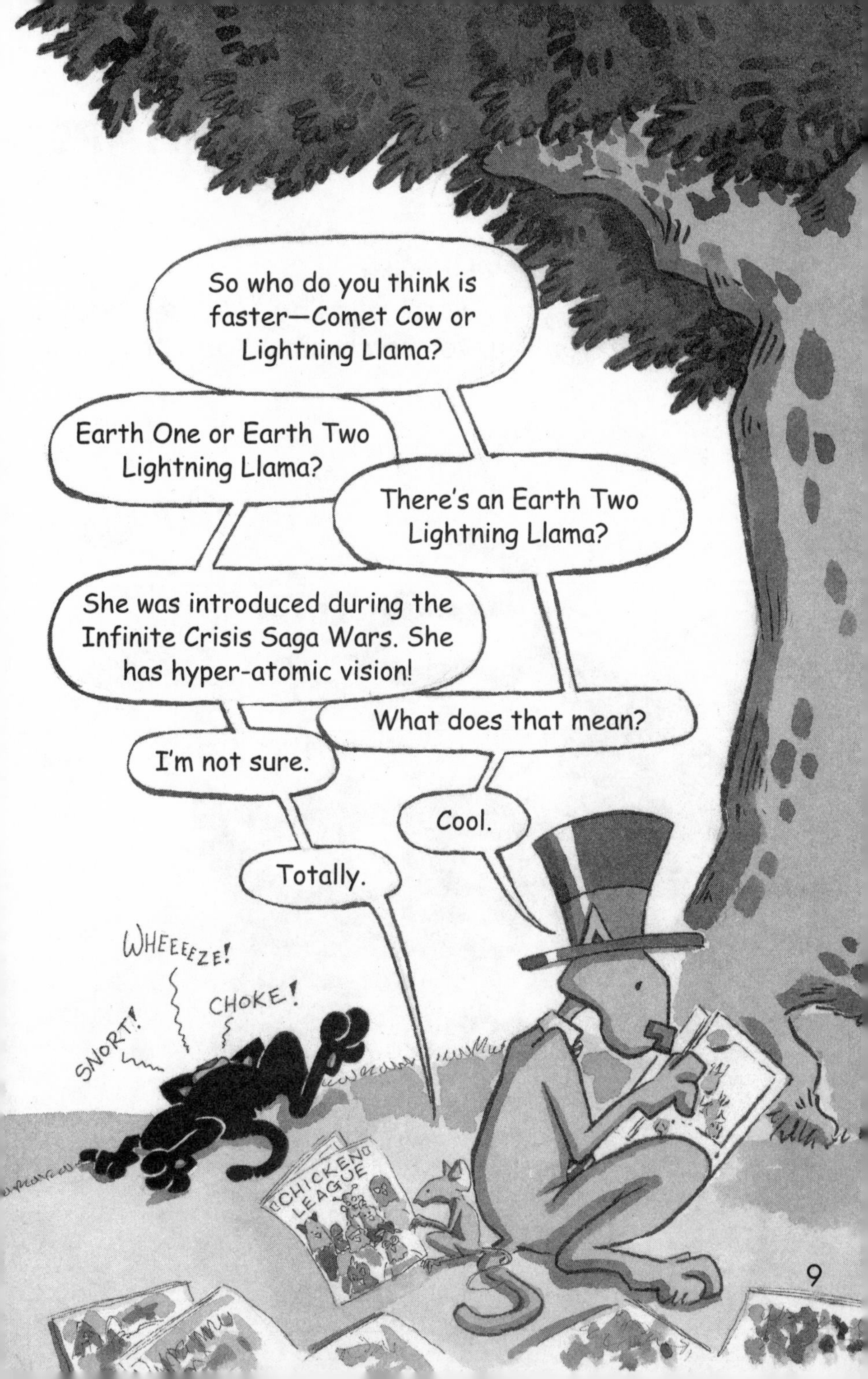
So who do you think is faster—Comet Cow or Lightning Llama?
Earth One or Earth Two Lightning Llama?
There's an Earth Two Lightning Llama?
She was introduced during the Infinite Crisis Saga Wars. She has hyper-atomic vision!
What does that mean?
I'm not sure.
Cool.
Totally.
WHEEEEZE!
CHOKE!
SNORT!
CHICKEN LEAGUE

•CHAPTER TWO•

JUST A LITTLE OUT OF SHAPE

Hi, Kitty.

Let me guess—you were chasing Mouse again, weren't you? You'll never catch him. You know that, don't you?

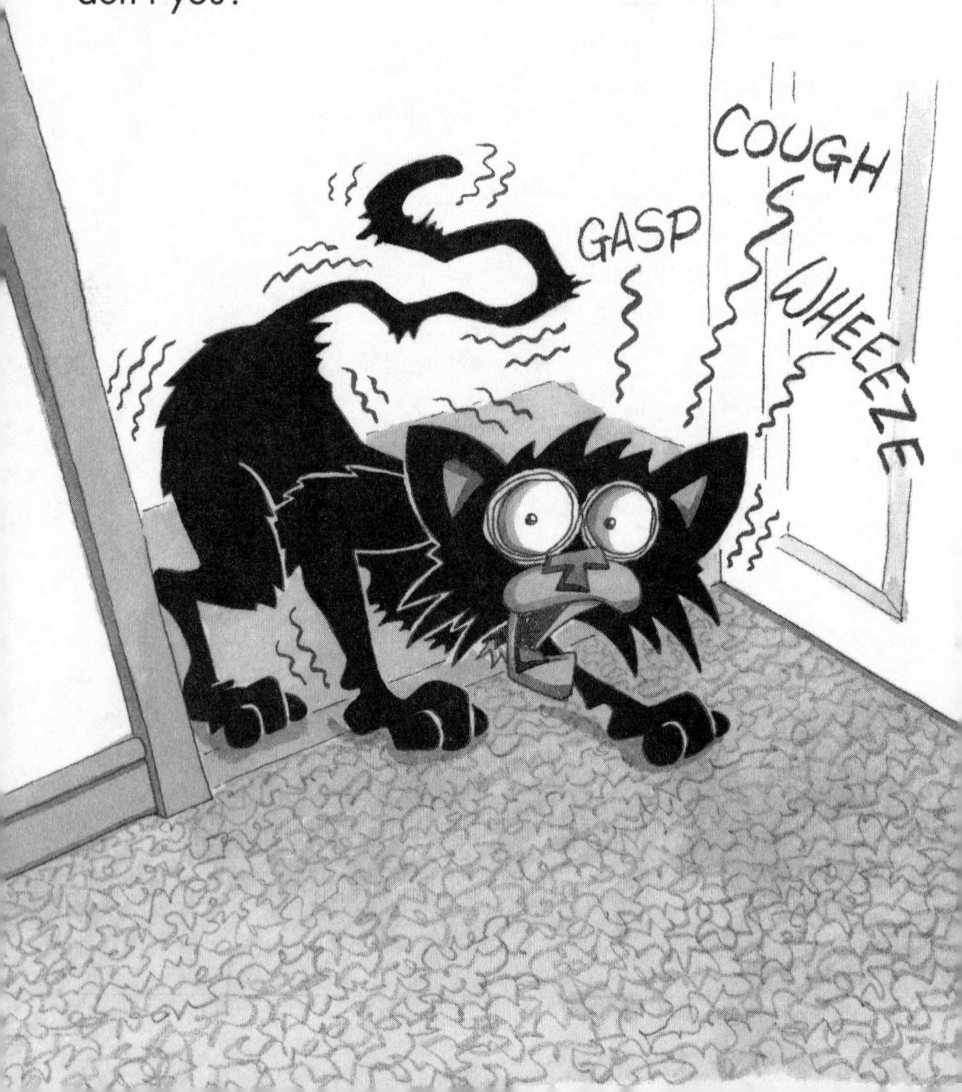
COUGH
GASP
WHEEEZE

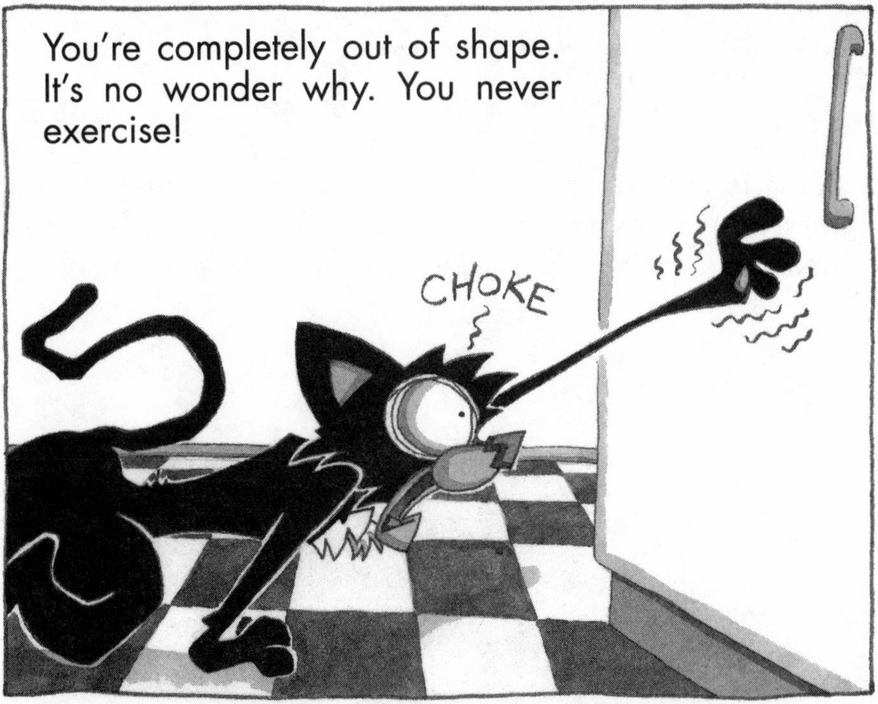
You're completely out of shape. It's no wonder why. You never exercise!
CHOKE

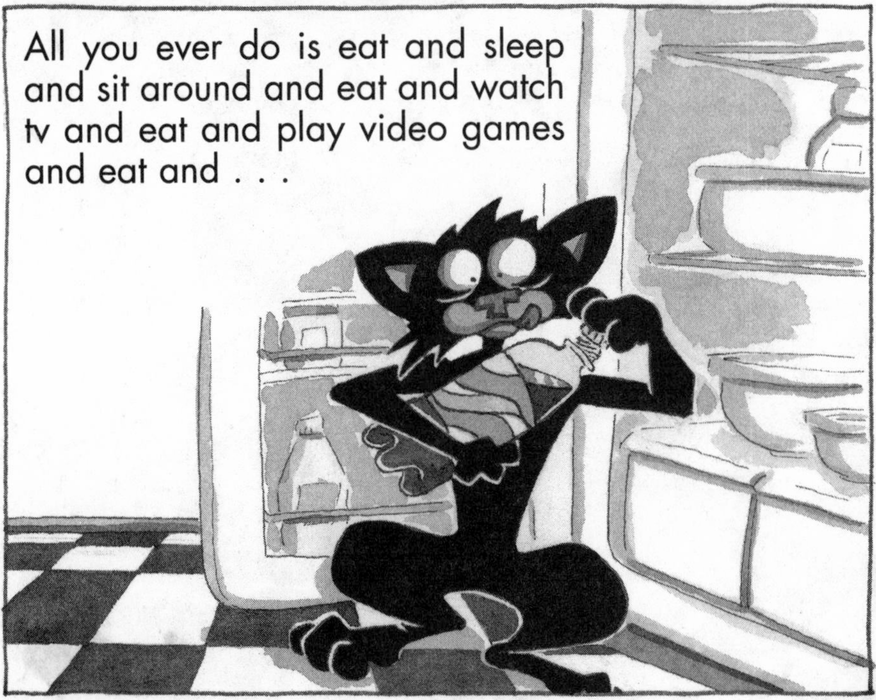
All you ever do is eat and sleep and sit around and eat and watch tv and eat and play video games and eat and . . .

KITTY!

Soda is the worst thing for you to drink when you're thirsty! You're dehydrated. Do you know what that means? It means that your body needs WATER.

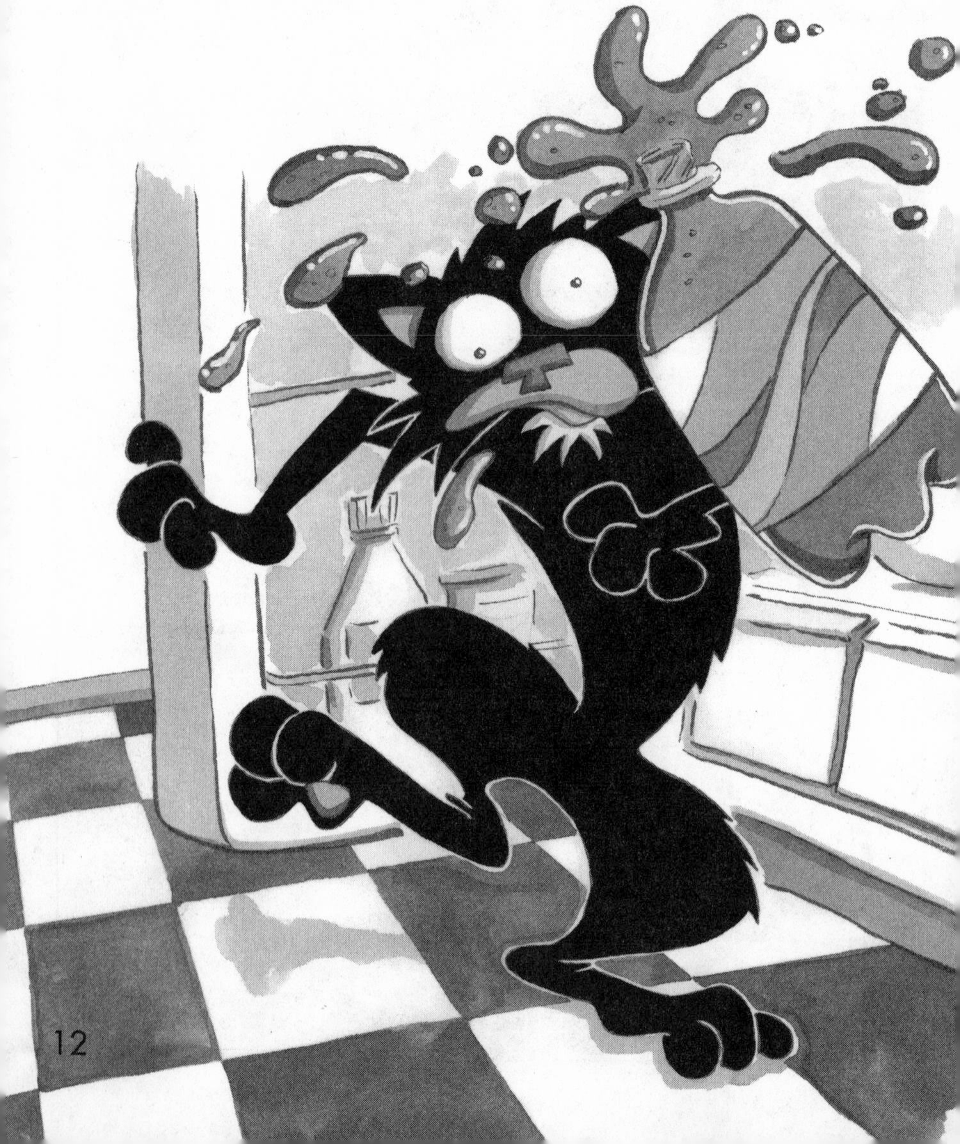

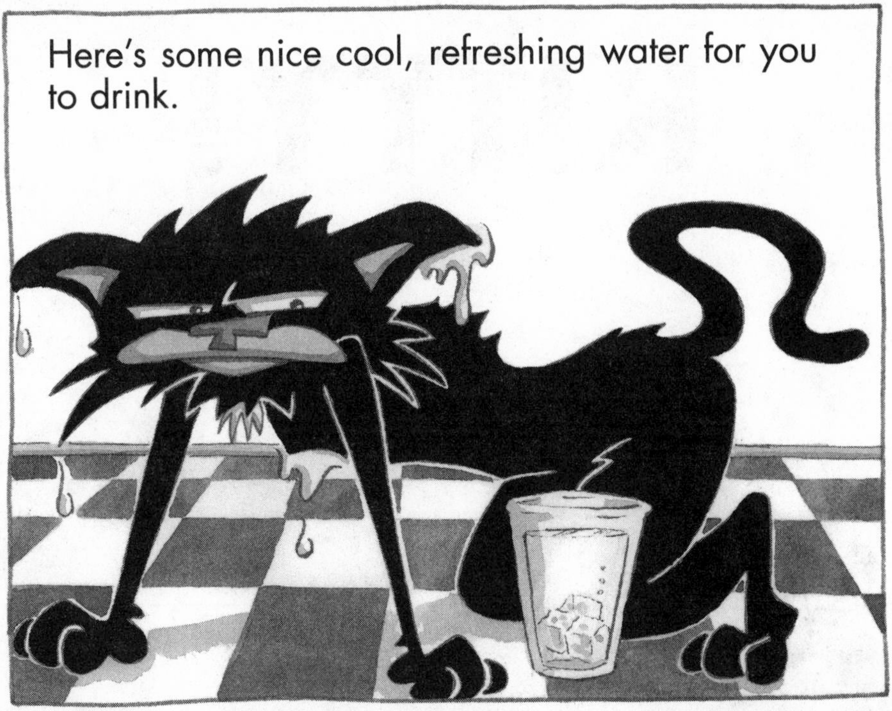
Here's some nice cool, refreshing water for you to drink.

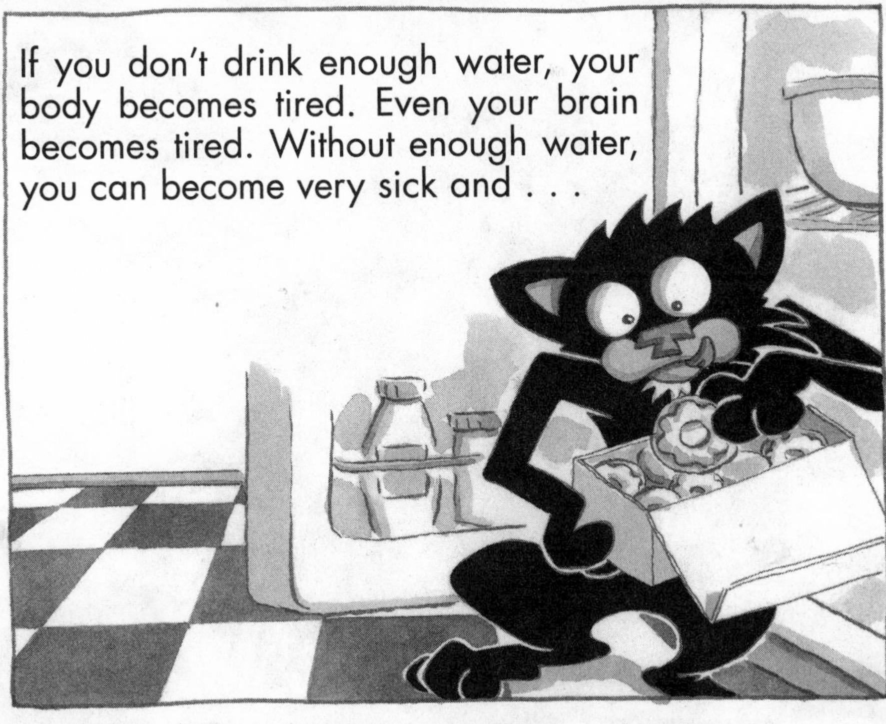
If you don't drink enough water, your body becomes tired. Even your brain becomes tired. Without enough water, you can become very sick and . . .

KITTY!

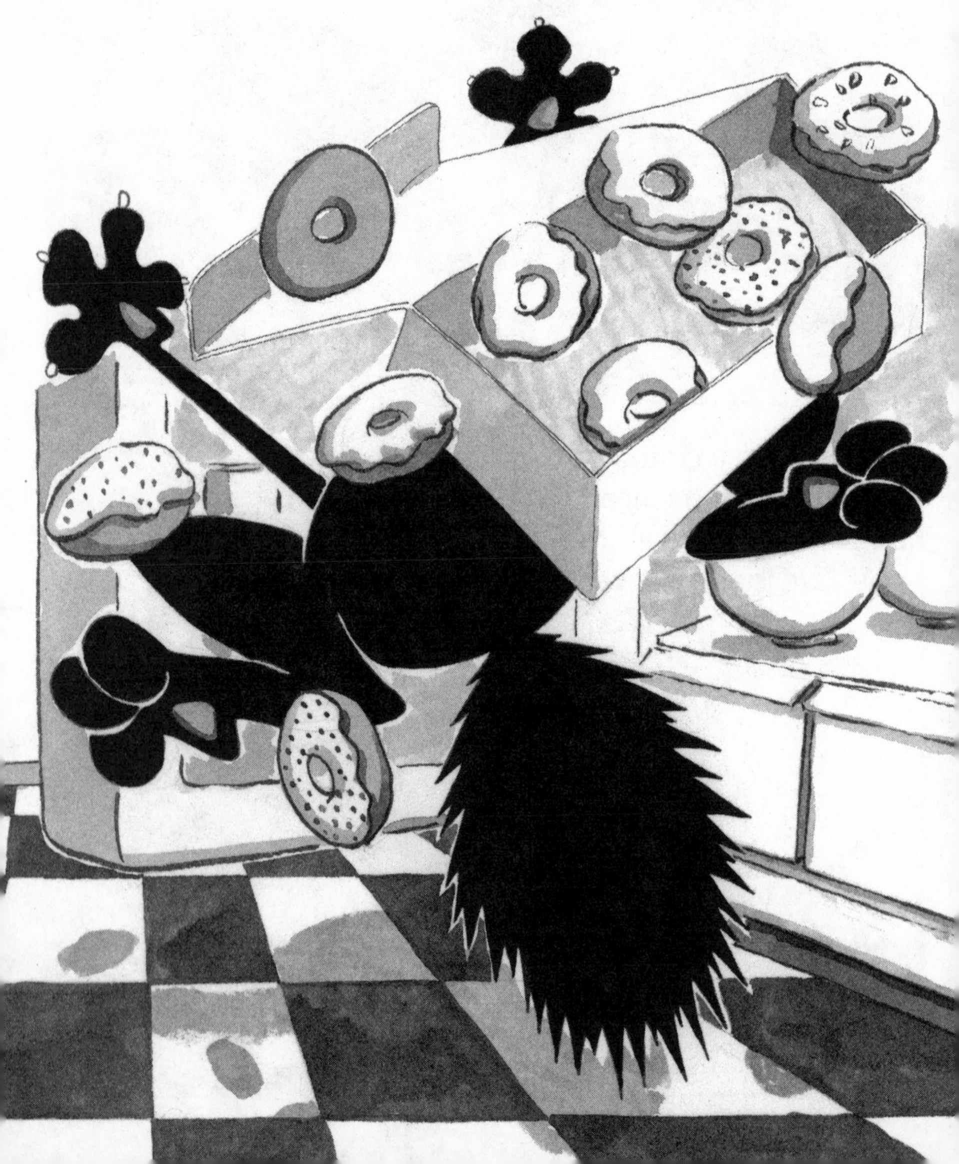

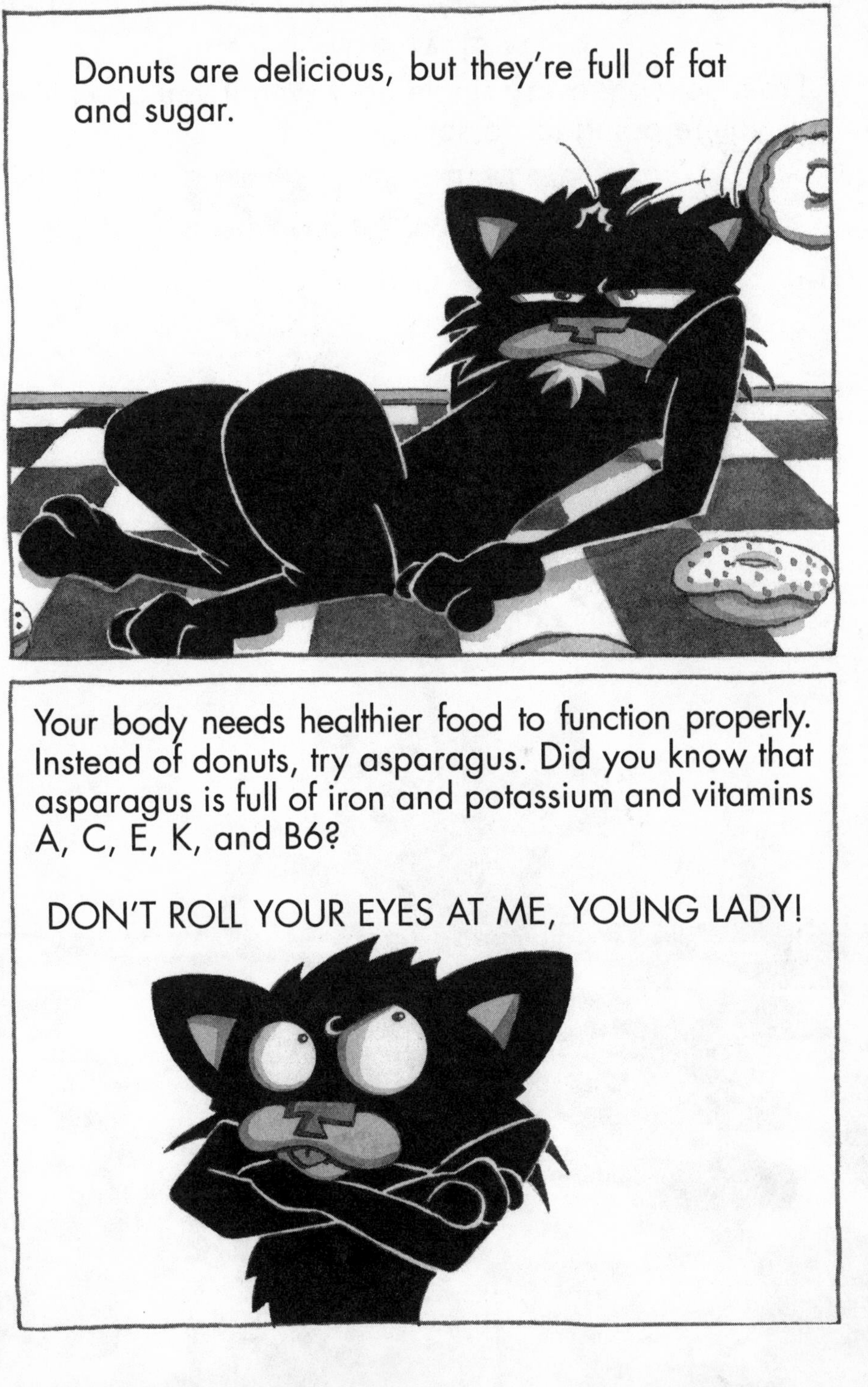
Donuts are delicious, but they're full of fat and sugar.
Your body needs healthier food to function properly. Instead of donuts, try asparagus. Did you know that asparagus is full of iron and potassium and vitamins A, C, E, K, and B6?
DON'T ROLL YOUR EYES AT ME, YOUNG LADY!

THAT'S IT!
From now on, every single day, even if you don't like it, you're going to do some . . .

EXERCISE!

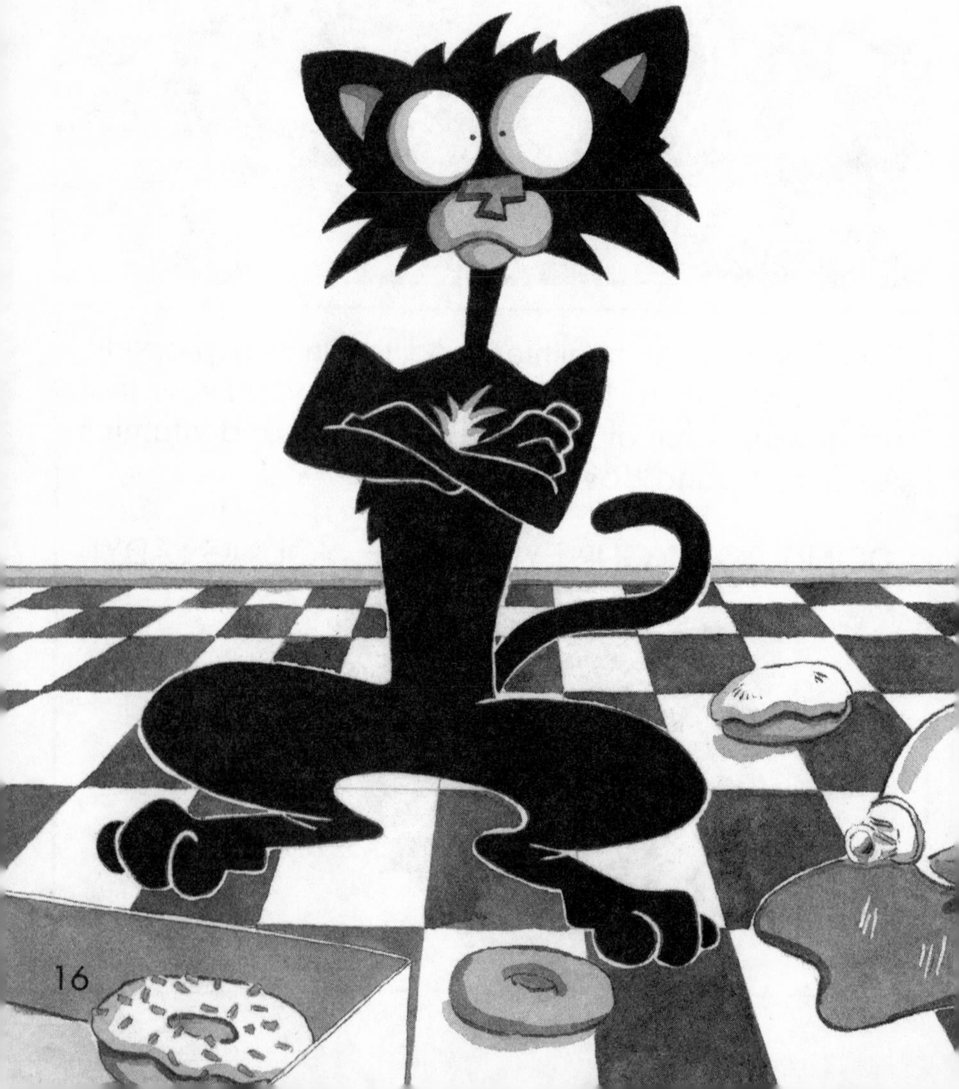

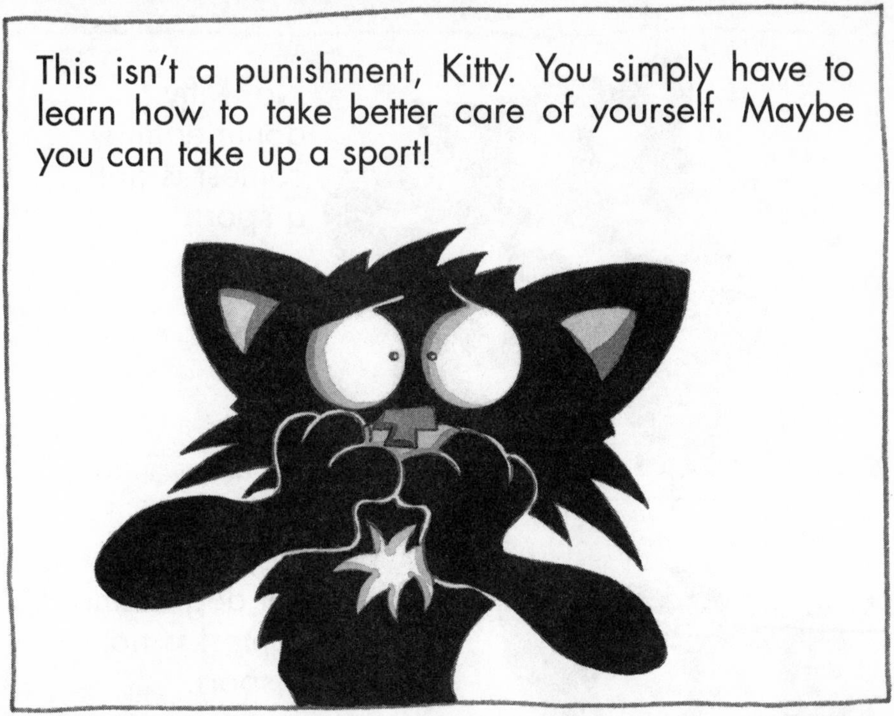
This isn't a punishment, Kitty. You simply have to learn how to take better care of yourself. Maybe you can take up a sport!

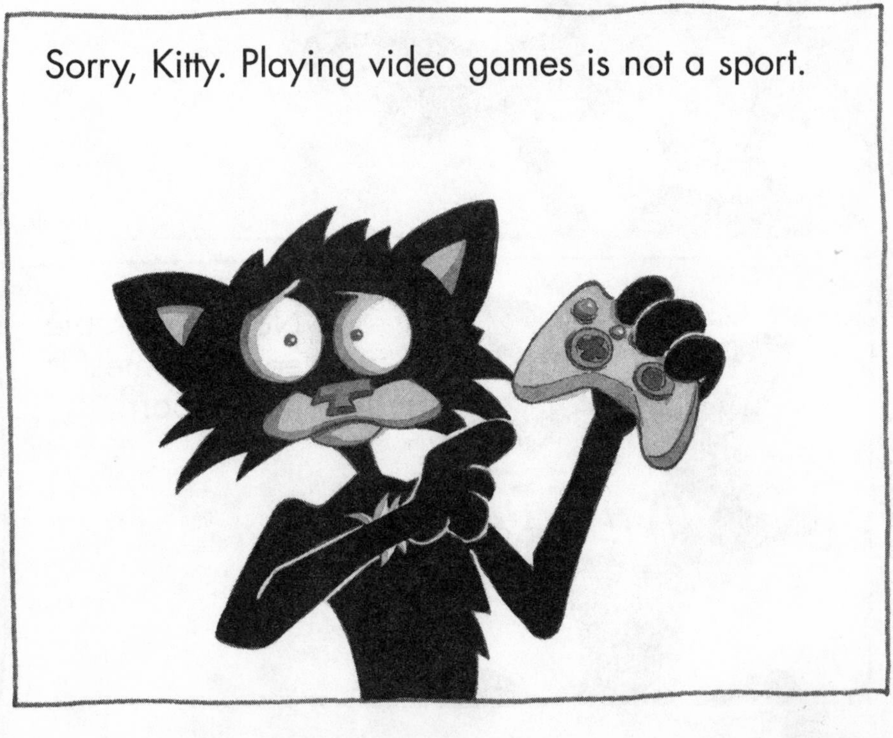
Sorry, Kitty. Playing video games is not a sport.

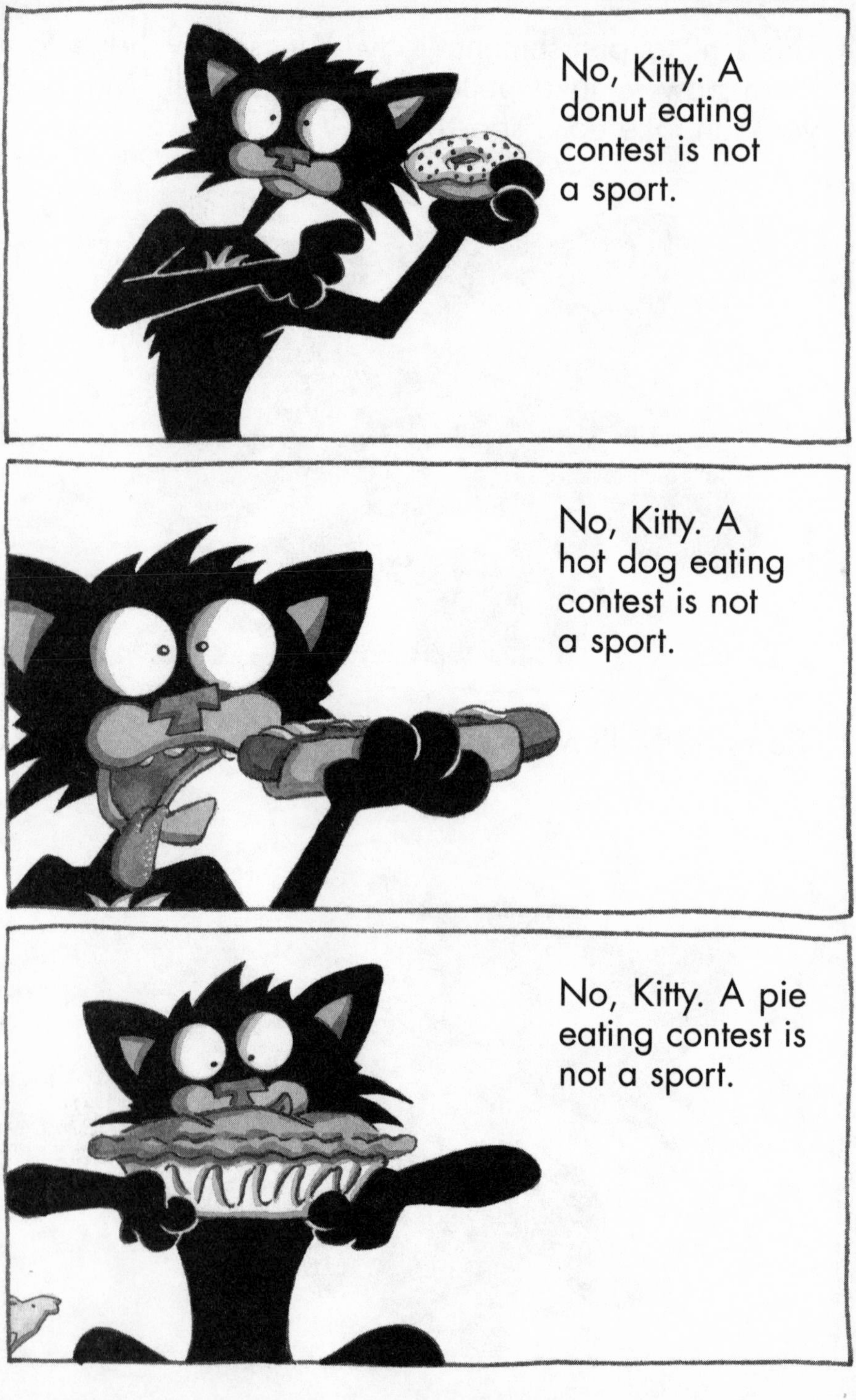
No, Kitty. A donut eating contest is not a sport.
No, Kitty. A hot dog eating contest is not a sport.
No, Kitty. A pie eating contest is not a sport.

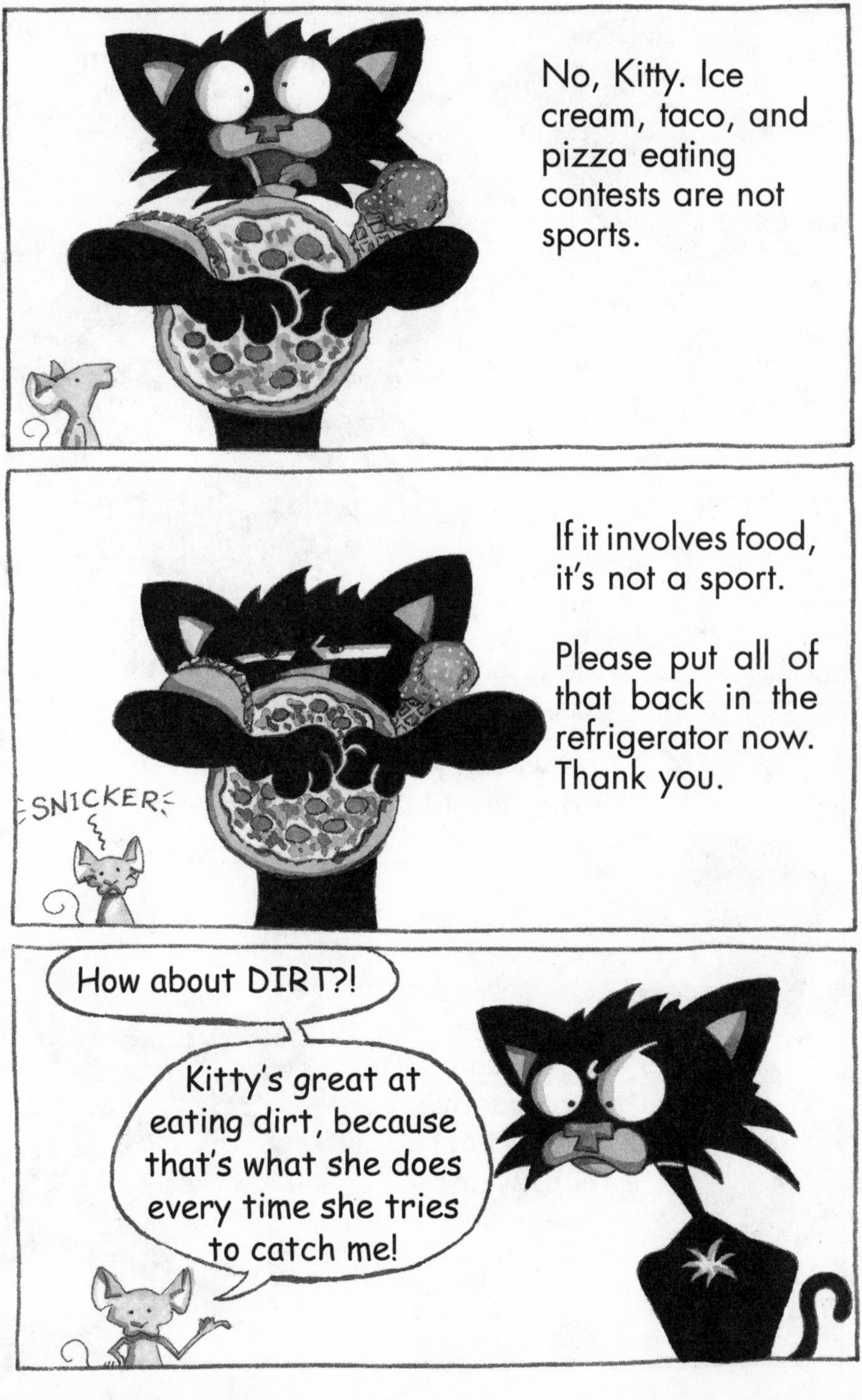
No, Kitty. Ice cream, taco, and pizza eating contests are not sports.
If it involves food, it's not a sport.
Please put all of that back in the refrigerator now. Thank you.
SNICKER
How about DIRT?!
Kitty's great at eating dirt, because that's what she does every time she tries to catch me!

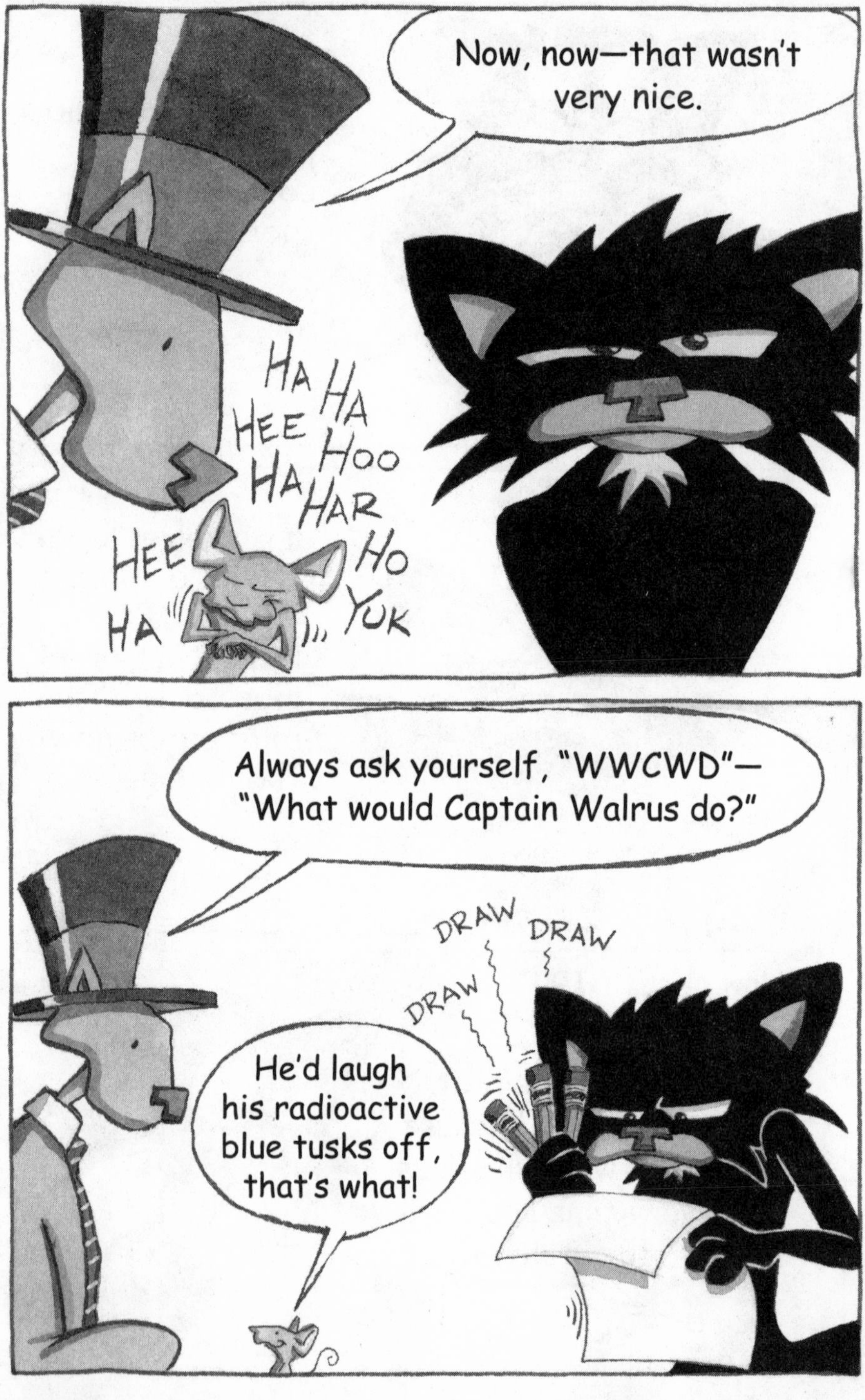
Now, now—that wasn't very nice.
HA HA
HEE HOO
HA HAR
HEE HO
HA YUK
Always ask yourself, "WWCWD"—"What would Captain Walrus do?"
DRAW DRAW DRAW
He'd laugh his radioactive blue tusks off, that's what!

No, Kitty. A mouse-eating contest is not a sport.

Do they even exist?

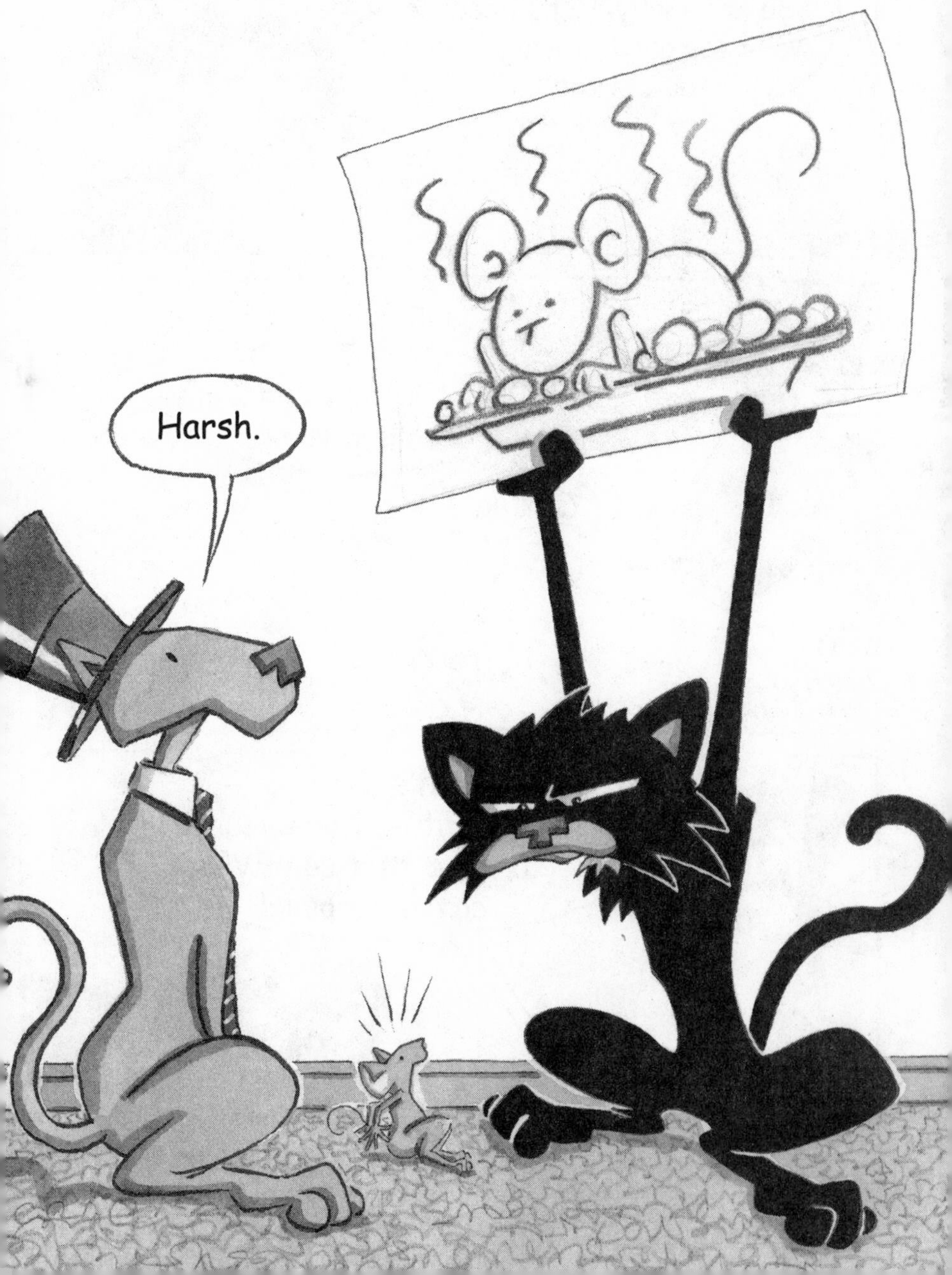
Harsh.

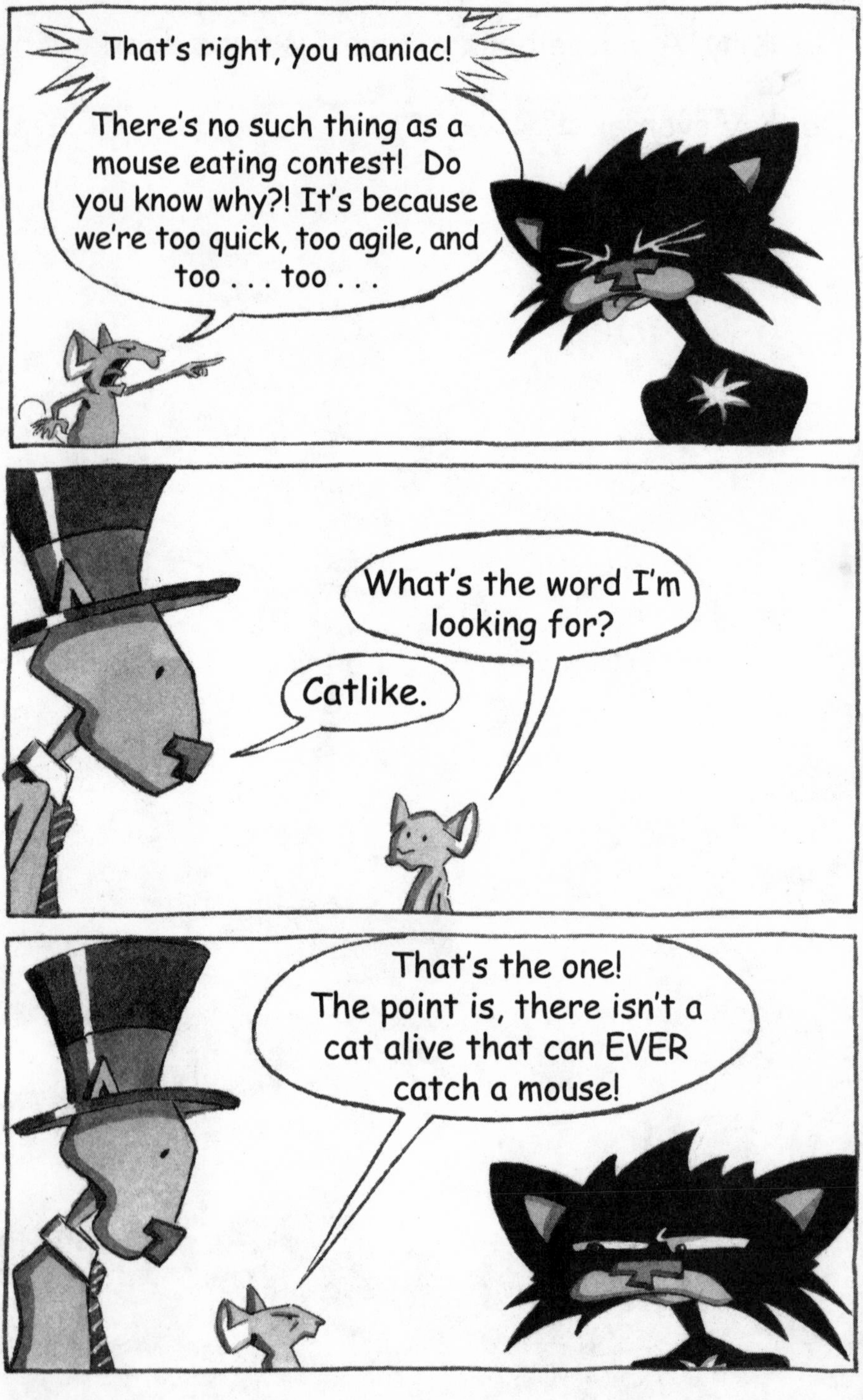
That's right, you maniac!
There's no such thing as a mouse eating contest! Do you know why?! It's because we're too quick, too agile, and too . . . too . . .
What's the word I'm looking for?
Catlike.
That's the one! The point is, there isn't a cat alive that can EVER catch a mouse!

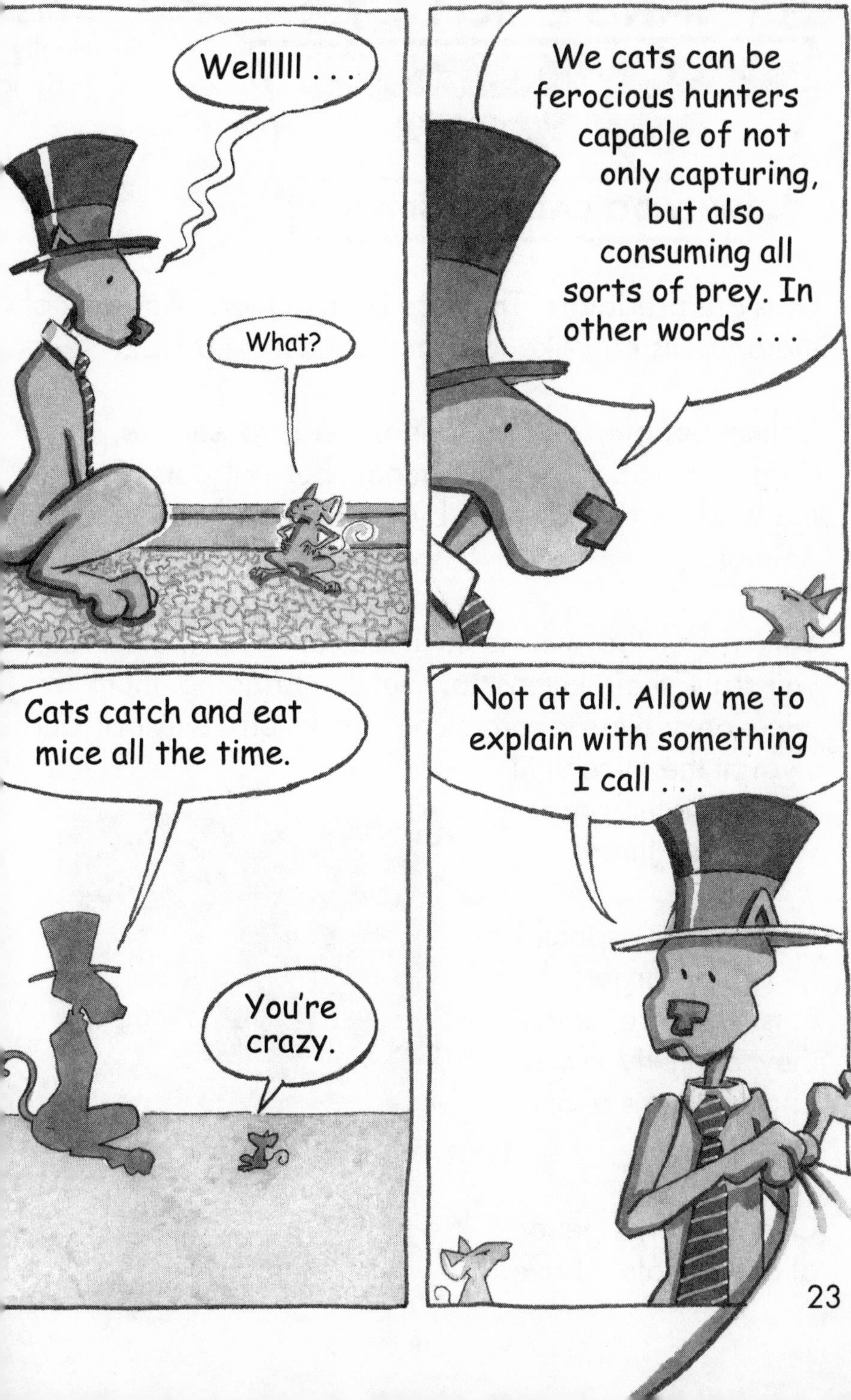
Welllllll . . .
What?
We cats can be ferocious hunters capable of not only capturing, but also consuming all sorts of prey. In other words . . .
Cats catch and eat mice all the time.
You're crazy.
Not at all. Allow me to explain with something I call . . .

STRANGE KITTY'S
UNCLE MURRAY'S FUN FACTS

WHY DO CATS CHASE MICE?

HEY! This usually thing

Cats are predators. They are born hunters. And one of the animals cats like to hunt the most are MICE.

Unlike people, cats must eat meat to survive. Even dogs can subsist without meat, but not cats. And in the wild, cats find meat by hunting and eating other animals.

Survival in the wild is so important that mother cats will train their kittens to hunt by bringing them live mice on which to practice. The kittens will bat and swat at the mice until they learn the proper way to kill them.

MICE—
• SMALL
• CAN'T FLY
• LOTS OF THEM
• TASTY

Mice are especially good targets for cats. They're small, they can't fly away, and there are a lot of them.

Over many generations, cats have

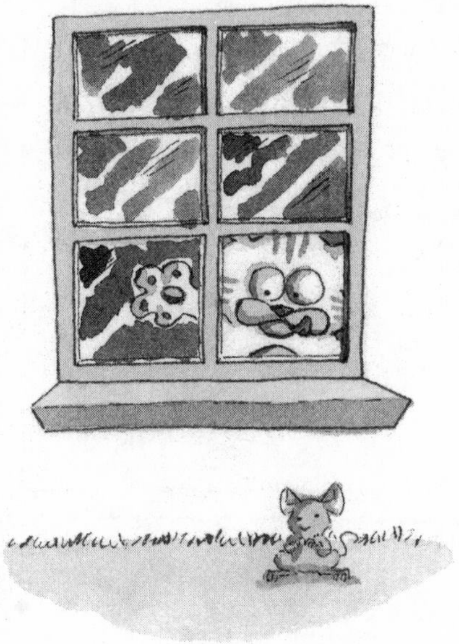

become extremely skilled at killing mice. Domesticated cats, ones that live with people as pets, kill up to 20.7 BILLION mice and other small animals every year worldwide. These, of course, are cats who have access to the outdoors. If you want to prevent your cat from killing other smaller animals, the solution is simple: Don't allow your cat to go outside. Ever.

Even if a cat is well fed and isn't at all hungry, it will still hunt and kill a mouse if the opportunity arises. It's instinct. It's in their nature to hunt, so they will.

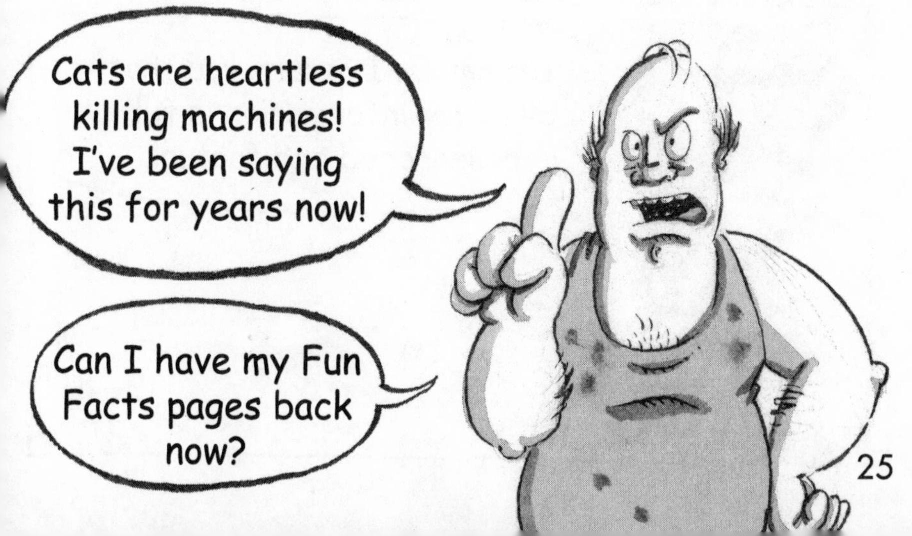
Cats are heartless killing machines! I've been saying this for years now!
Can I have my Fun Facts pages back now?

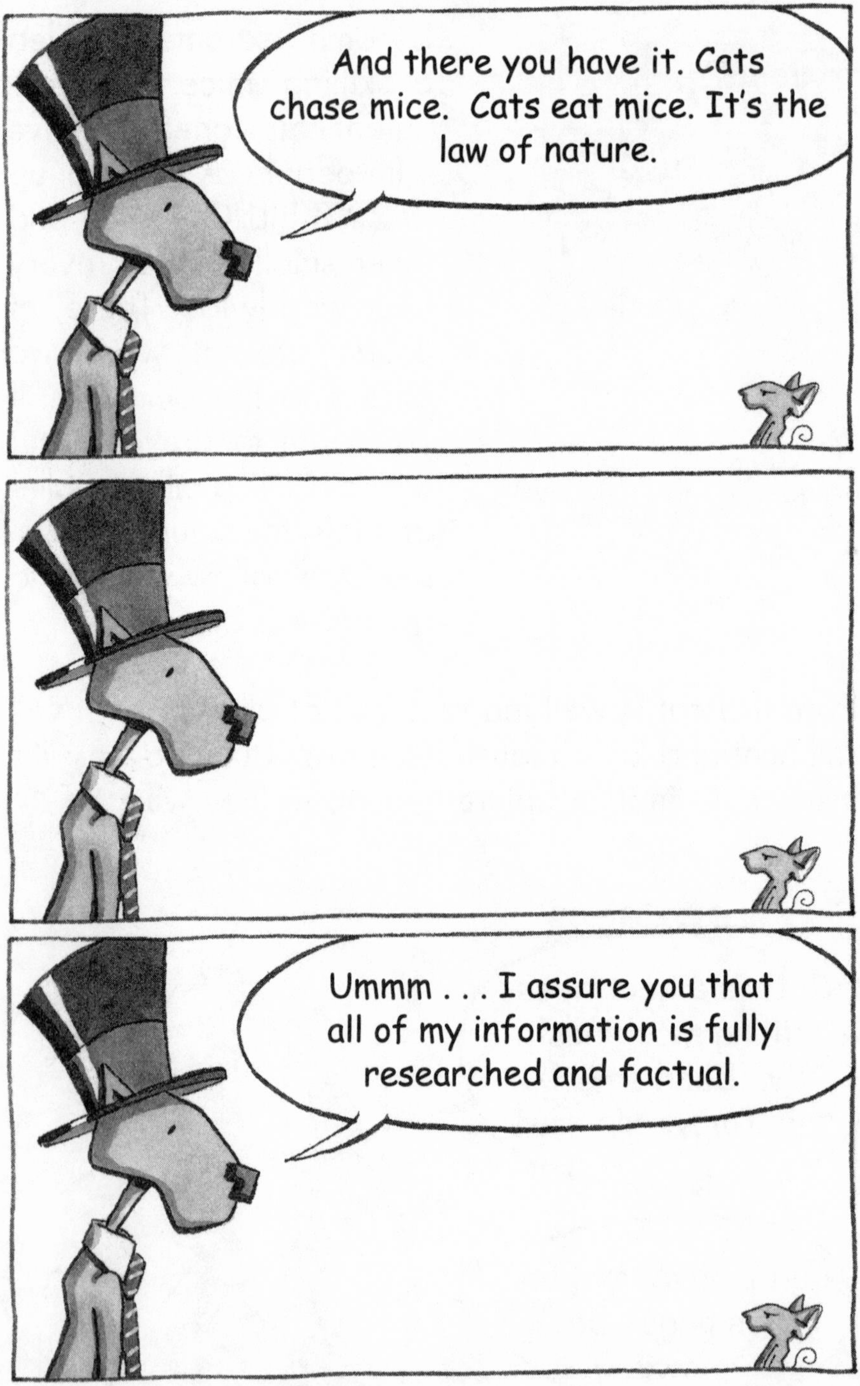
And there you have it. Cats chase mice. Cats eat mice. It's the law of nature.
Ummm . . . I assure you that all of my information is fully researched and factual.

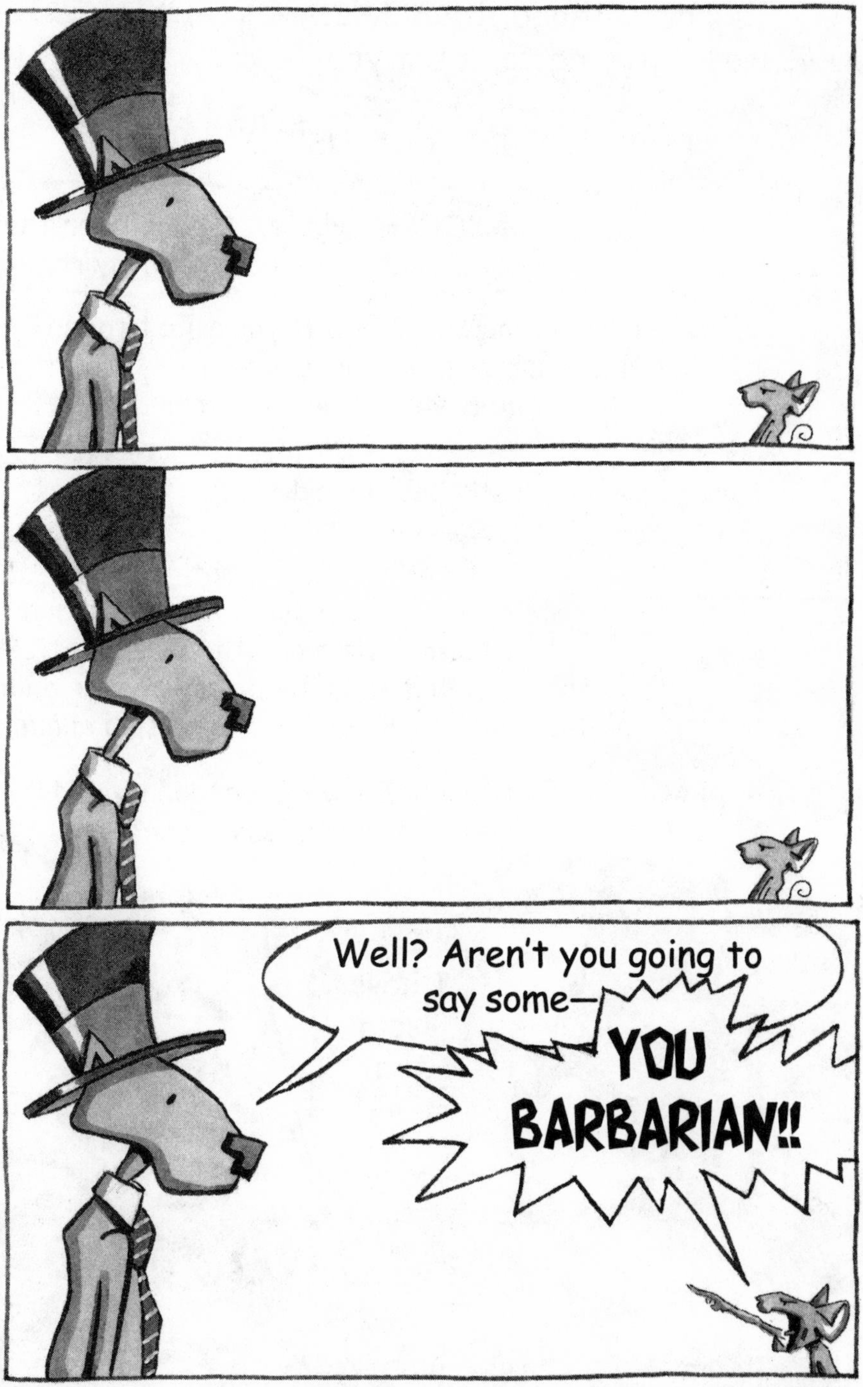
Well? Aren't you going to say some—
YOU BARBARIAN!!

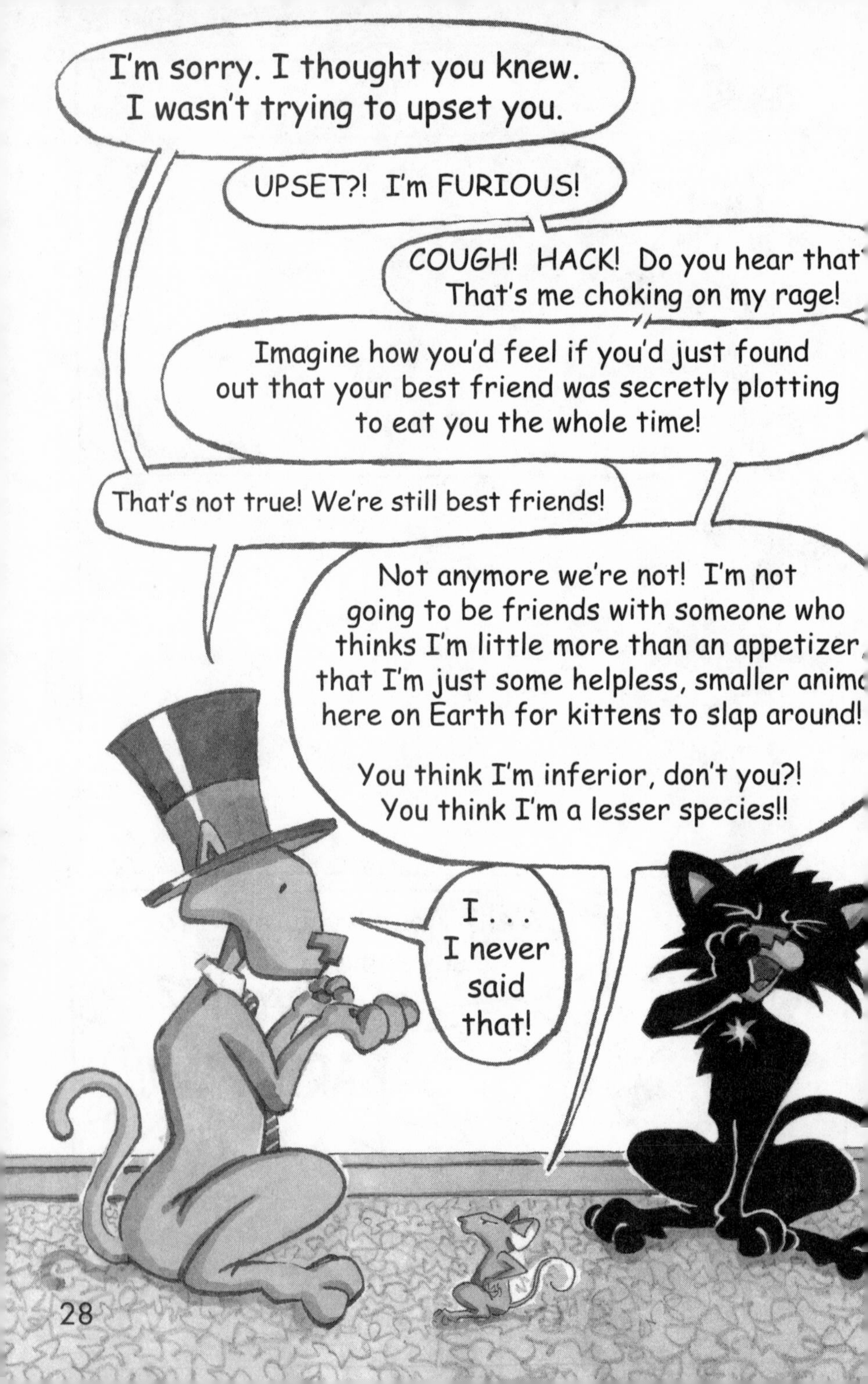
I'm sorry. I thought you knew. I wasn't trying to upset you.
UPSET?! I'm FURIOUS!
COUGH! HACK! Do you hear that? That's me choking on my rage!
Imagine how you'd feel if you'd just found out that your best friend was secretly plotting to eat you the whole time!
That's not true! We're still best friends!
Not anymore we're not! I'm not going to be friends with someone who thinks I'm little more than an appetizer, that I'm just some helpless, smaller animal here on Earth for kittens to slap around!
You think I'm inferior, don't you?! You think I'm a lesser species!!
I . . . I never said that!

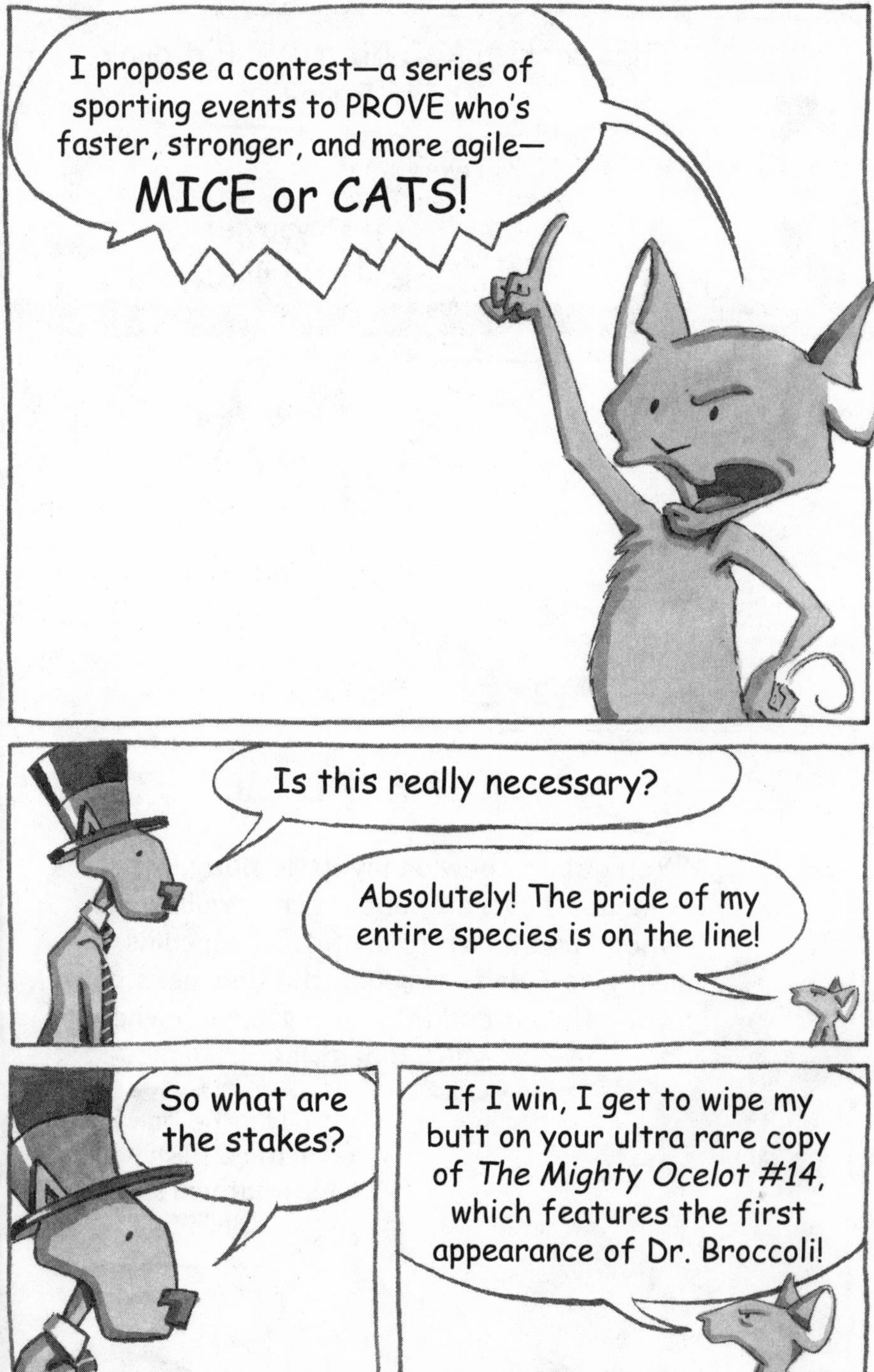

I propose a contest—a series of sporting events to PROVE who's faster, stronger, and more agile—MICE or CATS!
Is this really necessary?
Absolutely! The pride of my entire species is on the line!
So what are the stakes?
If I win, I get to wipe my butt on your ultra rare copy of *The Mighty Ocelot #14*, which features the first appearance of Dr. Broccoli!

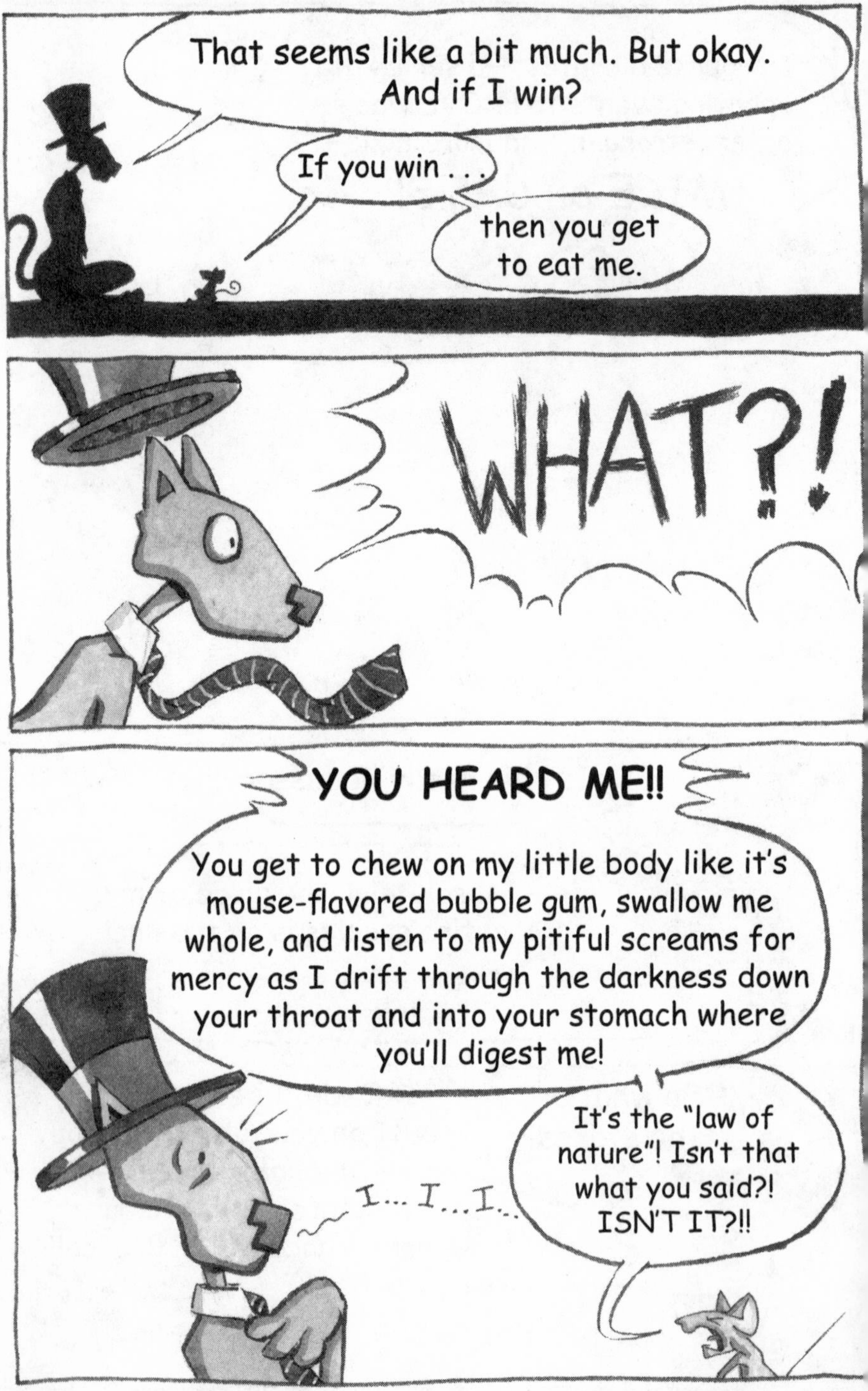
That seems like a bit much. But okay. And if I win?
If you win . . .
then you get to eat me.
WHAT?!
YOU HEARD ME!!
You get to chew on my little body like it's mouse-flavored bubble gum, swallow me whole, and listen to my pitiful screams for mercy as I drift through the darkness down your throat and into your stomach where you'll digest me!
I... I... I...
It's the "law of nature"! Isn't that what you said?! ISN'T IT?!!

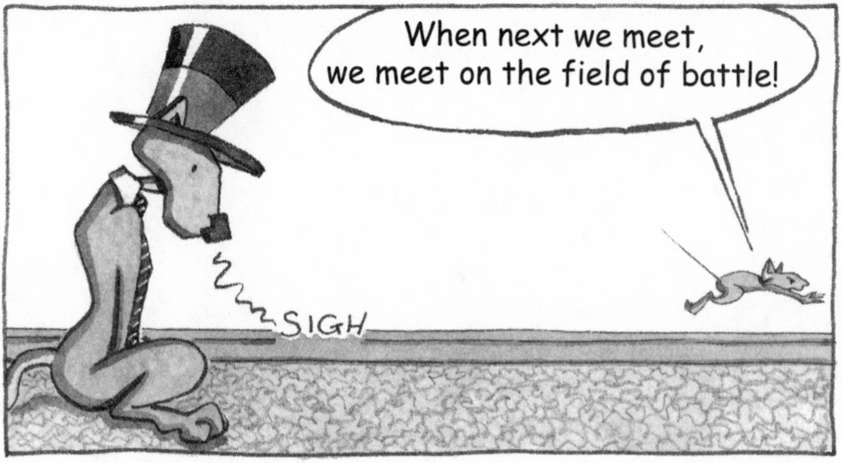
When next we meet,
we meet on the field of battle!
SIGH

Kitty!

Did you hear that? These contests are just the sort of thing you need! You'll be able to compete and exercise at the same time!

Kitty?

Where are you?

Kitty?

Kitty?

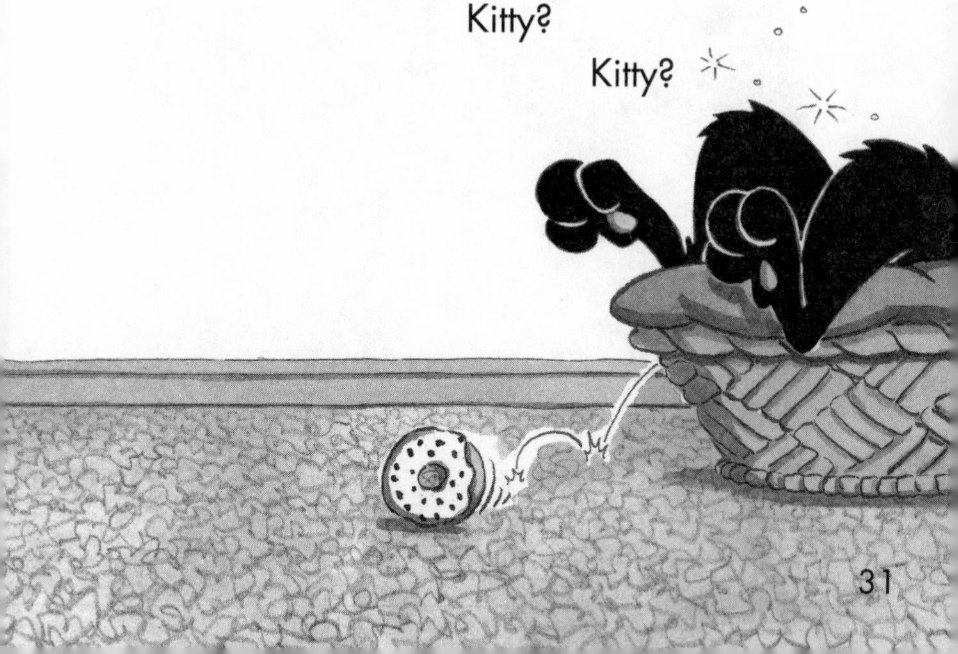

Oh, Kitty.

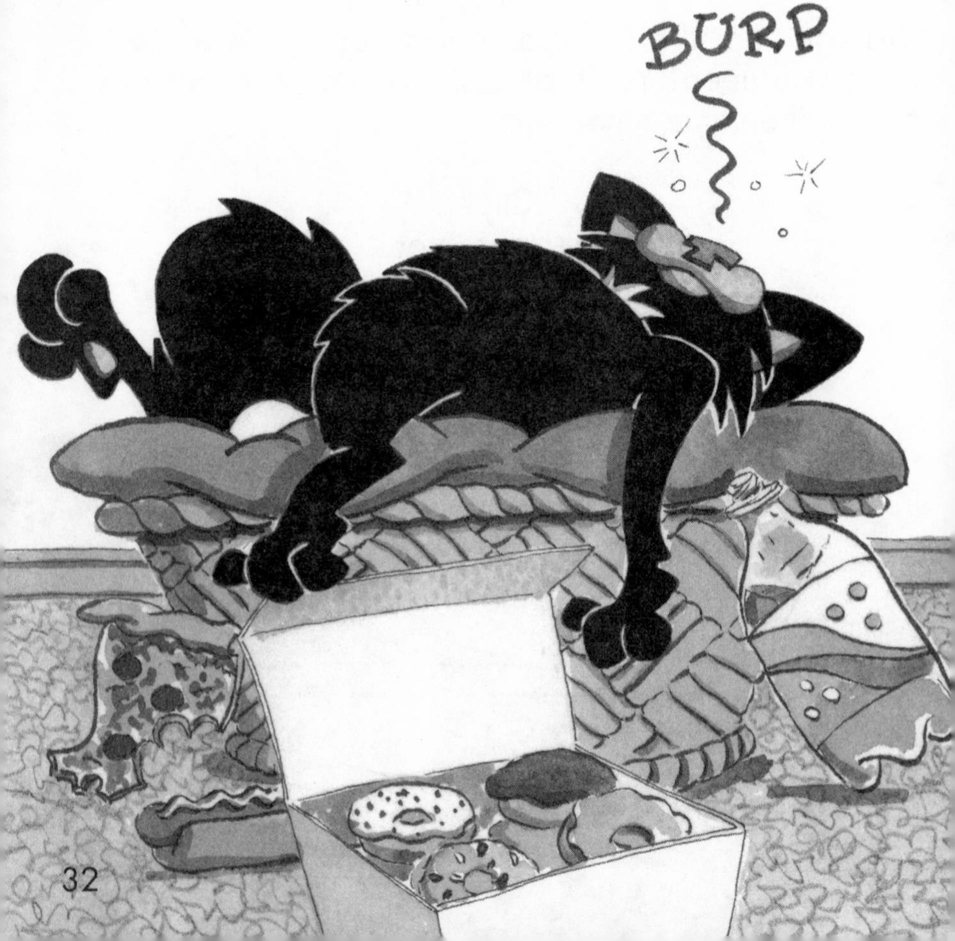
BURP

• CHAPTER THREE •

NEGOTIATIONS

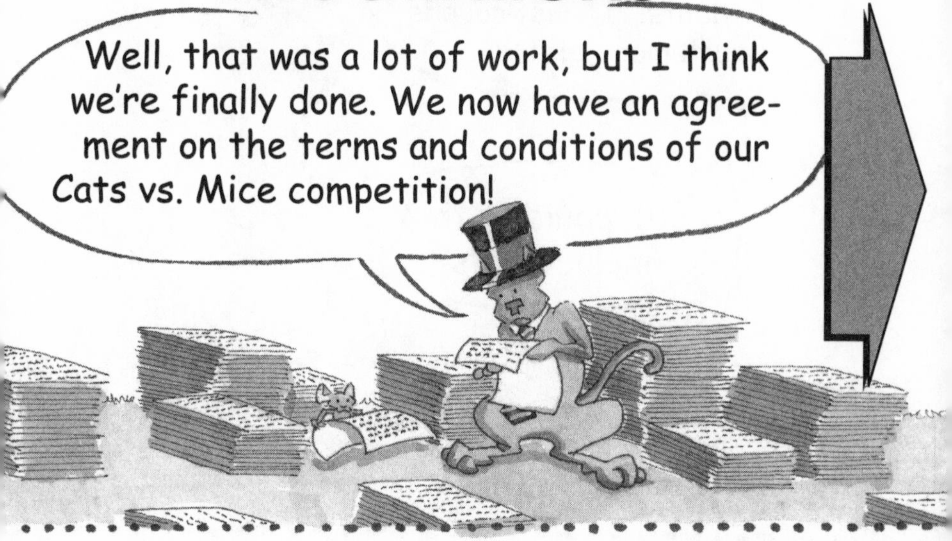
Well, that was a lot of work, but I think we're finally done. We now have an agreement on the terms and conditions of our Cats vs. Mice competition!

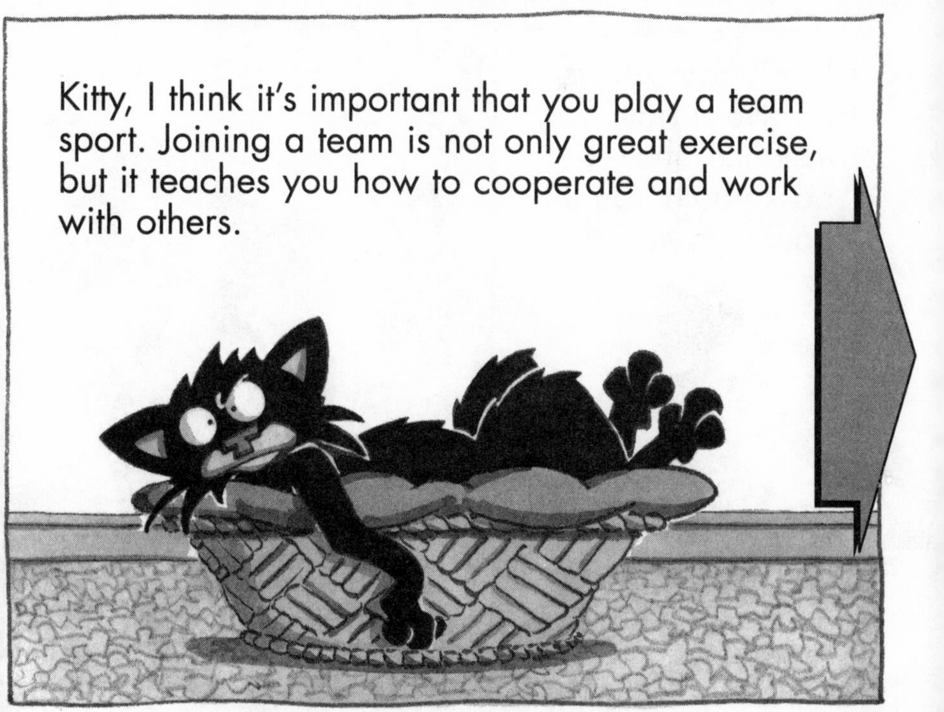
Kitty, I think it's important that you play a team sport. Joining a team is not only great exercise, but it teaches you how to cooperate and work with others.

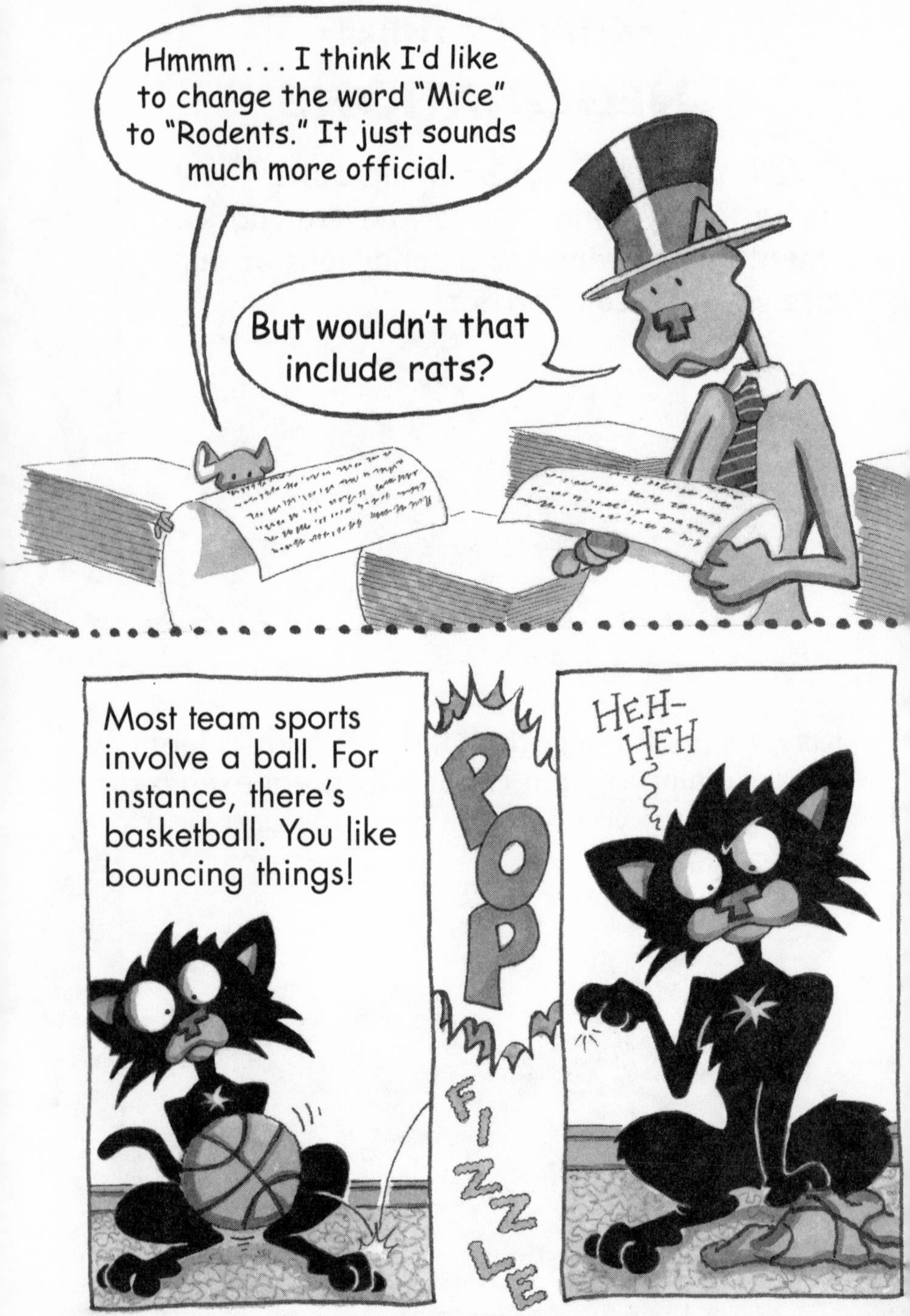
Hmmm . . . I think I'd like to change the word "Mice" to "Rodents." It just sounds much more official.
But wouldn't that include rats?
Most team sports involve a ball. For instance, there's basketball. You like bouncing things!
POP
FIZZLE
HEH-HEH

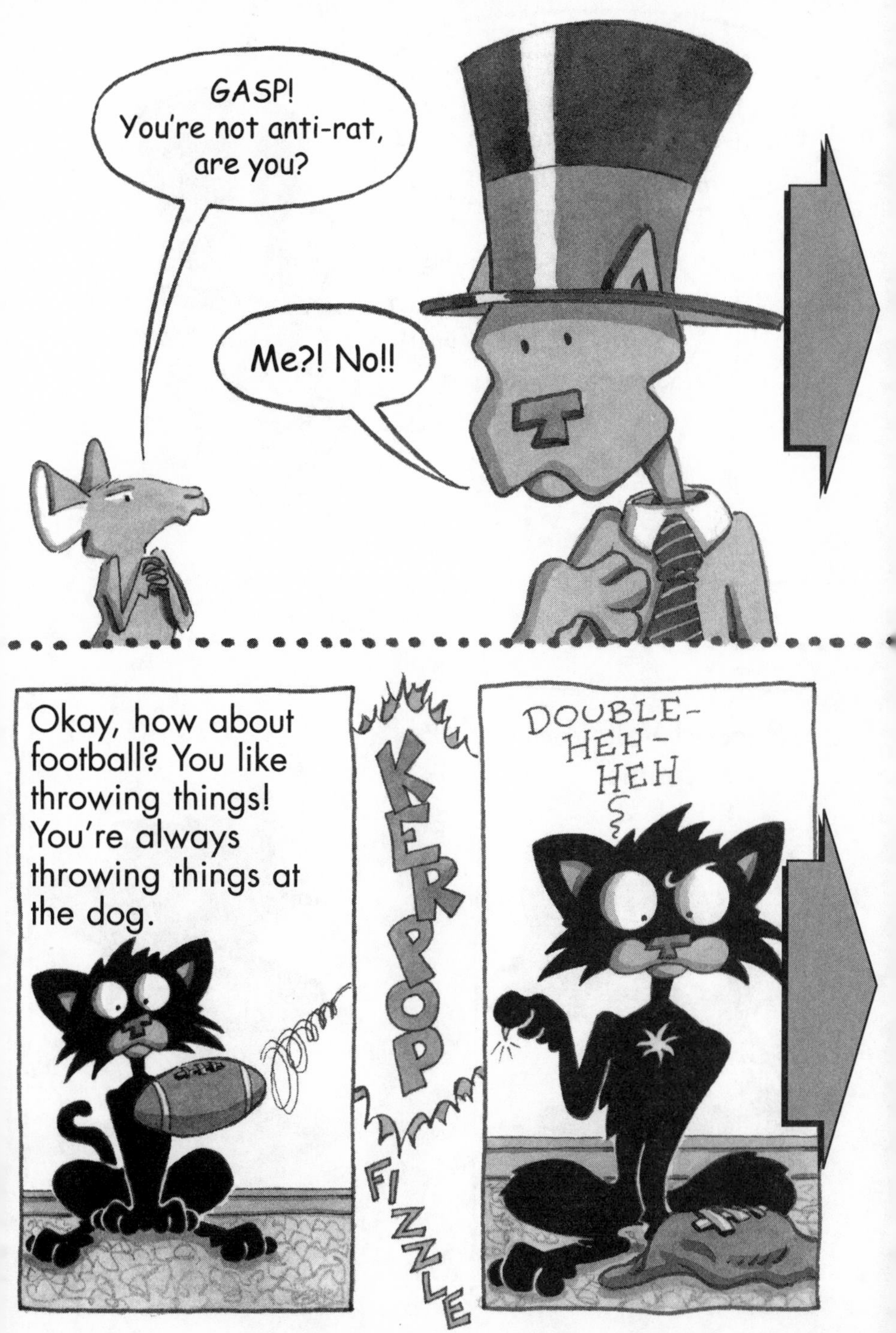
GASP!
You're not anti-rat, are you?
Me?! No!!
Okay, how about football? You like throwing things! You're always throwing things at the dog.
KERPOP
FIZZLE
DOUBLE-HEH-HEH

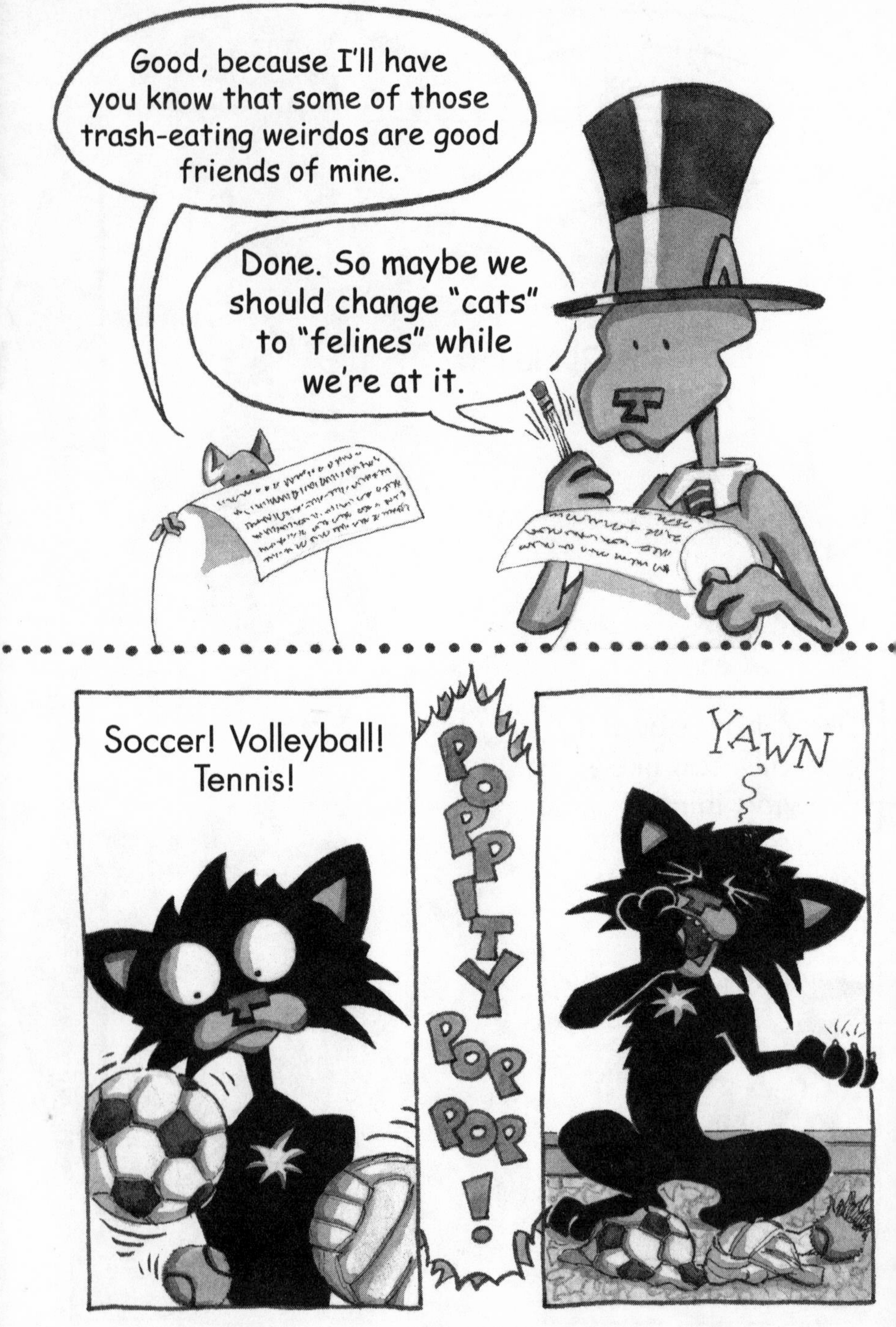
Good, because I'll have you know that some of those trash-eating weirdos are good friends of mine.
Done. So maybe we should change "cats" to "felines" while we're at it.
Soccer! Volleyball! Tennis!
POPPITY POP POP!
YAWN

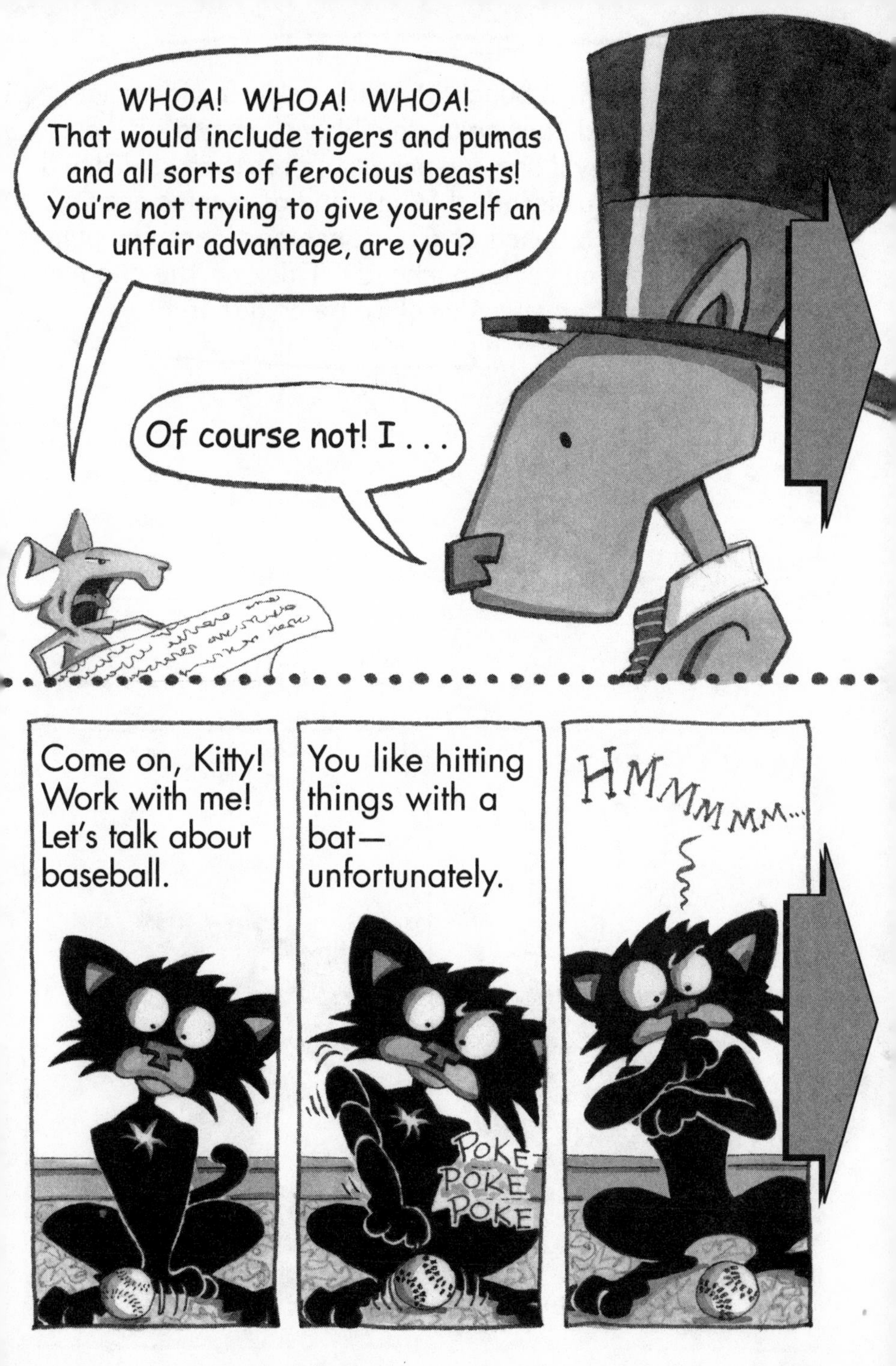
WHOA! WHOA! WHOA! That would include tigers and pumas and all sorts of ferocious beasts! You're not trying to give yourself an unfair advantage, are you?
Of course not! I . . .
Come on, Kitty! Work with me! Let's talk about baseball.
You like hitting things with a bat— unfortunately.
POKE POKE POKE
HMMMMMM...

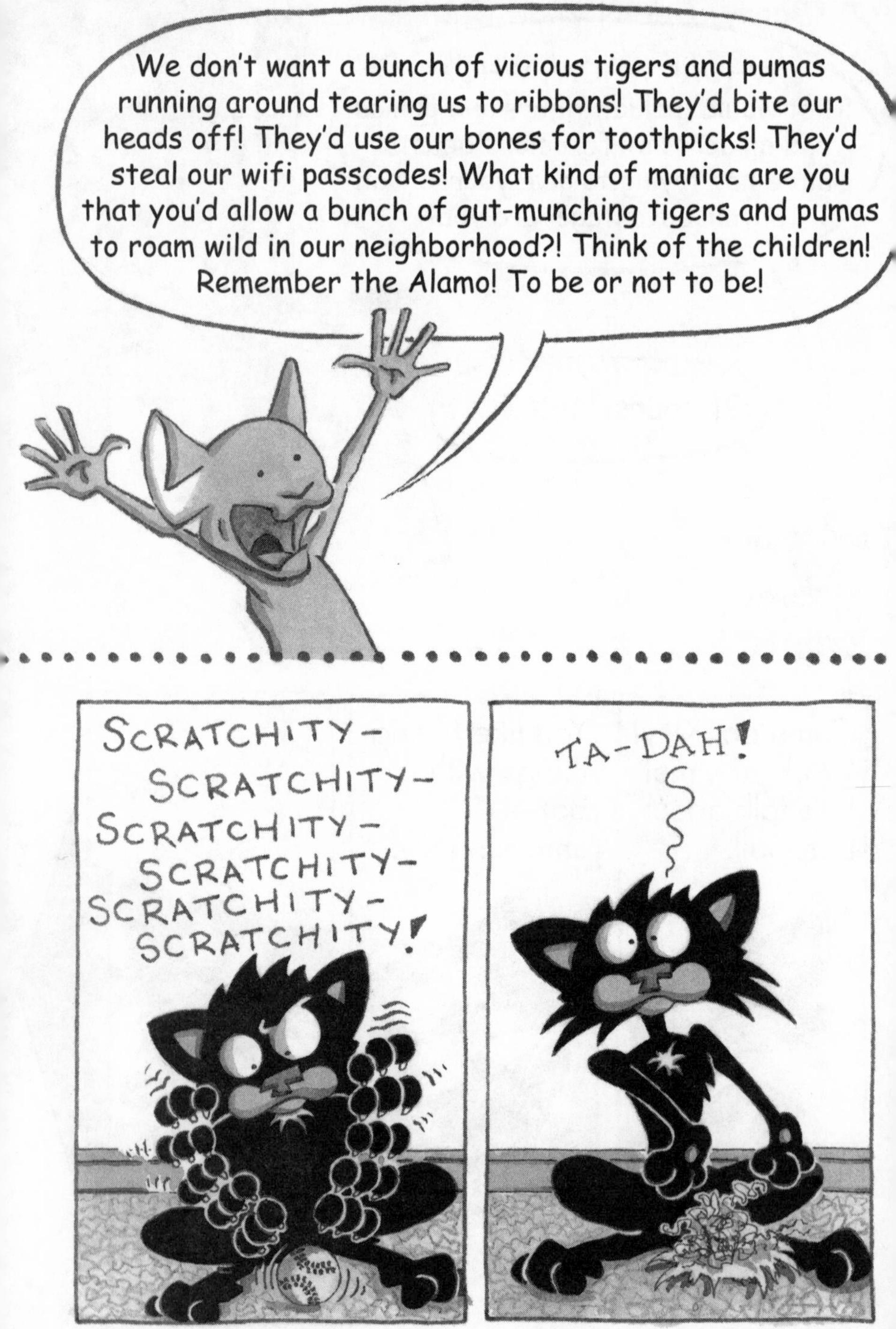
We don't want a bunch of vicious tigers and pumas running around tearing us to ribbons! They'd bite our heads off! They'd use our bones for toothpicks! They'd steal our wifi passcodes! What kind of maniac are you that you'd allow a bunch of gut-munching tigers and pumas to roam wild in our neighborhood?! Think of the children! Remember the Alamo! To be or not to be!
SCRATCHITY-SCRATCHITY-SCRATCHITY-SCRATCHITY-SCRATCHITY-SCRATCHITY!
TA-DAH!

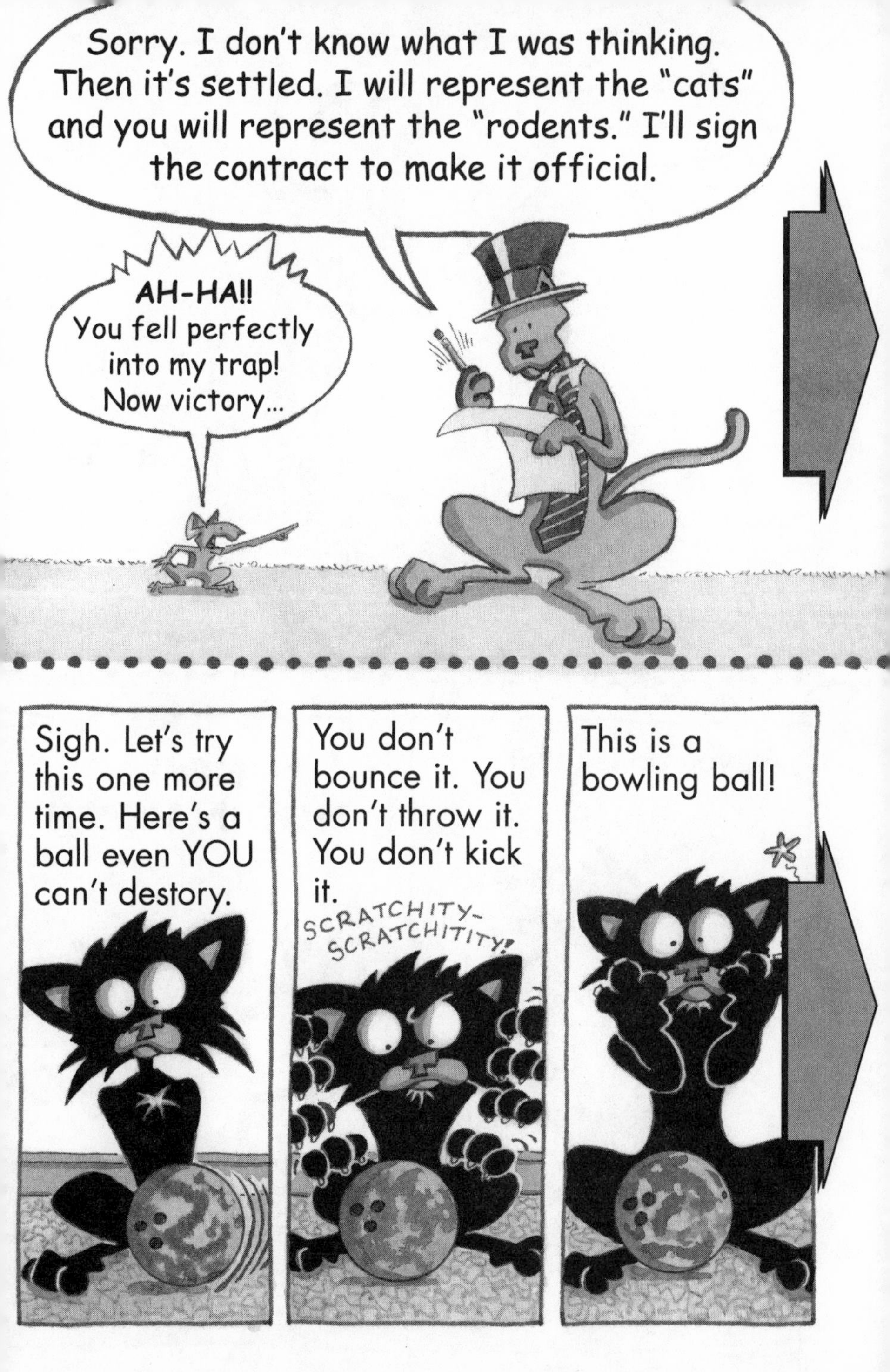
Sorry. I don't know what I was thinking. Then it's settled. I will represent the "cats" and you will represent the "rodents." I'll sign the contract to make it official.
AH-HA!! You fell perfectly into my trap! Now victory...
Sigh. Let's try this one more time. Here's a ball even YOU can't destory.
You don't bounce it. You don't throw it. You don't kick it.
SCRATCHITY-SCRATCHITITY!
This is a bowling ball!

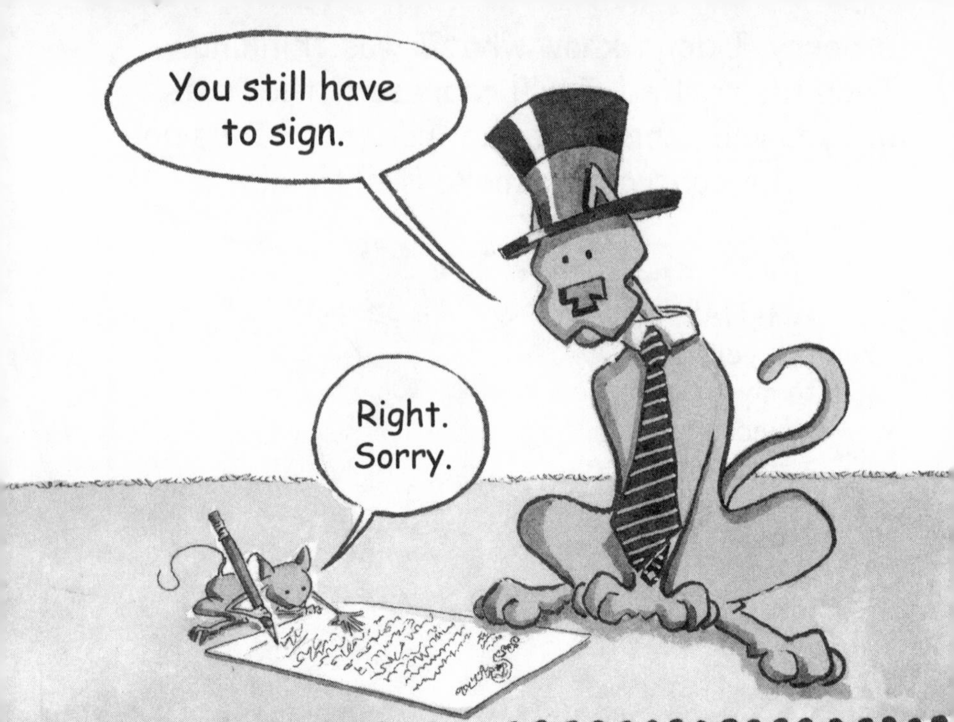
You still have to sign.
Right. Sorry.
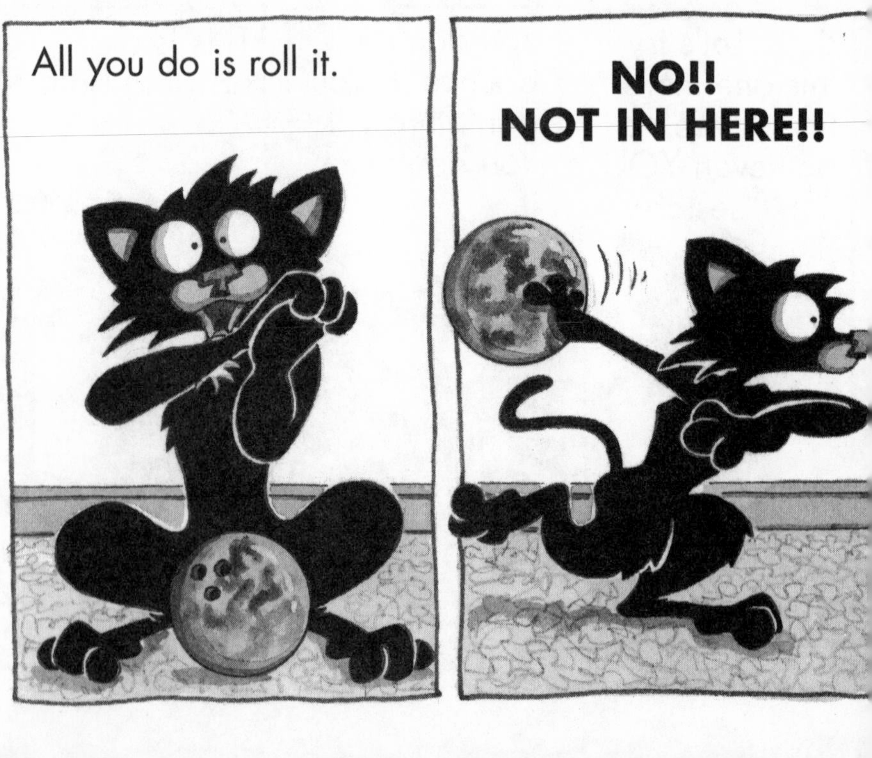
All you do is roll it.
NO!! NOT IN HERE!!

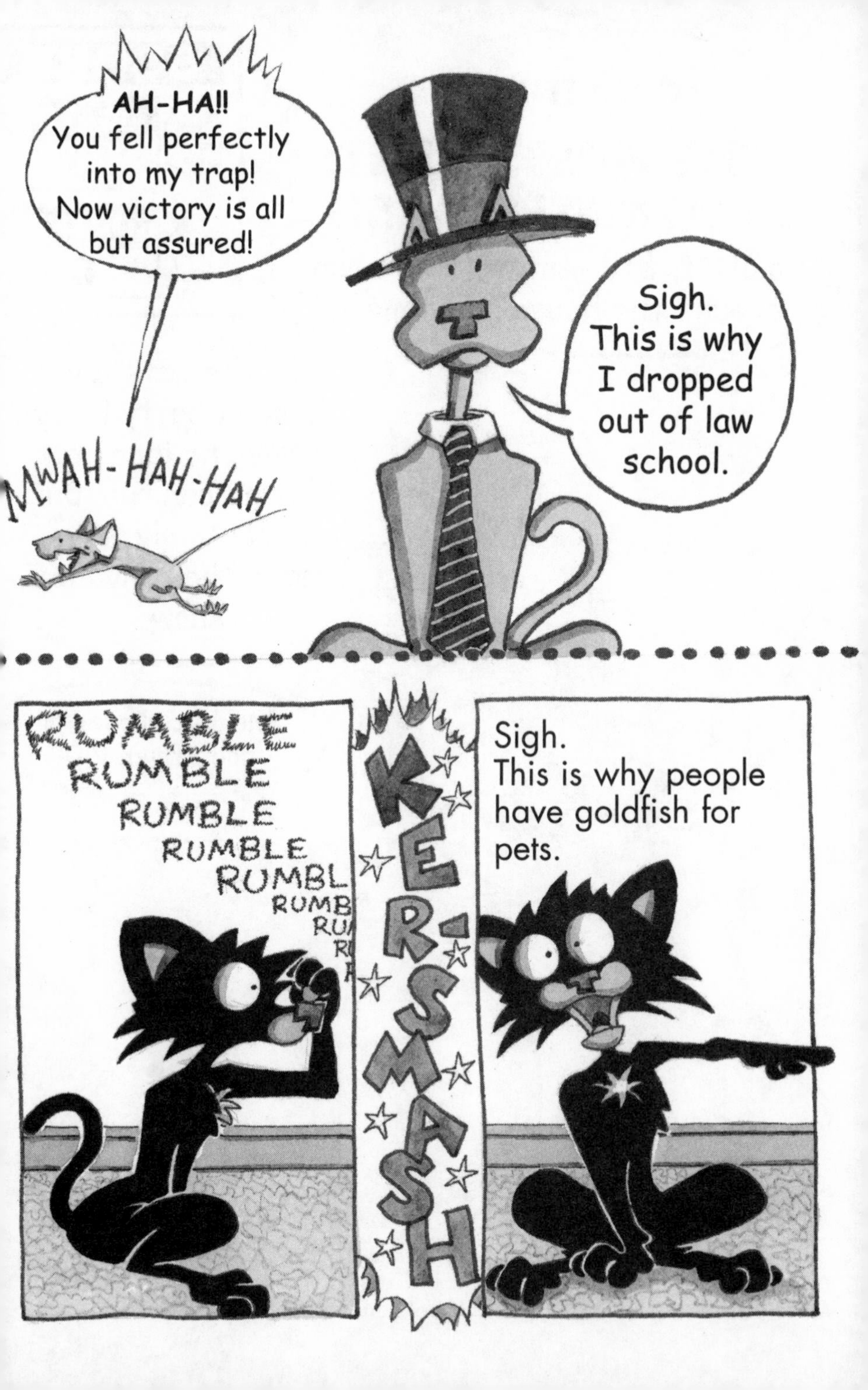
AH-HA!!
You fell perfectly into my trap! Now victory is all but assured!
MWAH-HAH-HAH
Sigh. This is why I dropped out of law school.
RUMBLE
RUMBLE
RUMBLE
RUMBLE
RUMBL
RUMB
KERSMASH
Sigh. This is why people have goldfish for pets.

• CHAPTER FOUR •

THE FIRST EVENT: 100-METER DASH

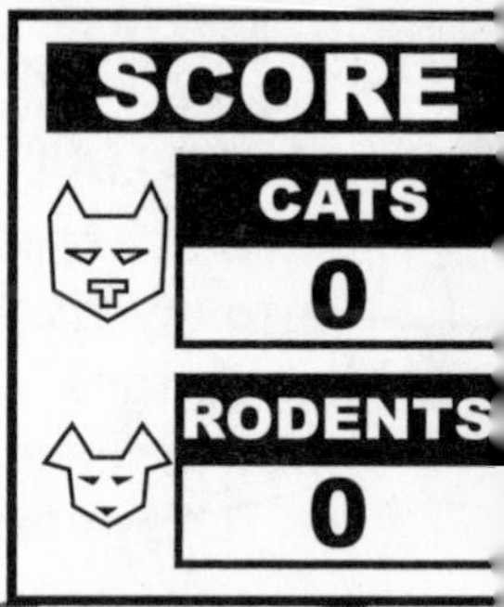
SCORE
CATS
0
RODENTS
0

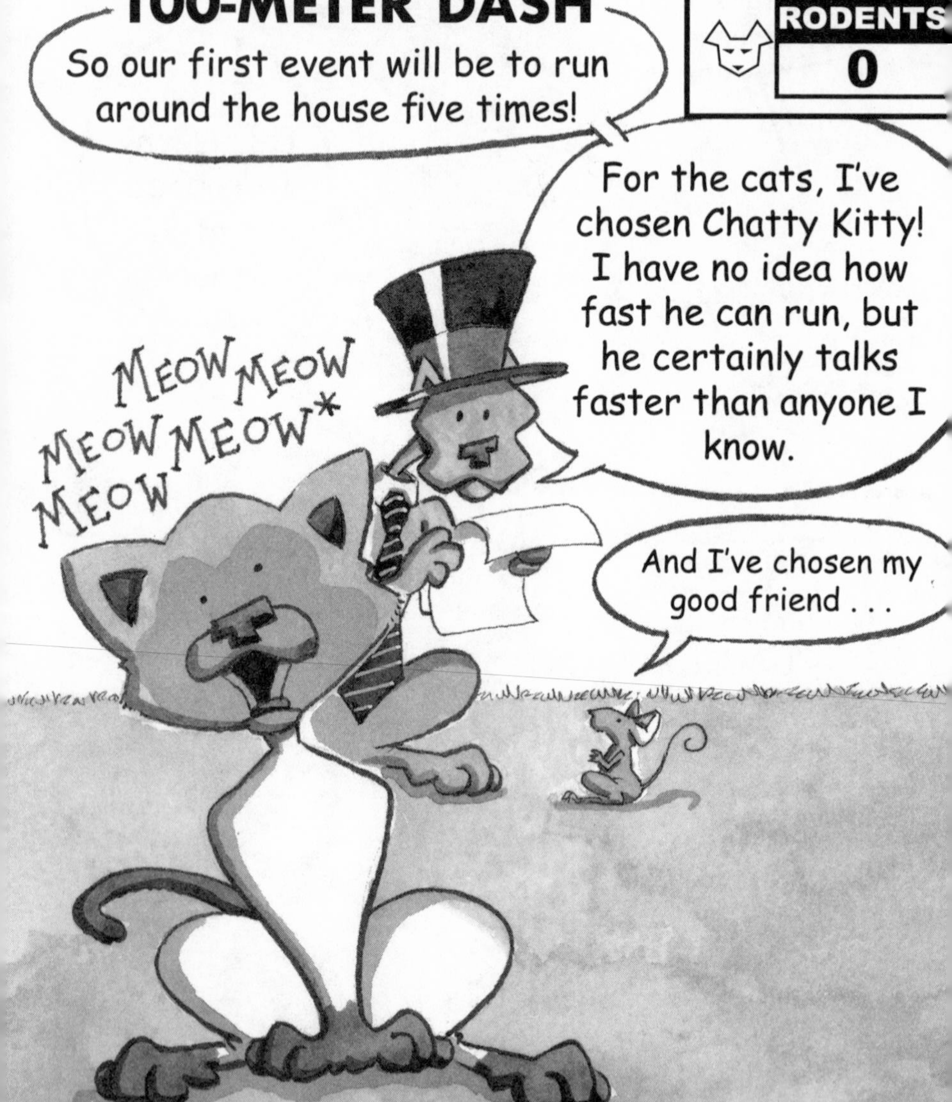
So our first event will be to run around the house five times!
For the cats, I've chosen Chatty Kitty! I have no idea how fast he can run, but he certainly talks faster than anyone I know.
MEOW MEOW MEOW MEOW* MEOW
And I've chosen my good friend . . .

* The average housecat can run as fast as 30 miles per hour in a short burst. Even if I could run that fast, I don't think I'd want to. I could be arrested for speeding inside a school zone.

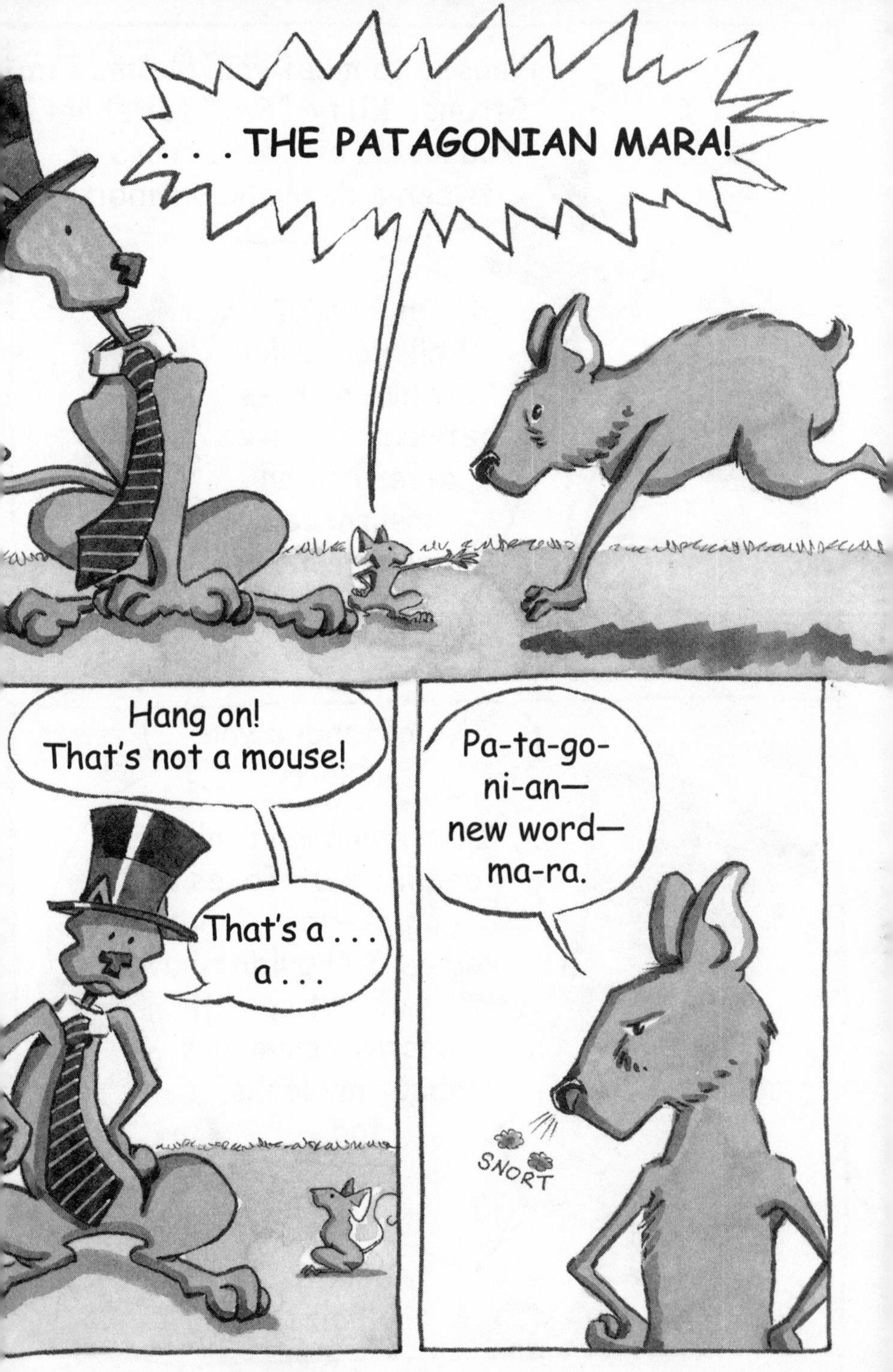
. . . THE PATAGONIAN MARA!
Hang on! That's not a mouse!
That's a . . . a . . .
Pa-ta-go-ni-an—new word—ma-ra.
SNORT

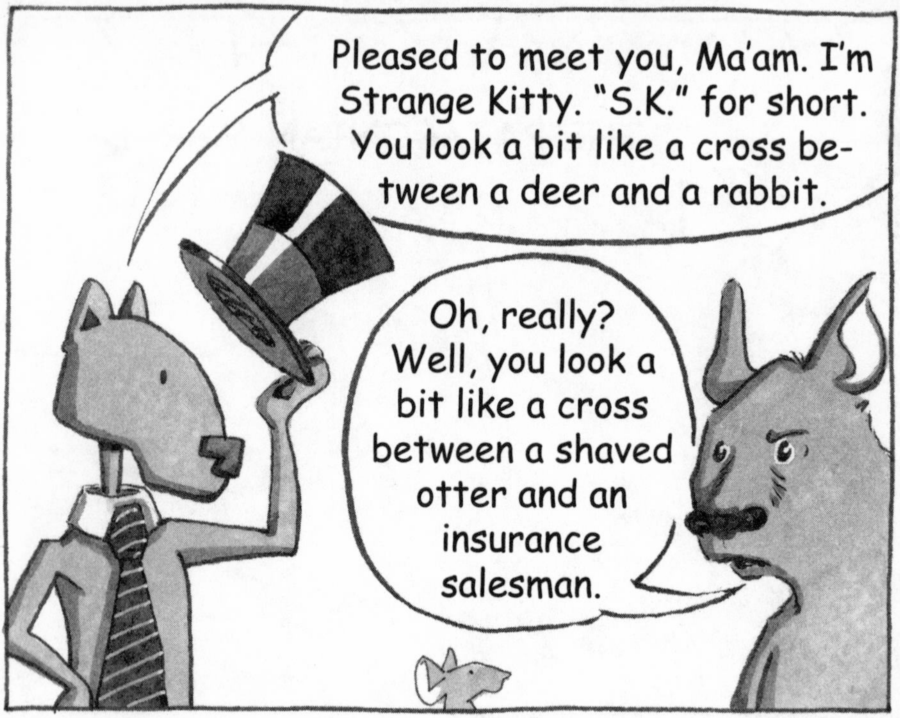
Pleased to meet you, Ma'am. I'm Strange Kitty. "S.K." for short. You look a bit like a cross between a deer and a rabbit.
Oh, really? Well, you look a bit like a cross between a shaved otter and an insurance salesman.

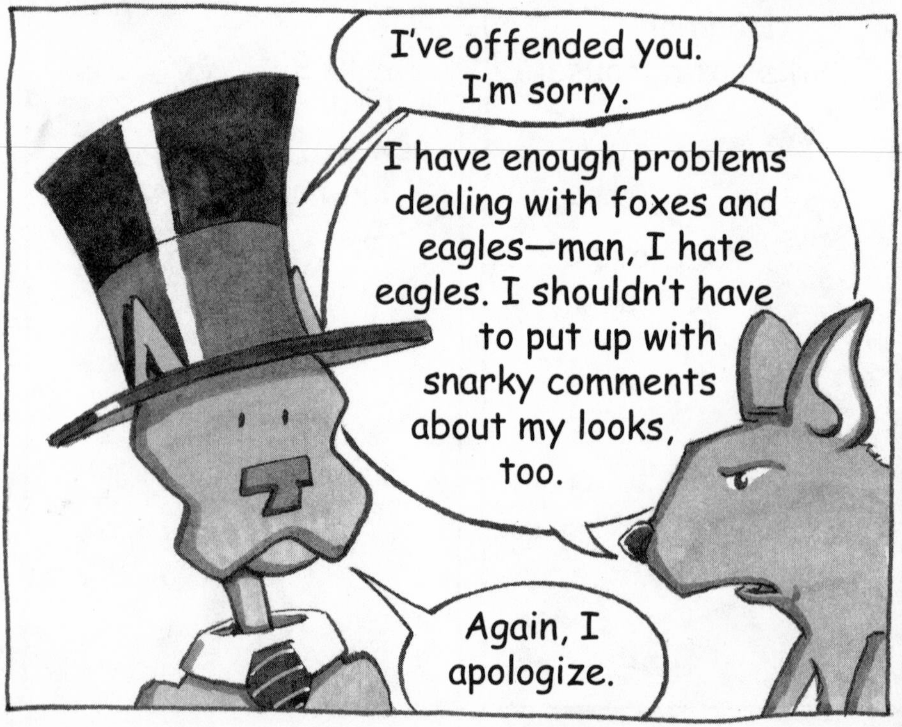
I've offended you. I'm sorry.
I have enough problems dealing with foxes and eagles—man, I hate eagles. I shouldn't have to put up with snarky comments about my looks, too.
Again, I apologize.

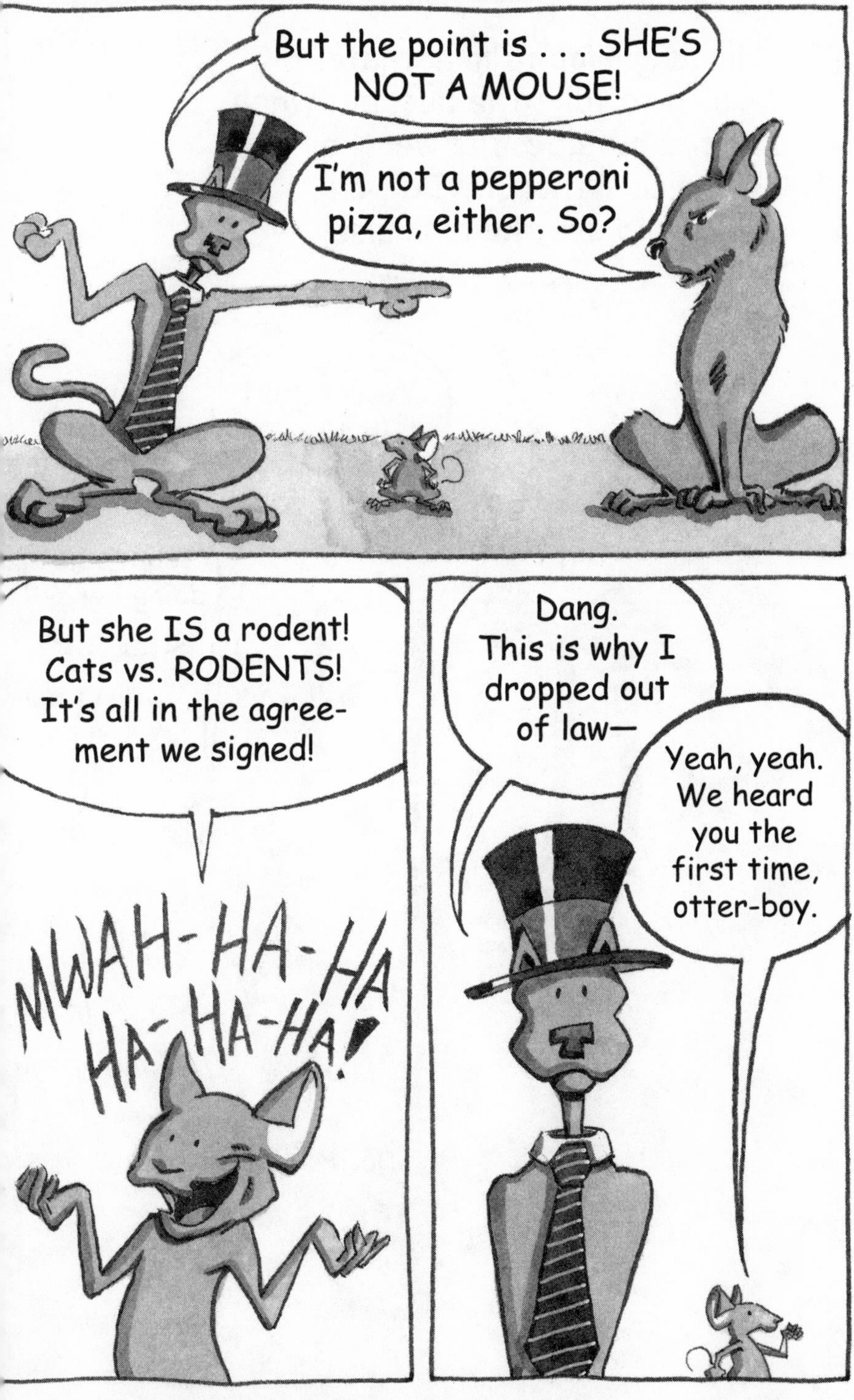
But the point is . . . SHE'S NOT A MOUSE!
I'm not a pepperoni pizza, either. So?
But she IS a rodent! Cats vs. RODENTS! It's all in the agree-ment we signed!
MWAH-HA-HA HA-HA-HA!
Dang. This is why I dropped out of law—
Yeah, yeah. We heard you the first time, otter-boy.

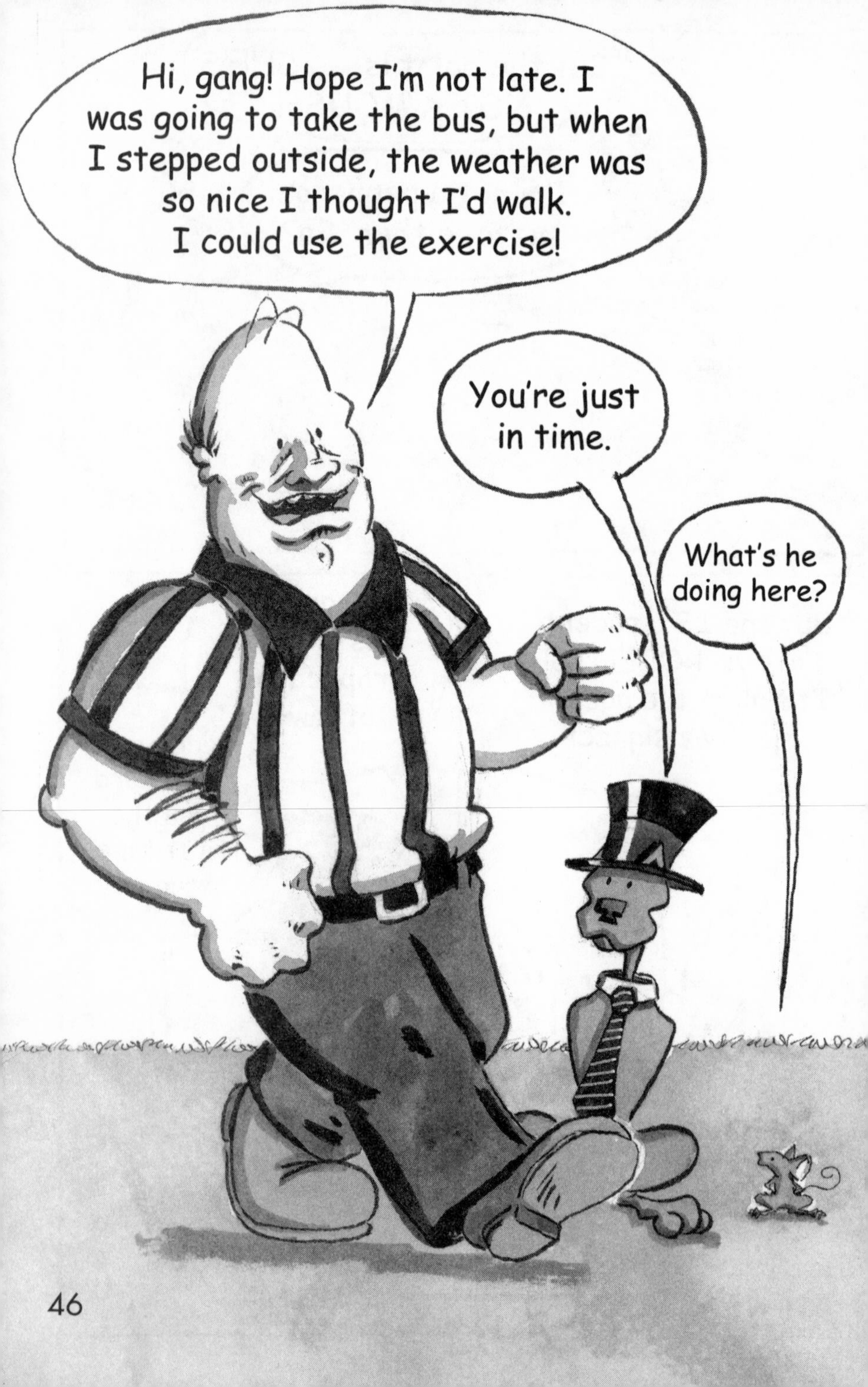
Hi, gang! Hope I'm not late. I was going to take the bus, but when I stepped outside, the weather was so nice I thought I'd walk. I could use the exercise!
You're just in time.
What's he doing here?

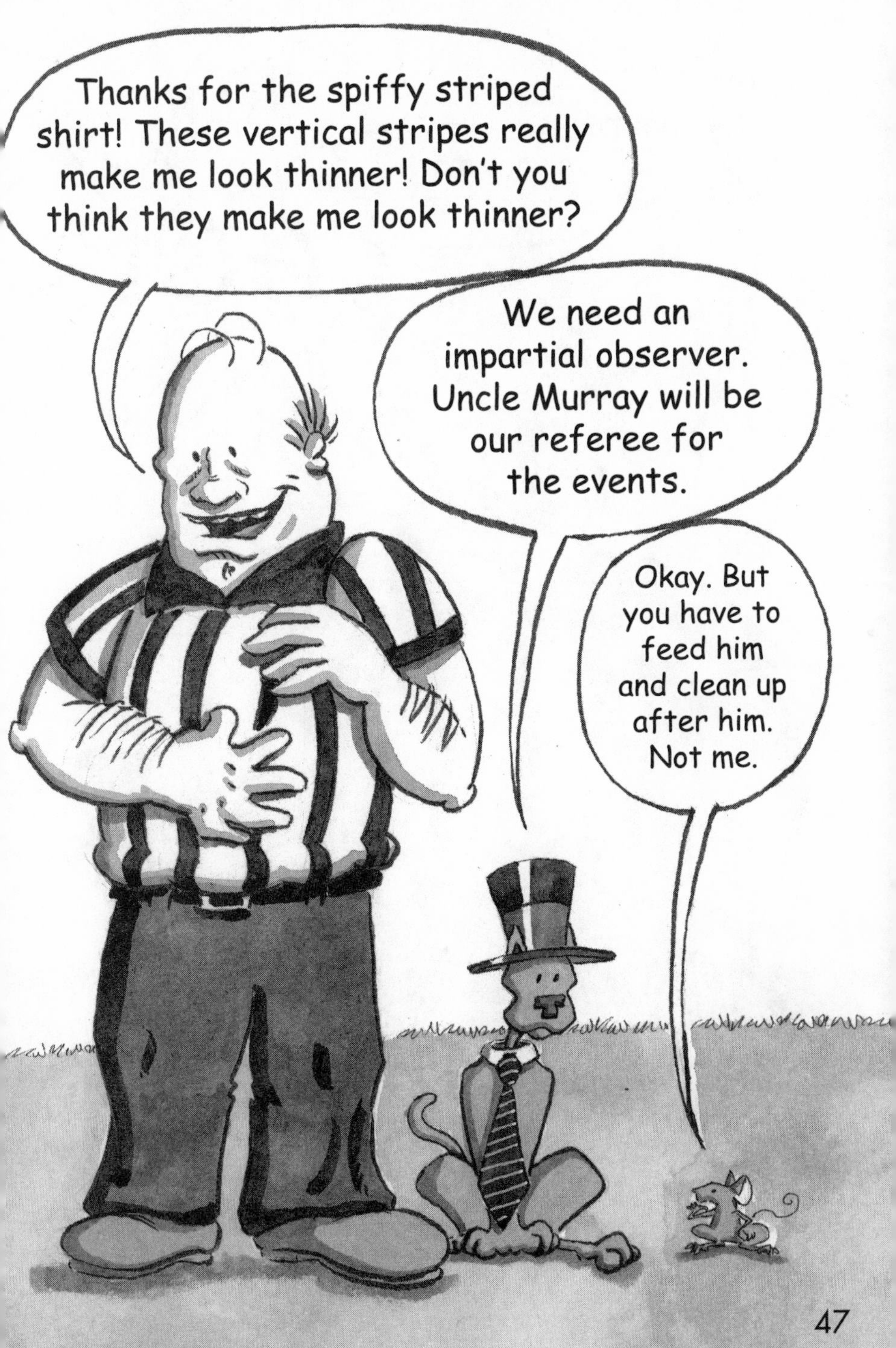
Thanks for the spiffy striped shirt! These vertical stripes really make me look thinner! Don't you think they make me look thinner?
We need an impartial observer. Uncle Murray will be our referee for the events.
Okay. But you have to feed him and clean up after him. Not me.

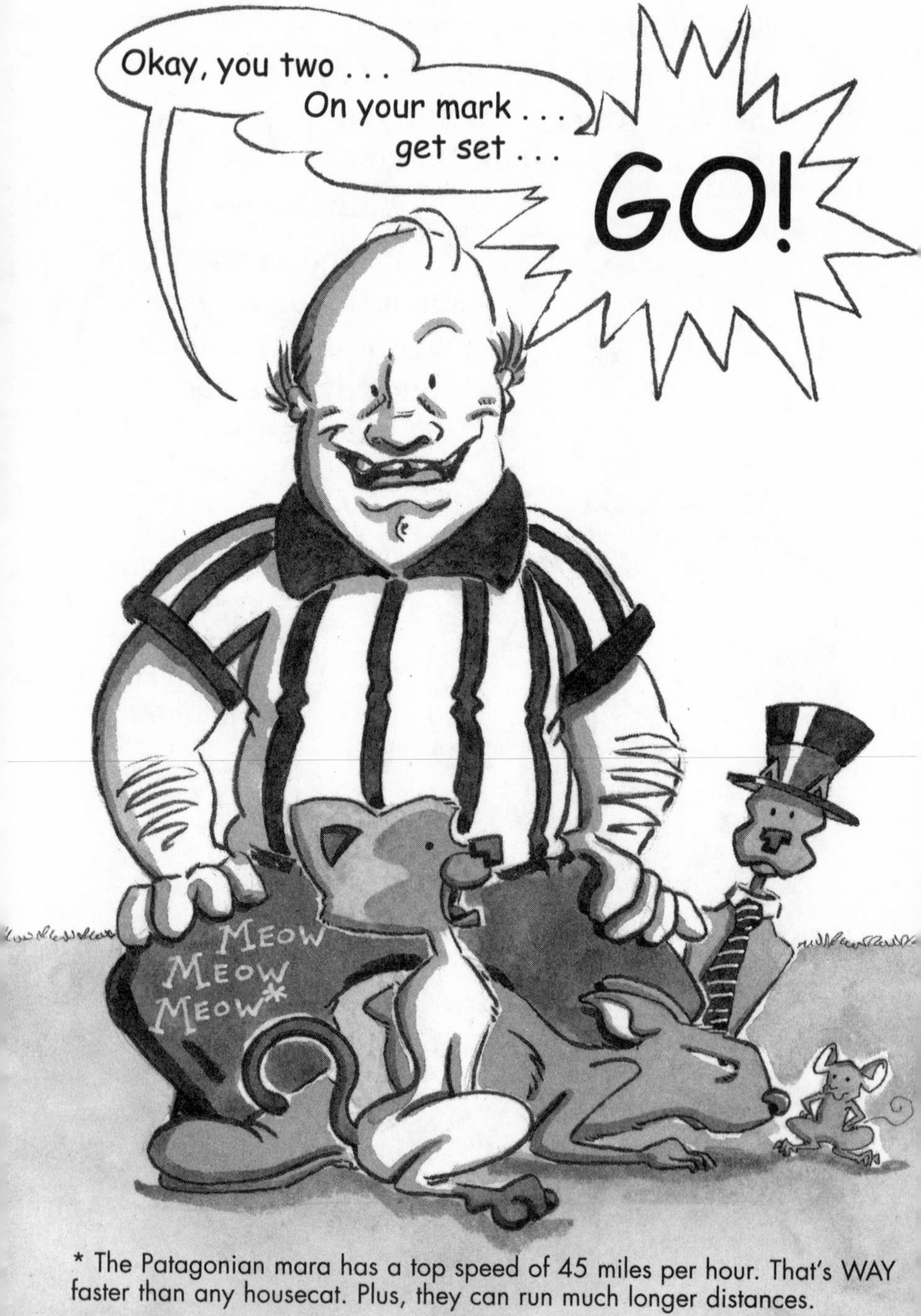
Okay, you two . . .
On your mark . . .
get set . . .
GO!
MEOW
MEOW
MEOW*

* The Patagonian mara has a top speed of 45 miles per hour. That's WAY faster than any housecat. Plus, they can run much longer distances.

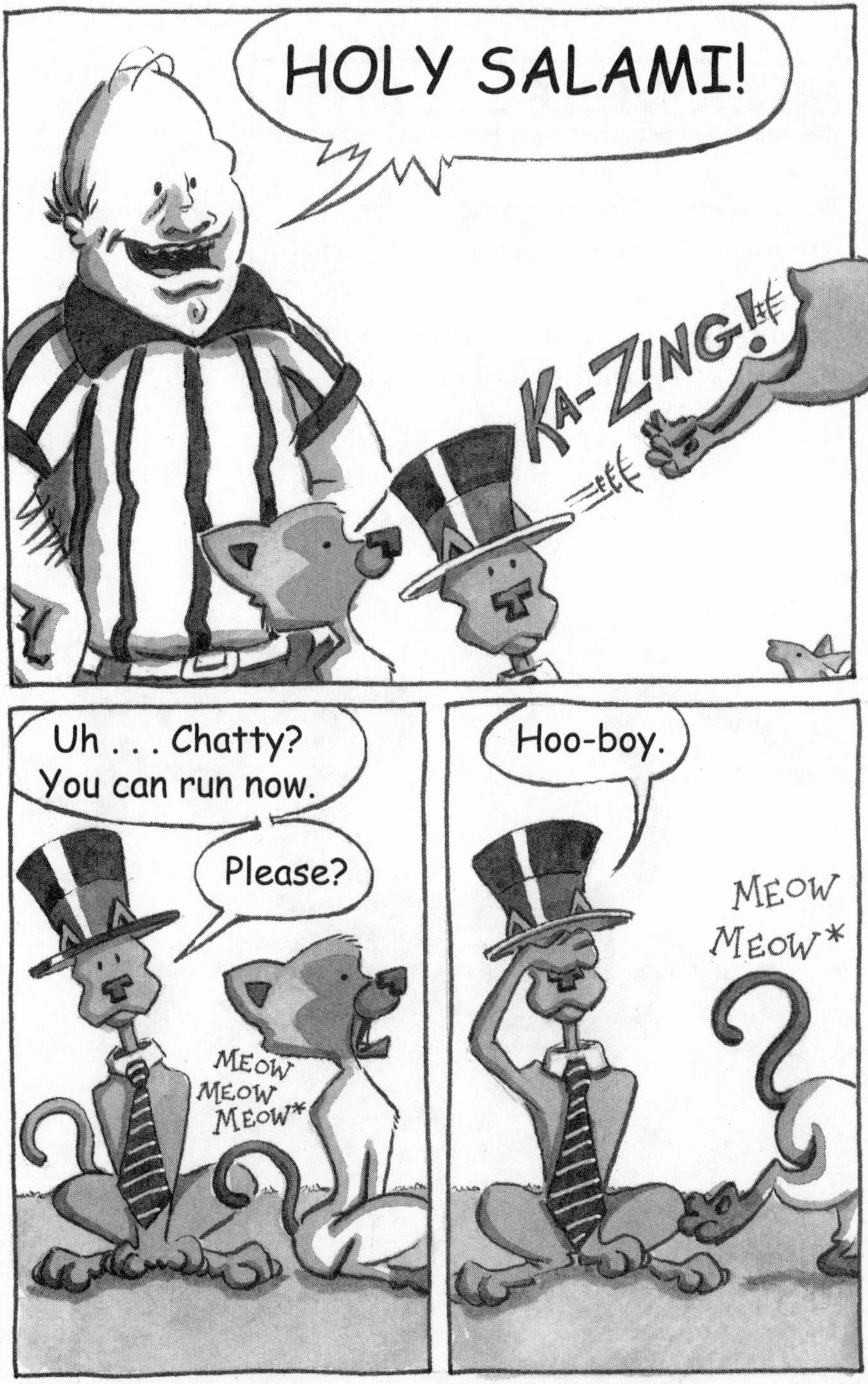
HOLY SALAMI!
KA-ZING!
Uh . . . Chatty? You can run now.
Please?
MEOW MEOW MEOW*
Hoo-boy.
MEOW MEOW*

* Yup. I was right. Way faster.

* I wonder if she's ever been pulled over for speeding in a school zone.

MEANWHILE . . . KITTY

Okay, Kitty. We're going to begin your new exercise regimen with some light jogging.

Jogging is like running, only you're not trying to go too fast. The point is to keep your body active.

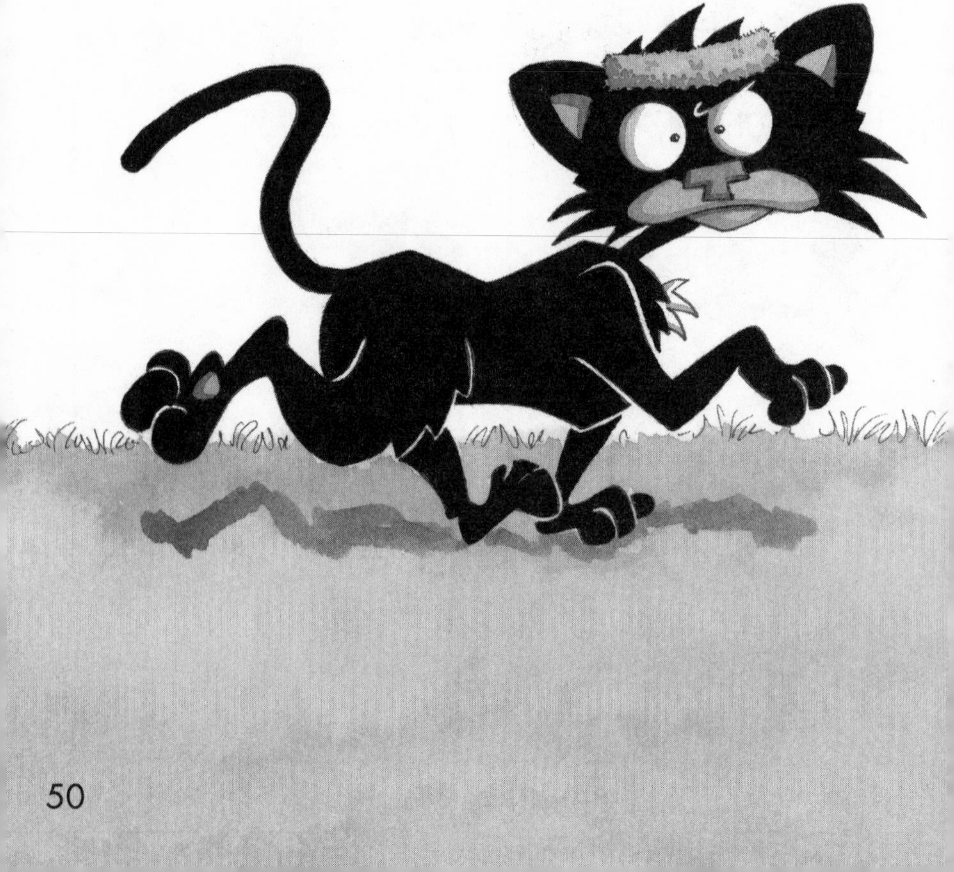

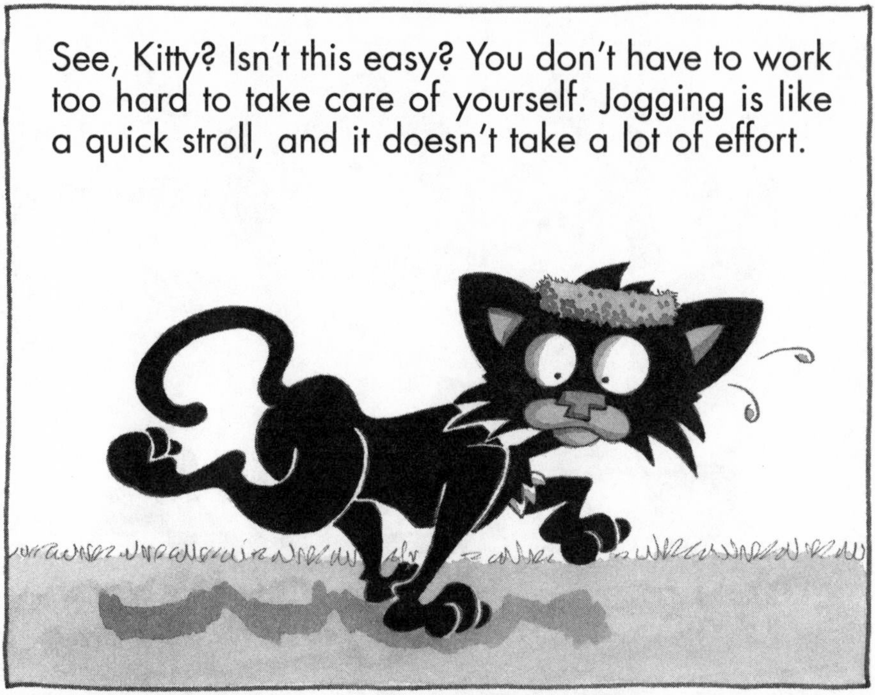
See, Kitty? Isn't this easy? You don't have to work too hard to take care of yourself. Jogging is like a quick stroll, and it doesn't take a lot of effort.

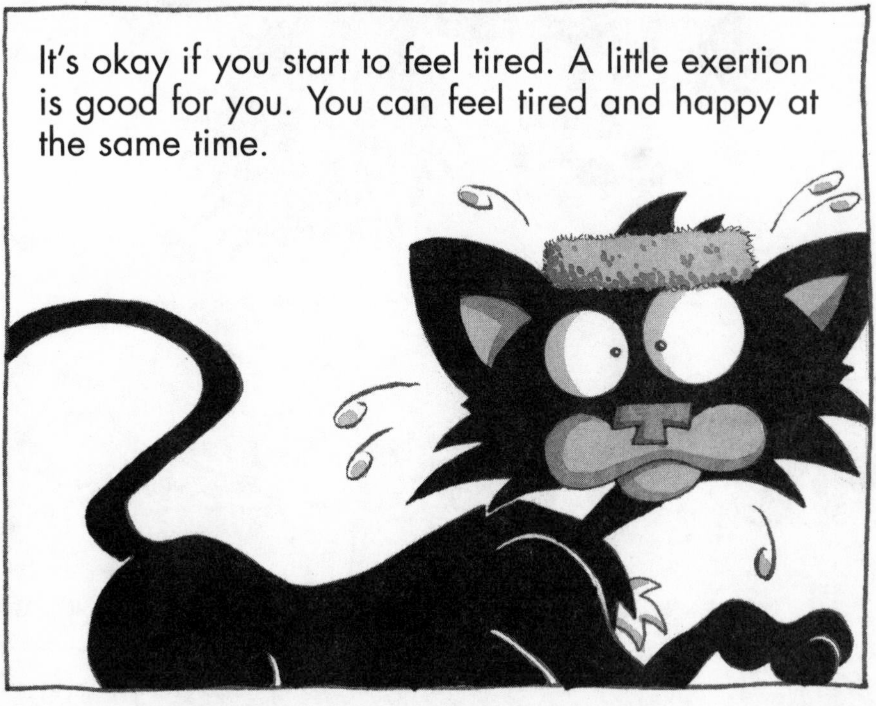
It's okay if you start to feel tired. A little exertion is good for you. You can feel tired and happy at the same time.

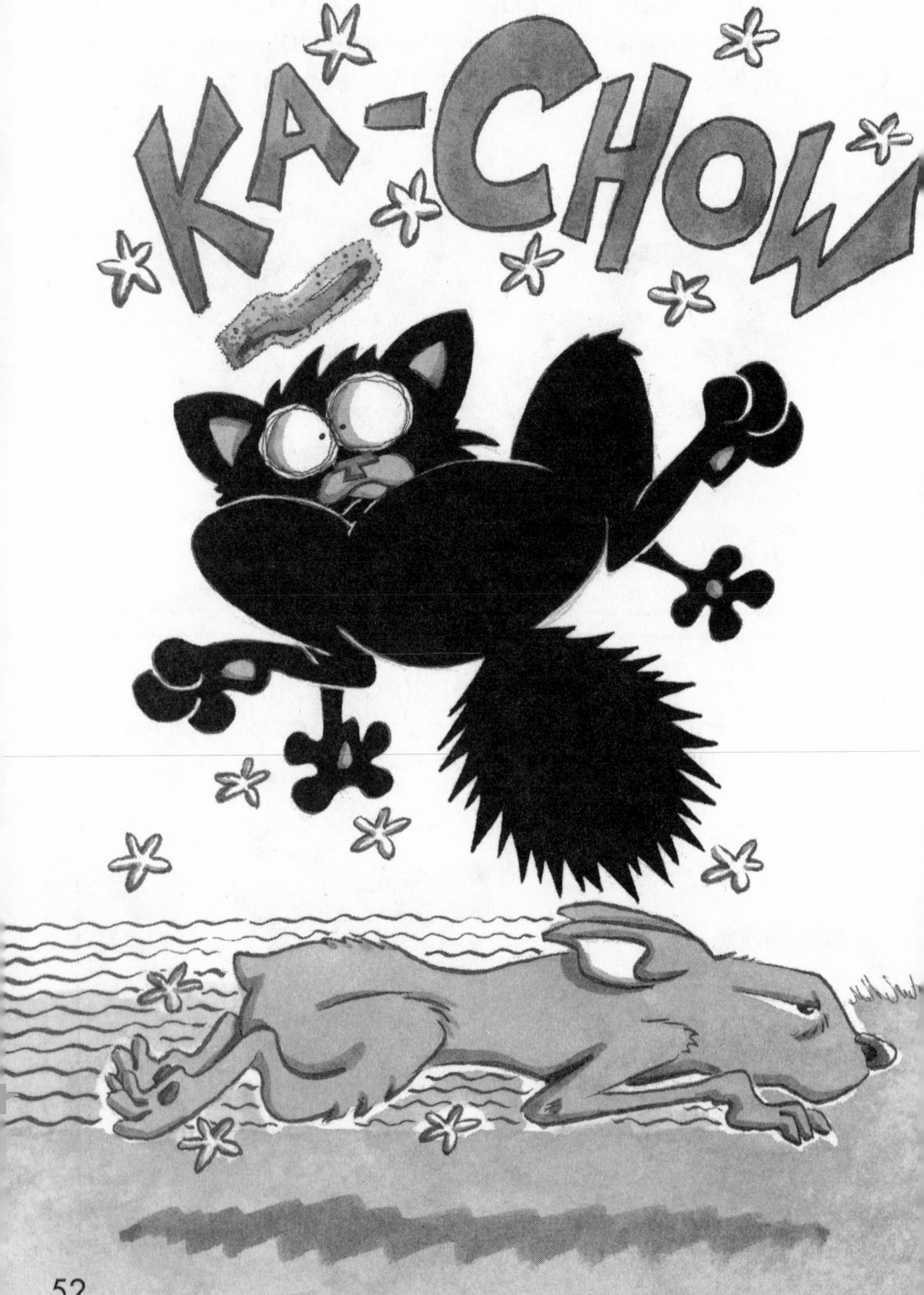
KA-CHOW

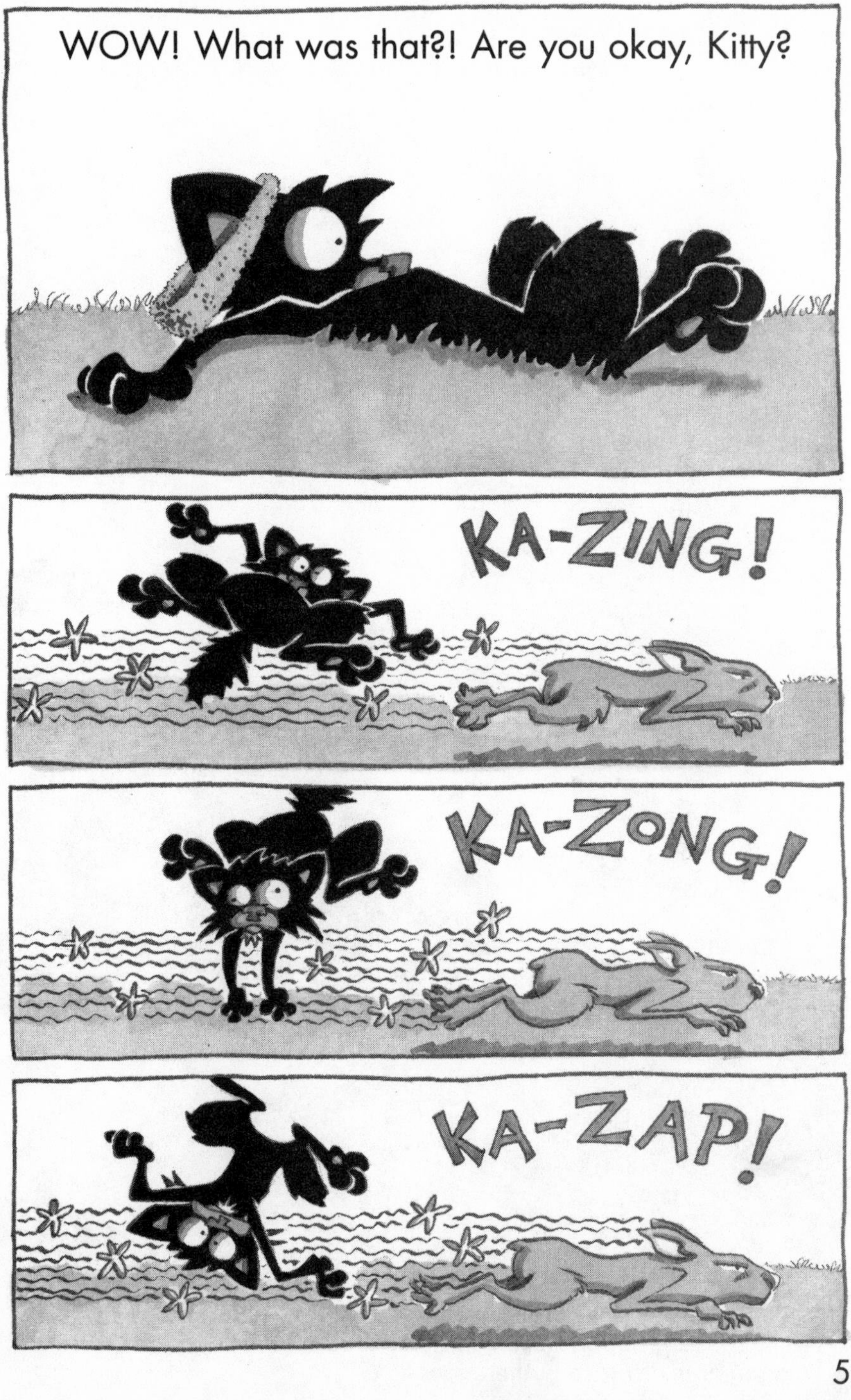
WOW! What was that?! Are you okay, Kitty?
KA-ZING!
KA-ZONG!
KA-ZAP!

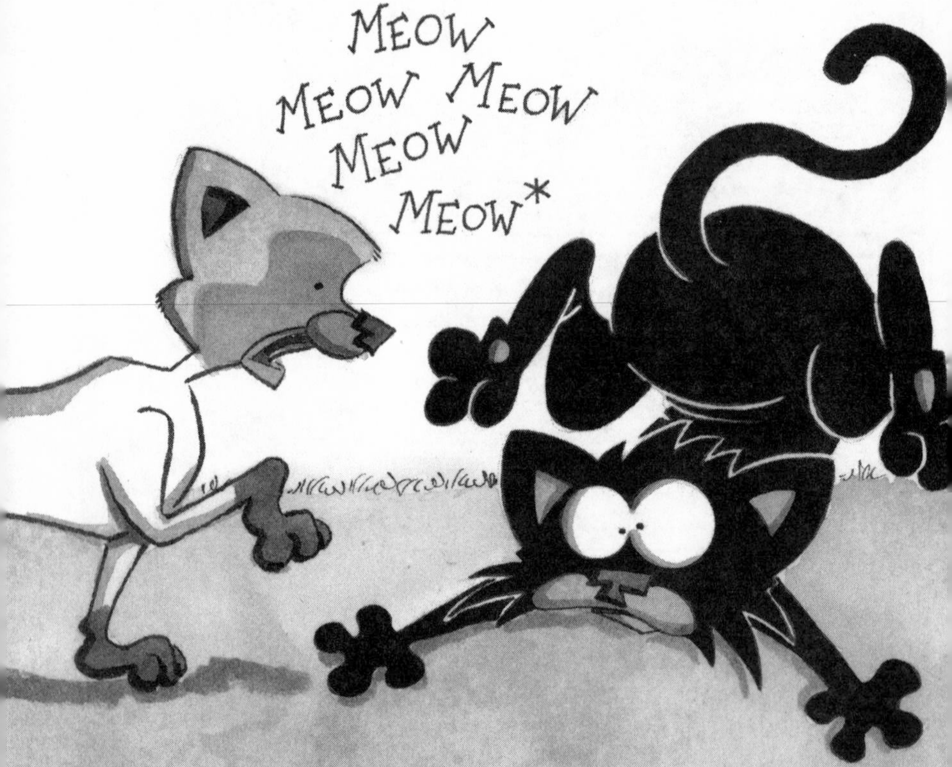
MEOW
MEOW MEOW
MEOW
MEOW*

* Hello. You're probably getting this a lot today, but did you happen to see a Patagonian mara race by here four times?

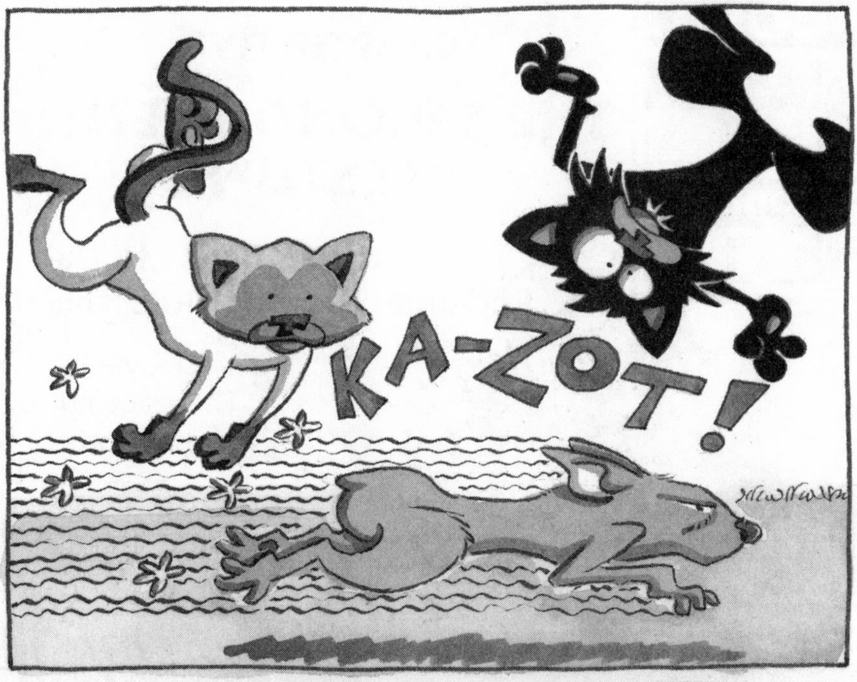
KA-ZOT!

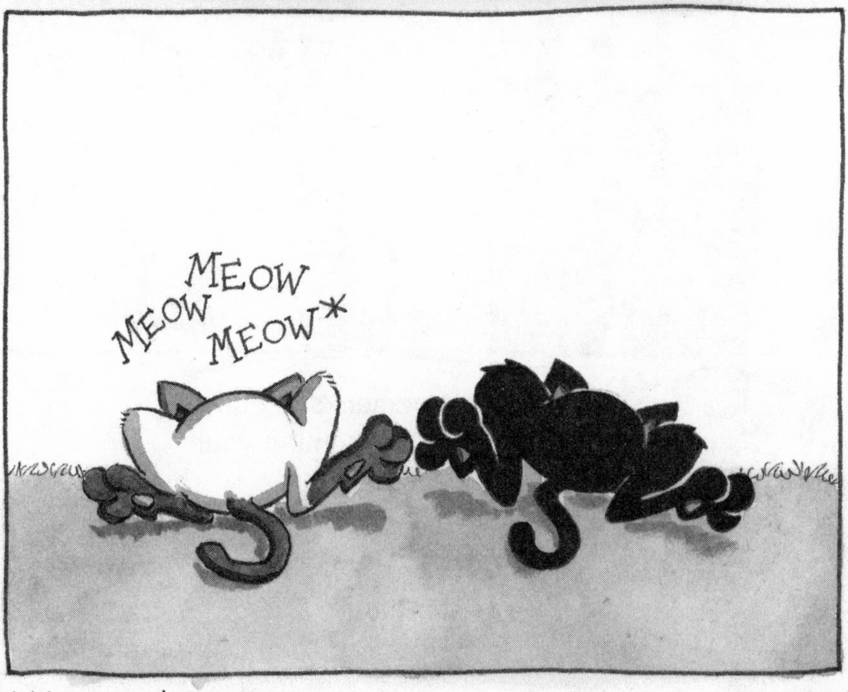
MEOW
MEOW
MEOW*

* Never mind.

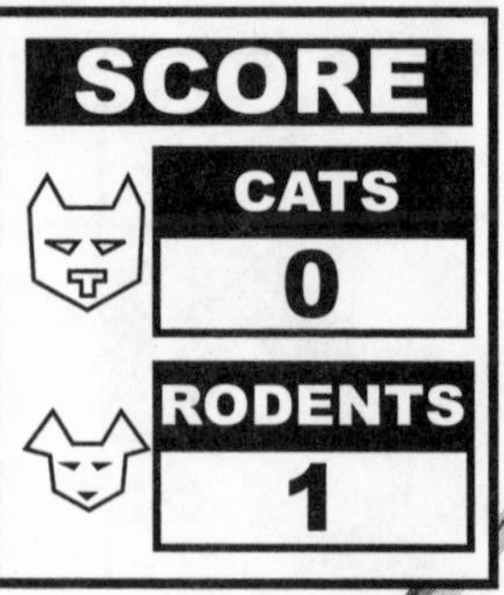
SCORE
CATS
0
RODENTS
1

•CHAPTER FIVE•

THE SECOND EVENT: WRESTLING

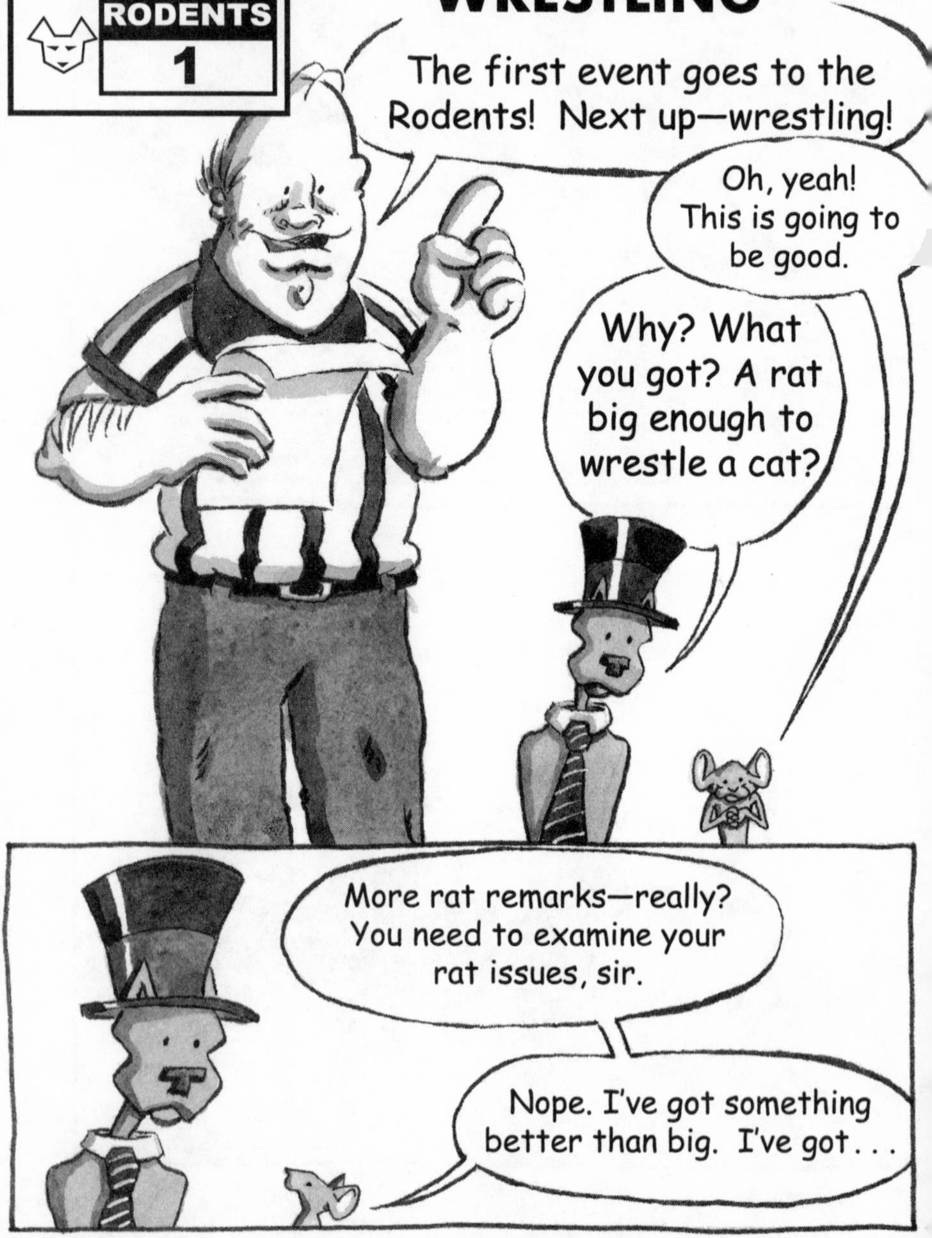
The first event goes to the Rodents! Next up—wrestling!
Oh, yeah! This is going to be good.
Why? What you got? A rat big enough to wrestle a cat?
More rat remarks—really? You need to examine your rat issues, sir.
Nope. I've got something better than big. I've got . . .

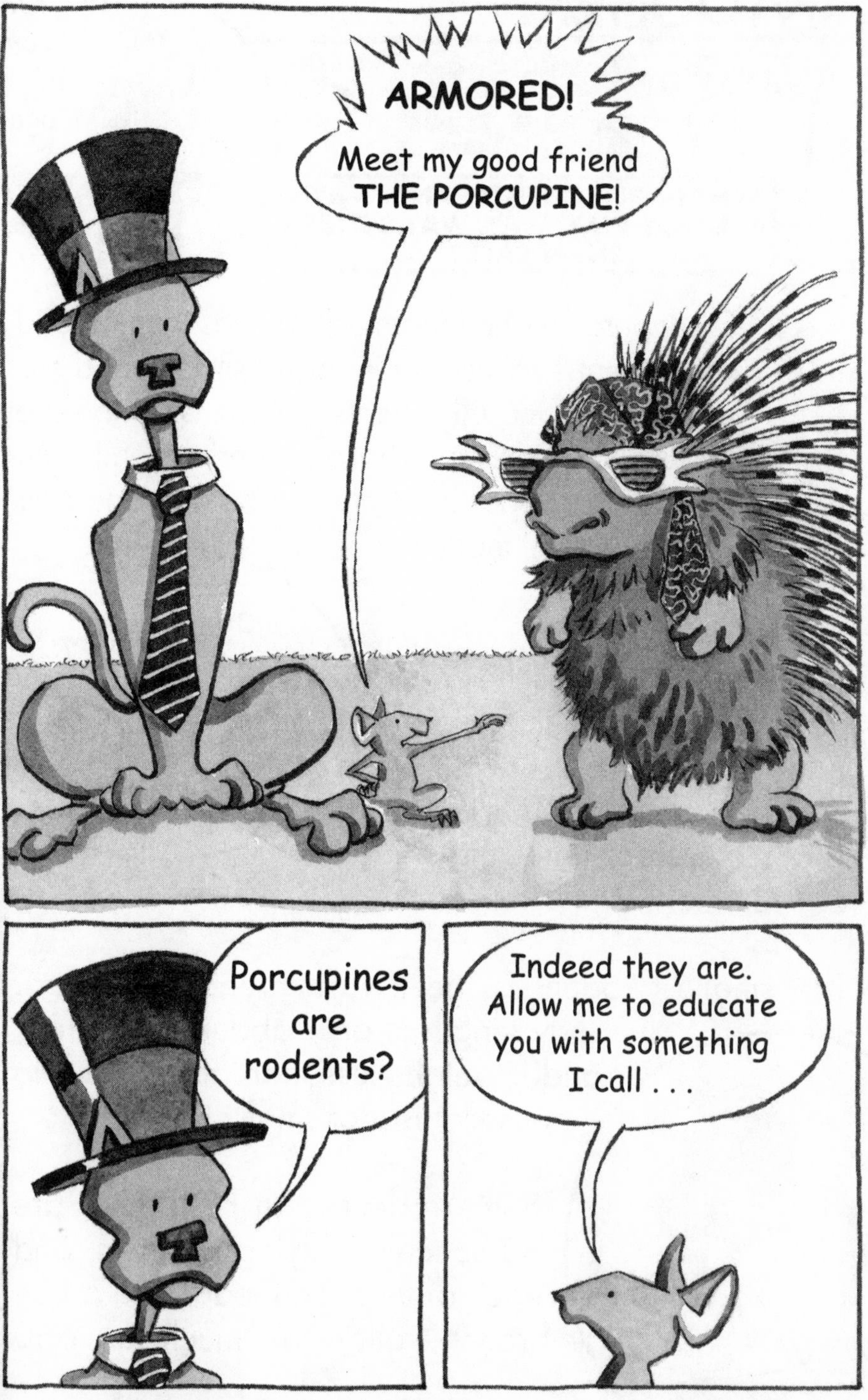
ARMORED!
Meet my good friend THE PORCUPINE!
Porcupines are rodents?
Indeed they are. Allow me to educate you with something I call . . .

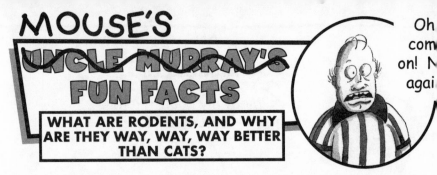

MOUSE'S

UNCLE MURRAY'S FUN FACTS

WHAT ARE RODENTS, AND WHY ARE THEY WAY, WAY, WAY BETTER THAN CATS?

Oh
com
on! N
agai

Forty percent of all mammal species in the world are rodents! We come in many shapes and sizes, but the thing all rodents have in common are two pairs of incisors (sharp powerful teeth), one pair on the upper front of our jaw and one pair on the bottom, that never stop growing!

The biggest rodent is the capybara. They look a little like gigantic guinea pigs and can weigh as much as 200 pounds! That's over four times the weight of even the biggest housecat.

CAPYBARA

The smallest rodent is the dwarf three-toed jerboa. Its body length is only about 1.7 inches, and it weighs less than an ounce. No housecat is that small.

DWARF JERBOA

(ACTUAL SIZE)

Some rodents can FLY! There are 43 species of flying squirrels, and each of them can leap from a tree branch, glide as much as 660 feet through the air, and land effortlessly on another branch. If you dropped a cat from the top of a tall tree, it would fall like a bag of wet bananas until it hit the ground with a dull *thud*.

Some rodents practically live in WATER! Beavers, for instance, can hold their breath underwater for 15 minutes! A colony of beavers can build a dam that will block an entire river. Do you know what happens when you get a cat even slightly wet? One little drop of water, and they go insane. Pathetic!

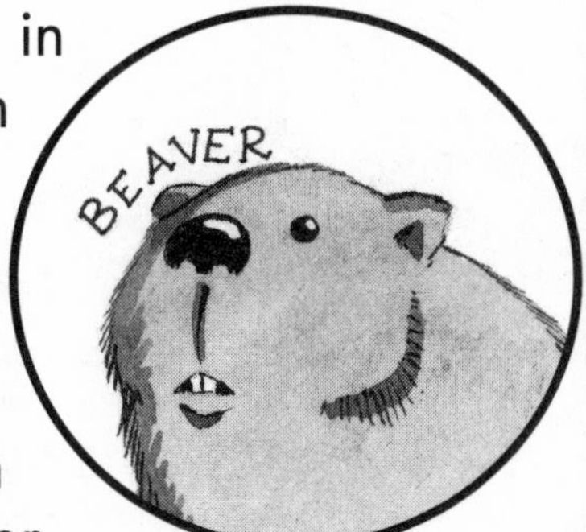
BEAVER

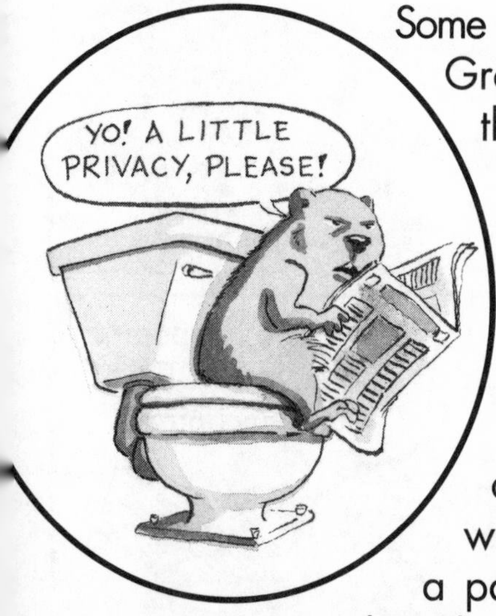
YO! A LITTLE PRIVACY, PLEASE!

Some rodents live UNDERGROUND! Groundhogs build burrows that can be as long as 60 feet with several chambers, or rooms. They'll even build a special chamber where they can poop. That's right—groundhogs build bathrooms! Cats will do their business wherever there's a patch of sand or dirt. They don't care!

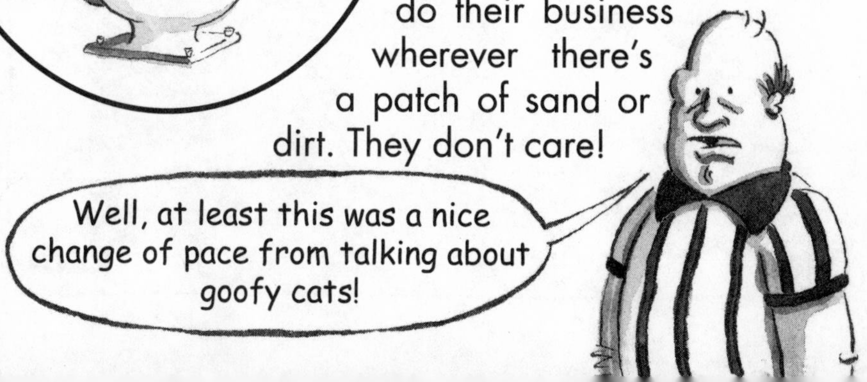
Well, at least this was a nice change of pace from talking about goofy cats!

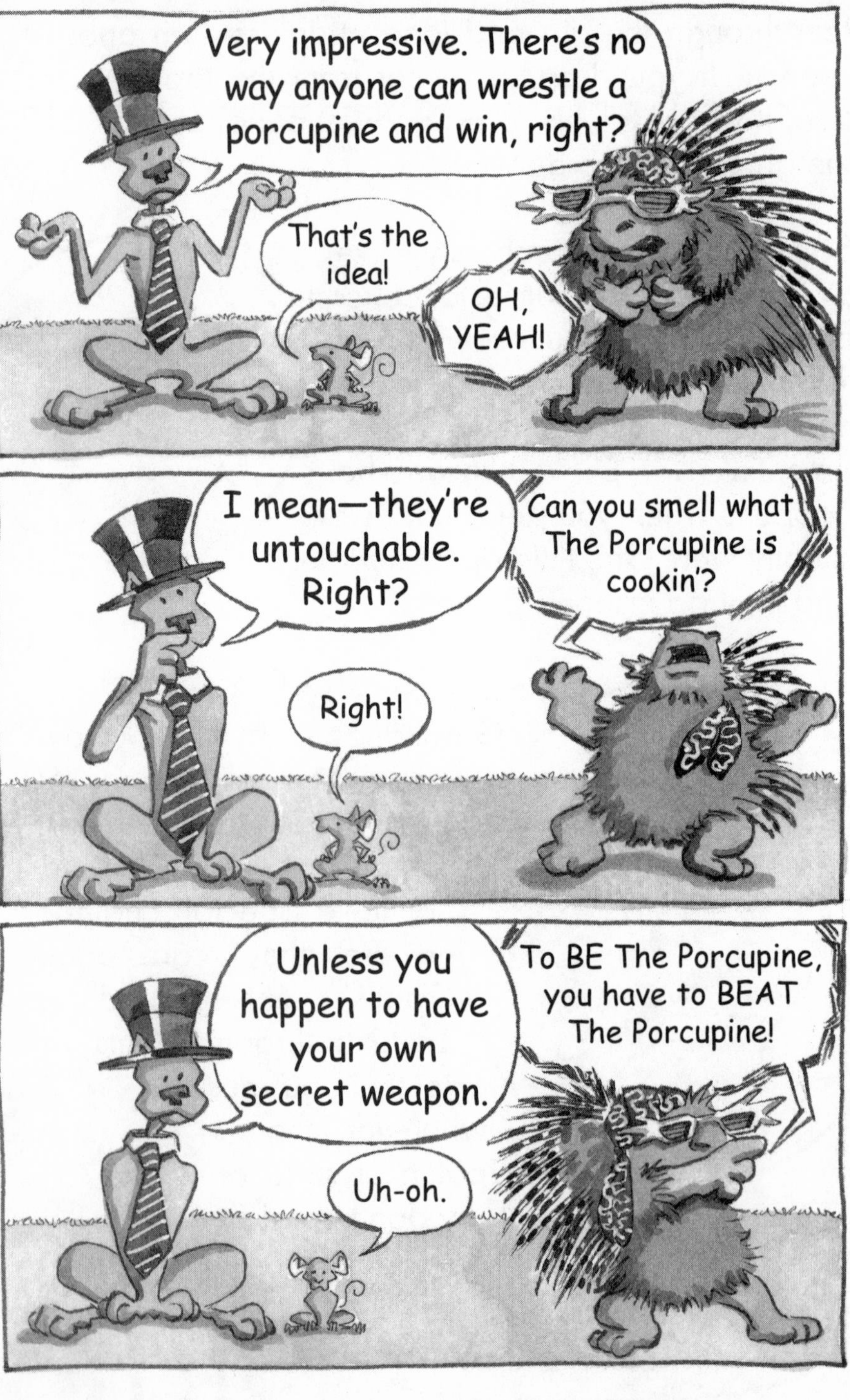
Very impressive. There's no way anyone can wrestle a porcupine and win, right?
That's the idea!
OH, YEAH!
I mean—they're untouchable. Right?
Can you smell what The Porcupine is cookin'?
Right!
Unless you happen to have your own secret weapon.
To BE The Porcupine, you have to BEAT The Porcupine!
Uh-oh.

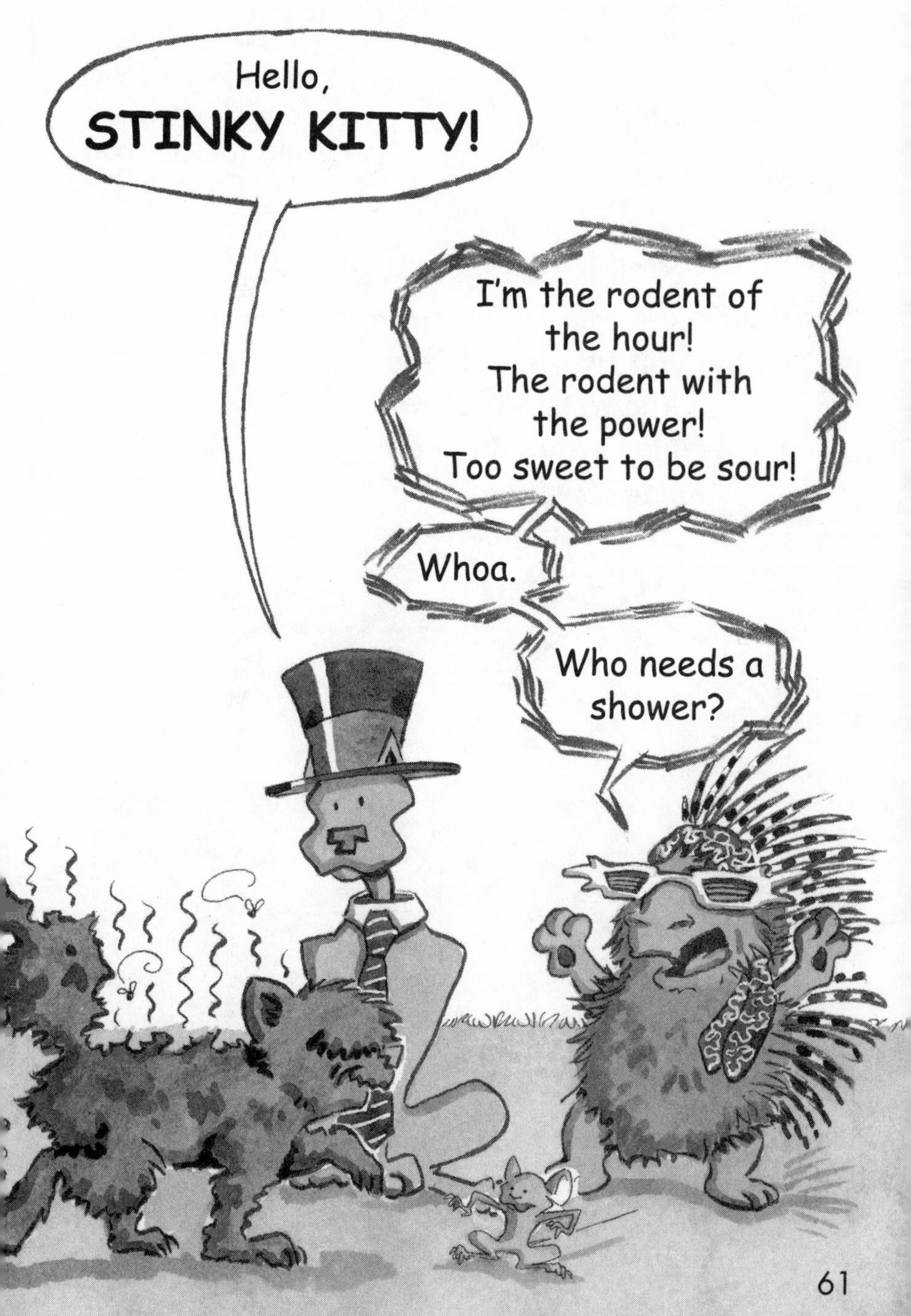
Hello, **STINKY KITTY!**
I'm the rodent of the hour! The rodent with the power! Too sweet to be sour!
Whoa.
Who needs a shower?

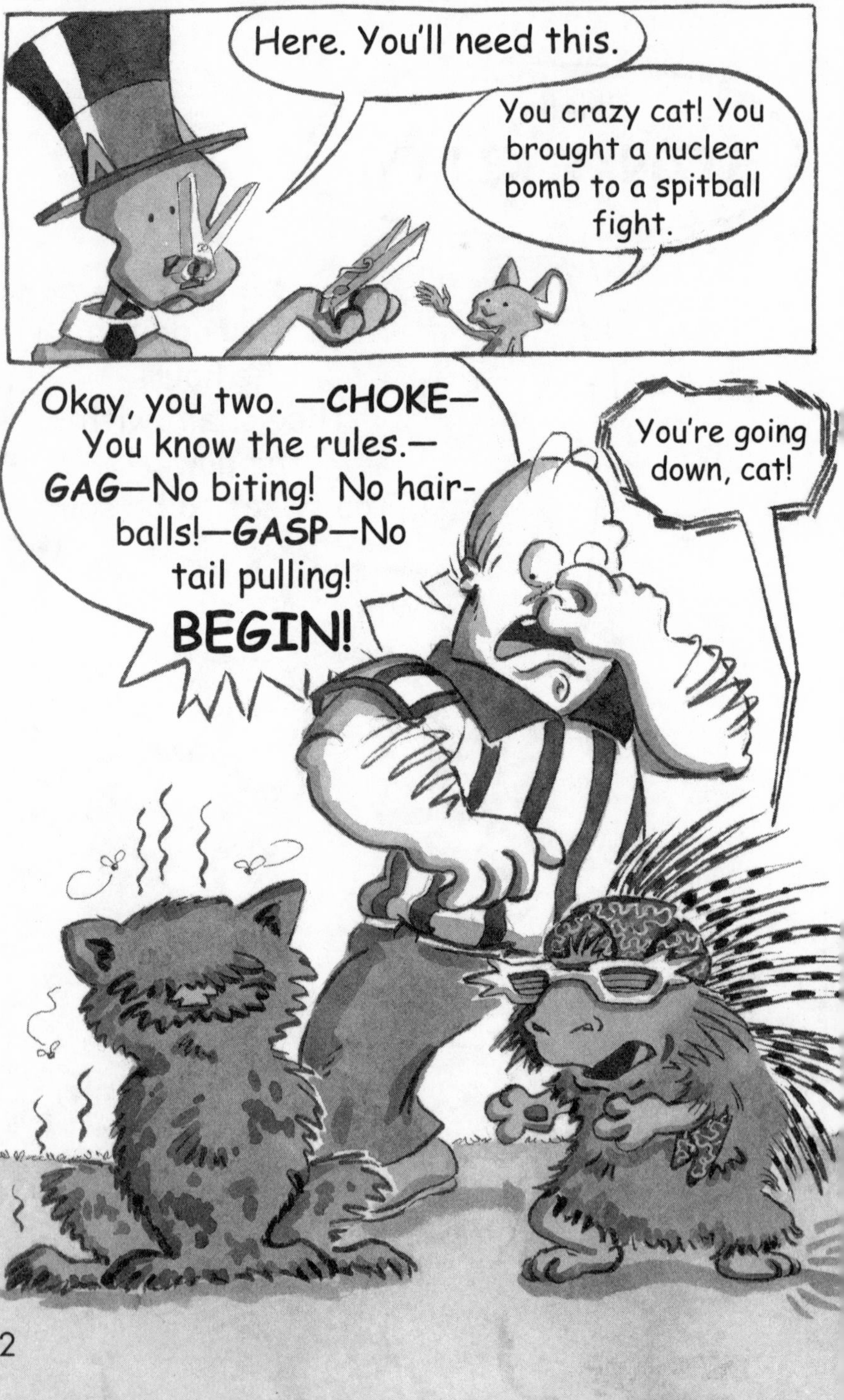
Here. You'll need this.
You crazy cat! You brought a nuclear bomb to a spitball fight.
Okay, you two. —CHOKE— You know the rules.—GAG—No biting! No hair-balls!—GASP—No tail pulling! BEGIN!
You're going down, cat!

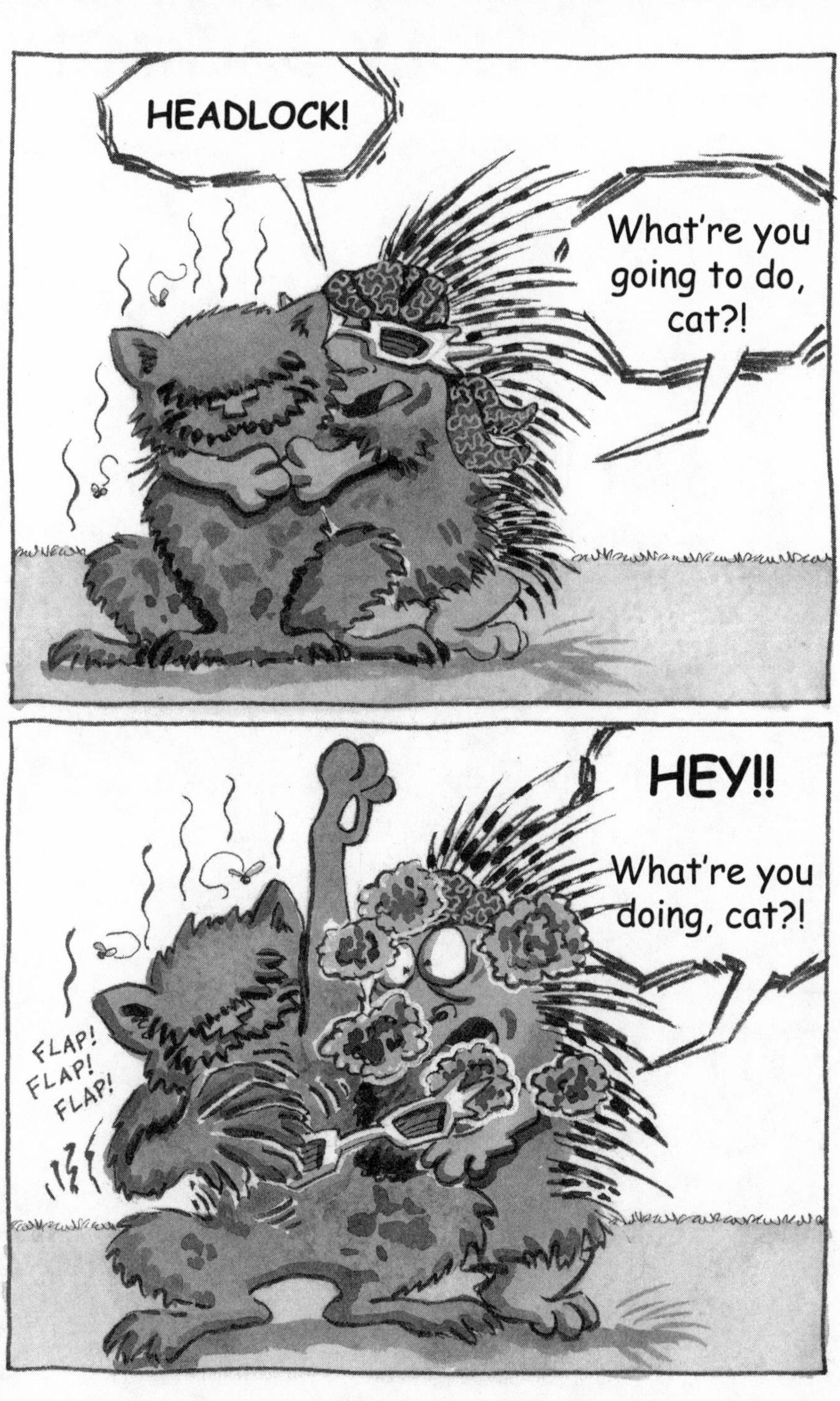
HEADLOCK!
What're you going to do, cat?!
HEY!!
What're you doing, cat?!
FLAP! FLAP! FLAP!

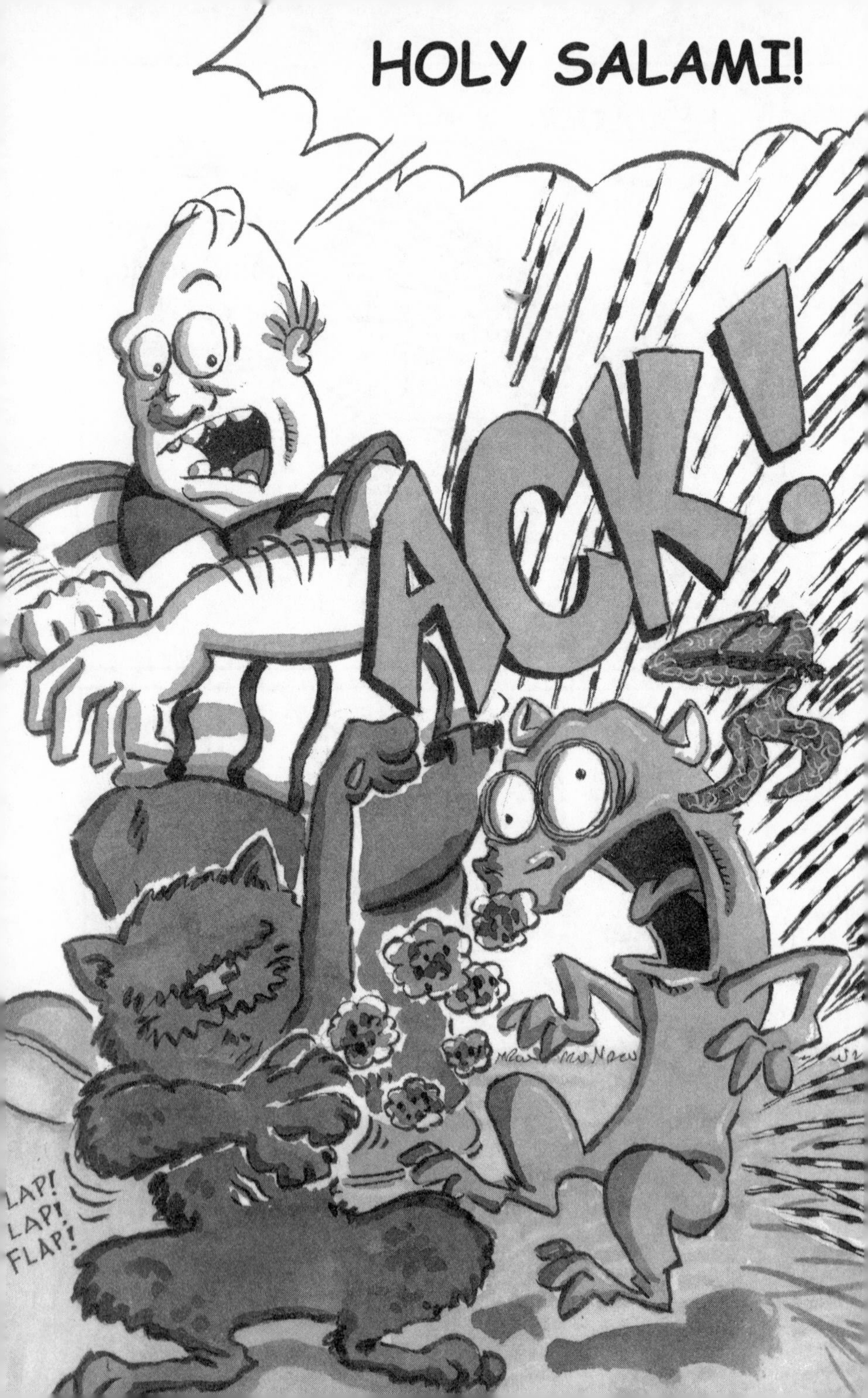
HOLY SALAMI!
ACK!
LAP!
LAP!
FLAP!

MEANWHILE . . . KITTY

Kitty, sometimes the games we play are also a great way to exercise. Like jump rope!

Try it, Kitty!

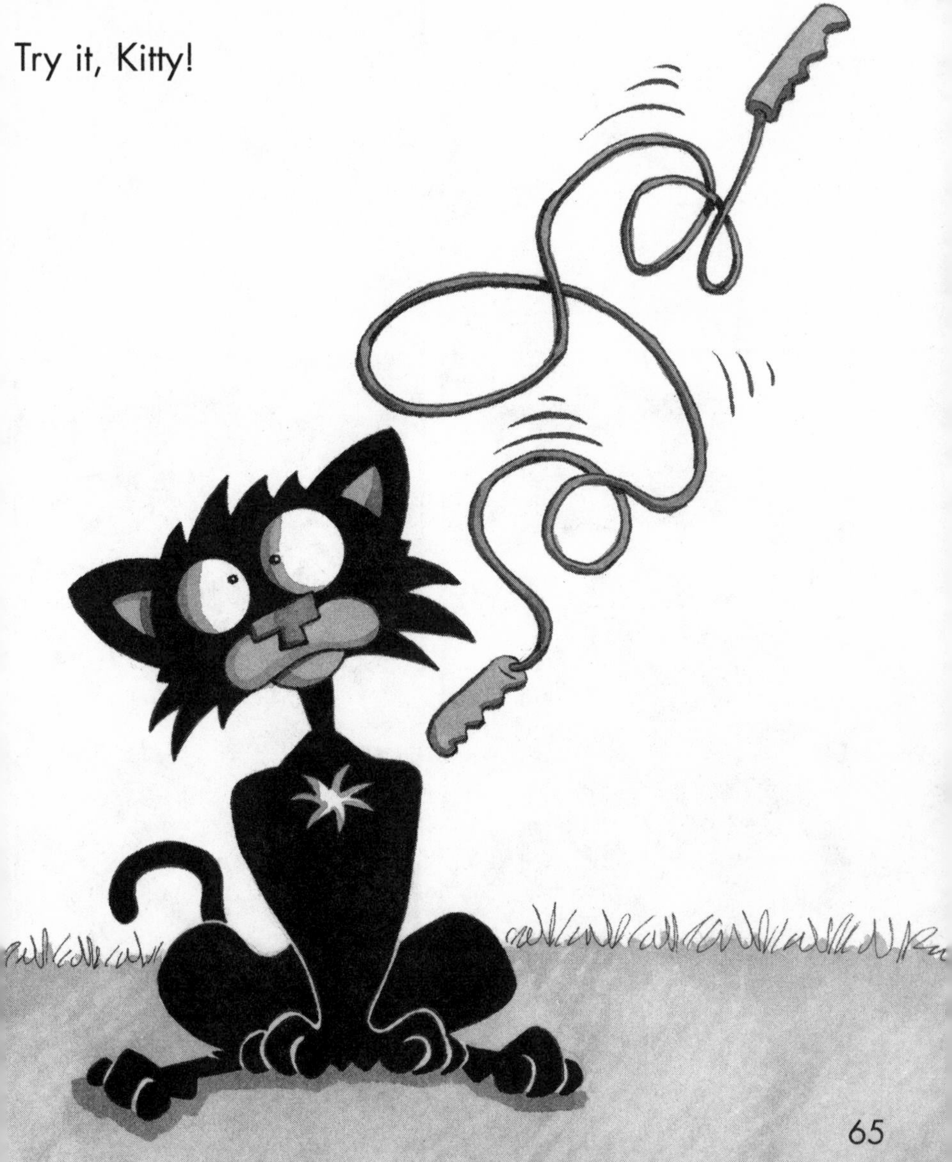

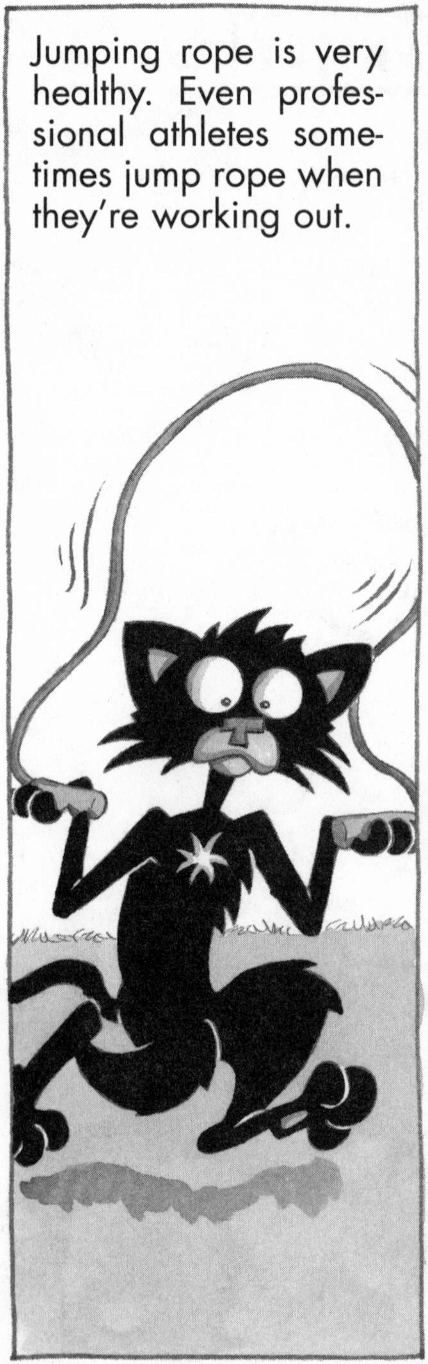
Jumping rope is very healthy. Even professional athletes sometimes jump rope when they're working out.

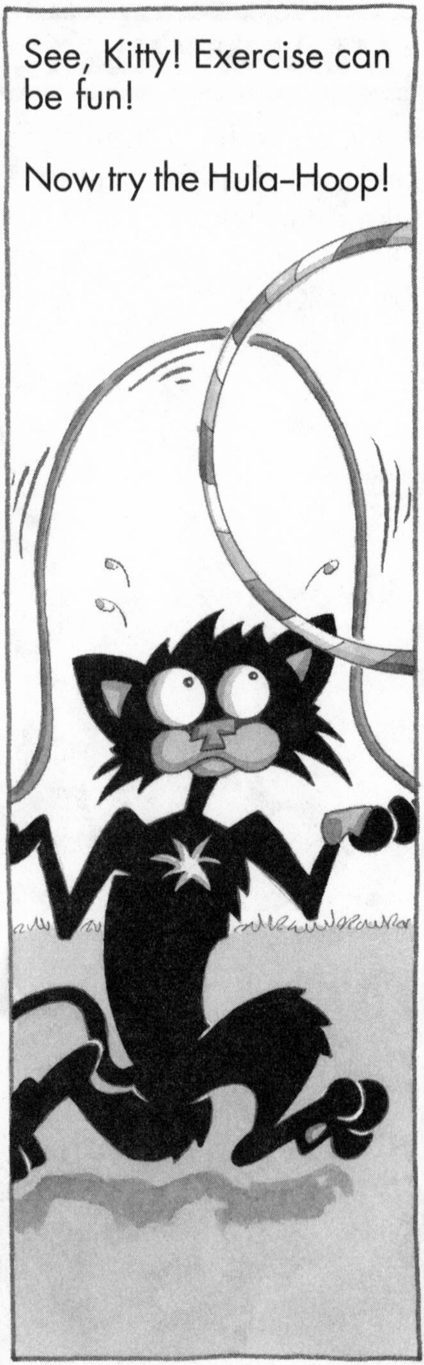
See, Kitty! Exercise can be fun!
Now try the Hula-Hoop!

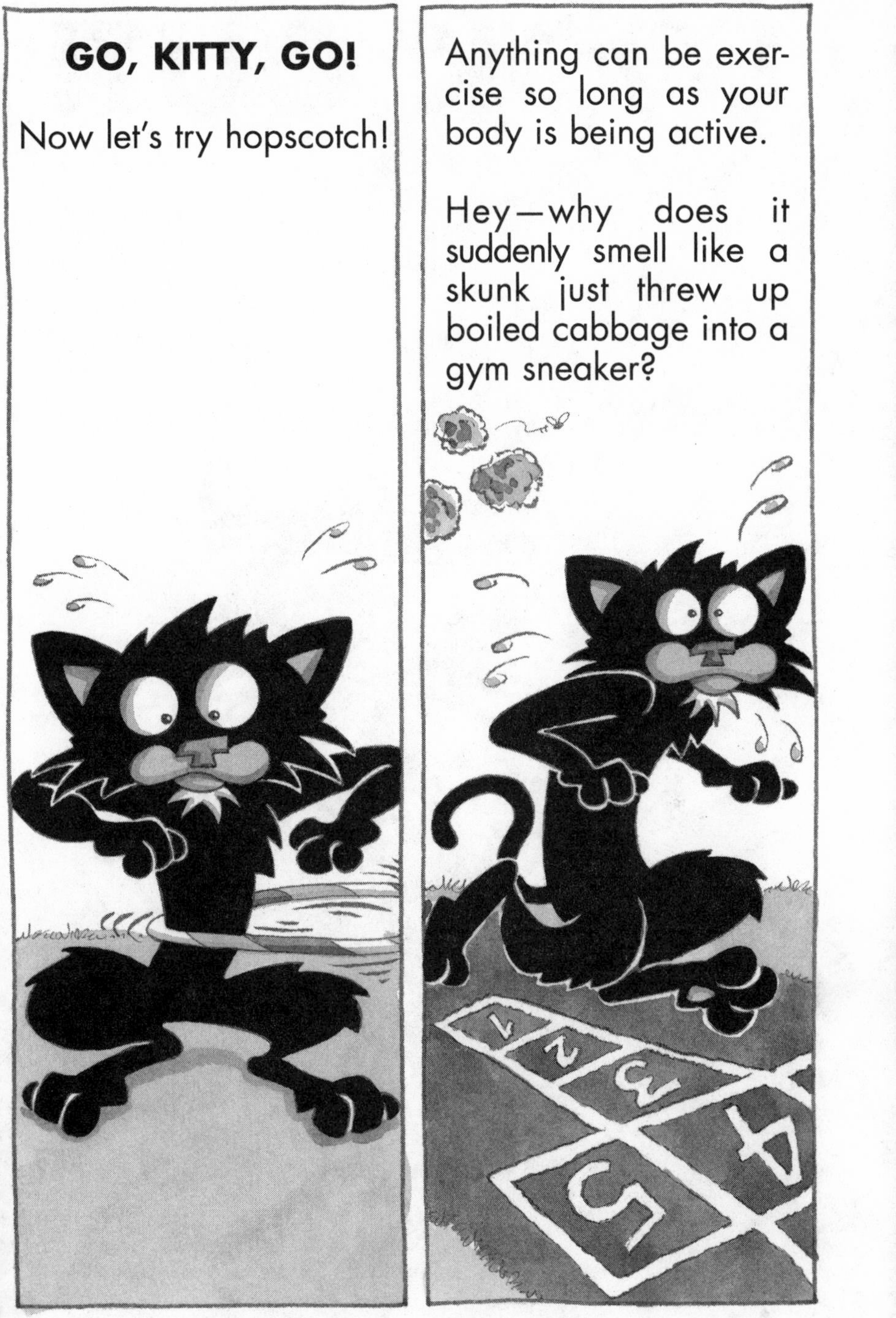
GO, KITTY, GO!
Now let's try hopscotch!
Anything can be exercise so long as your body is being active.
Hey—why does it suddenly smell like a skunk just threw up boiled cabbage into a gym sneaker?

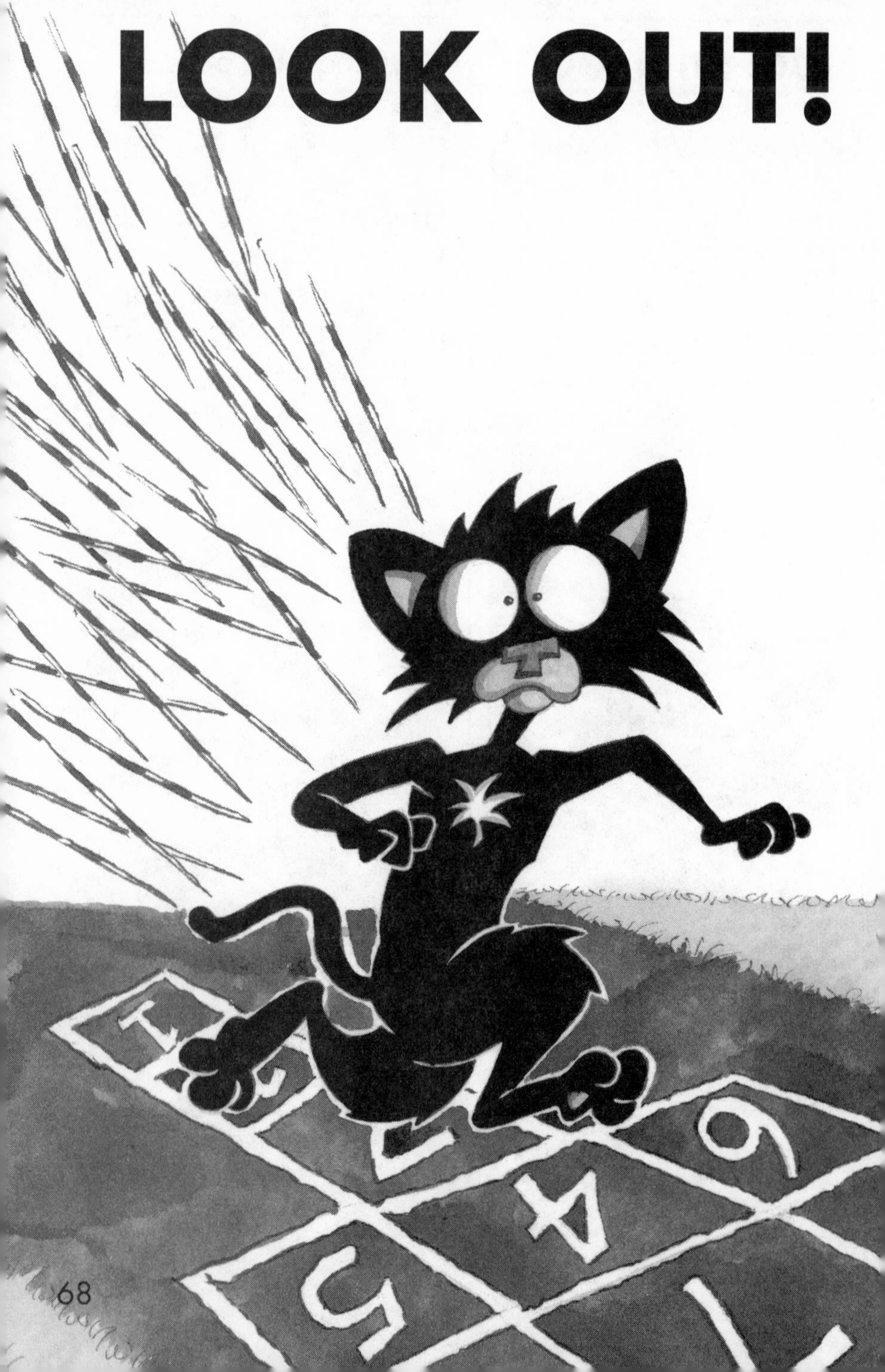
LOOK OUT!

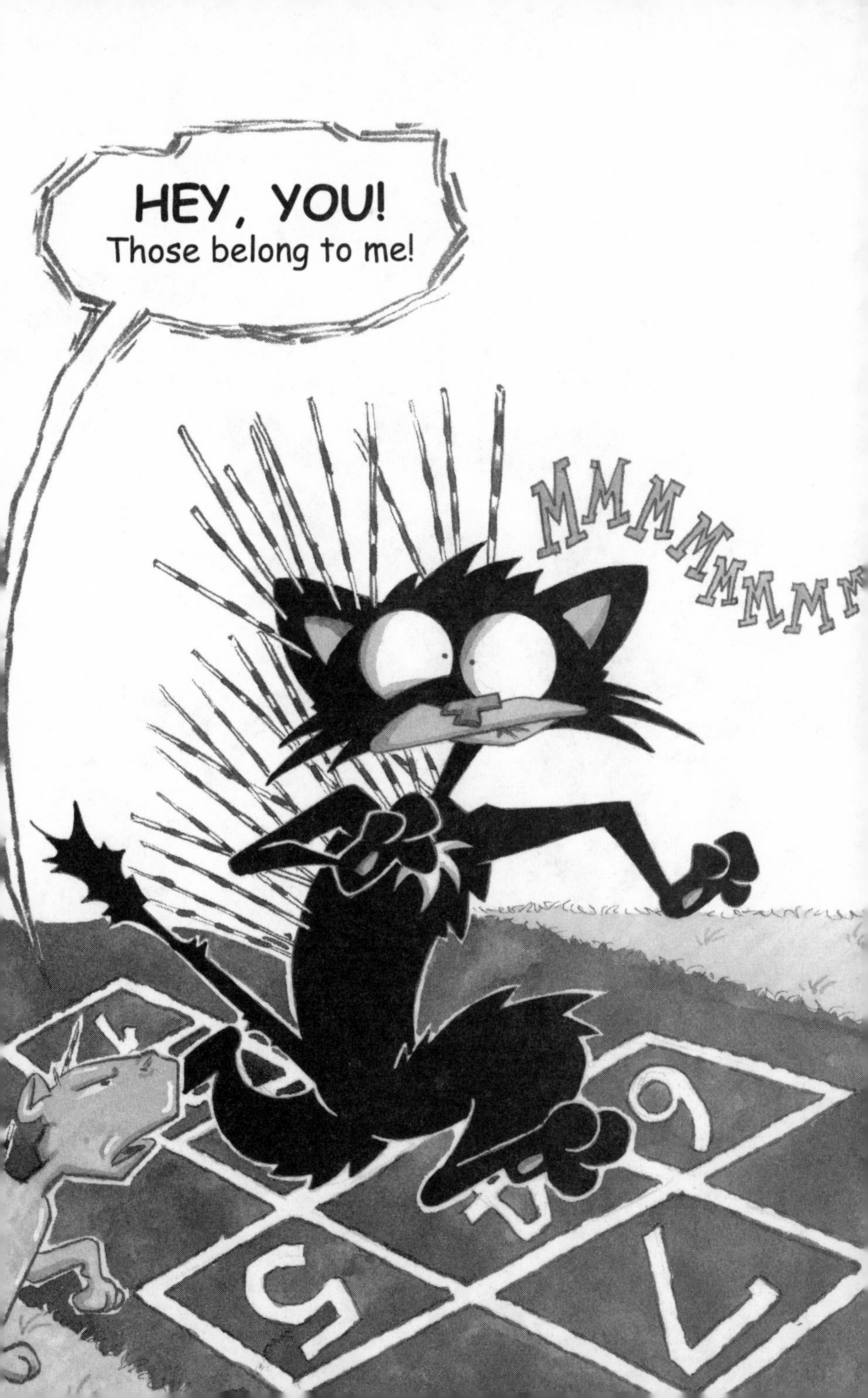
HEY, YOU!
Those belong to me!
MMMMMMMMF

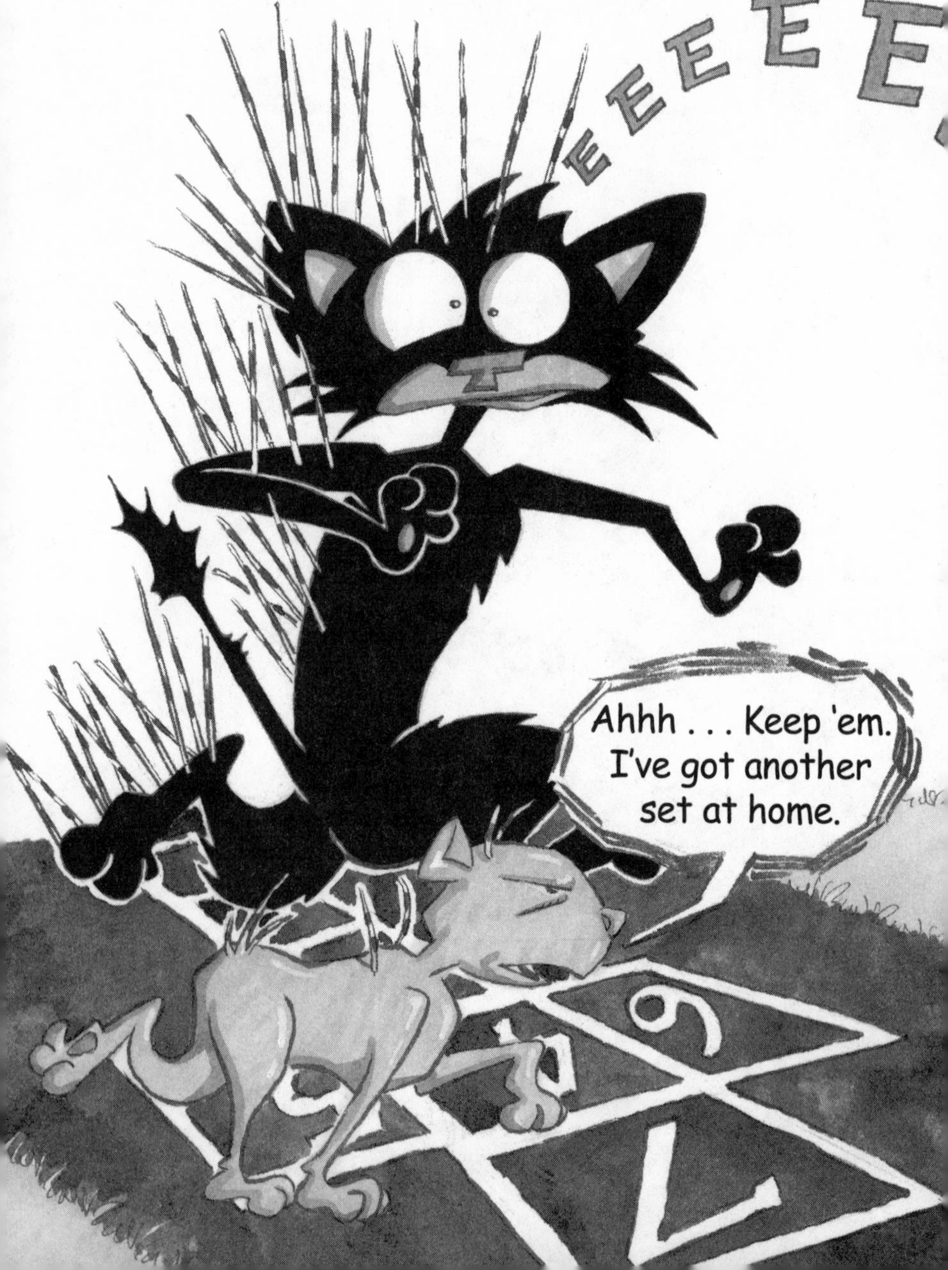
EEEEE
Ahhh . . . Keep 'em. I've got another set at home.

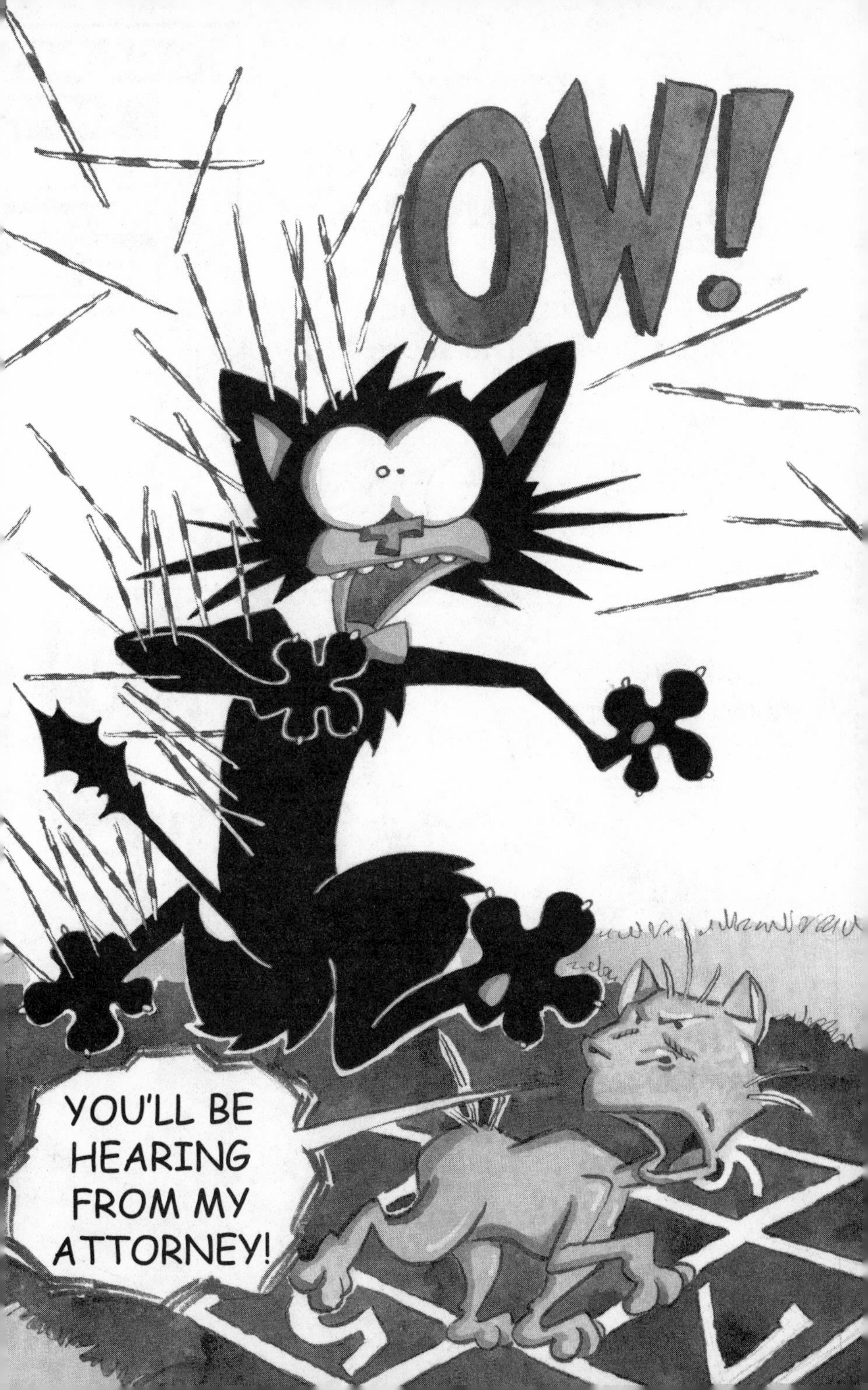
OW!
YOU'LL BE HEARING FROM MY ATTORNEY!

• CHAPTER SIX •

THE THIRD EVENT: TAE KWON DO

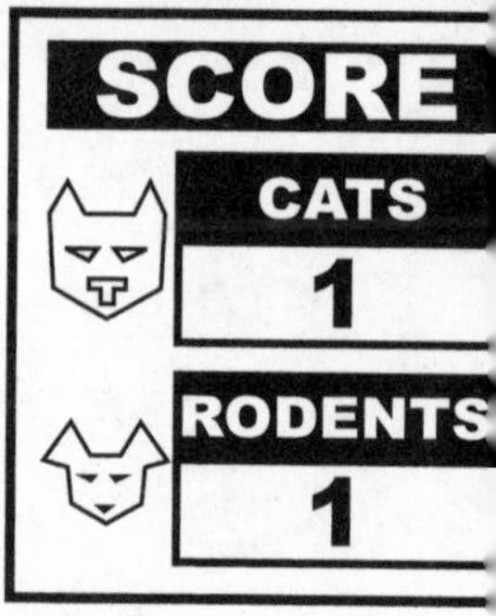
SCORE
CATS
1
RODENTS
1

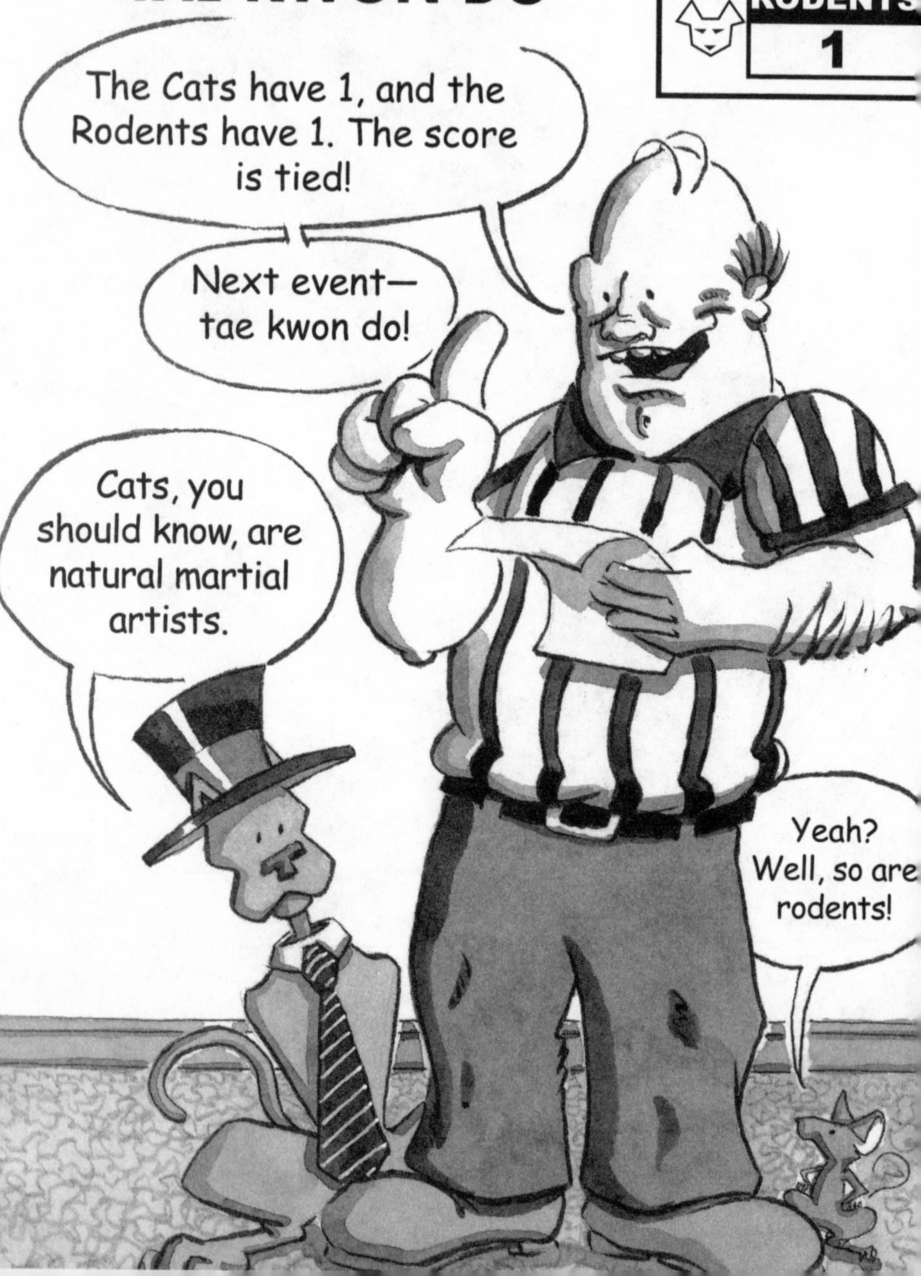
The Cats have 1, and the Rodents have 1. The score is tied!
Next event—tae kwon do!
Cats, you should know, are natural martial artists.
Yeah? Well, so are rodents!

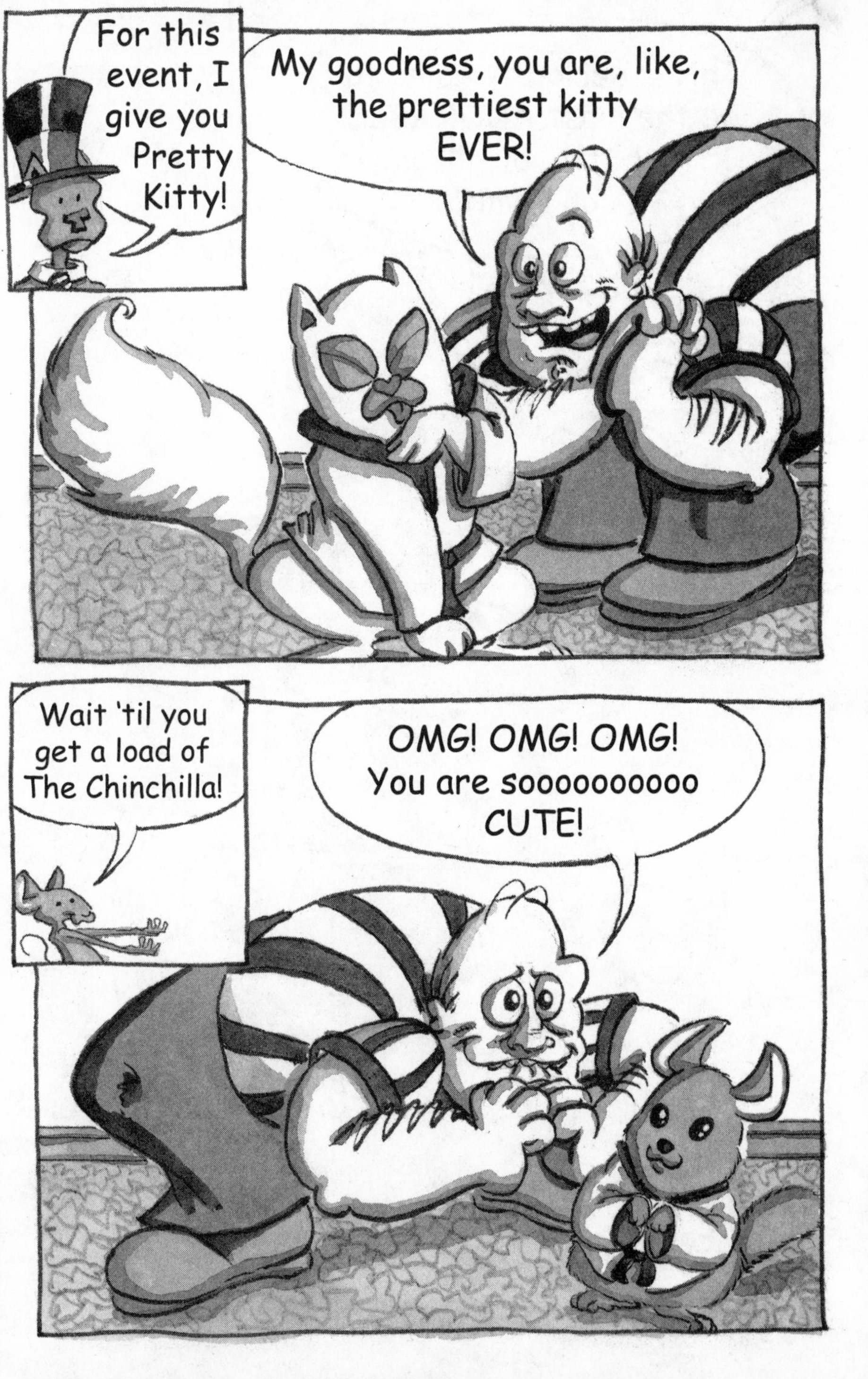

For this event, I give you Pretty Kitty!
My goodness, you are, like, the prettiest kitty EVER!
Wait 'til you get a load of The Chinchilla!
OMG! OMG! OMG! You are sooooooooooo CUTE!

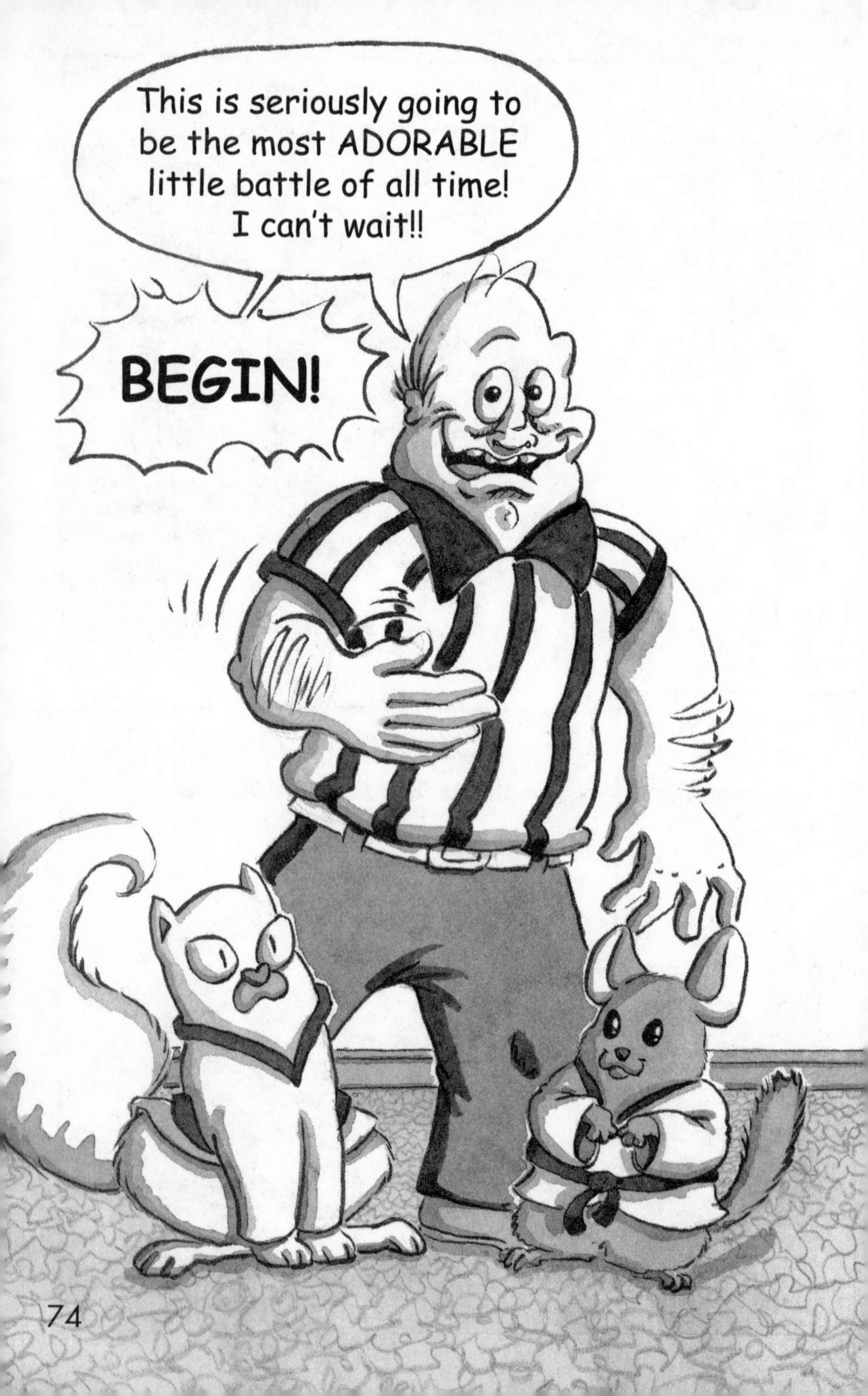
This is seriously going to be the most ADORABLE little battle of all time! I can't wait!!
BEGIN!

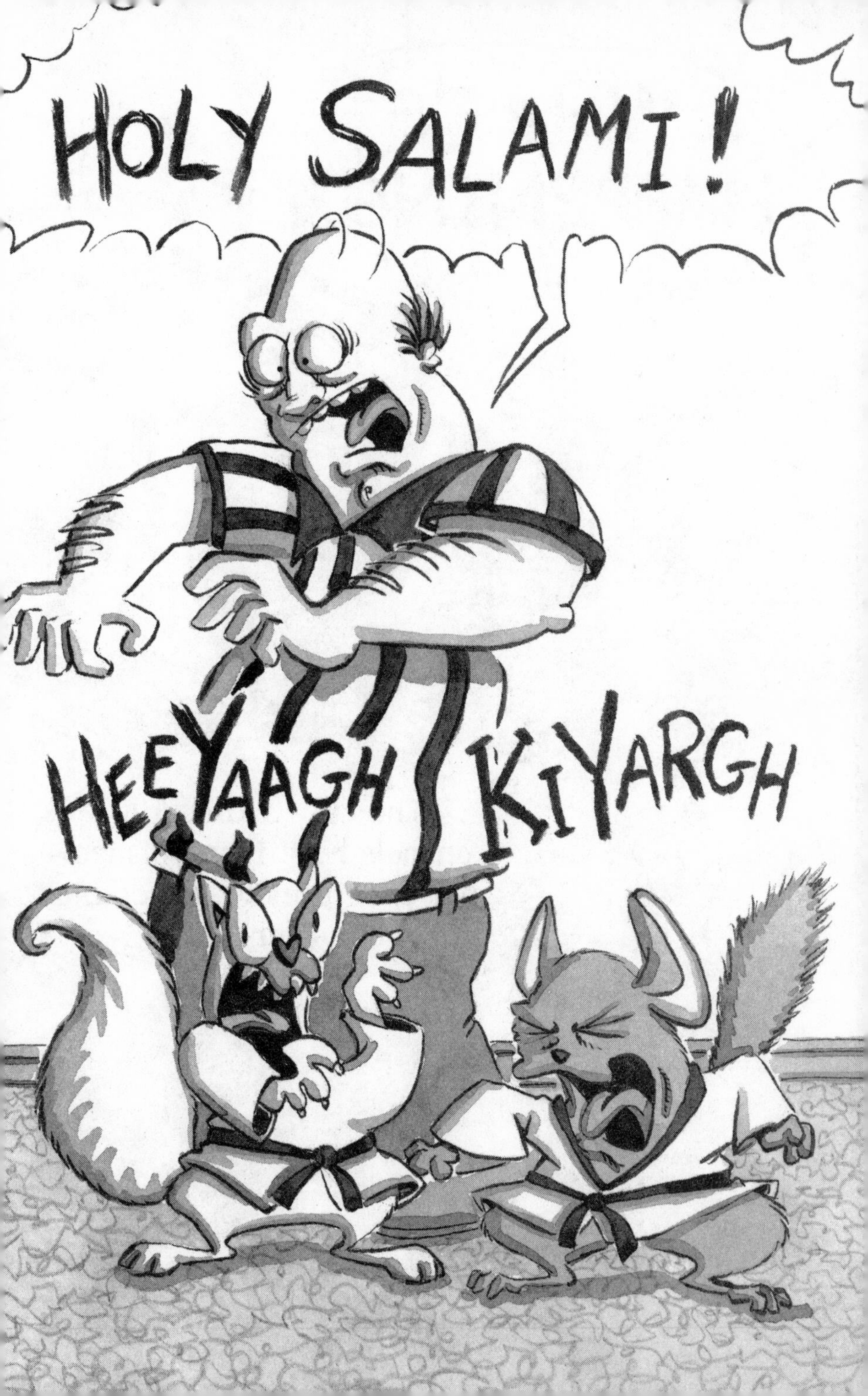
HOLY SALAMI!
HEEYAAGH
KIYARGH

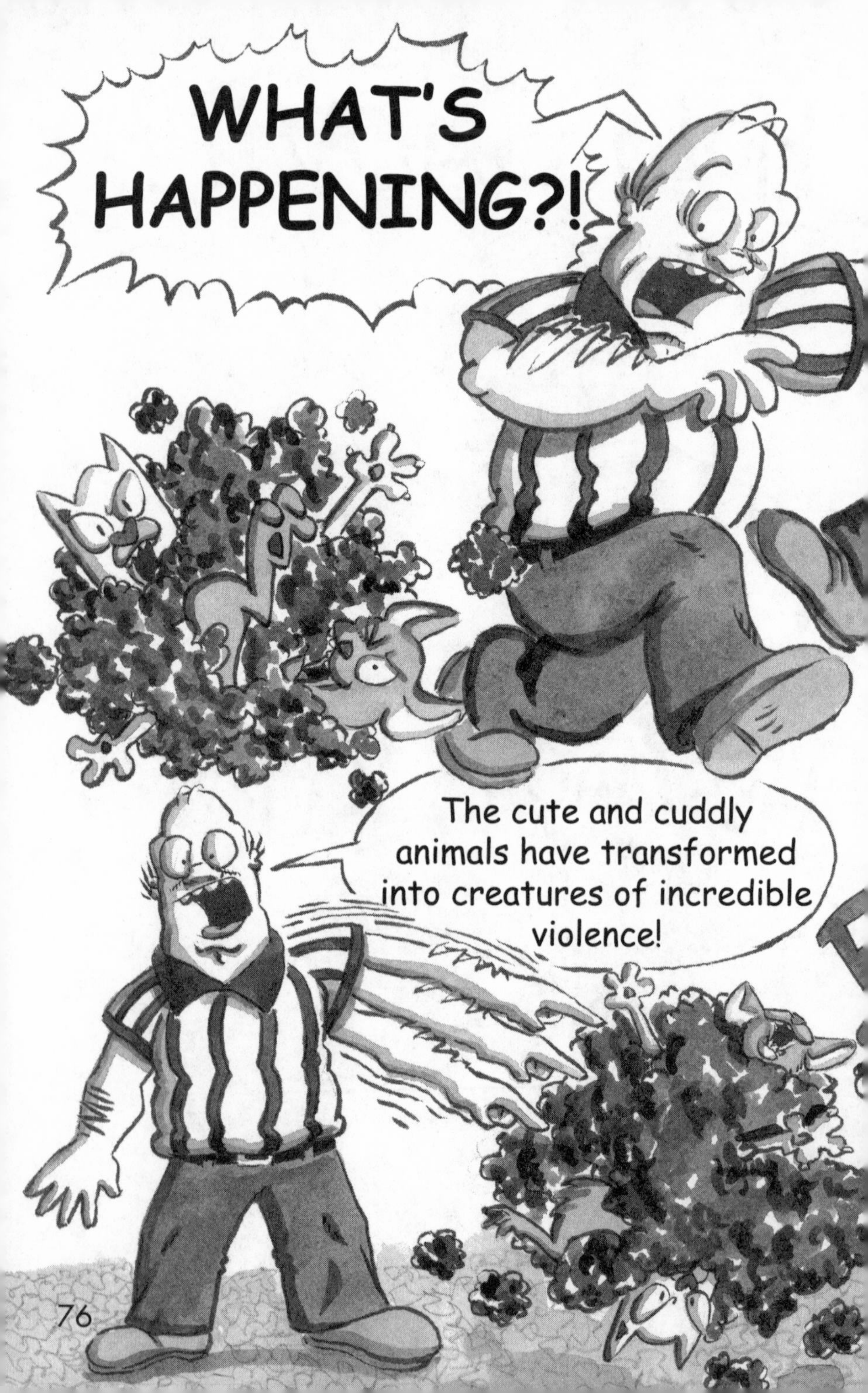
WHAT'S HAPPENING?!
The cute and cuddly animals have transformed into creatures of incredible violence!

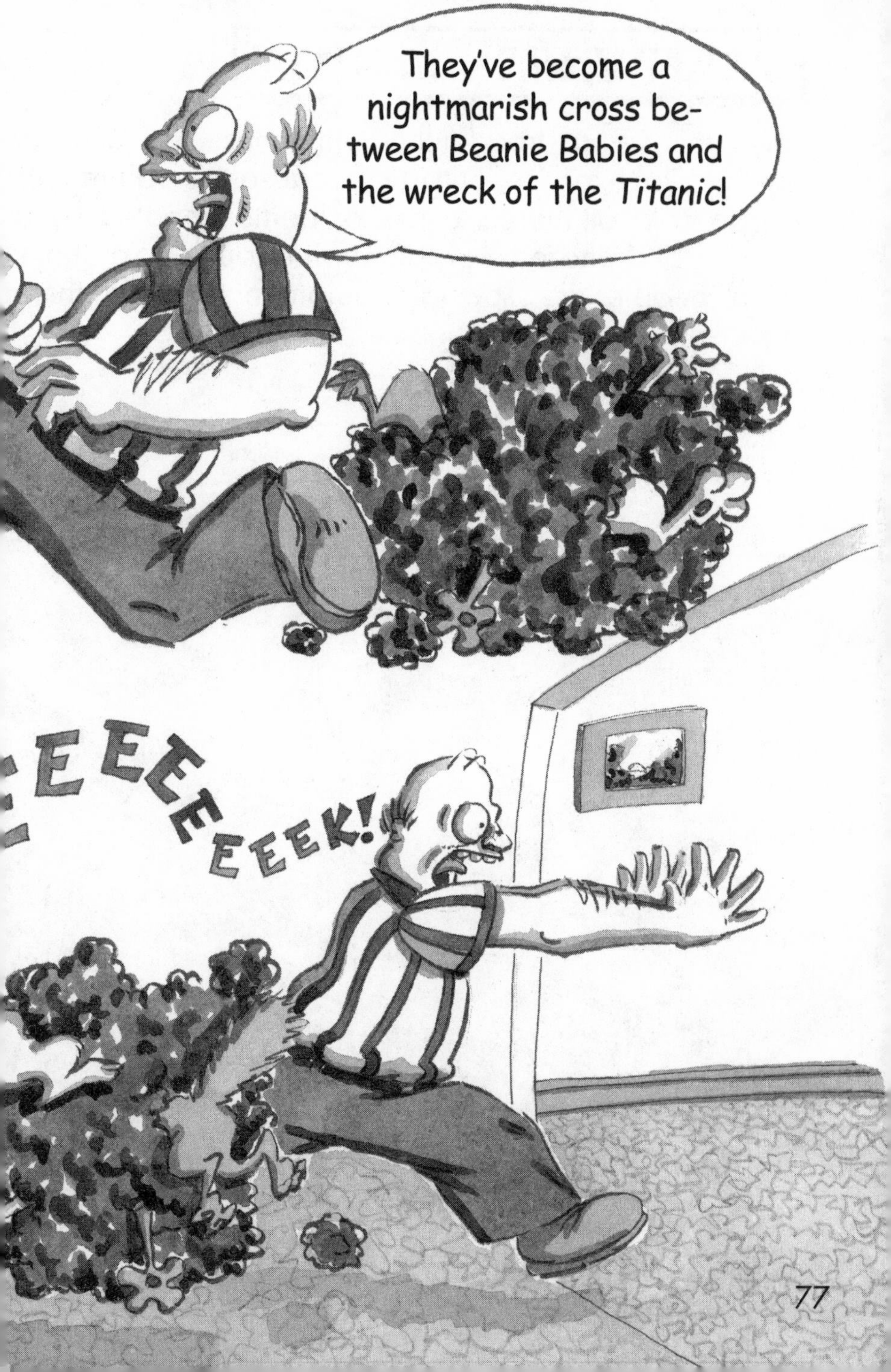

They've become a nightmarish cross between Beanie Babies and the wreck of the *Titanic*!
EEEEEEEEEK!

MEANWHILE . . . KITTY

Kitty, this is a treadmill. Sometimes it's just not possible to exercise outside because it's raining or it's too cold or there's a risk of being impaled by a shower of hundreds of porcupine quills. So that's when people use special equipment to help them exercise inside.

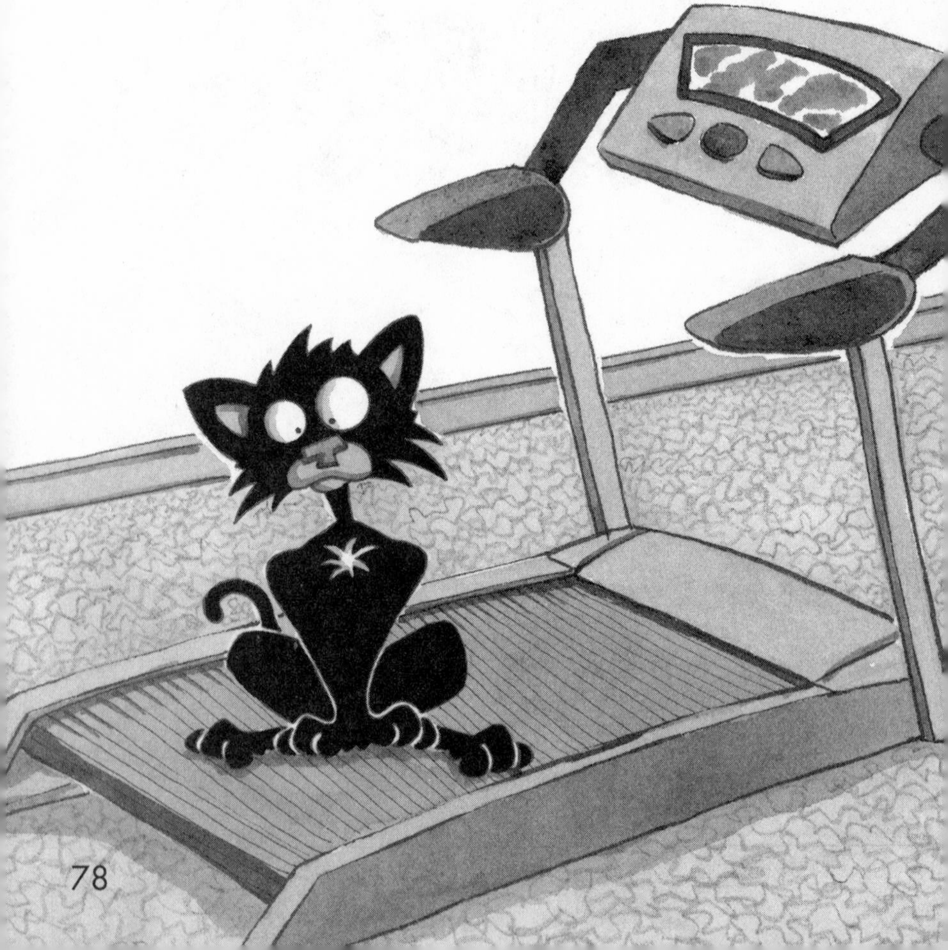

The track on the floor of this treadmill will move to make you feel like you're walking when you're really staying in one place.

There are similar pieces of exercise equipment to make you feel like you're riding a bike or climbing stairs or even rowing a boat.

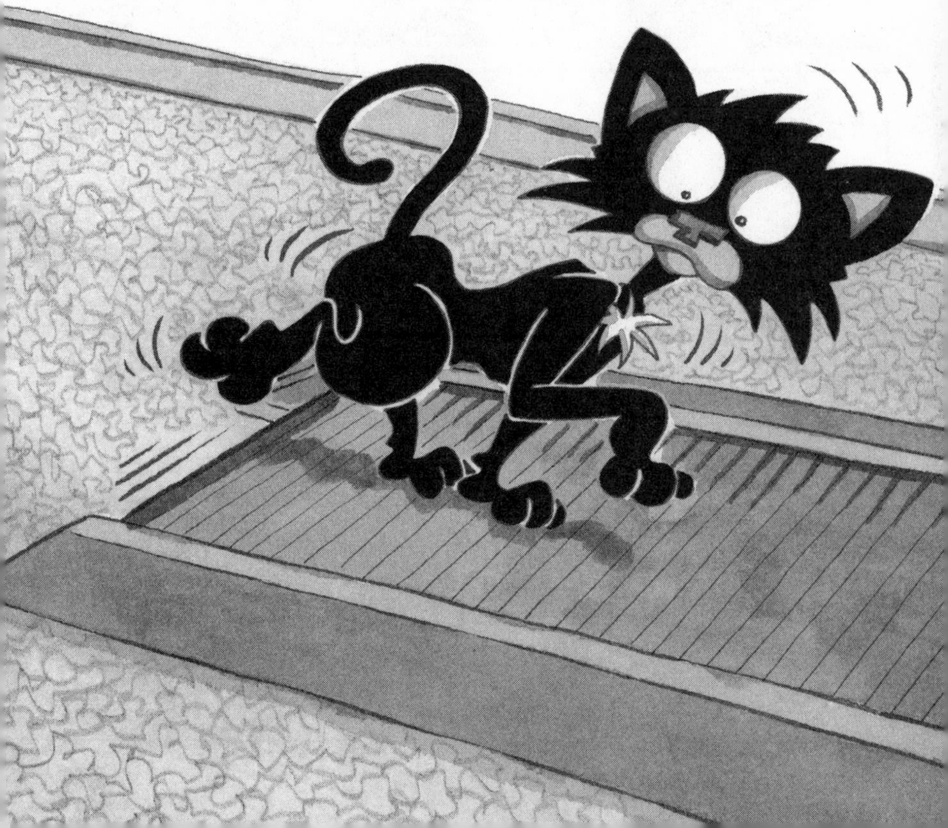

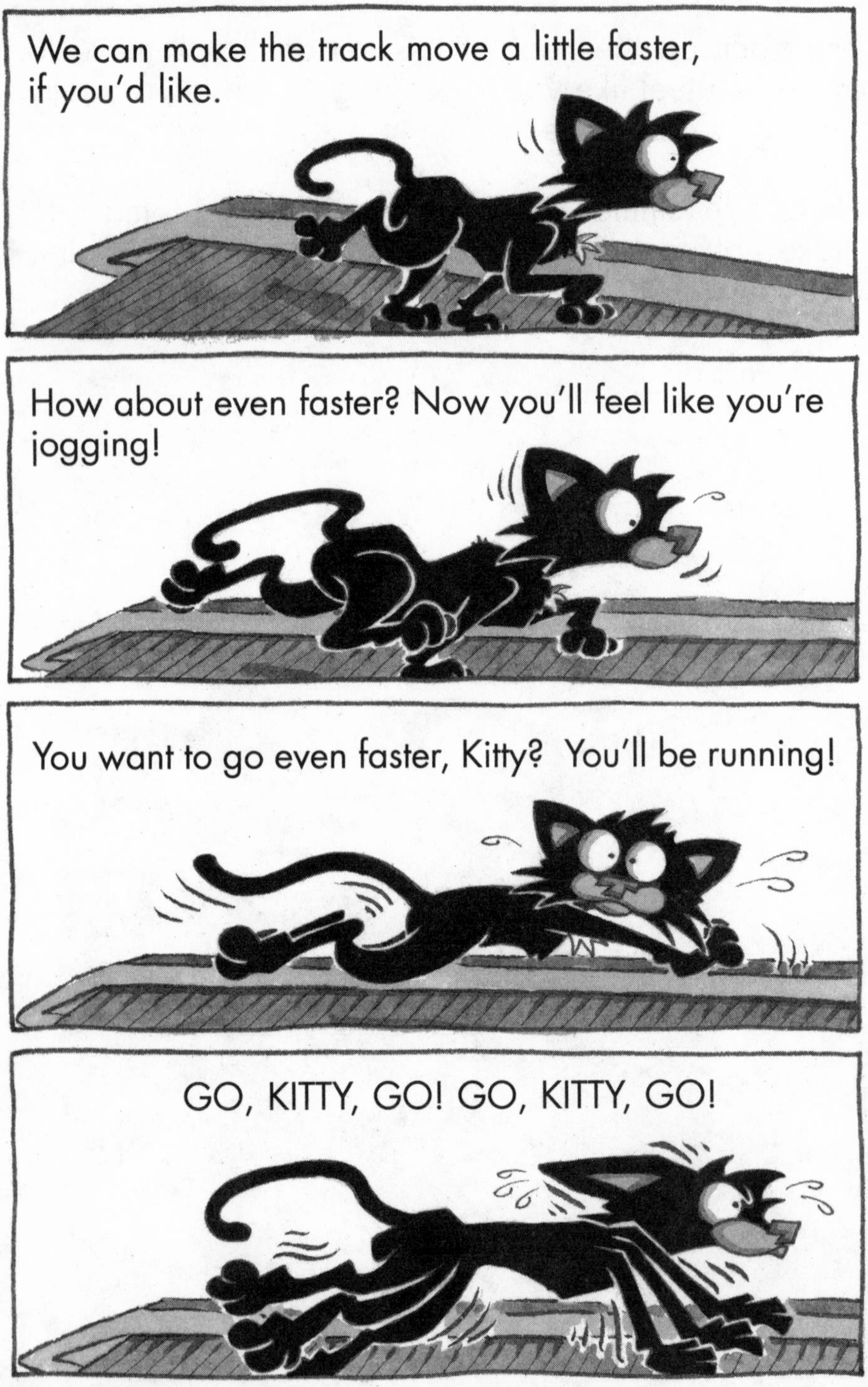
We can make the track move a little faster, if you'd like.
How about even faster? Now you'll feel like you're jogging!
You want to go even faster, Kitty? You'll be running!
GO, KITTY, GO! GO, KITTY, GO!

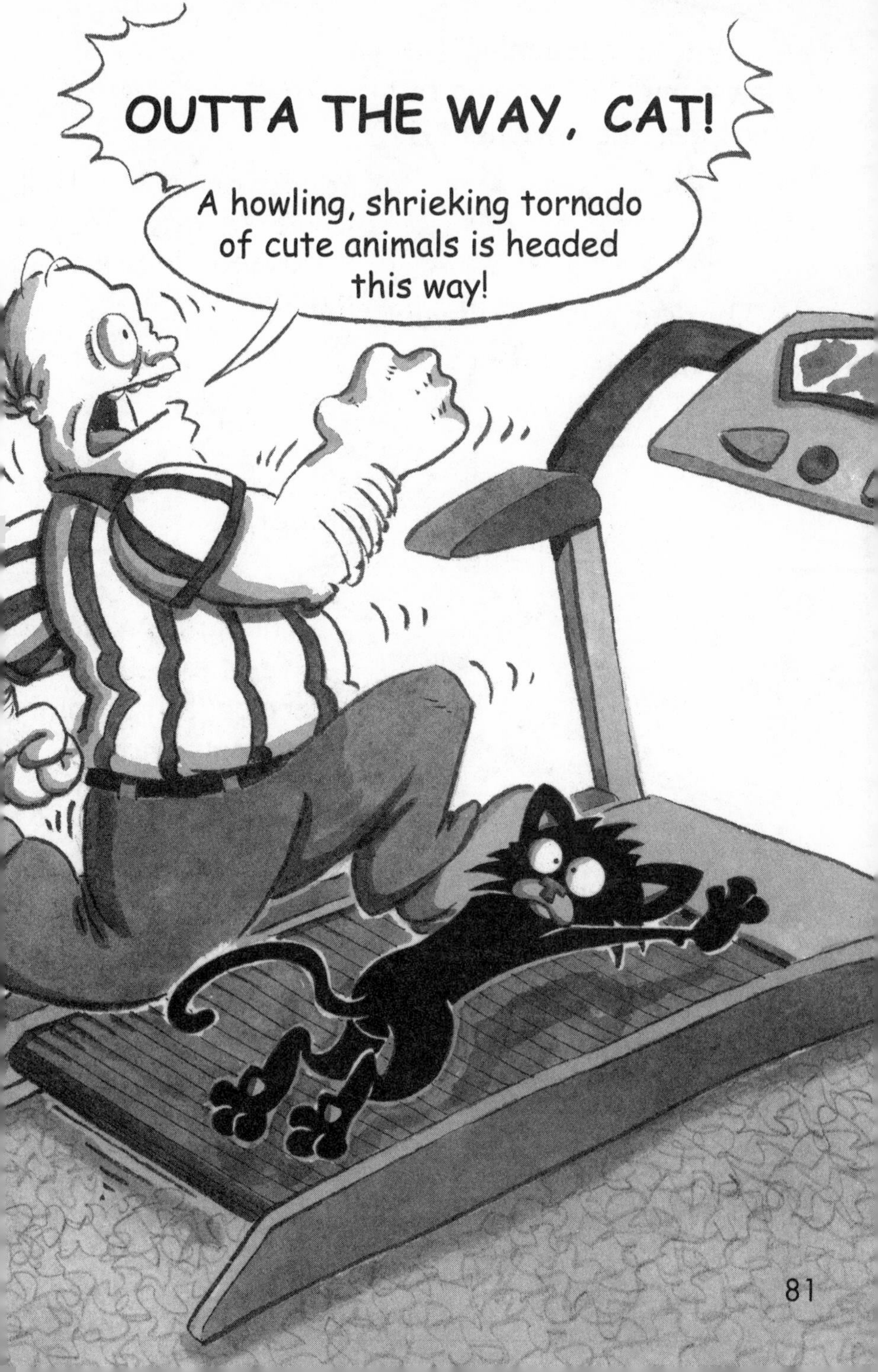
OUTTA THE WAY, CAT!
A howling, shrieking tornado of cute animals is headed this way!

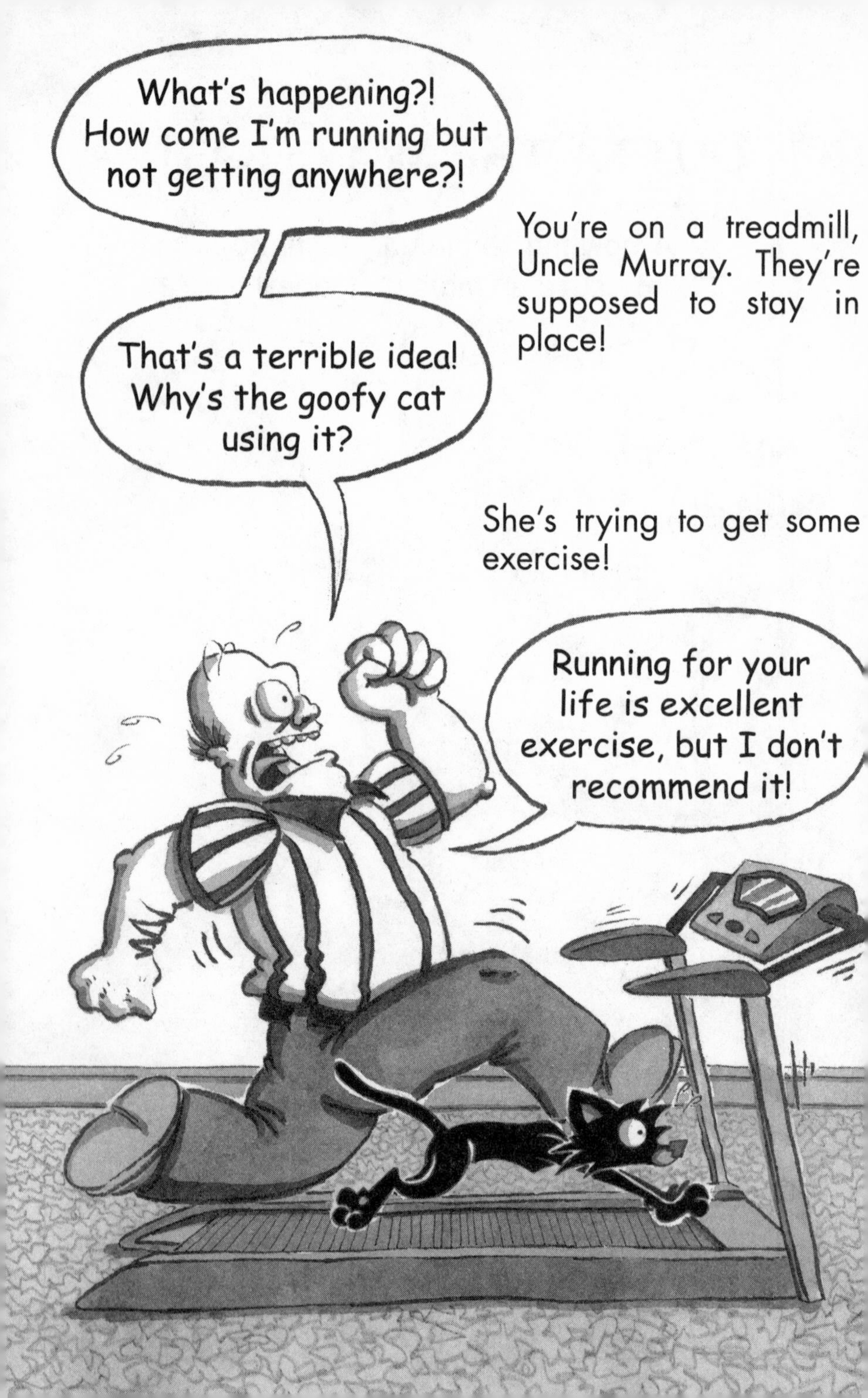
What's happening?! How come I'm running but not getting anywhere?!
You're on a treadmill, Uncle Murray. They're supposed to stay in place!
That's a terrible idea! Why's the goofy cat using it?
She's trying to get some exercise!
Running for your life is excellent exercise, but I don't recommend it!

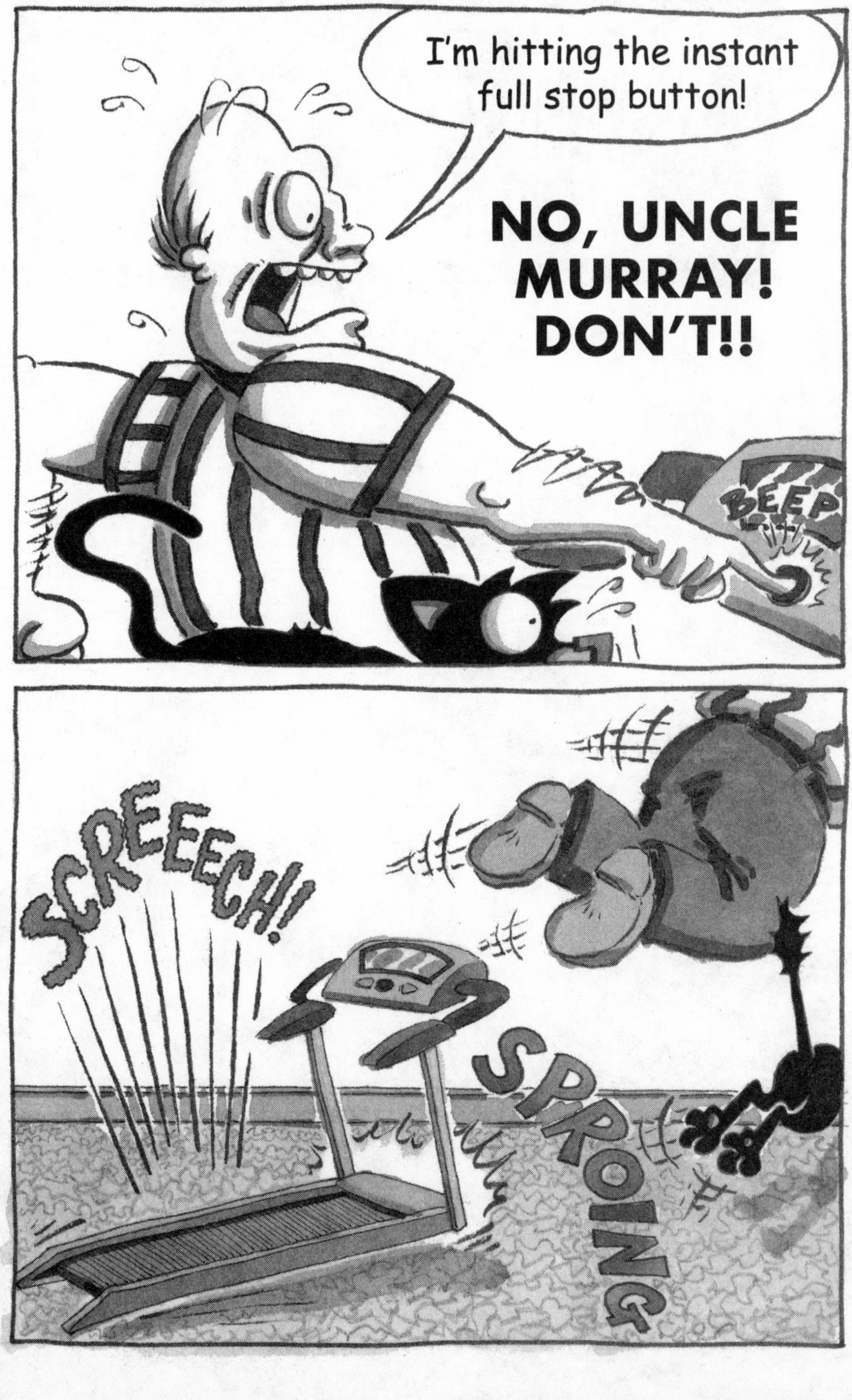
I'm hitting the instant full stop button!
NO, UNCLE MURRAY! DON'T!!
BEEP
SCREEECH!
SPROING

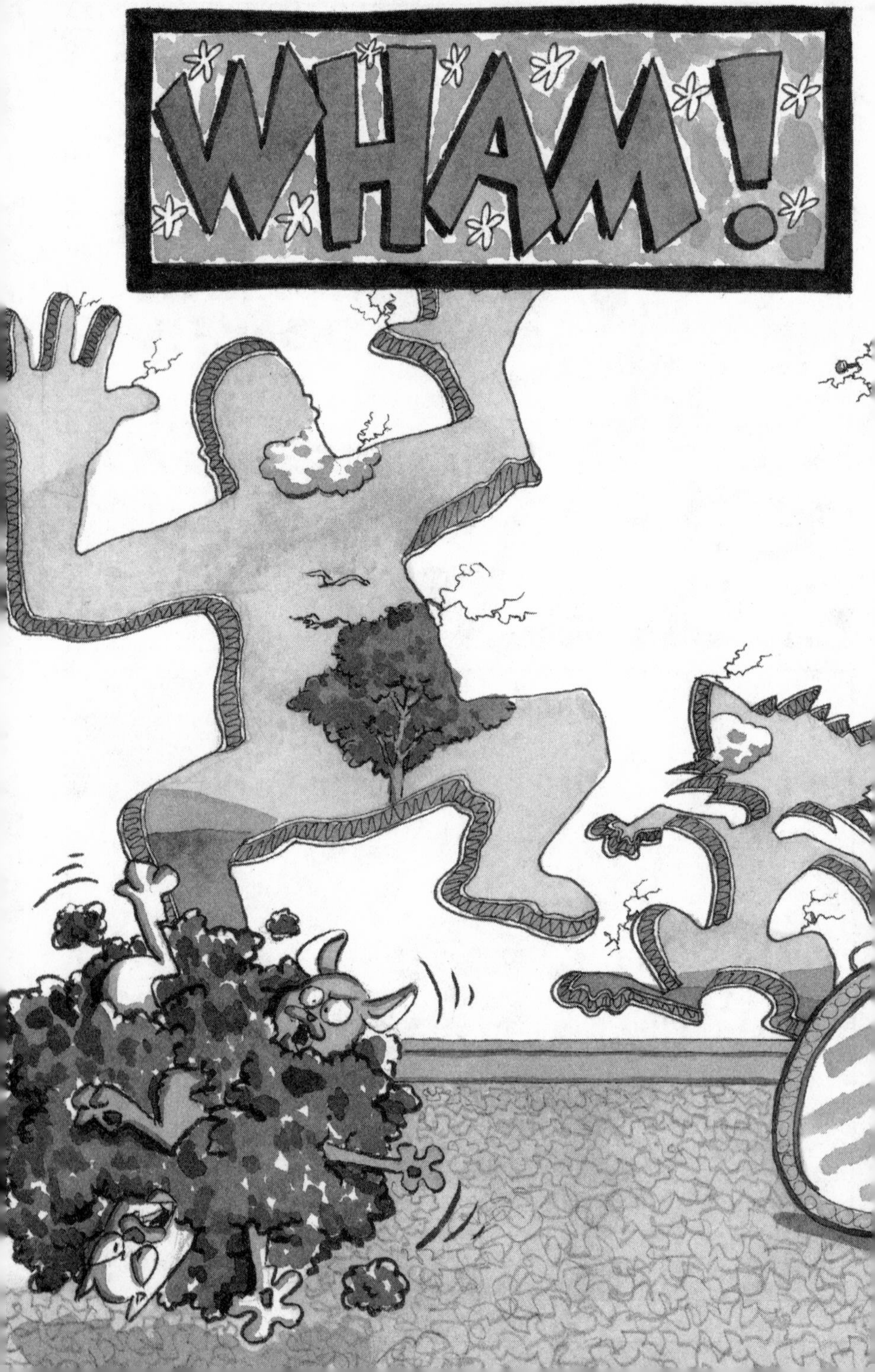
WHAM!

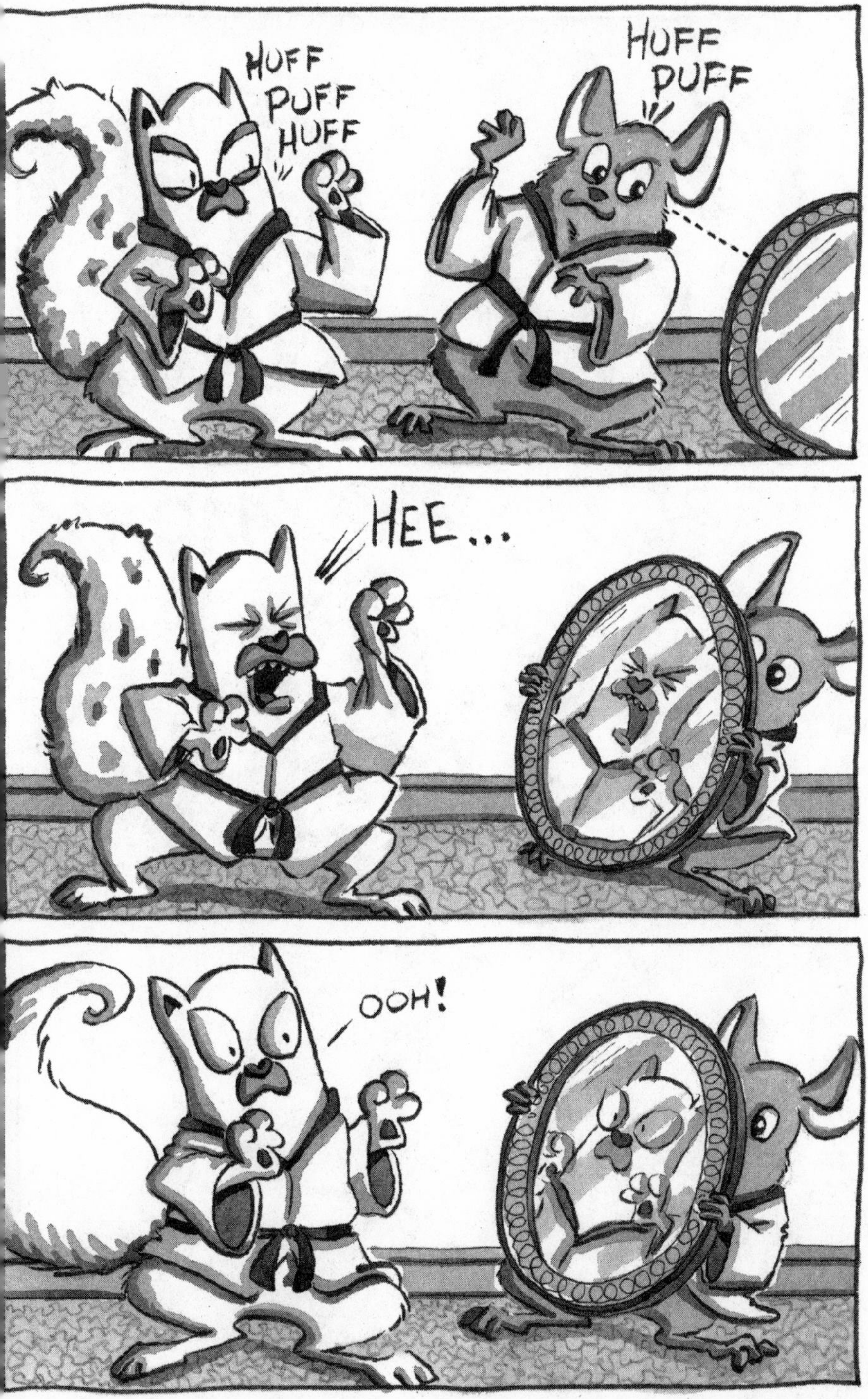
HUFF
PUFF
HUFF
HUFF
PUFF
HEE...
OOH!

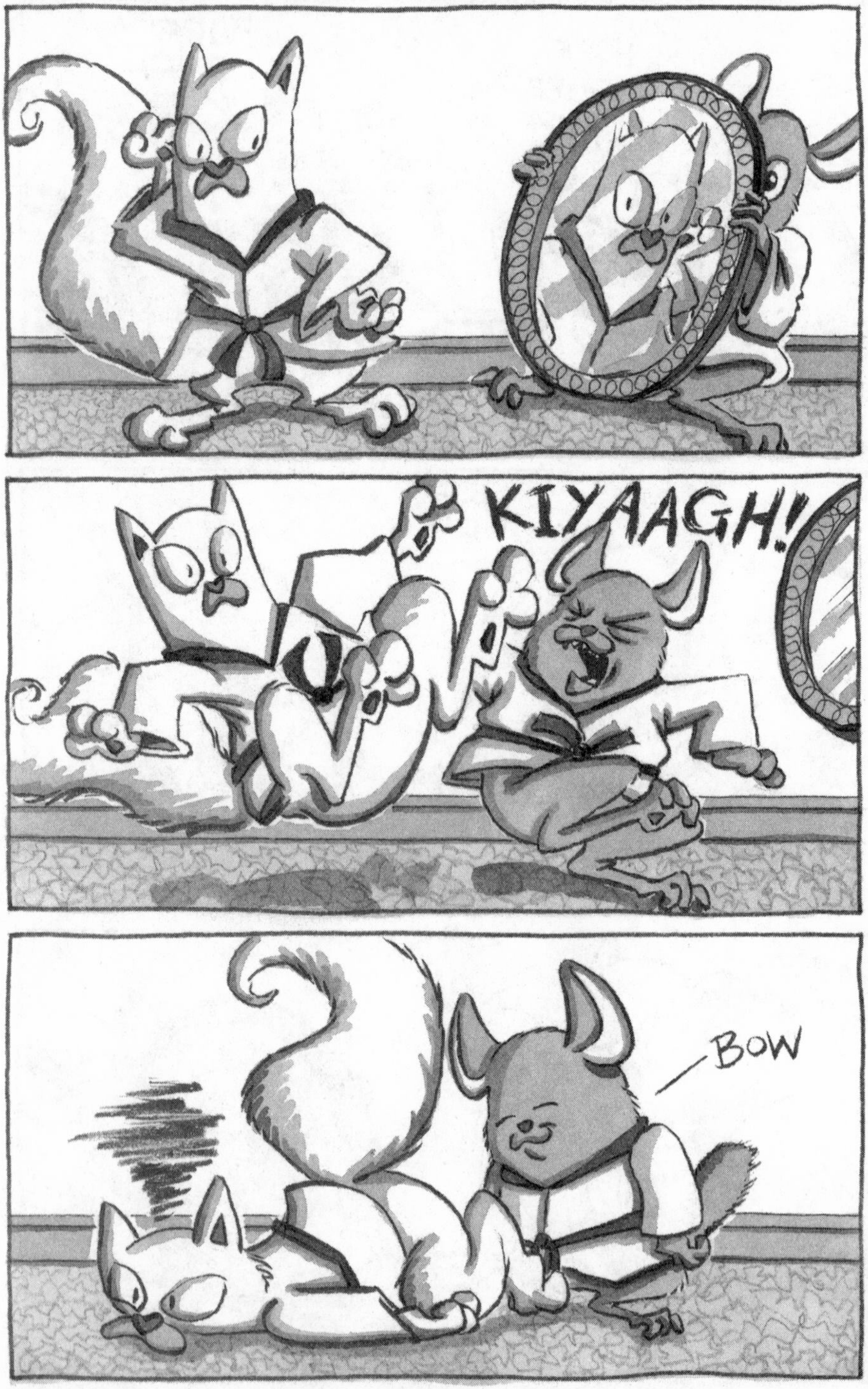
KIYAAGH!
BOW

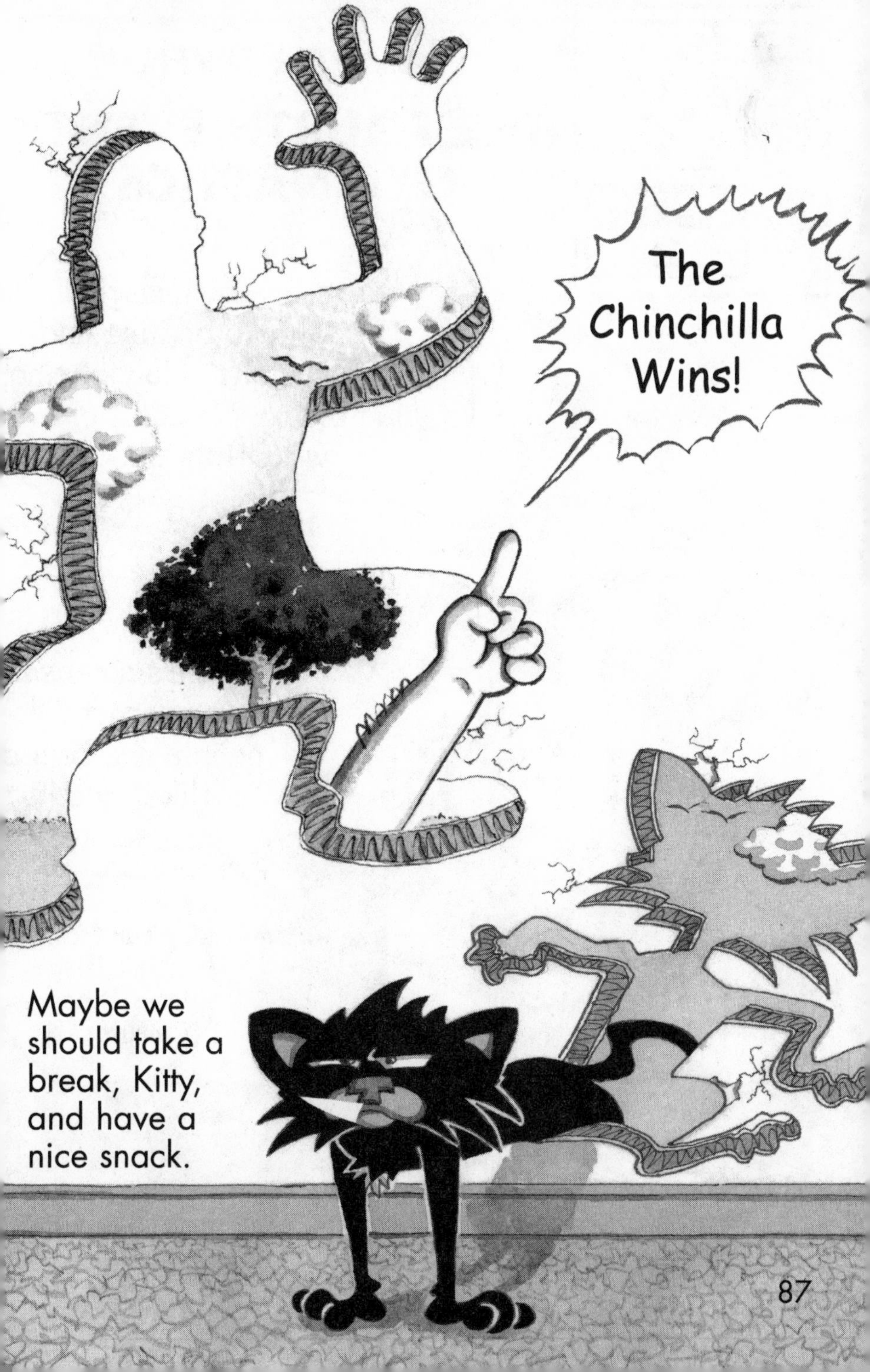
The Chinchilla Wins!

Maybe we should take a break, Kitty, and have a nice snack.

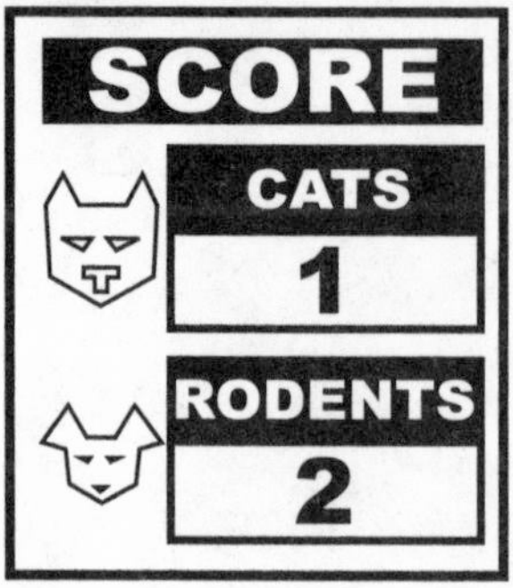
SCORE
CATS
1
RODENTS
2

•CHAPTER SEVEN•

THE FOURTH EVENT: GYMNASTICS

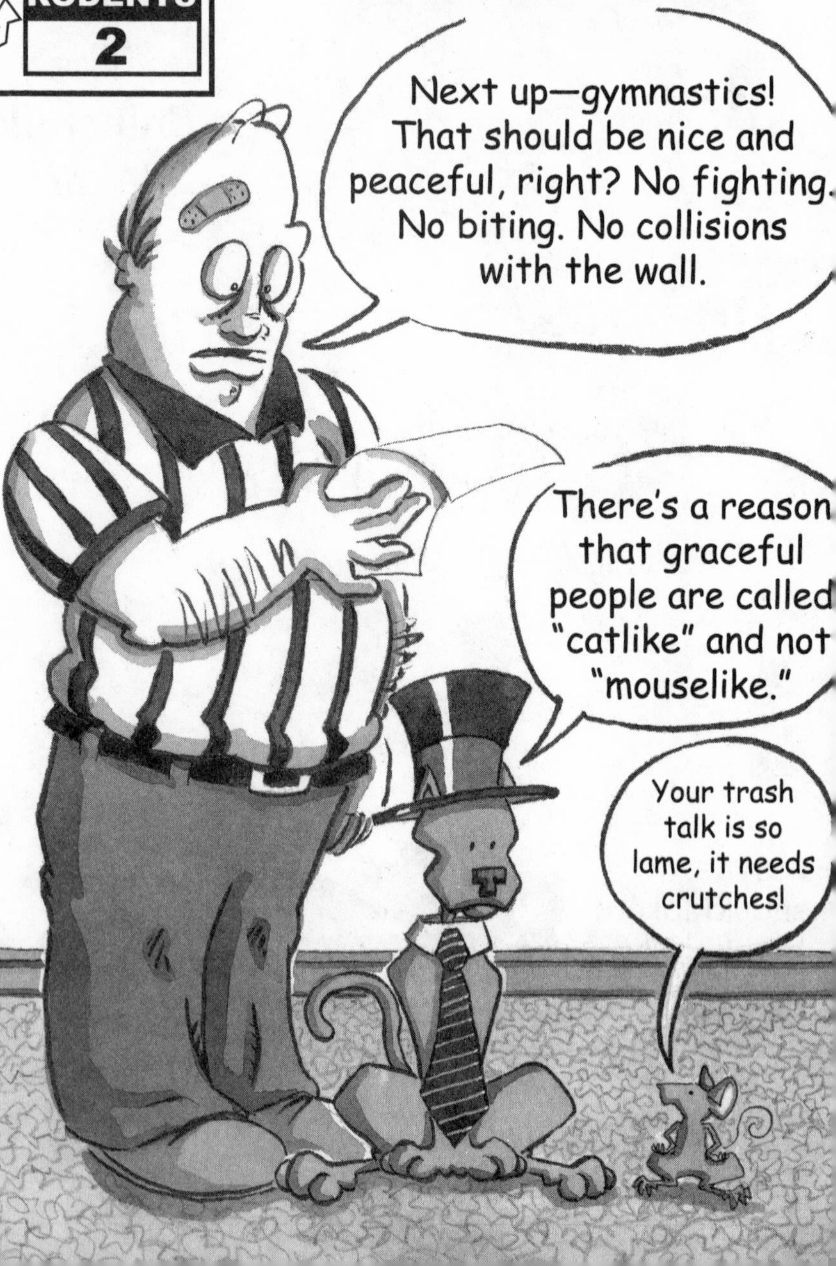
Next up—gymnastics! That should be nice and peaceful, right? No fighting. No biting. No collisions with the wall.
There's a reason that graceful people are called "catlike" and not "mouselike."
Your trash talk is so lame, it needs crutches!

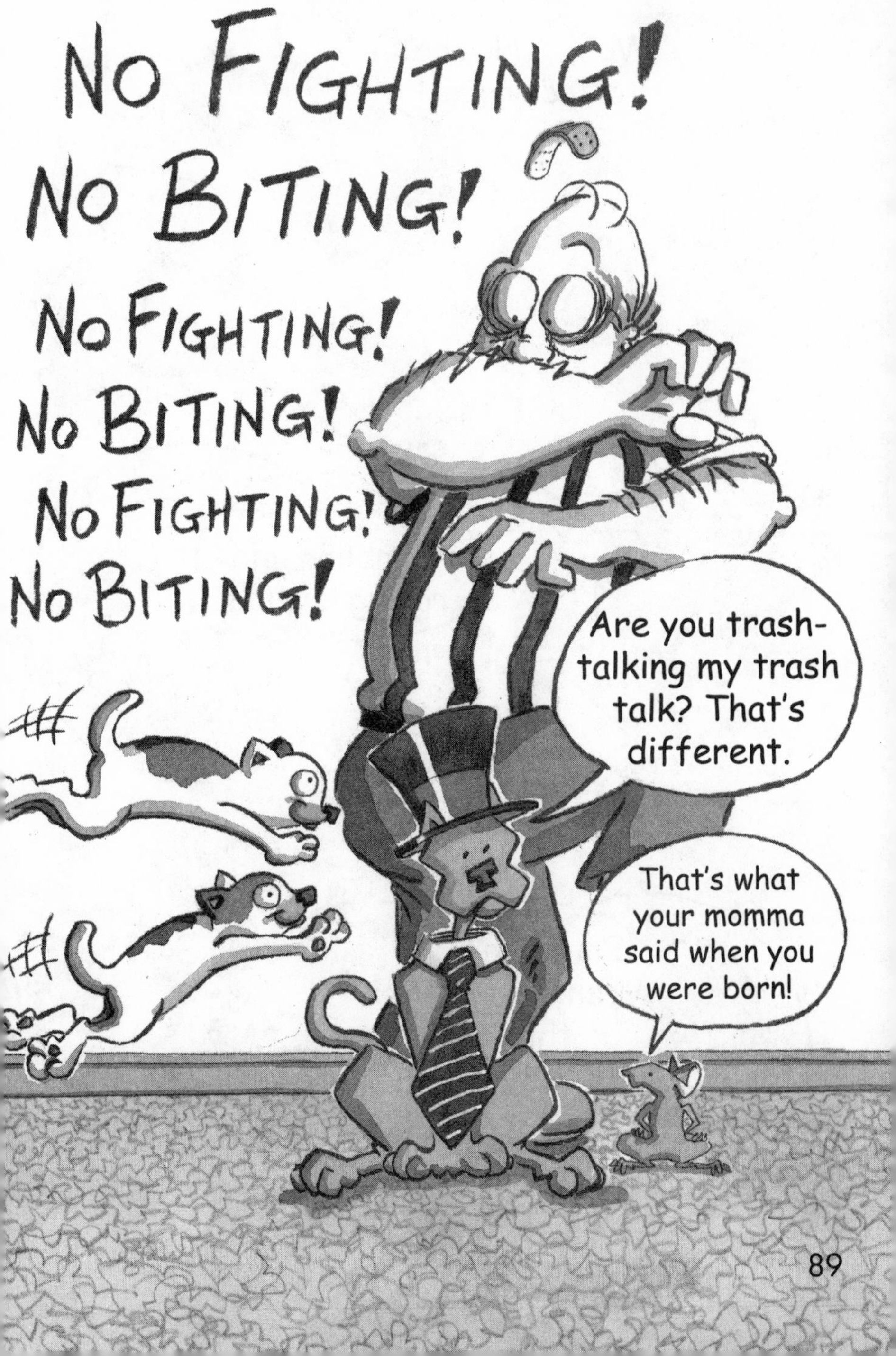
NO FIGHTING!
NO BITING!
NO FIGHTING!
NO BITING!
NO FIGHTING!
NO BITING!
Are you trash-talking my trash talk? That's different.
That's what your momma said when you were born!

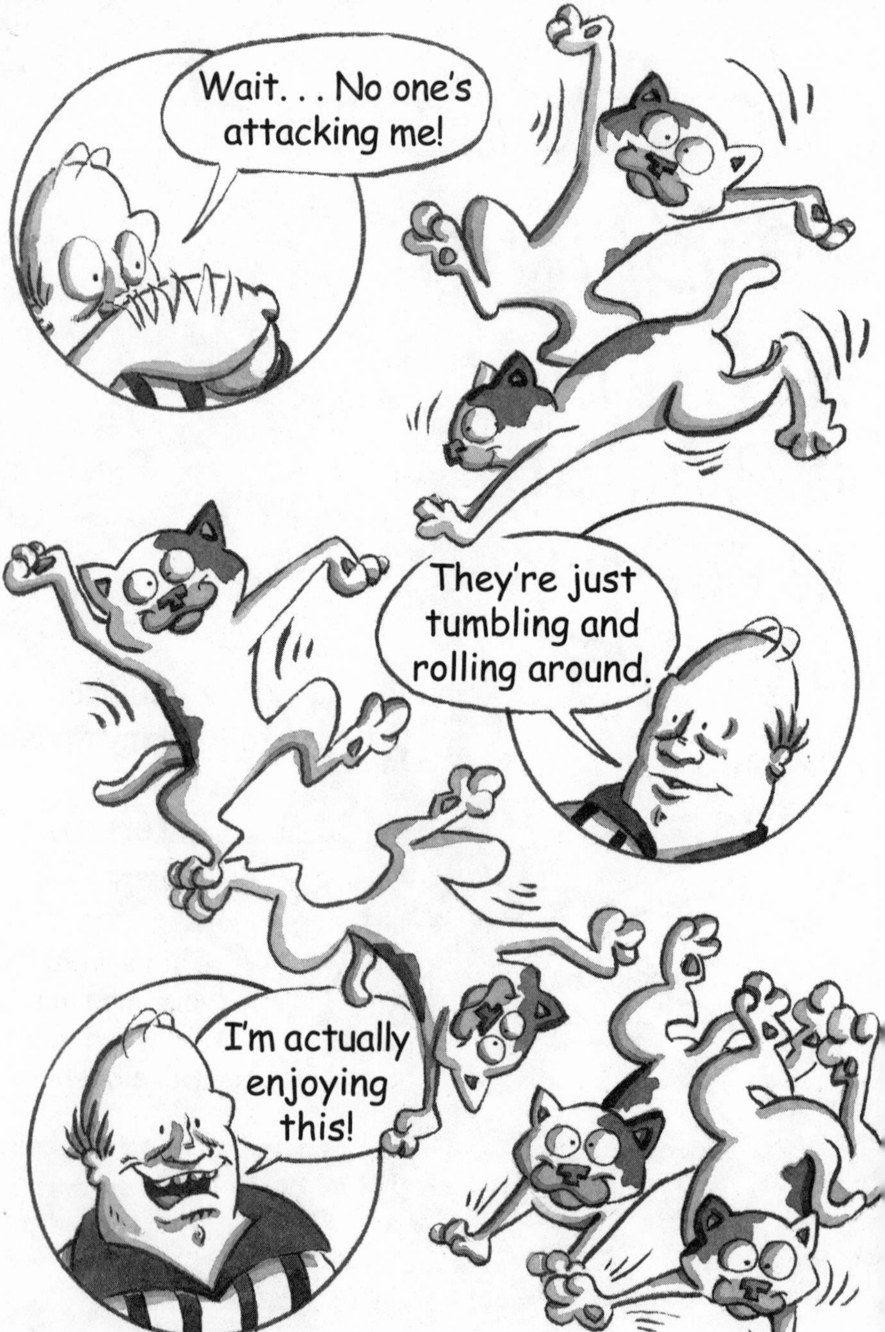
Wait. . . No one's attacking me!
They're just tumbling and rolling around.
I'm actually enjoying this!

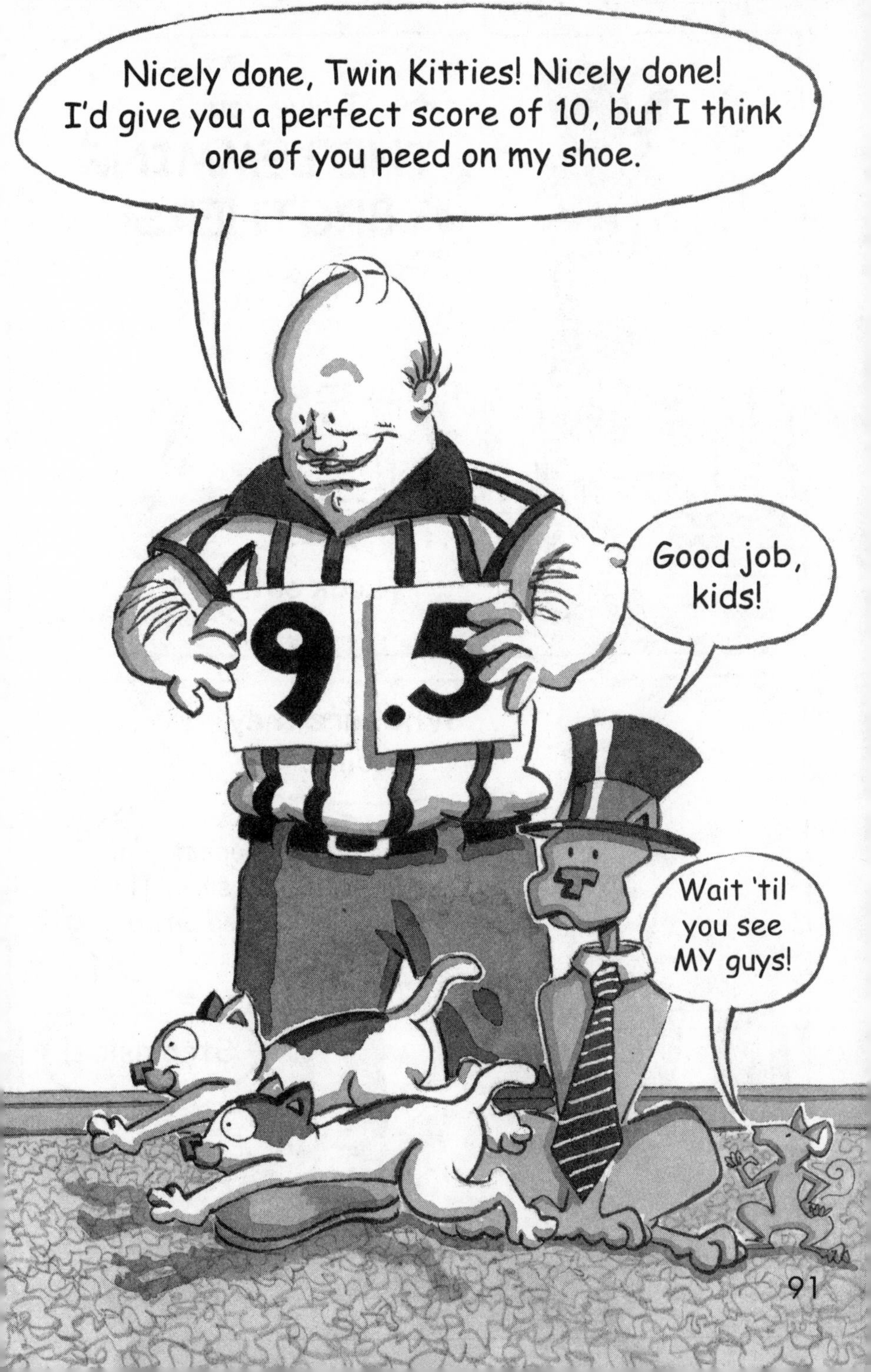
Nicely done, Twin Kitties! Nicely done! I'd give you a perfect score of 10, but I think one of you peed on my shoe.
9.5
Good job, kids!
Wait 'til you see MY guys!

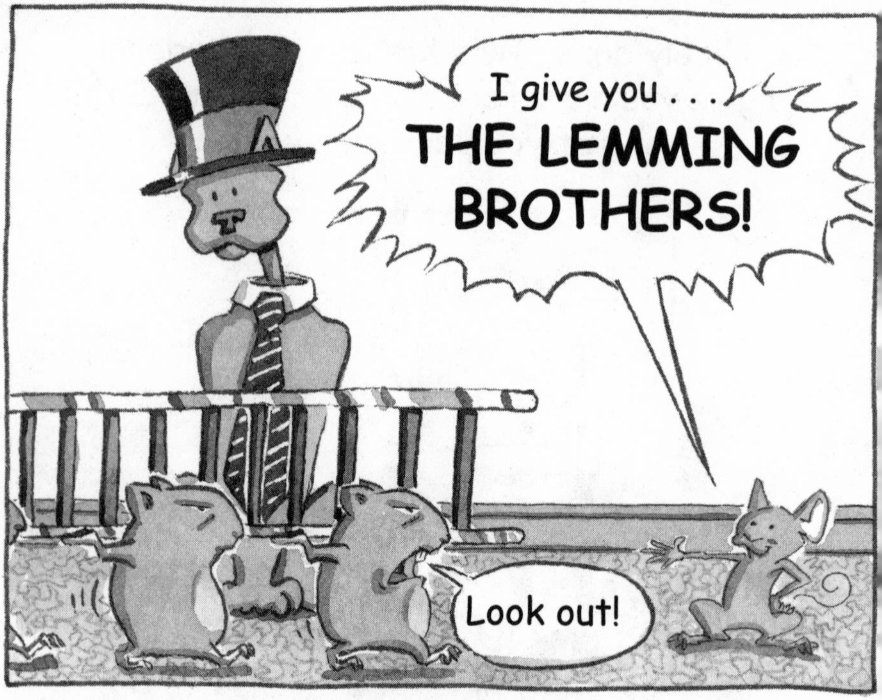
I give you . . .
THE LEMMING BROTHERS!
Look out!

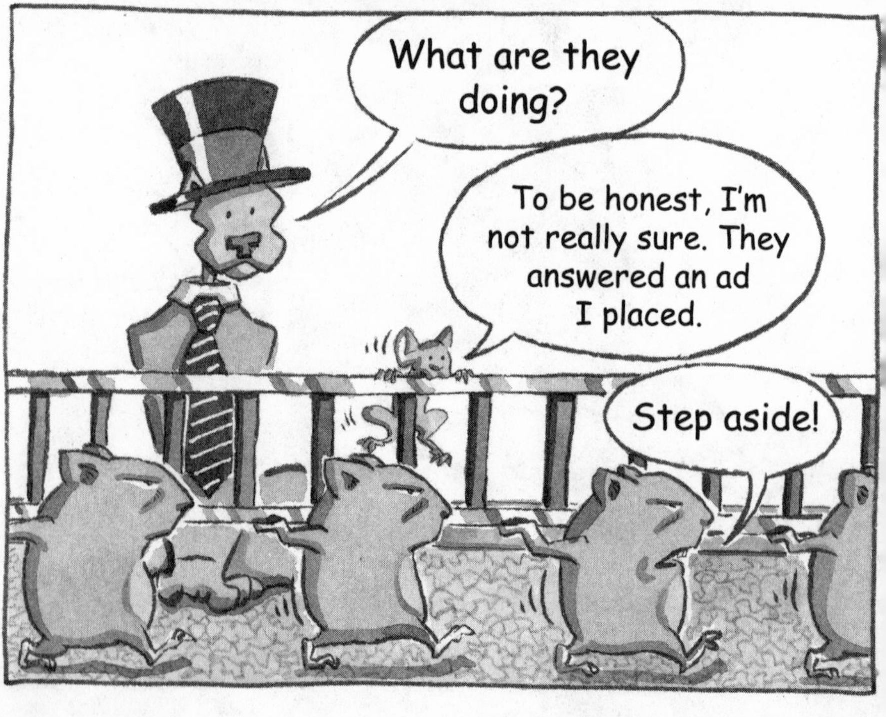
What are they doing?
To be honest, I'm not really sure. They answered an ad I placed.
Step aside!

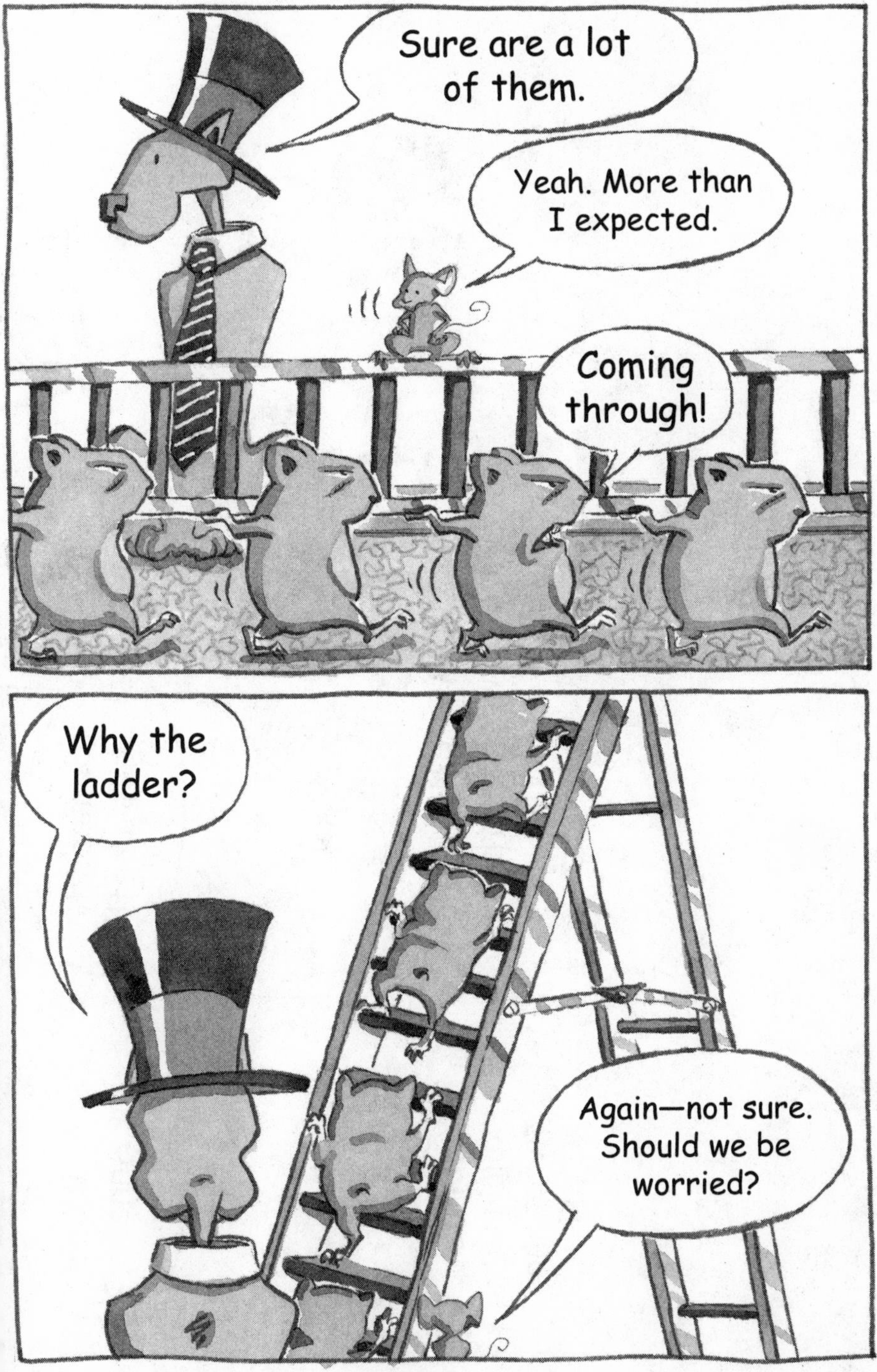
Sure are a lot of them.
Yeah. More than I expected.
Coming through!
Why the ladder?
Again—not sure. Should we be worried?

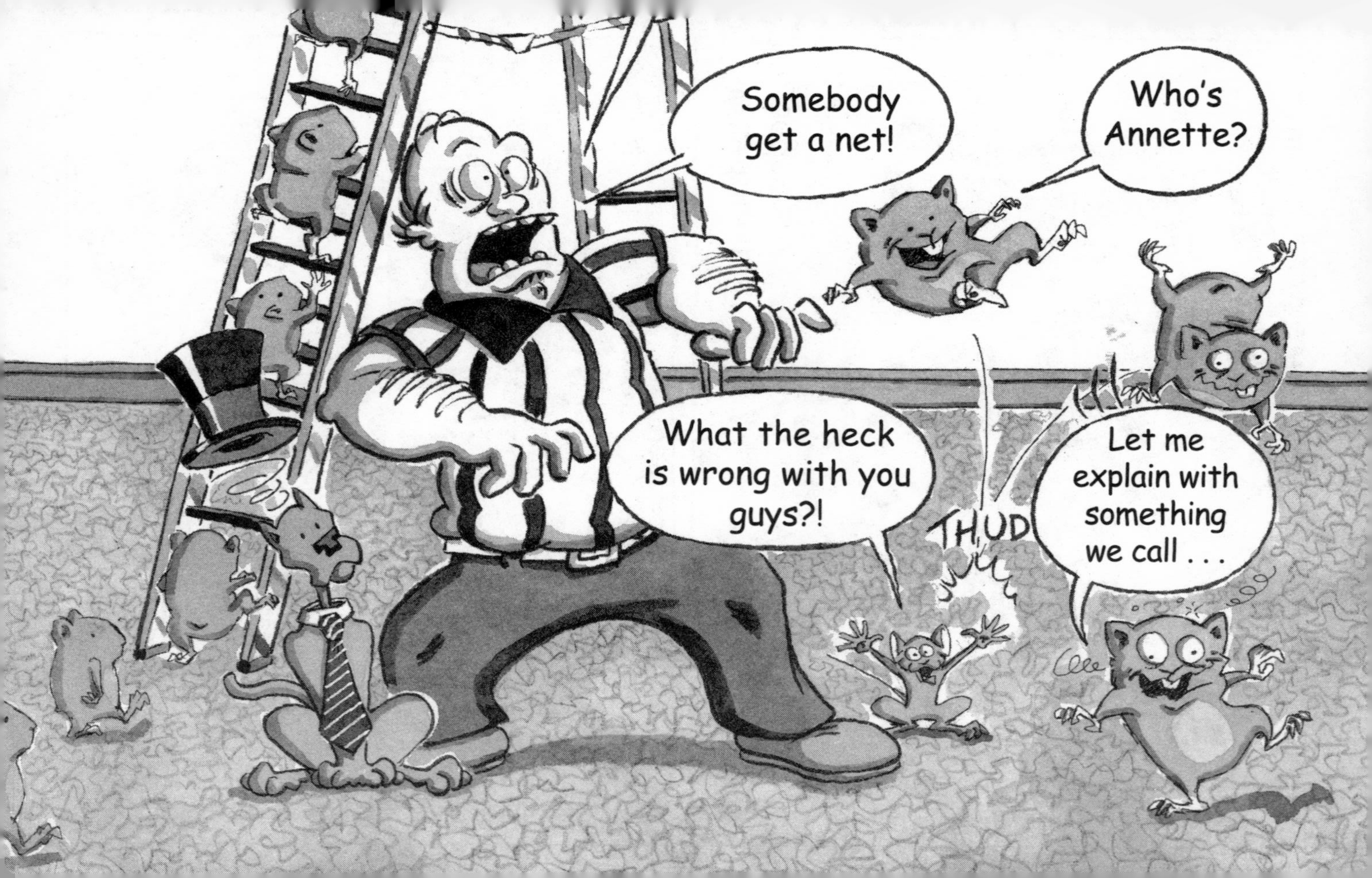
Somebody get a net!
Who's Annette?
What the heck is wrong with you guys?!
THUD
Let me explain with something we call . . .

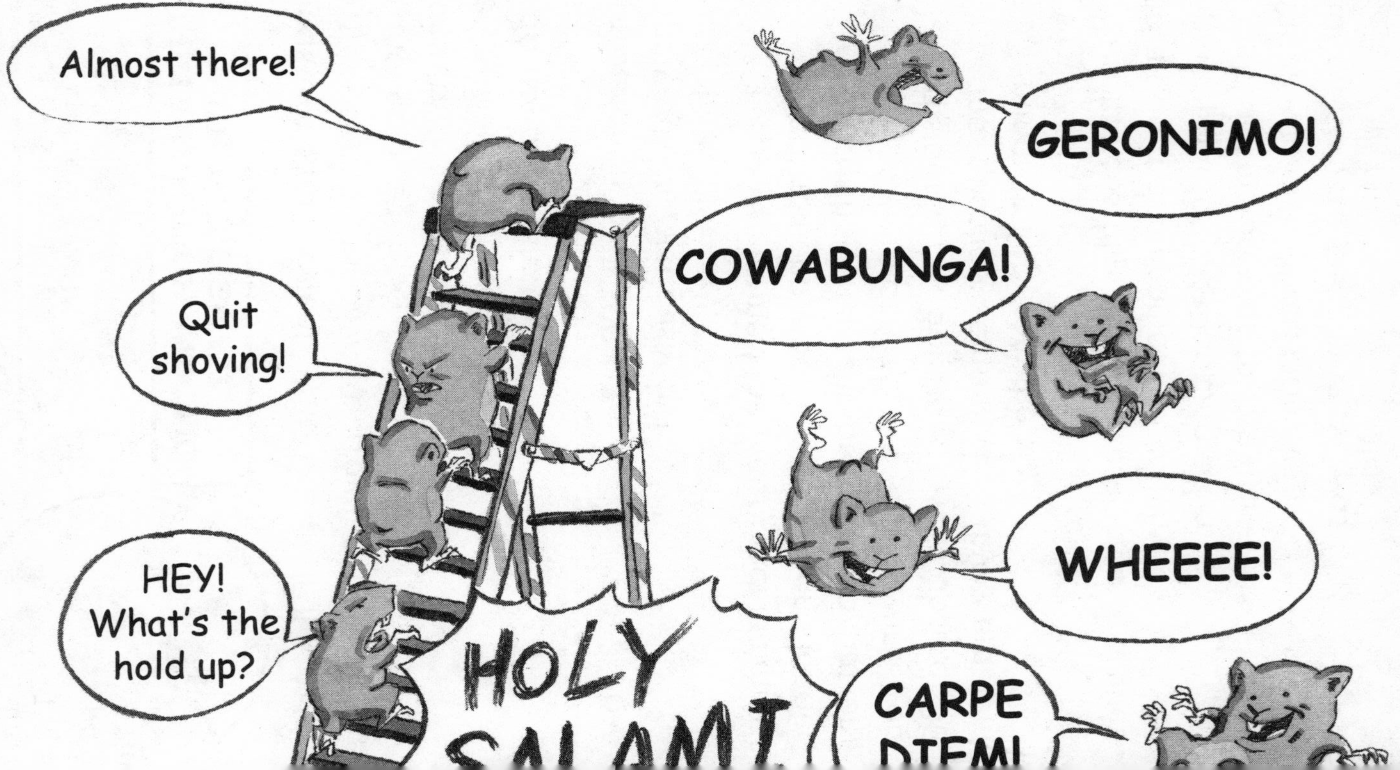
Almost there!
Quit shoving!
HEY! What's the hold up?
HOLY
GERONIMO!
COWABUNGA!
WHEEEEE!
CARPE

THE LEMMING BROS' ~~UNCLE MURRAY'S~~ FUN FACTS

WHAT THE HECK IS WRONG WITH THESE GUYS?

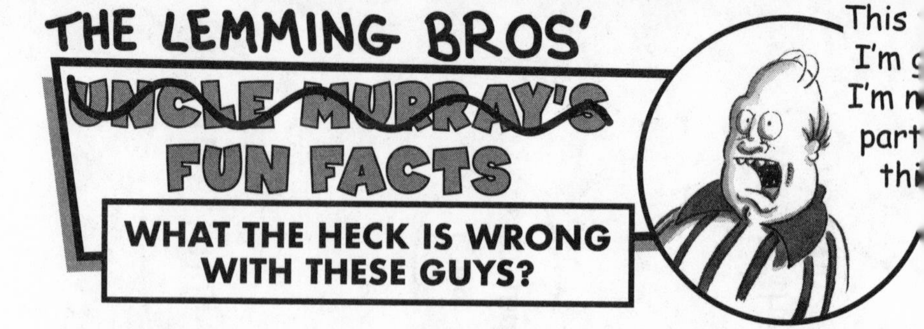
This
I'm
I'm
part

Lemmings are small rodents who live near the Arctic where they spend their lives burrowing through the snow and cold earth to forage for plants and berries. Because they're so used to the cold, Lemmings do not hibernate.

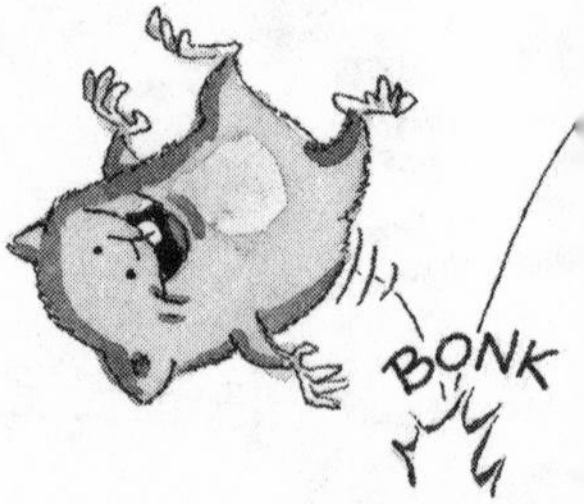
BONK

A rumor began in the 1500s that lemmings would mysteriously fall from the sky. Wise men even formed the theory that lemmings were somehow born in the sky and landed on Earth. Other scholars believed that lemmings were carried over by the wind from distant lands. Both ideas were absurd. But the question remained: Why were lemmings falling from the sky?

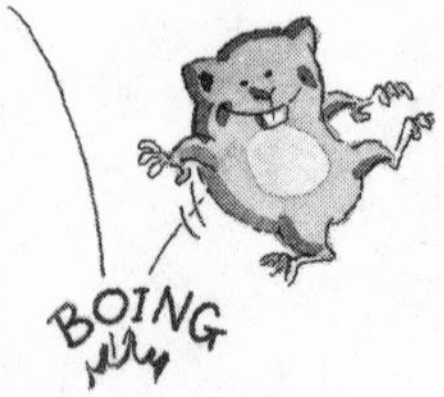
BOING

In 1958, a famous film studio investigated this question and made a documentary in which lemmings appeared to be leaping off a cliff to their doom. So was this the answer? No. It was discovered many years later that off camera the film crew was

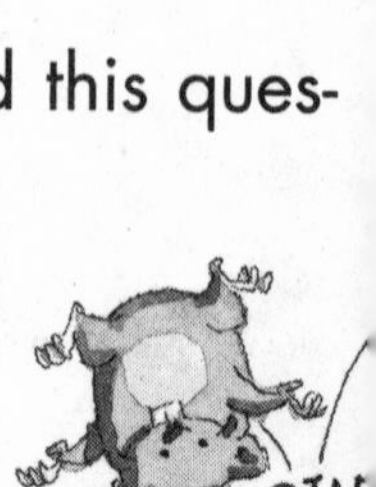

pushing the lemmings over the edge. The film was a lie, but it created a rumor that lemmings regularly leap off cliffs on purpose. The TRUTH is that lemmings reproduce very quickly and are sometimes clumsy.

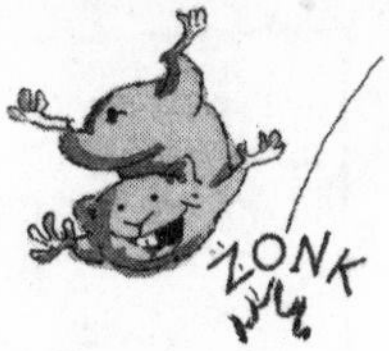
ZONK

A lemming population can grow to be three thousand times its size in just four years. This is not surprising considering that a female lemming can become pregnant at just two weeks old. During those times where there are too many lemmings for even the lemmings to be comfortable, they disperse. They travel in every direction to find more room, more food, and new homes.

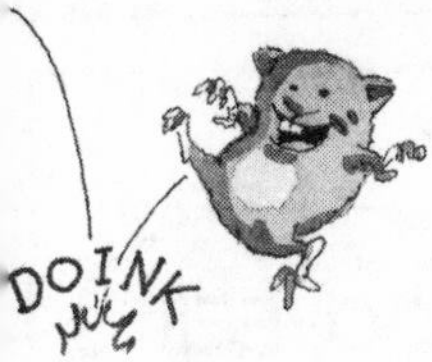
DOINK

Sometimes their travels will take them to lakes and rivers. But they don't stop. They push ahead and swim, even if some of them don't make it across.

And sometimes their travels will take them to steep slopes where, not being terribly agile, they tumble and roll and sometimes accidentally fall off a cliff, possibly landing in front of a wise man from the 1500s who is confused by what he's just seen.

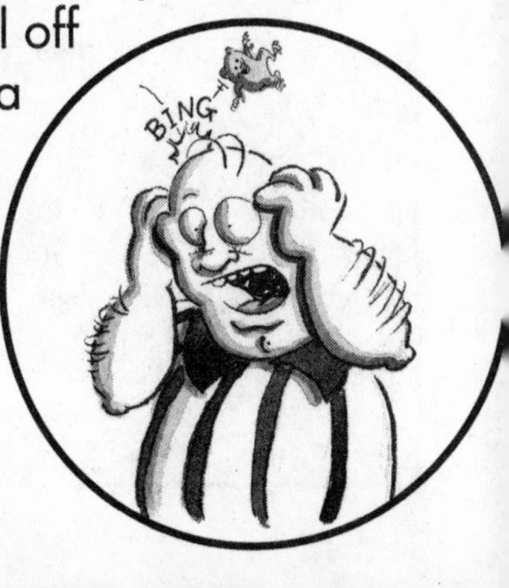
BING
Keep the Fun Facts!
I just want a helmet!

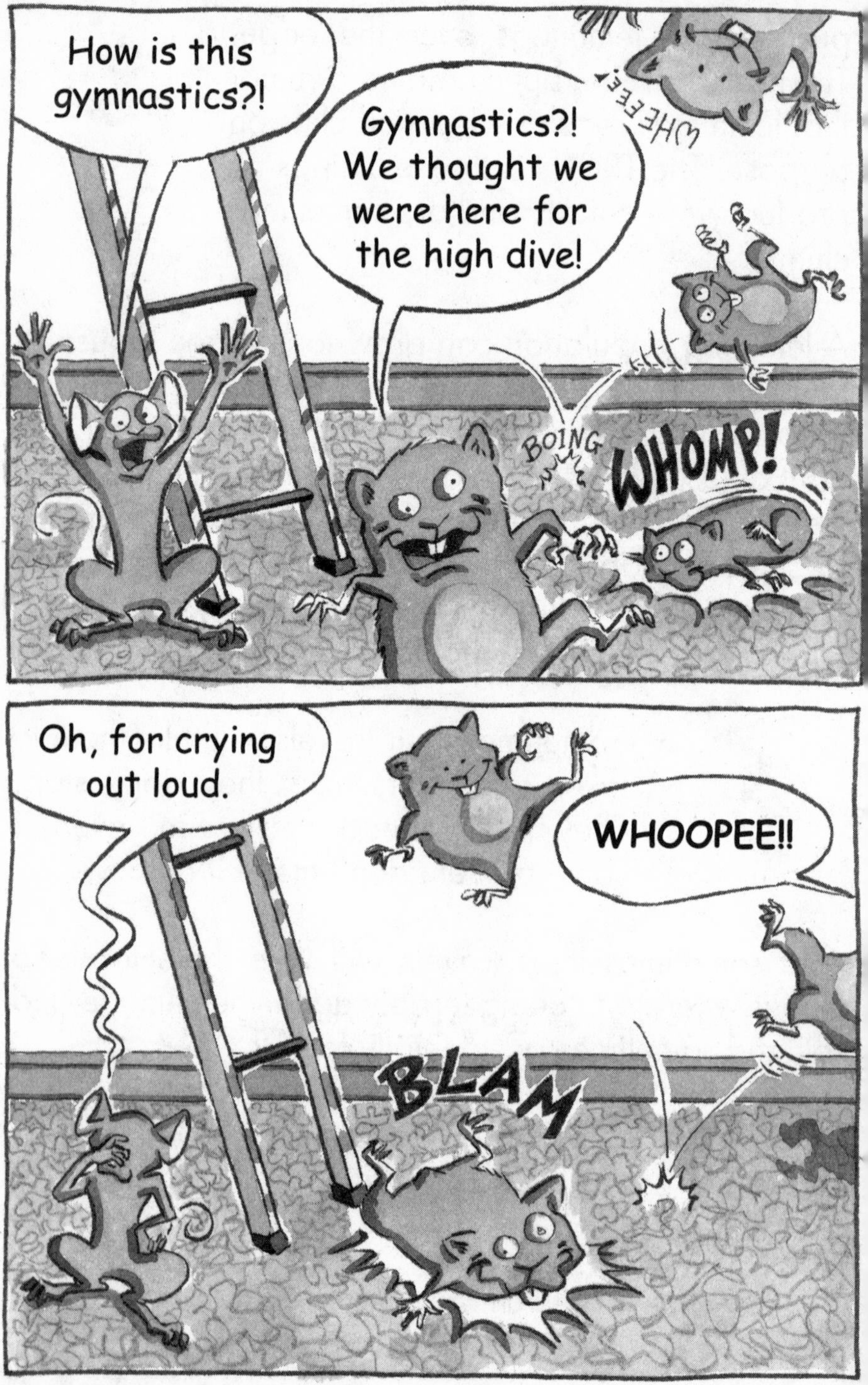
How is this gymnastics?!
WHEEEE!
Gymnastics?! We thought we were here for the high dive!
BOING
WHOMP!
Oh, for crying out loud.
WHOOPEE!!
BLAM

MEANWHILE . . . KITTY

One way to keep your body in good shape is to exercise every day. But another way that's just as important is to eat healthy food. This means avoiding foods that are heavy with fats and sugar and eating a balanced diet of meats, grains, fruits and . . .

VEGETABLES.

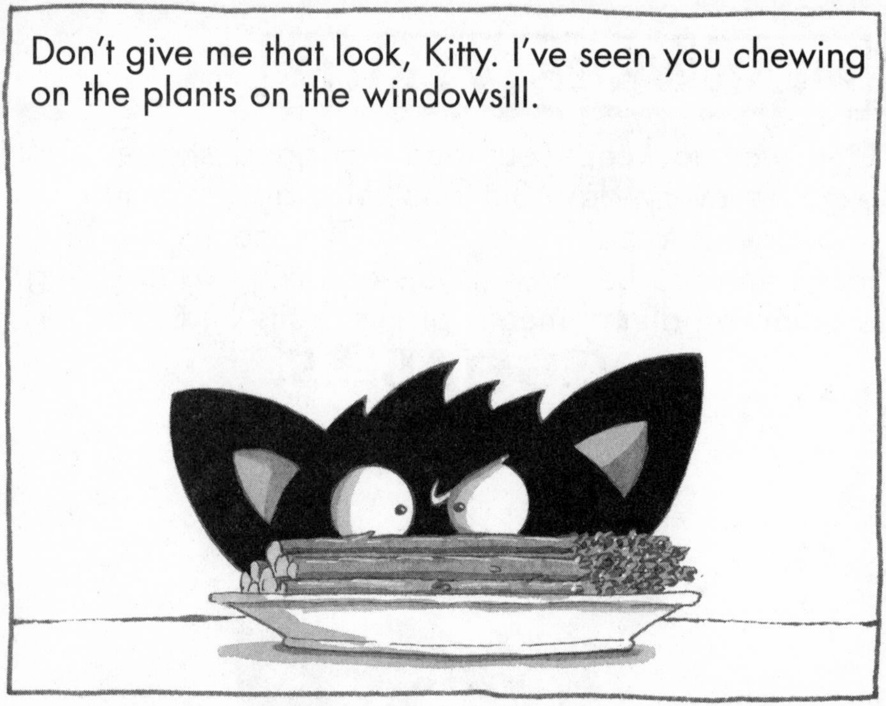
Don't give me that look, Kitty. I've seen you chewing on the plants on the windowsill.

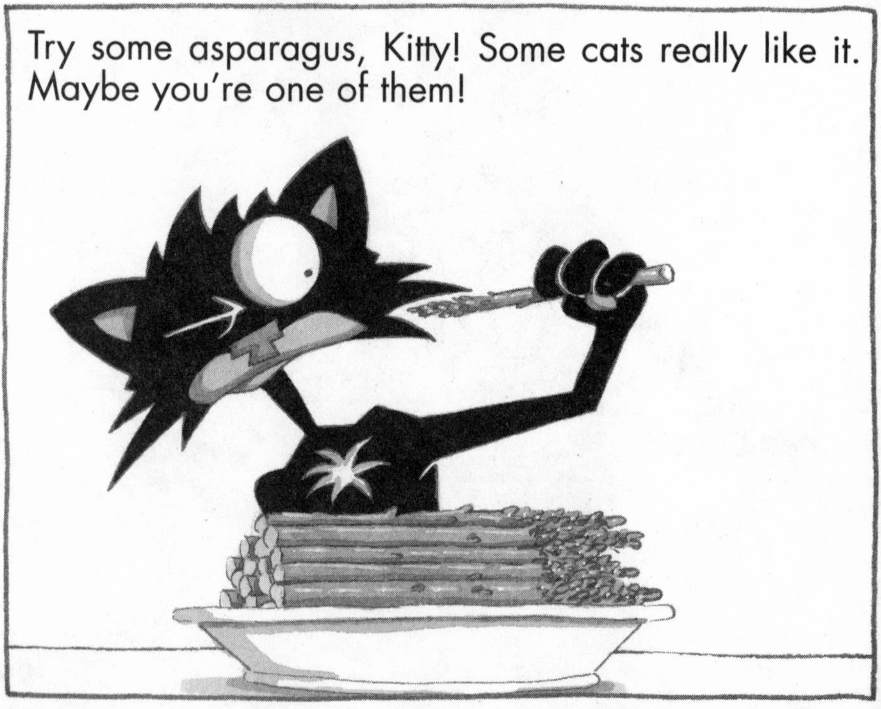
Try some asparagus, Kitty! Some cats really like it. Maybe you're one of them!

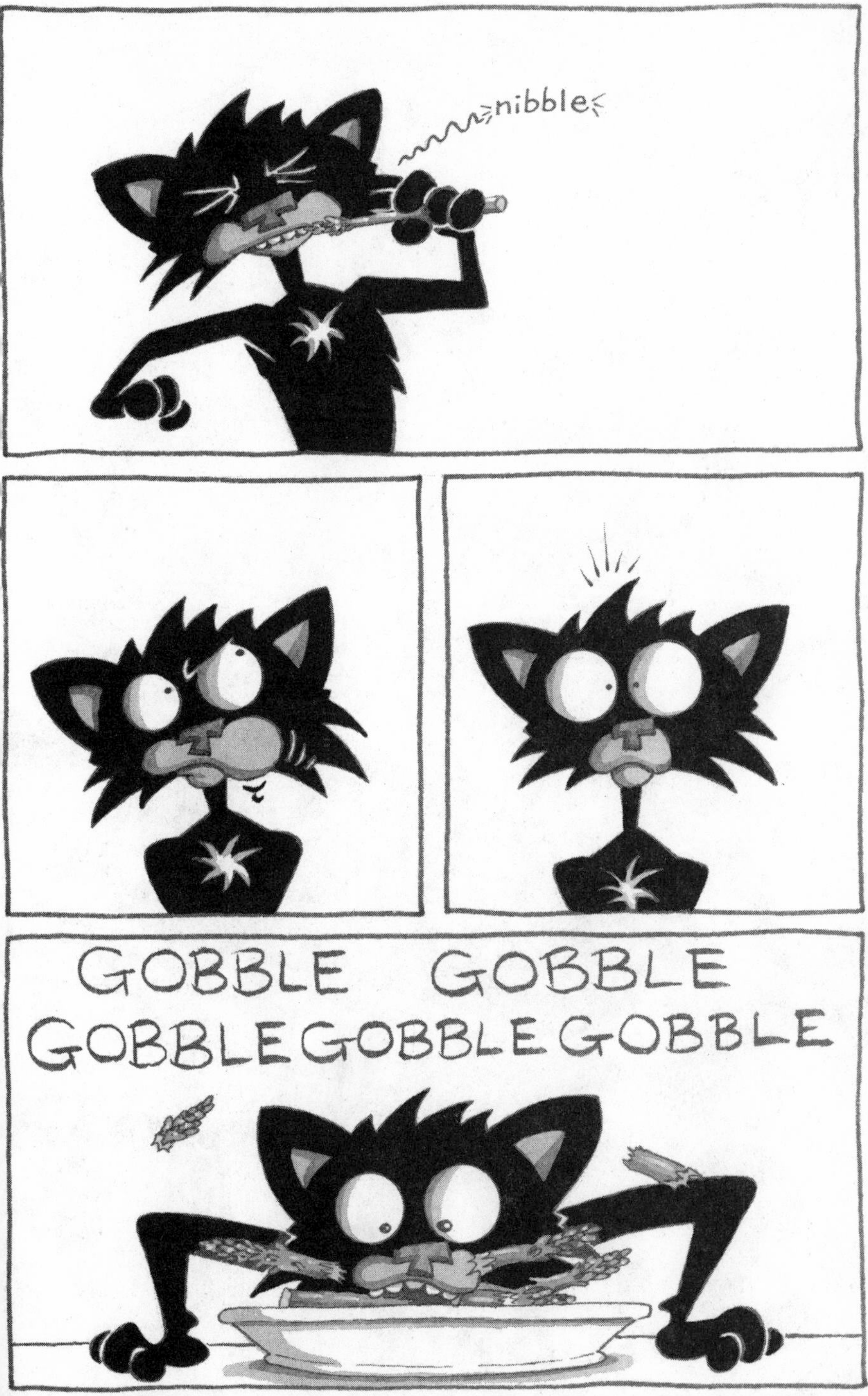
nibble
GOBBLE GOBBLE
GOBBLE GOBBLE GOBBLE

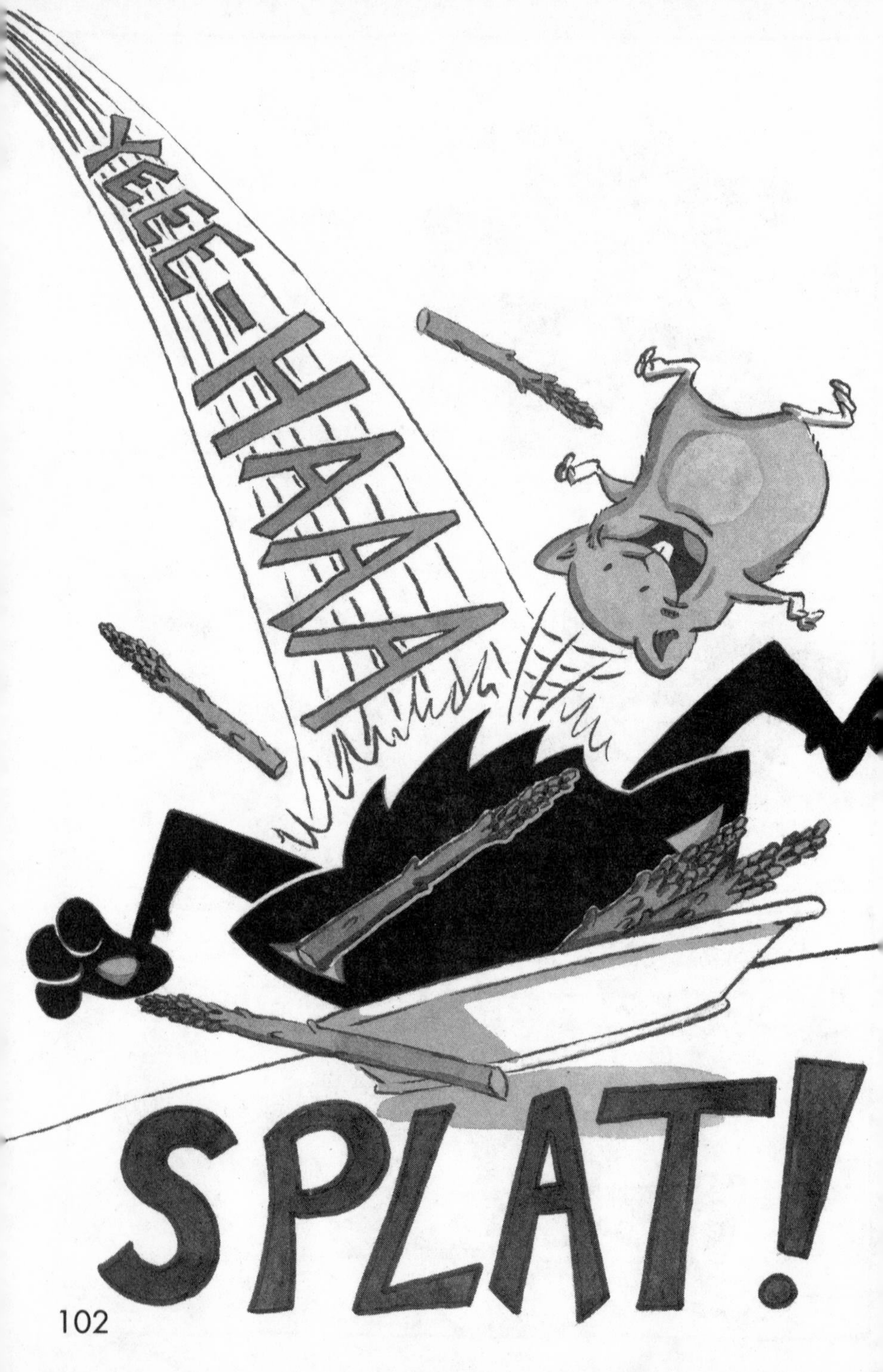
YEEE-HAAA
SPLAT!

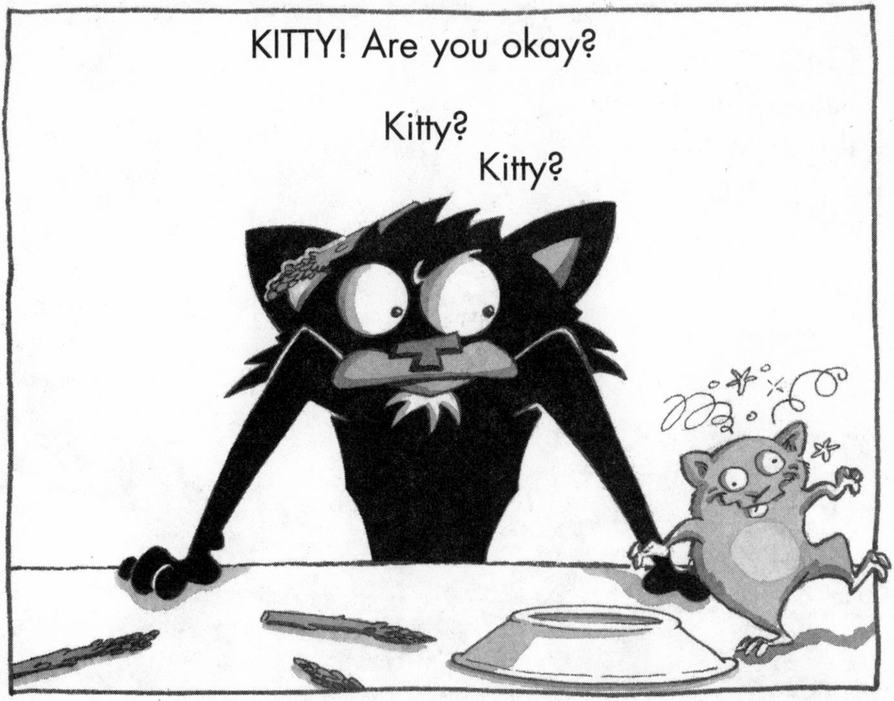
KITTY! Are you okay?
Kitty?
Kitty?

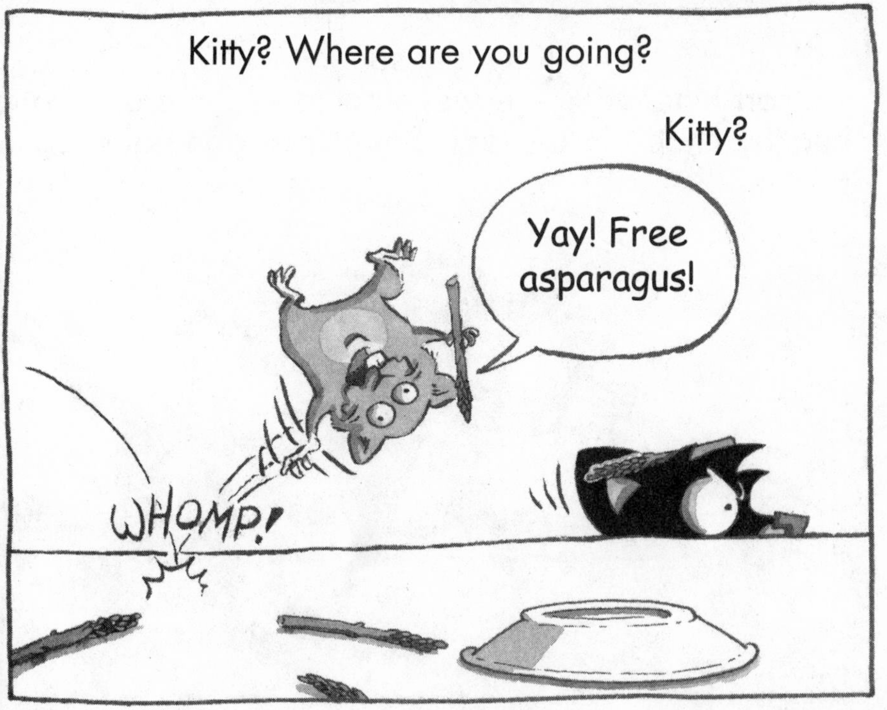
Kitty? Where are you going?
Kitty?
Yay! Free asparagus!
WHOMP!

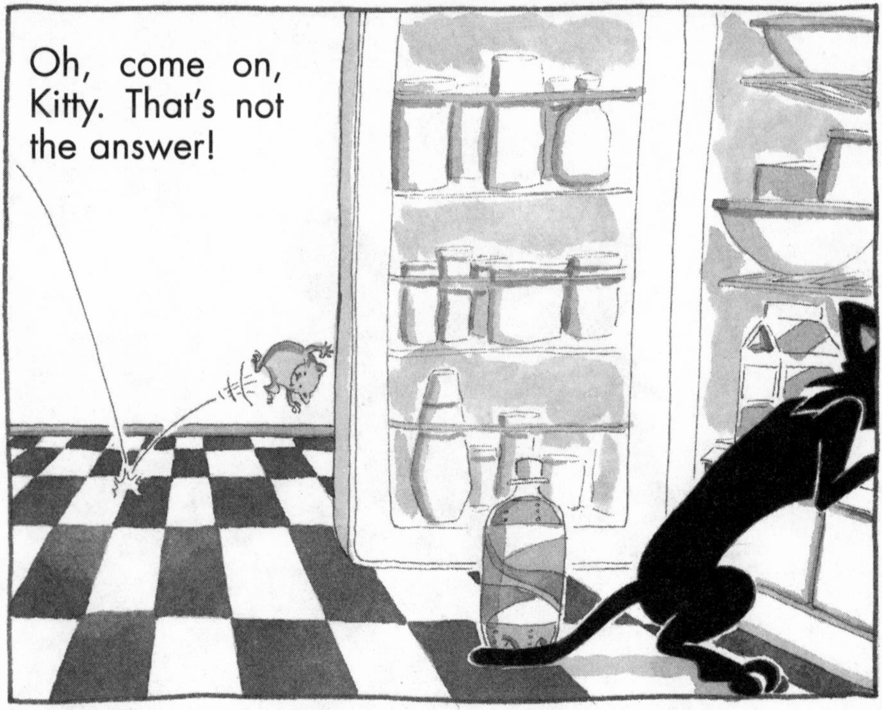
Oh, come on, Kitty. That's not the answer!

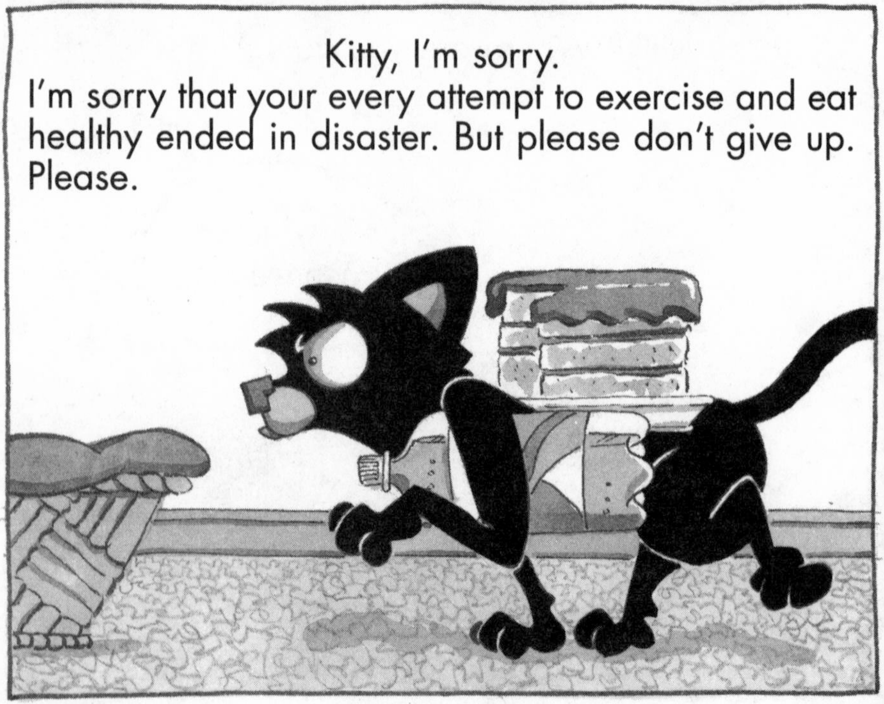
Kitty, I'm sorry.
I'm sorry that your every attempt to exercise and eat healthy ended in disaster. But please don't give up. Please.

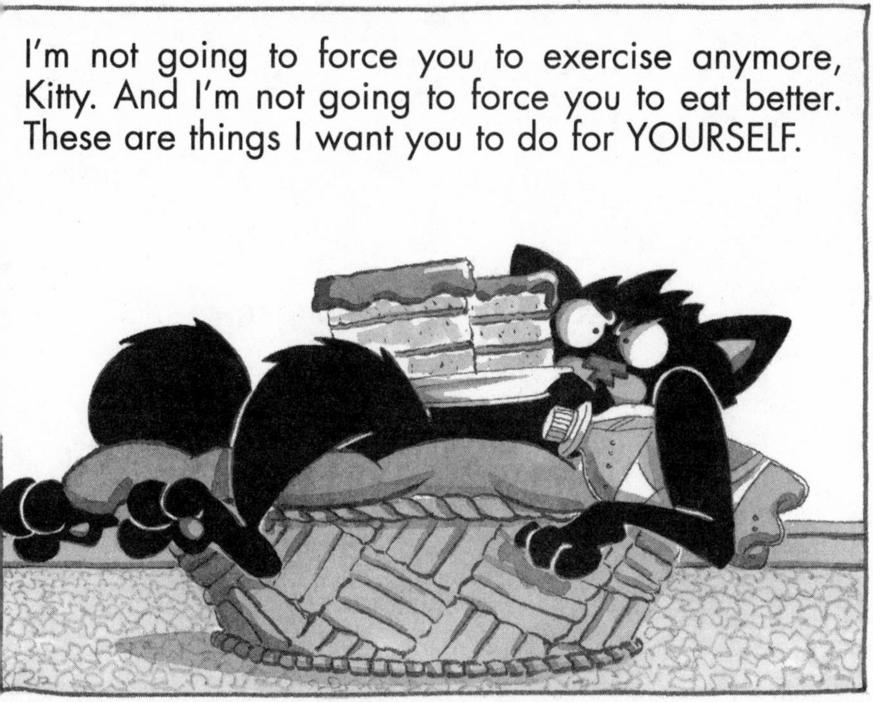
I'm not going to force you to exercise anymore, Kitty. And I'm not going to force you to eat better. These are things I want you to do for YOURSELF.

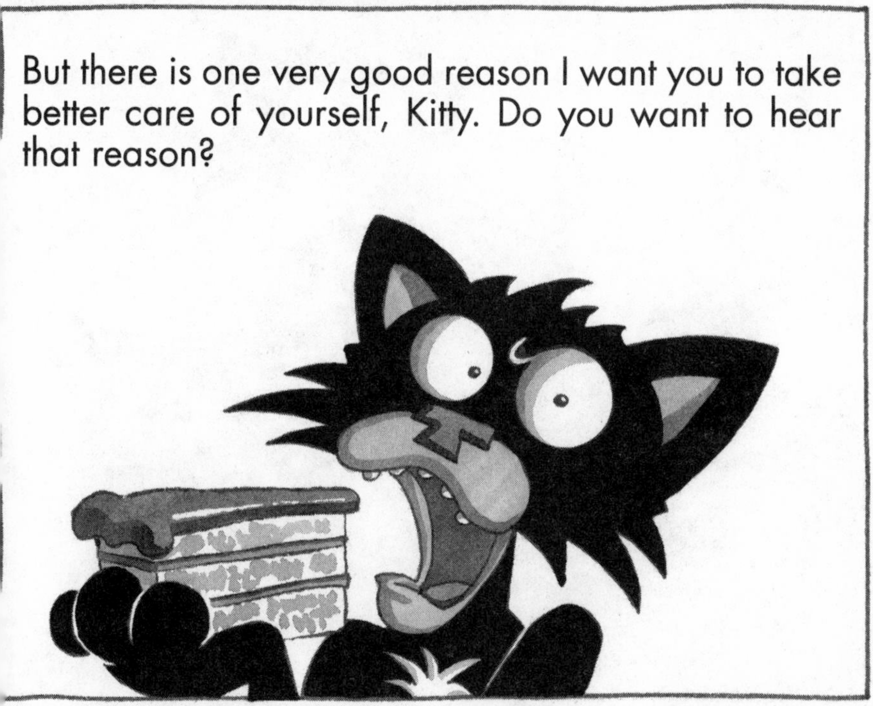
But there is one very good reason I want you to take better care of yourself, Kitty. Do you want to hear that reason?

I want you to live longer.

It's true. Exercise and proper food help to keep your body healthy. And the healthier your body, the longer you live. I don't know of a simpler way to put it.

You worked hard today, Kitty, and I'm proud of you for it. You deserve a rest. Please promise me you'll think about what I told you and maybe . . . just maybe . . . find a way to stay active.

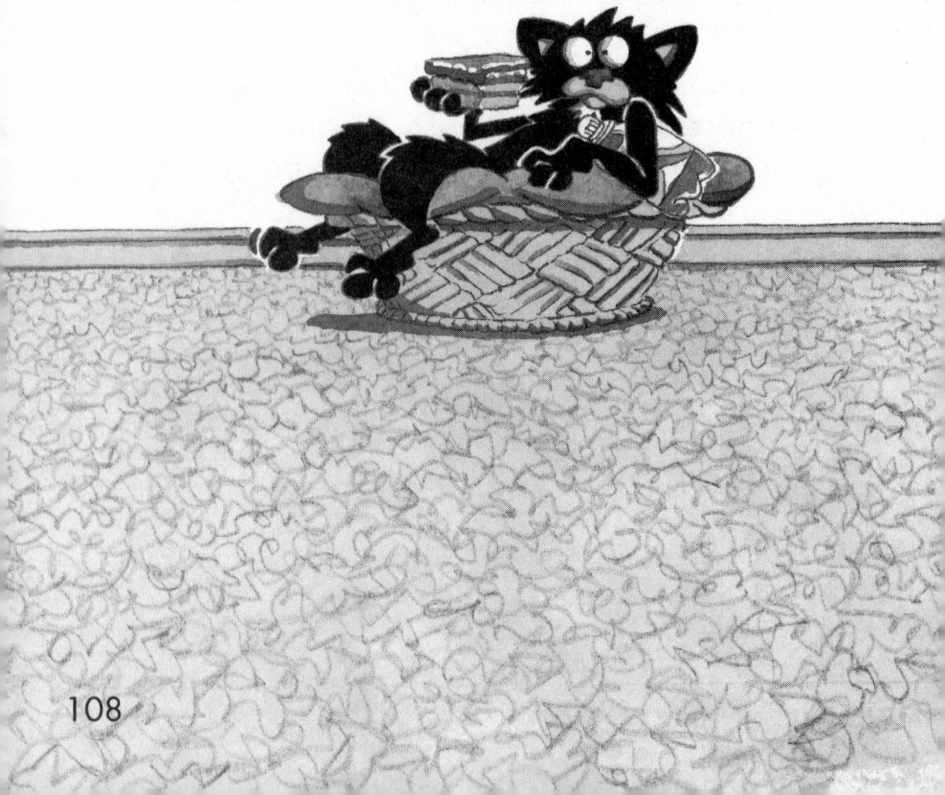

• CHAPTER EIGHT •

THE FINAL EVENT

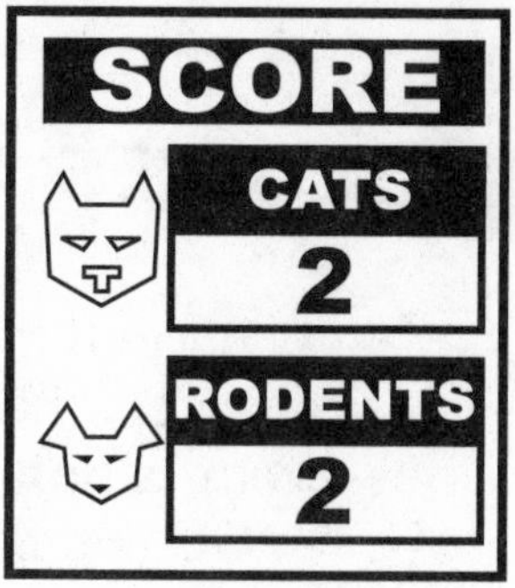
SCORE
CATS
2
RODENTS
2

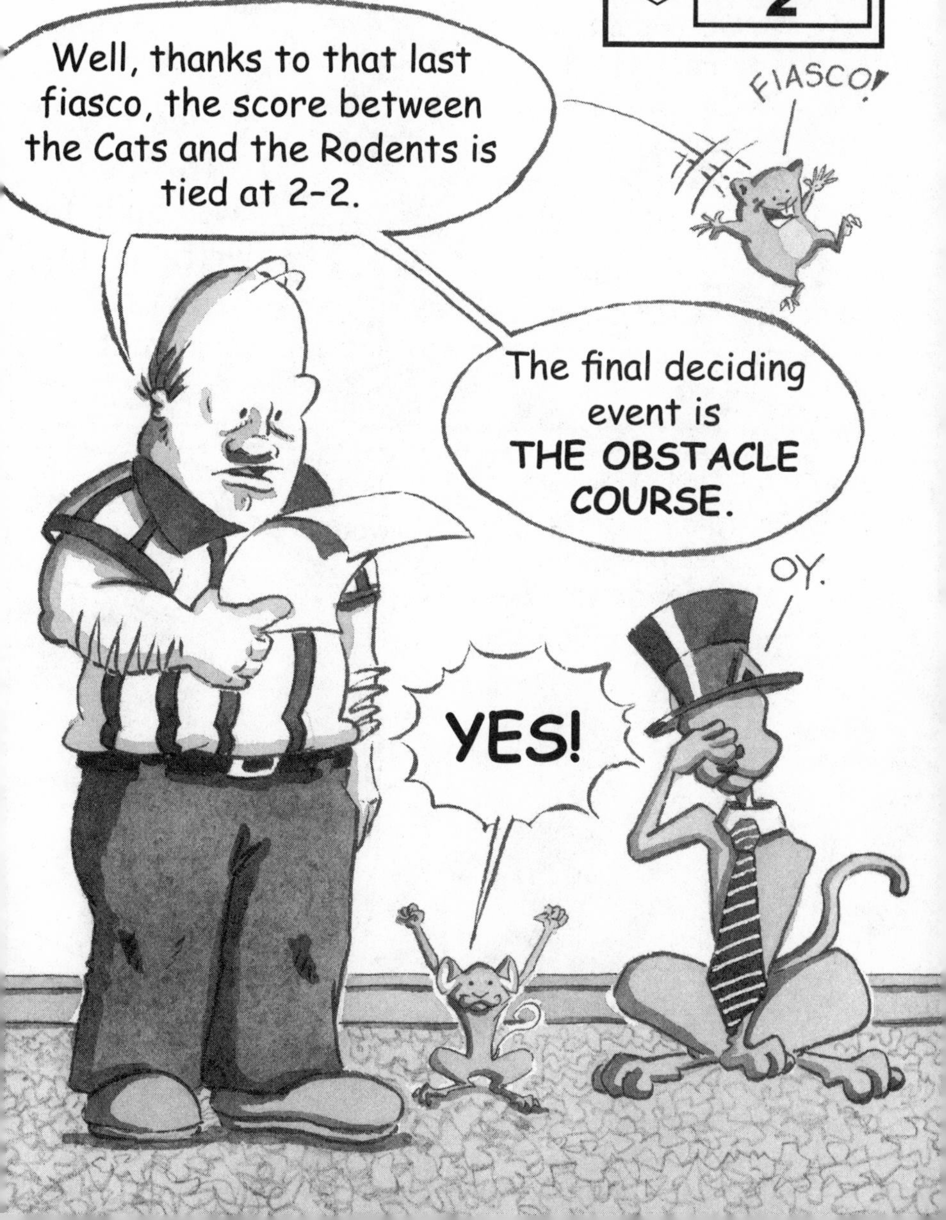
Well, thanks to that last fiasco, the score between the Cats and the Rodents is tied at 2–2.
FIASCO!
The final deciding event is THE OBSTACLE COURSE.
OY.
YES!

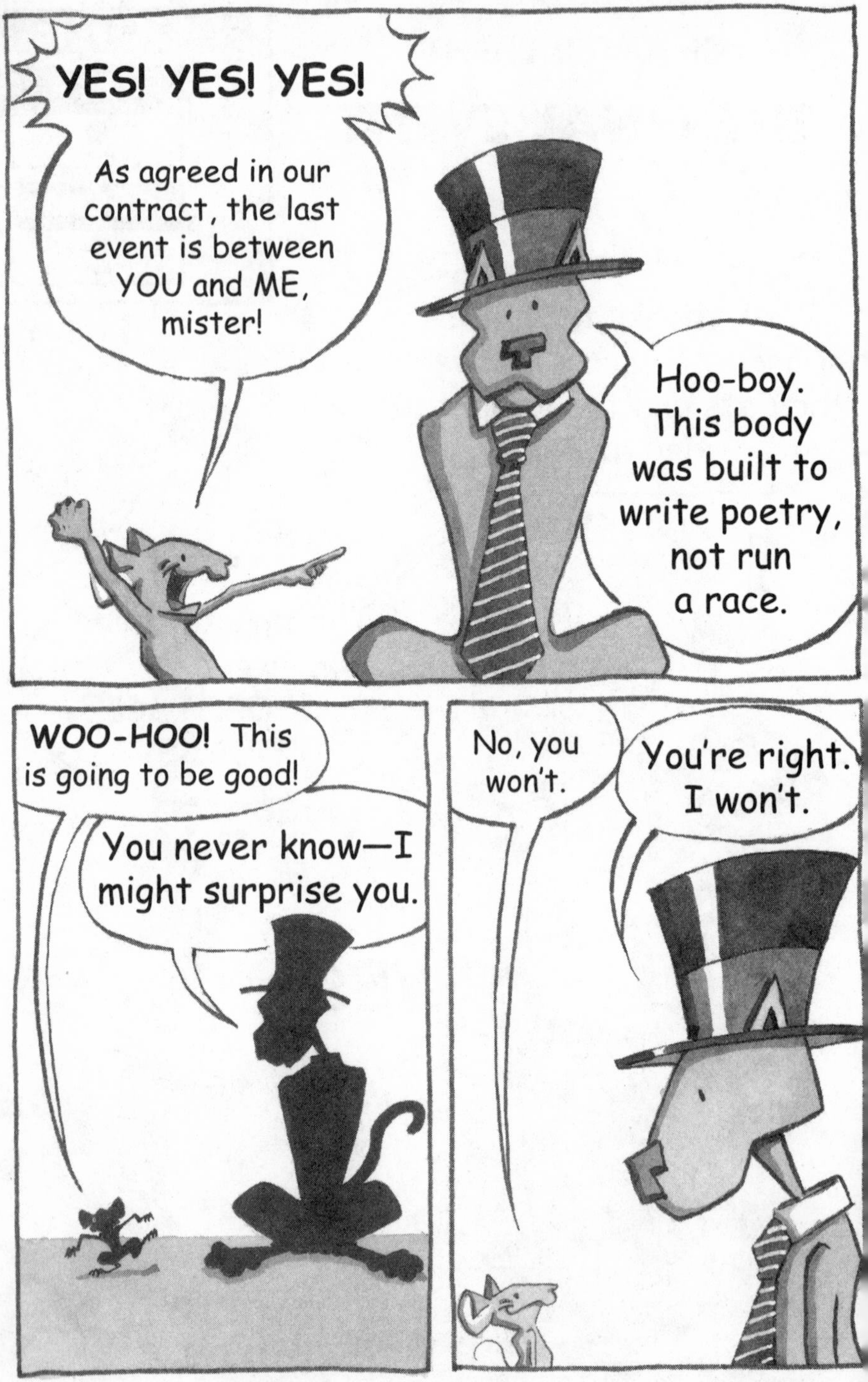
YES! YES! YES!
As agreed in our contract, the last event is between YOU and ME, mister!
Hoo-boy. This body was built to write poetry, not run a race.
WOO-HOO! This is going to be good!
You never know—I might surprise you.
No, you won't.
You're right. I won't.

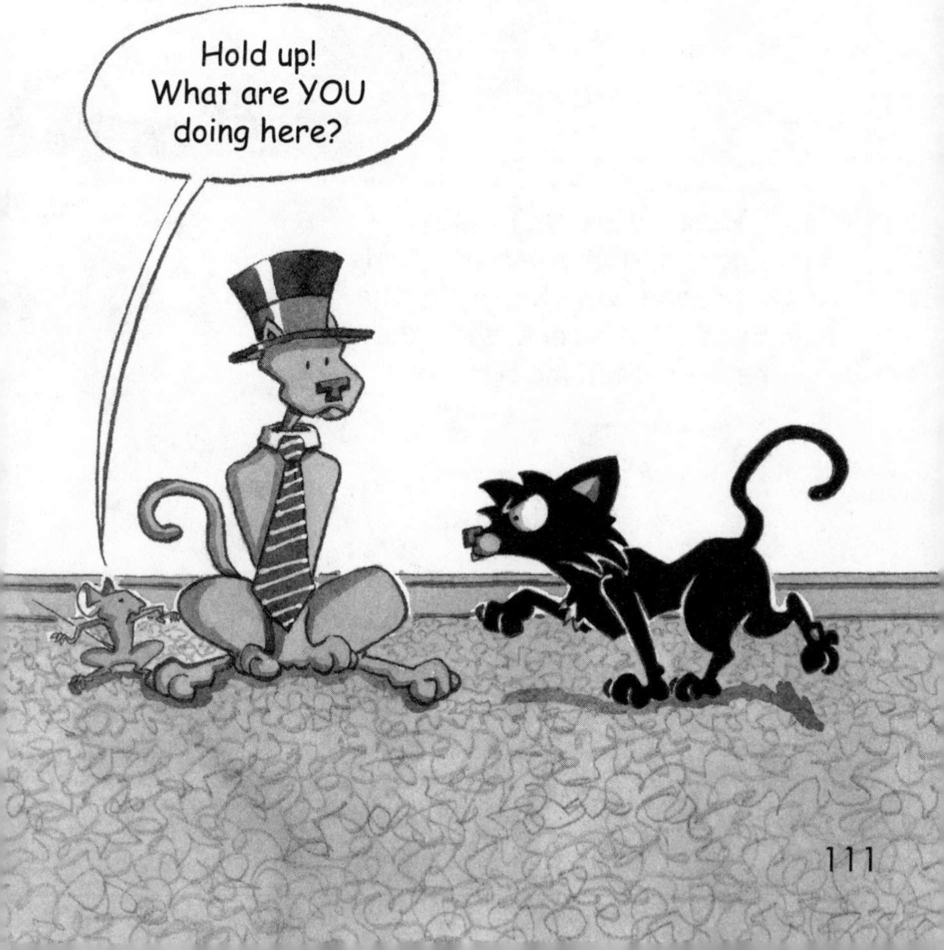
Hold up! What are YOU doing here?

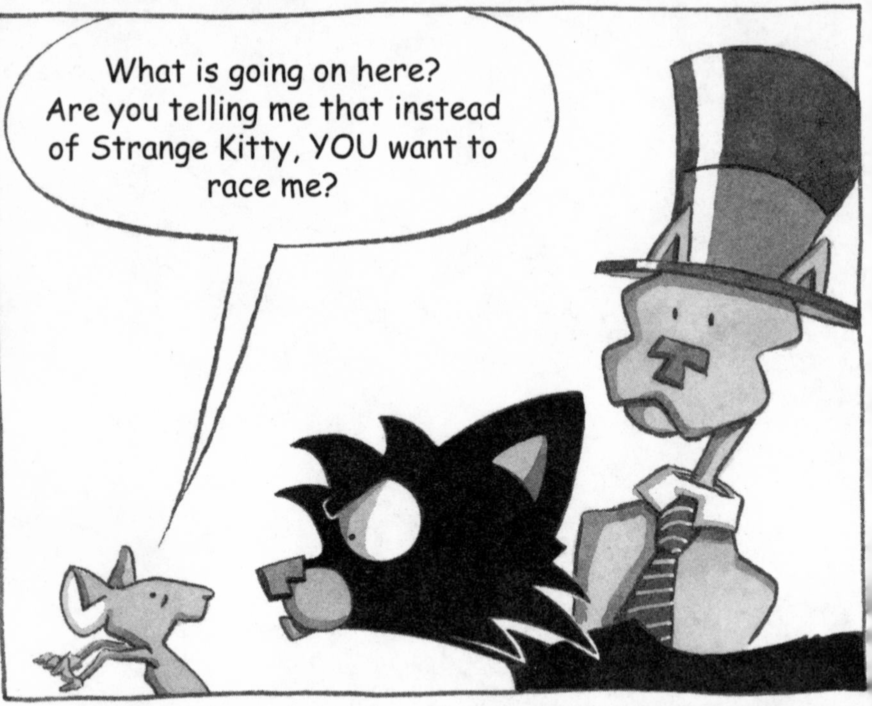
What is going on here? Are you telling me that instead of Strange Kitty, YOU want to race me?

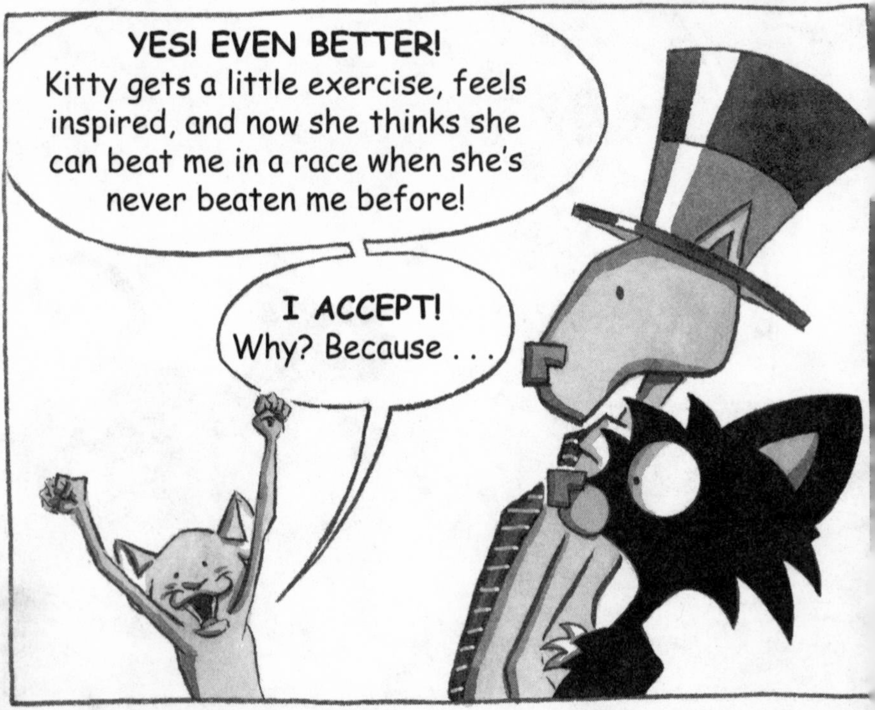
YES! EVEN BETTER! Kitty gets a little exercise, feels inspired, and now she thinks she can beat me in a race when she's never beaten me before!
I ACCEPT! Why? Because . . .

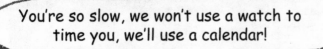

You're so slow, we won't use a watch to time you, we'll use a calendar!

You're so sickly, you'd lose a race to a sloth covered in molasses running uphill!

You're so clumsy, you'd trip on your own shadow!

You're so weak, you couldn't lift helium!

You're so lazy, you were expelled from kindergarten for sleeping through naptime!

Don't take it personally. He's so mean, he'd trash-talk his momma on her birthday.

You're so out of shape, you can't do a sit-up, a push-up, a pull-up, a dress-up, a shut-up, a throw-up, or even a ketchup!

And you're ugly!

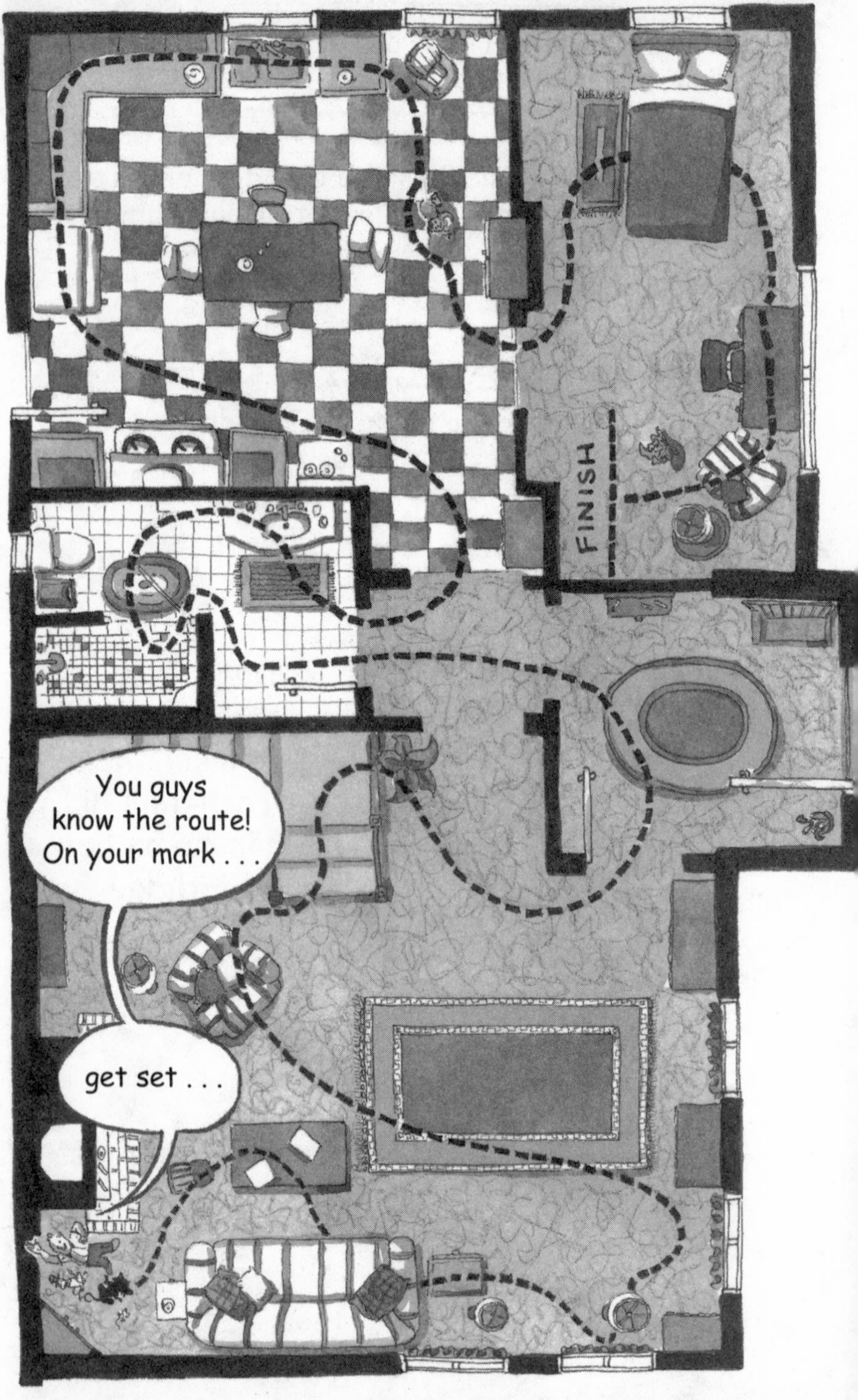

You guys know the route! On your mark . . .
get set . . .
FINISH

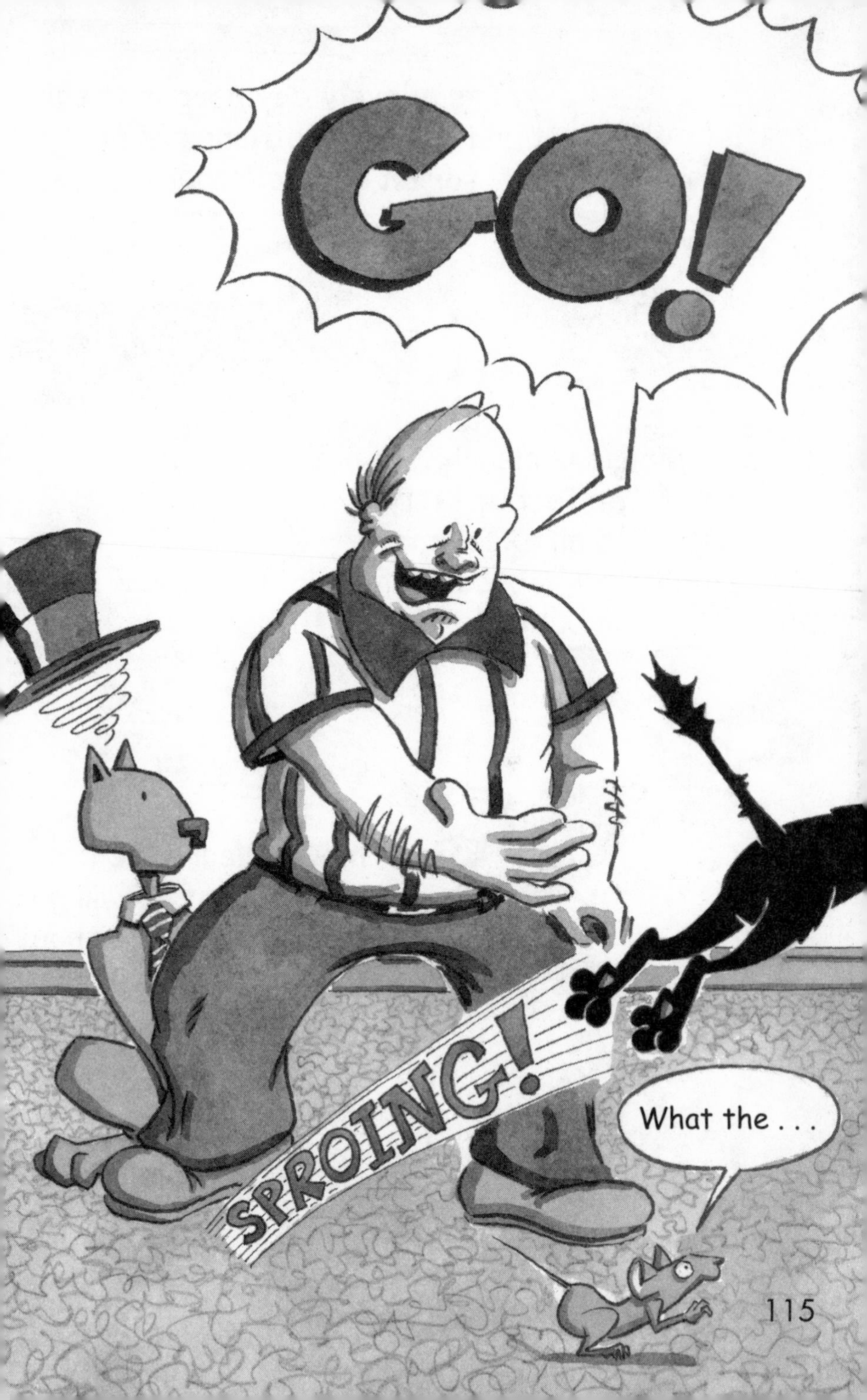
GO!
SPROING!
What the . . .

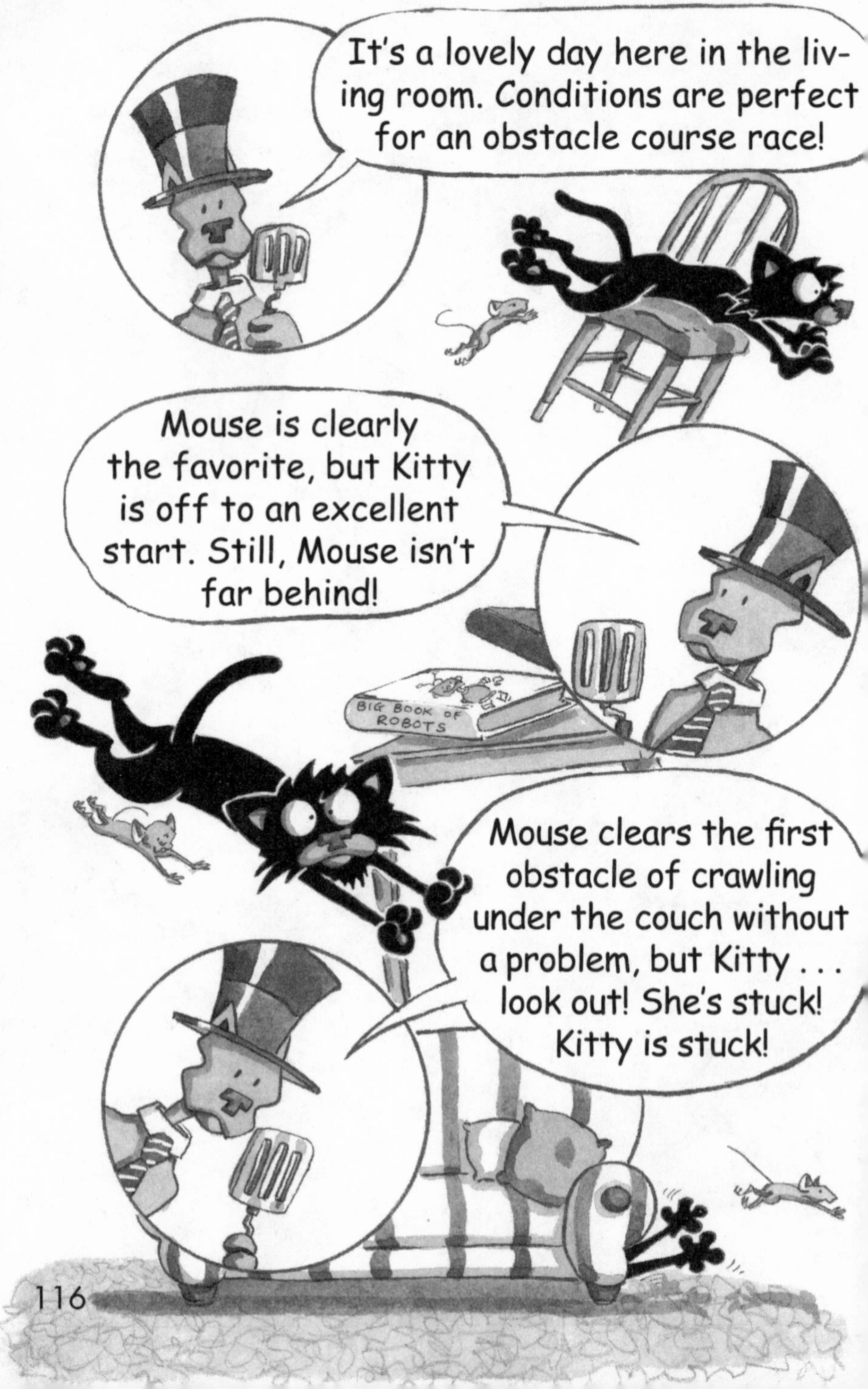
It's a lovely day here in the living room. Conditions are perfect for an obstacle course race!
Mouse is clearly the favorite, but Kitty is off to an excellent start. Still, Mouse isn't far behind!
BIG BOOK OF ROBOTS
Mouse clears the first obstacle of crawling under the couch without a problem, but Kitty . . . look out! She's stuck! Kitty is stuck!

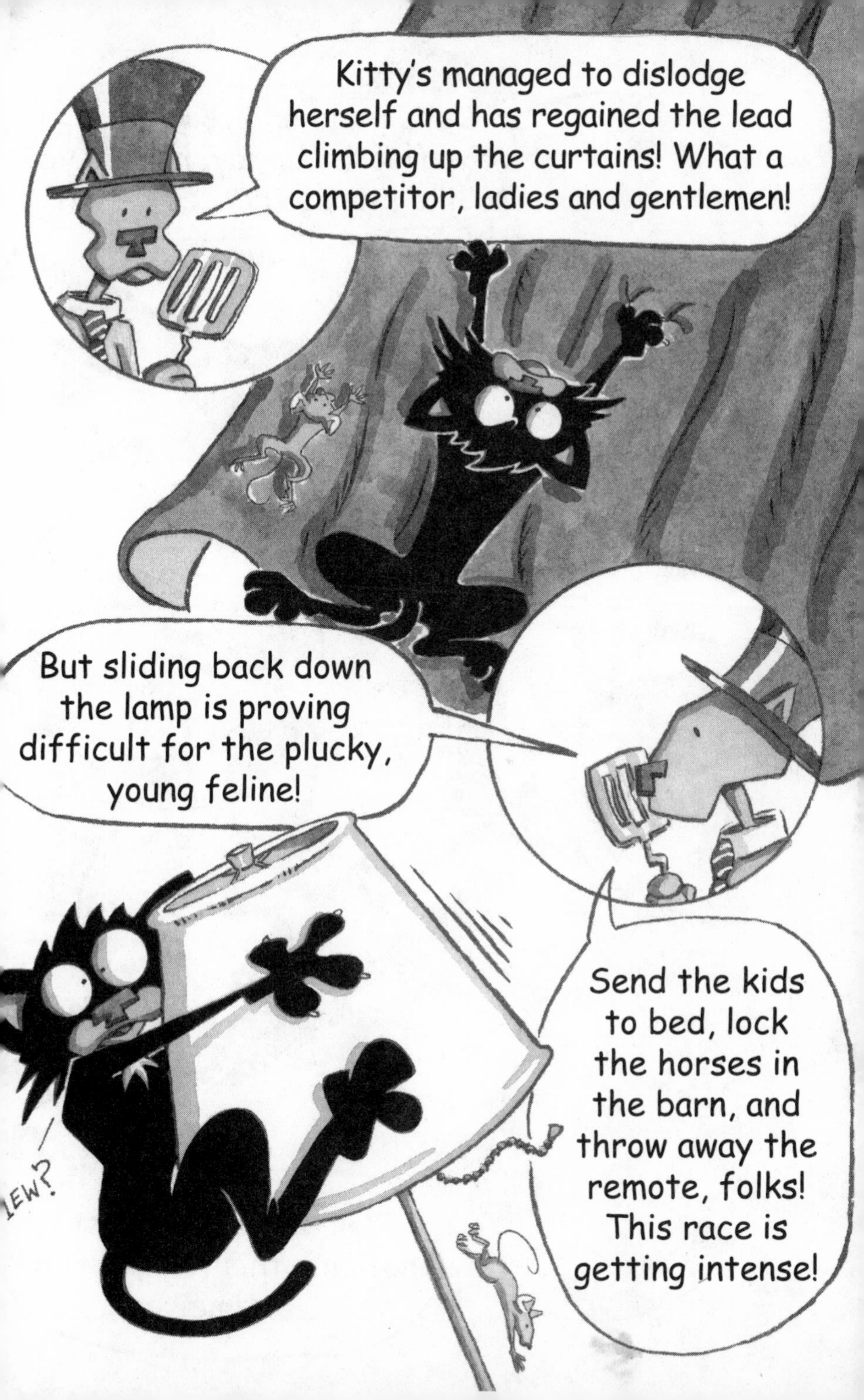
Kitty's managed to dislodge herself and has regained the lead climbing up the curtains! What a competitor, ladies and gentlemen!
But sliding back down the lamp is proving difficult for the plucky, young feline!
Send the kids to bed, lock the horses in the barn, and throw away the remote, folks! This race is getting intense!
EW?

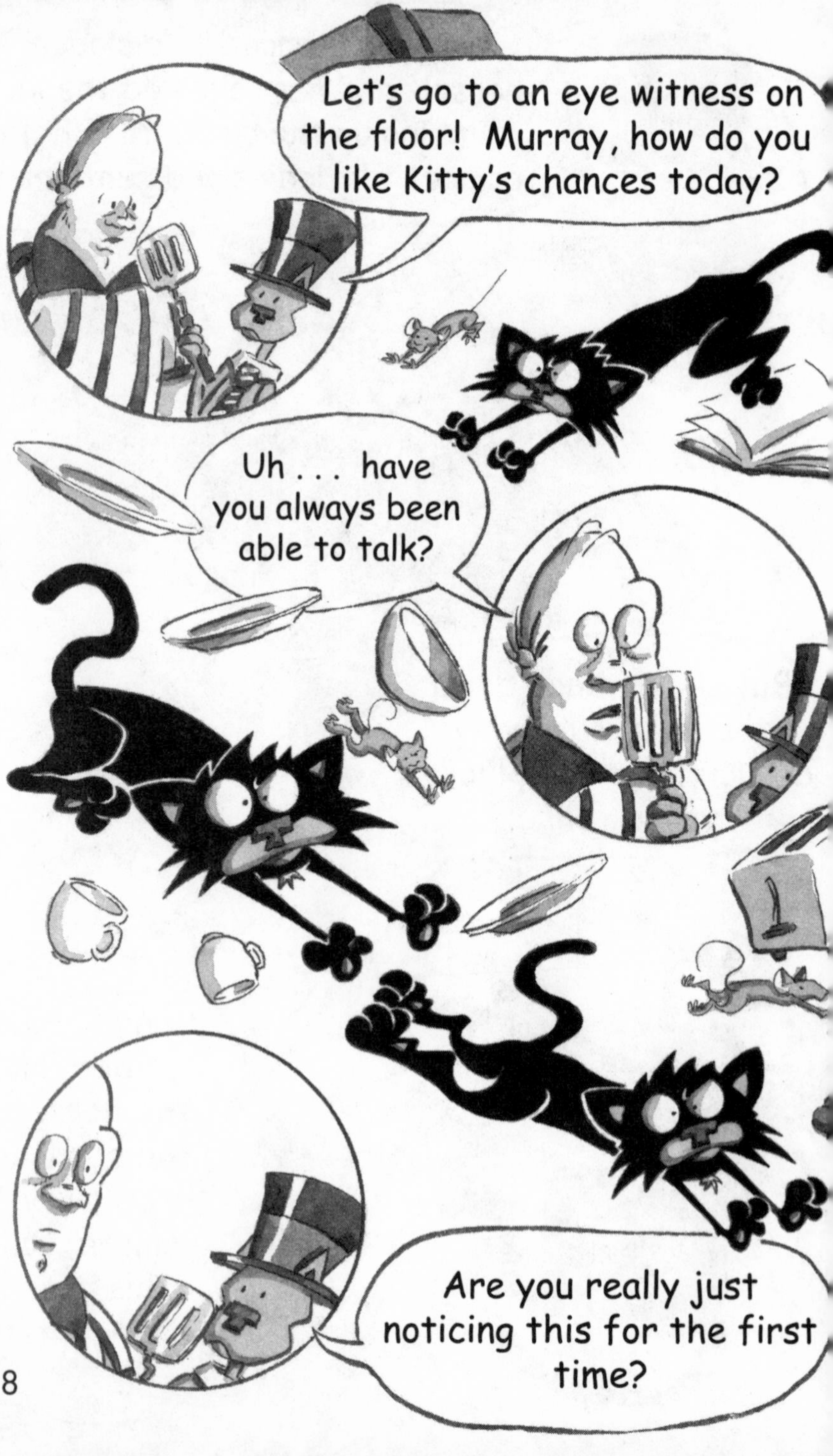
Let's go to an eye witness on the floor! Murray, how do you like Kitty's chances today?
Uh . . . have you always been able to talk?
Are you really just noticing this for the first time?

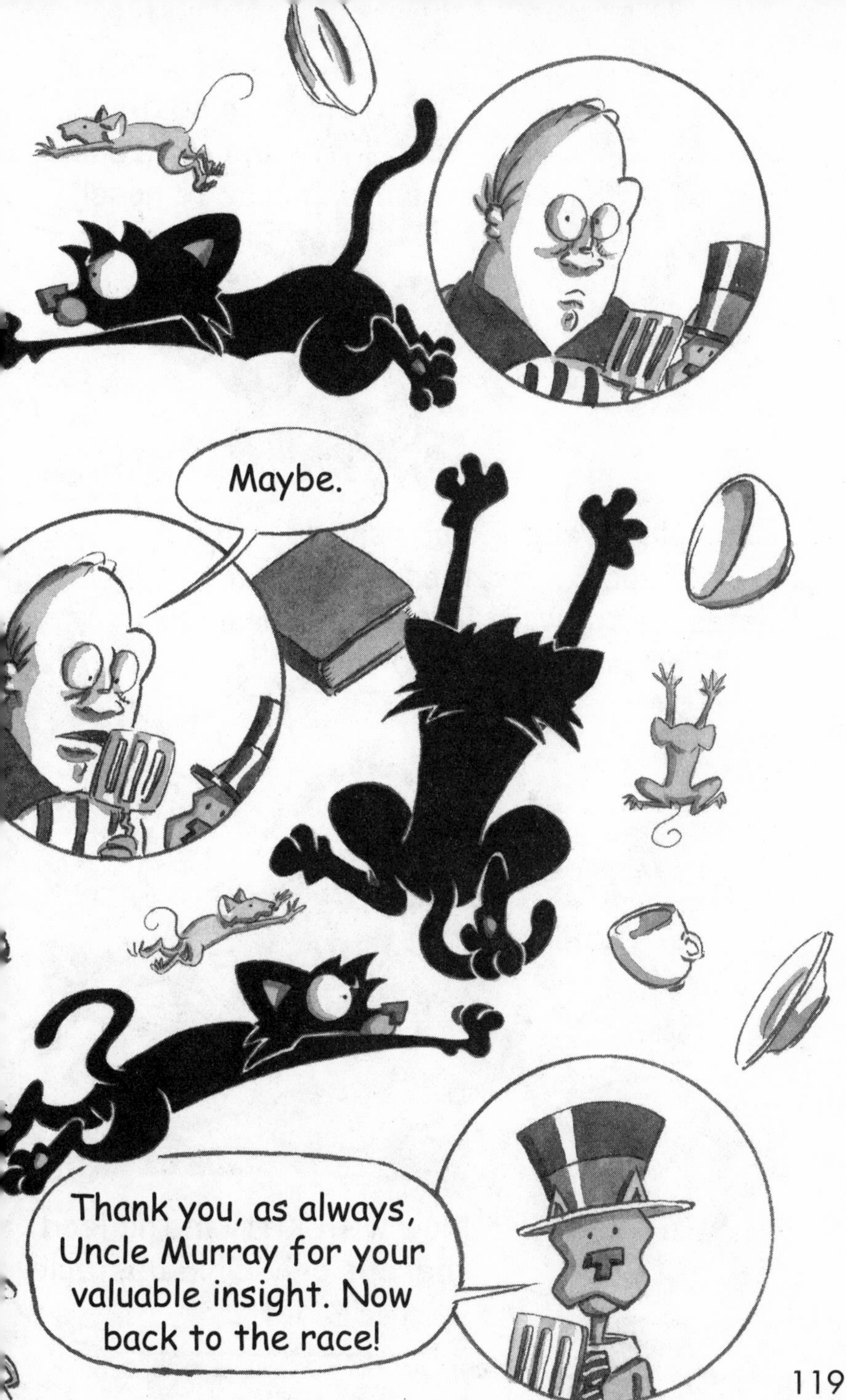
Maybe.
Thank you, as always, Uncle Murray for your valuable insight. Now back to the race!

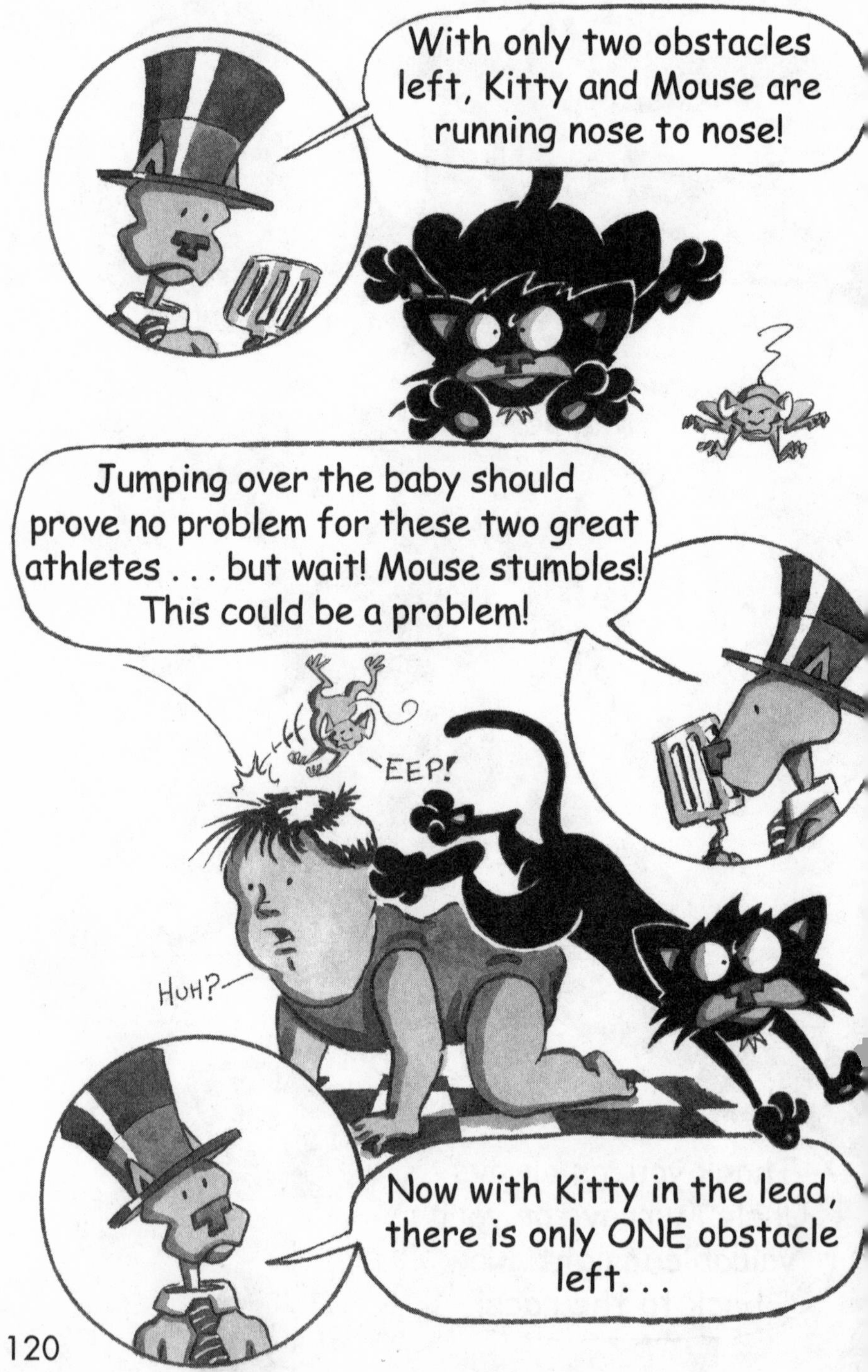

With only two obstacles left, Kitty and Mouse are running nose to nose!
Jumping over the baby should prove no problem for these two great athletes . . . but wait! Mouse stumbles! This could be a problem!
EEP!
HUH?
Now with Kitty in the lead, there is only ONE obstacle left. . .

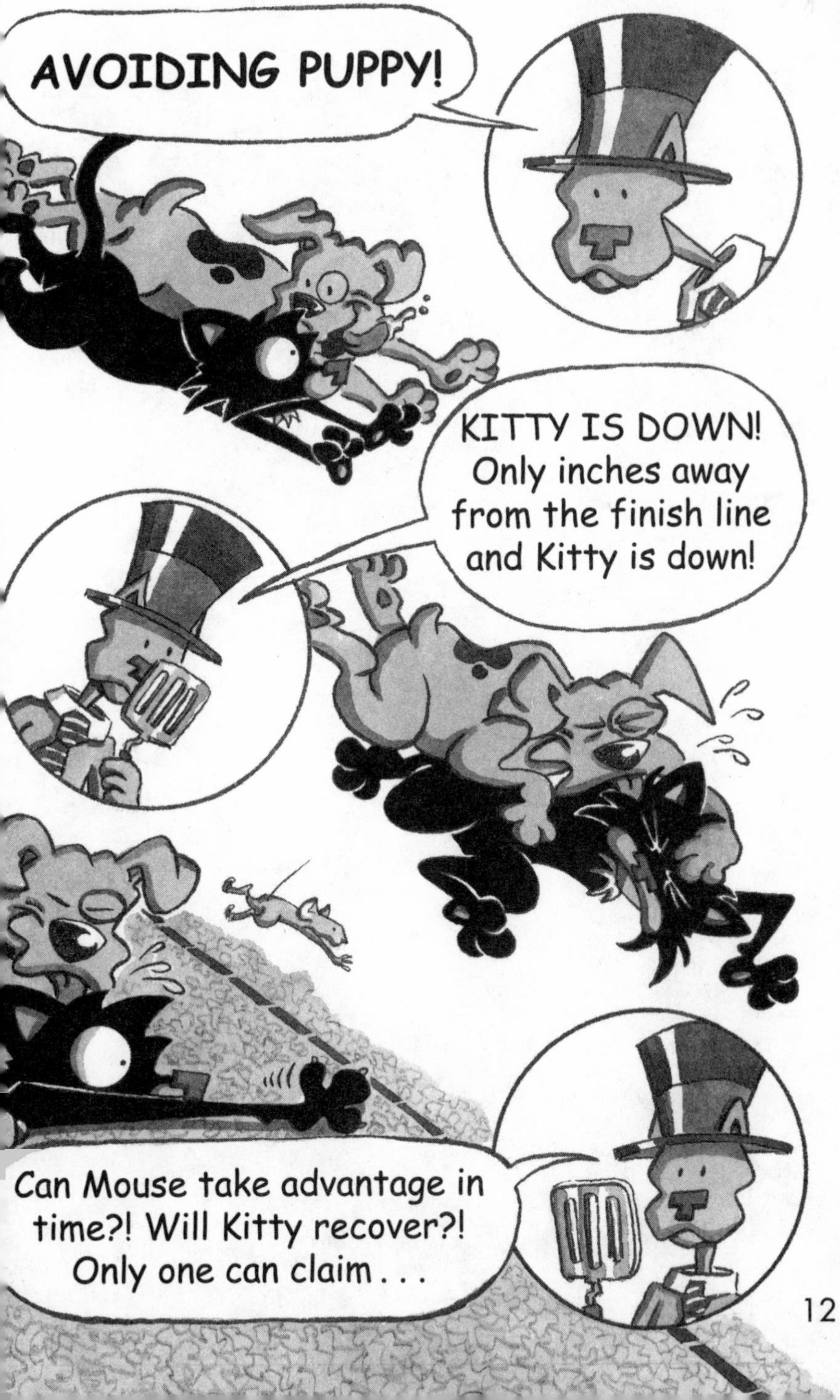
AVOIDING PUPPY!
KITTY IS DOWN! Only inches away from the finish line and Kitty is down!
Can Mouse take advantage in time?! Will Kitty recover?! Only one can claim . . .

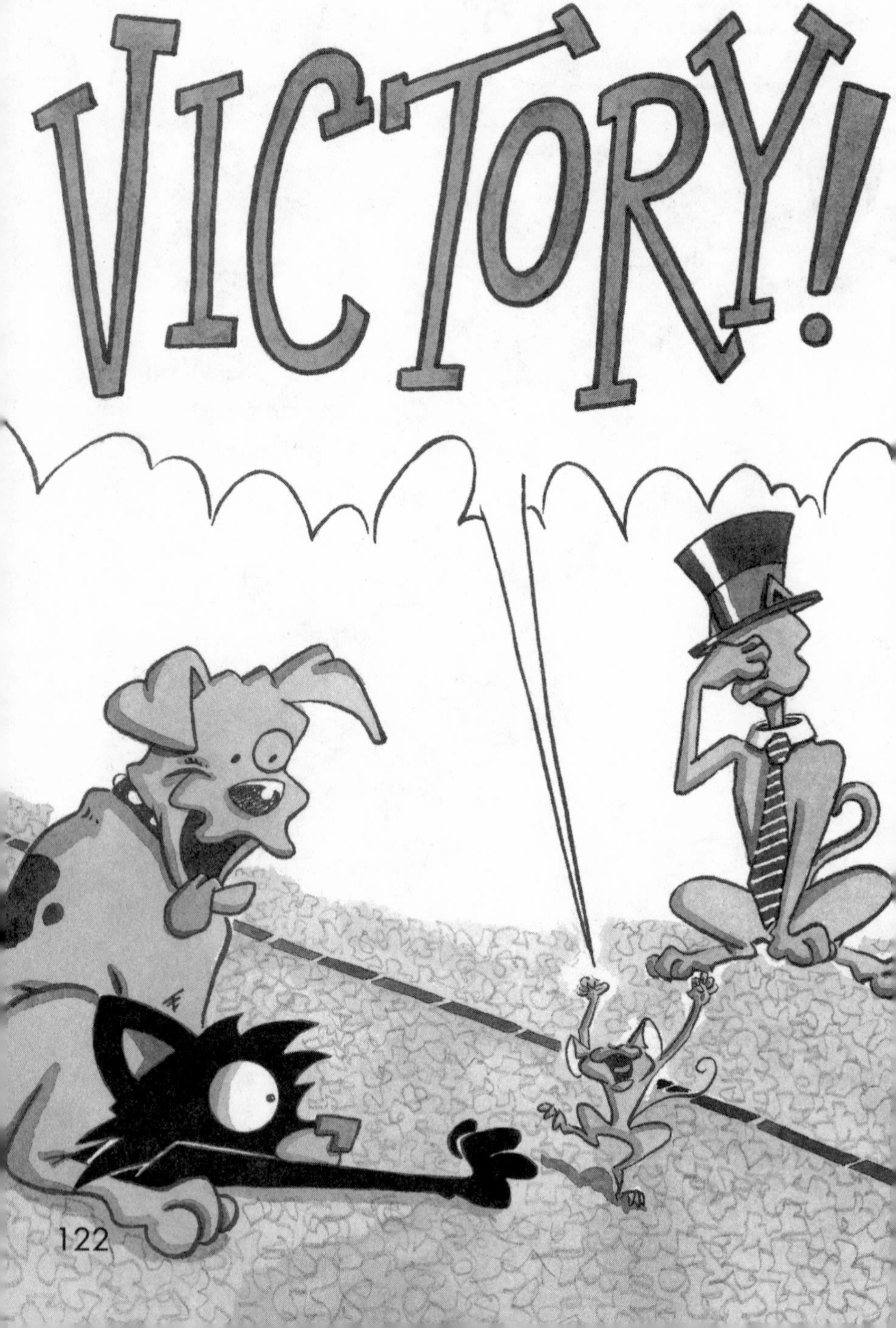
VICTORY!

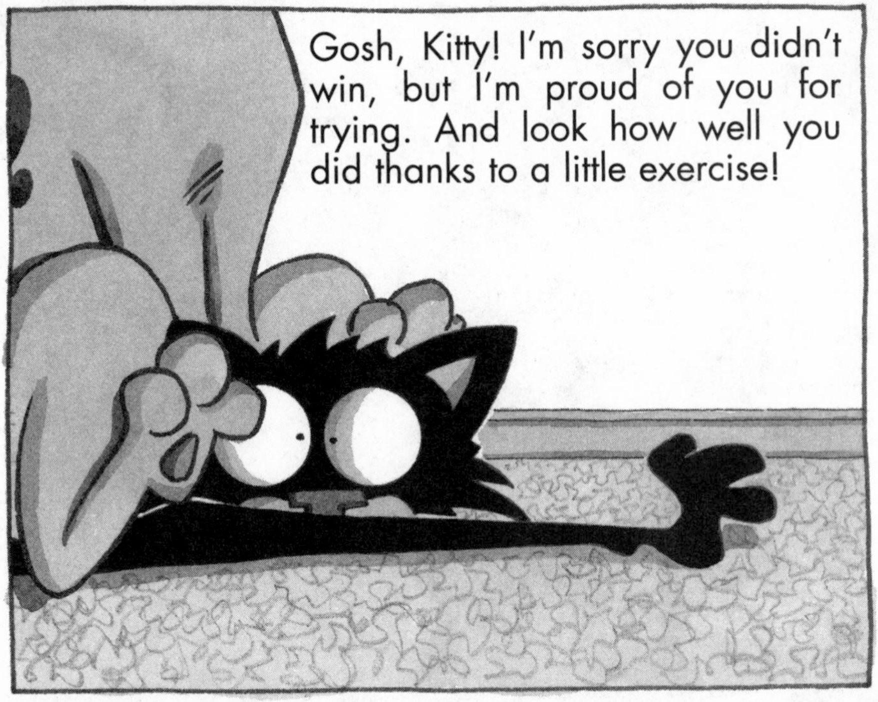
Gosh, Kitty! I'm sorry you didn't win, but I'm proud of you for trying. And look how well you did thanks to a little exercise!

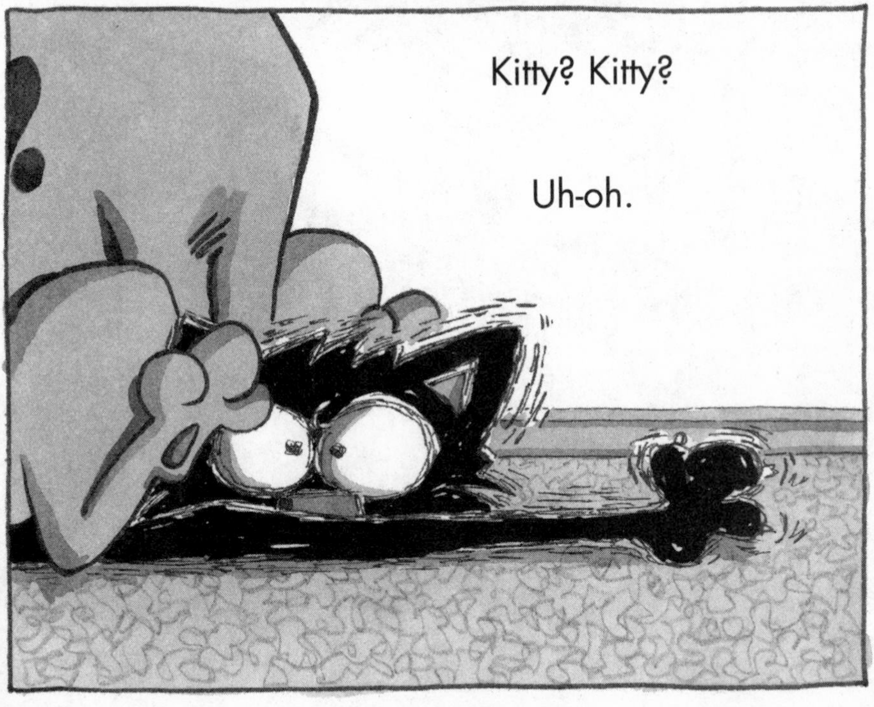
Kitty? Kitty?
Uh-oh.

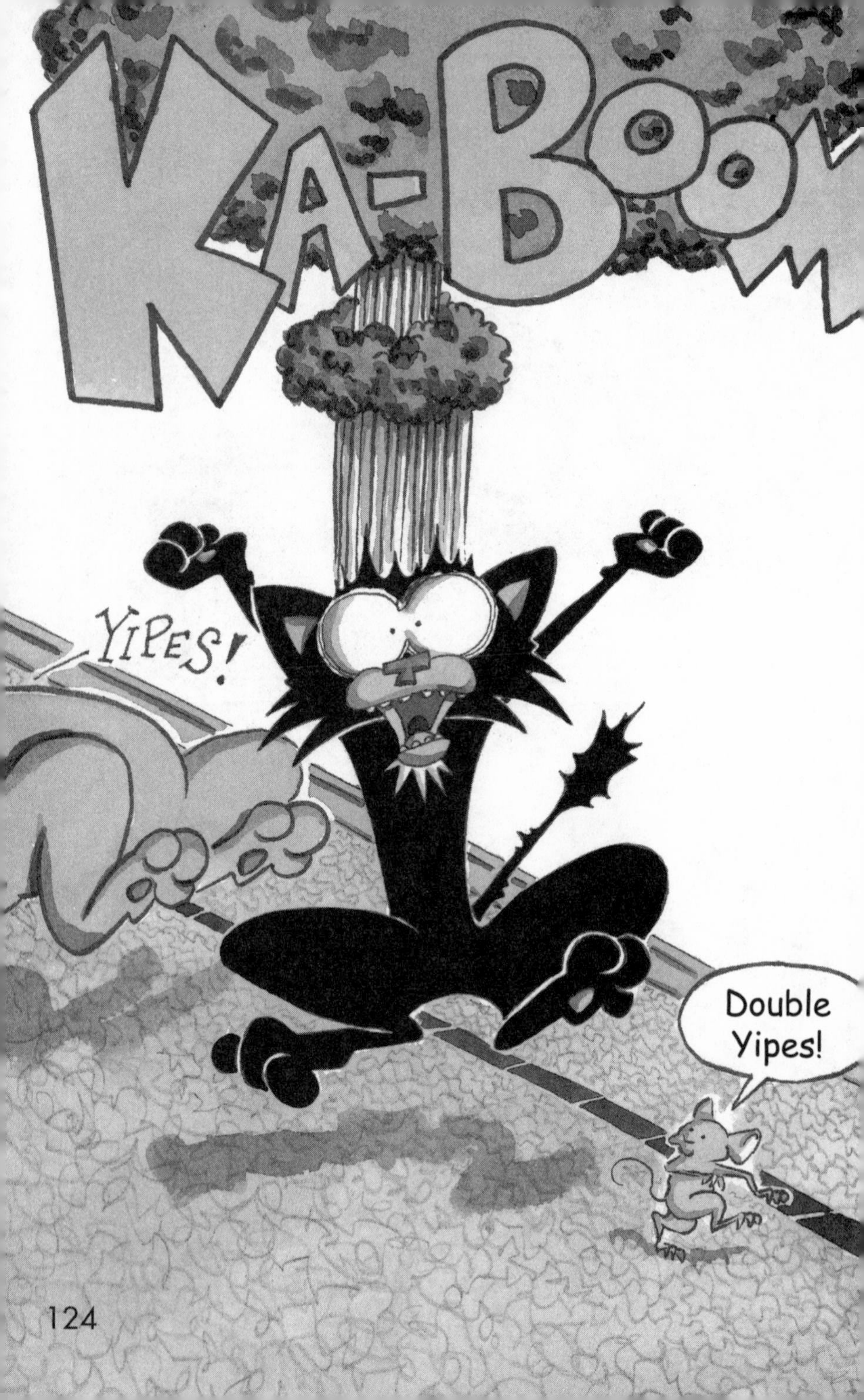
KA-BOOM
YIPES!
Double Yipes!

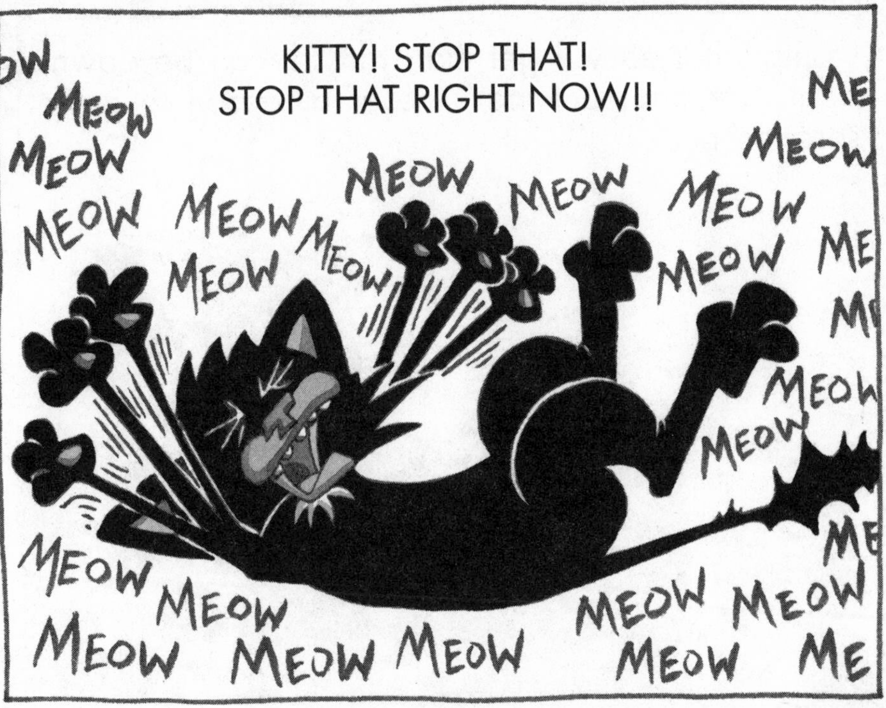
KITTY! STOP THAT!
STOP THAT RIGHT NOW!!

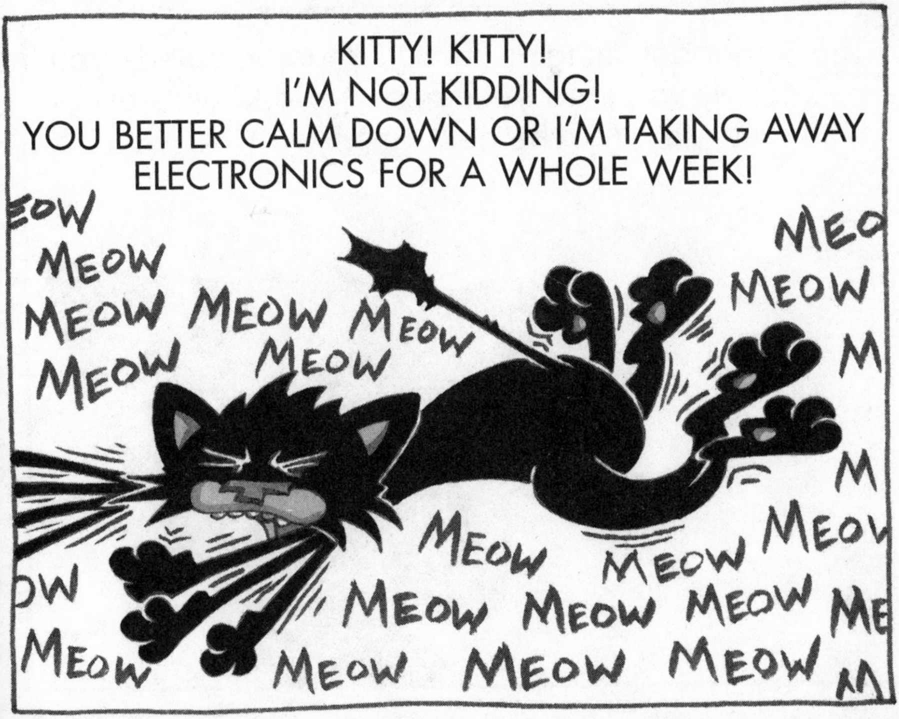
KITTY! KITTY!
I'M NOT KIDDING!
YOU BETTER CALM DOWN OR I'M TAKING AWAY
ELECTRONICS FOR A WHOLE WEEK!

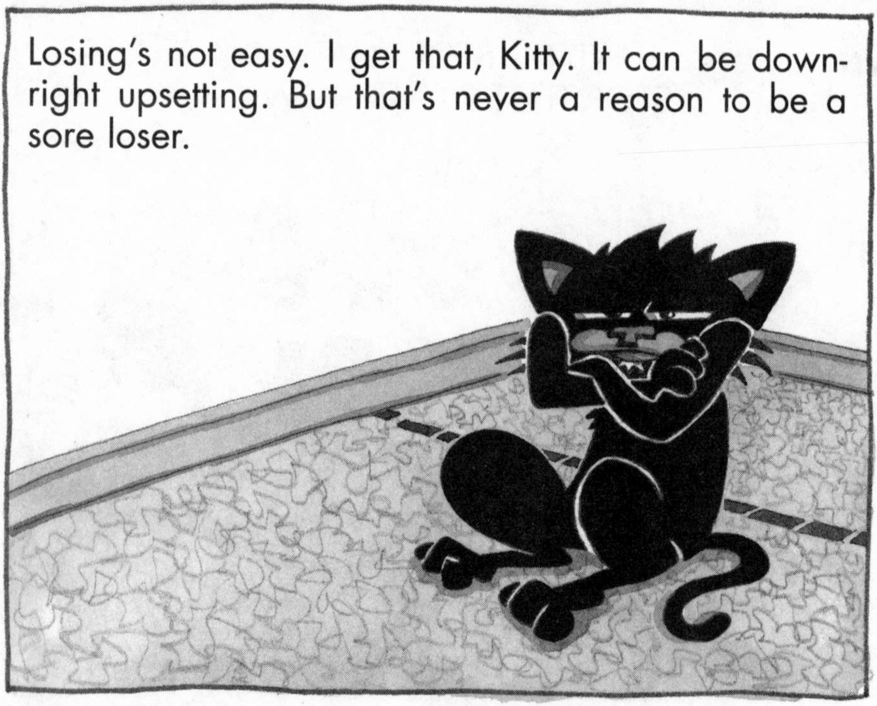
Losing's not easy. I get that, Kitty. It can be downright upsetting. But that's never a reason to be a sore loser.

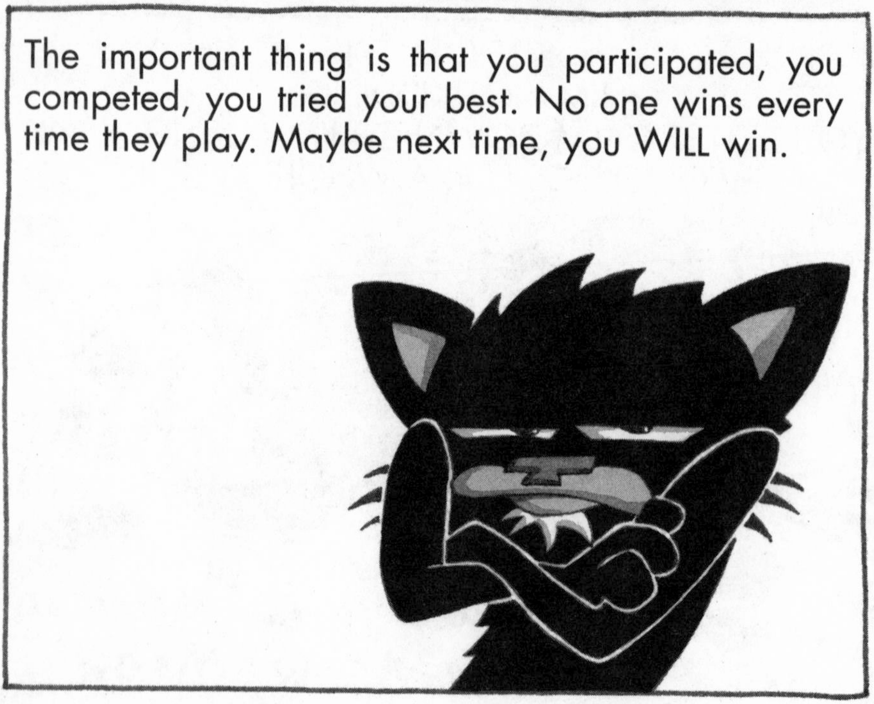
The important thing is that you participated, you competed, you tried your best. No one wins every time they play. Maybe next time, you WILL win.

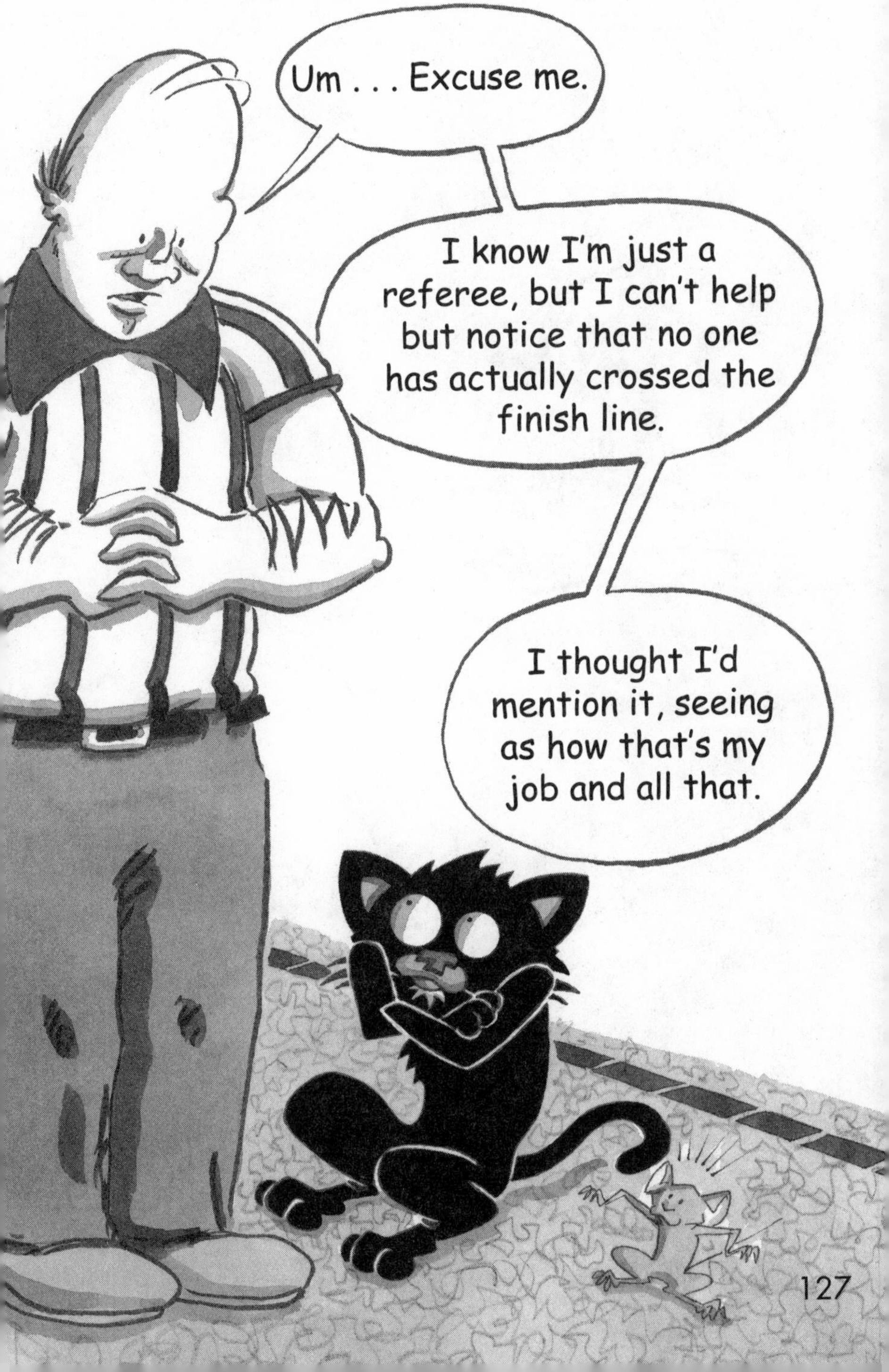
Um . . . Excuse me.
I know I'm just a referee, but I can't help but notice that no one has actually crossed the finish line.
I thought I'd mention it, seeing as how that's my job and all that.

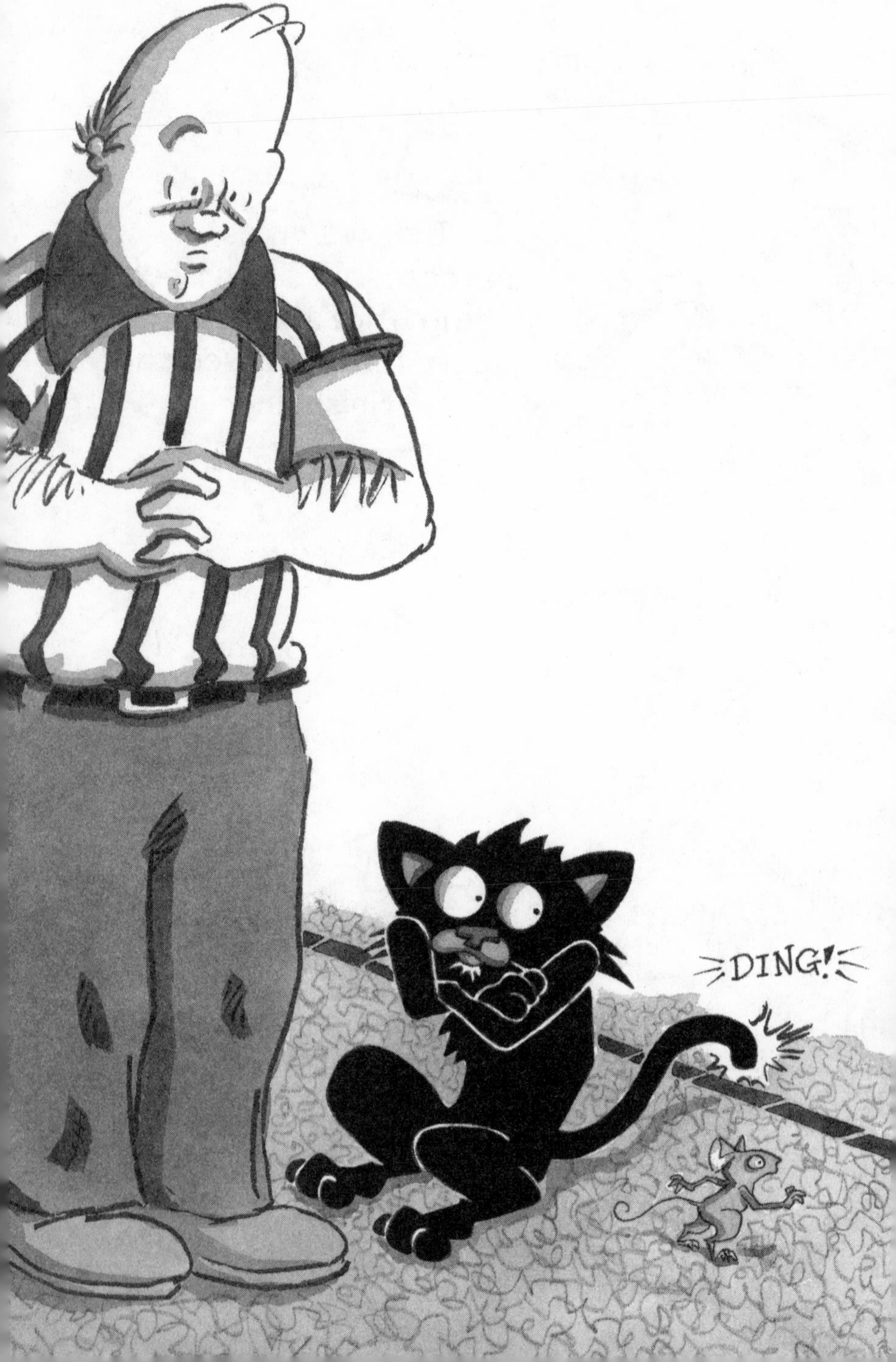
DING!

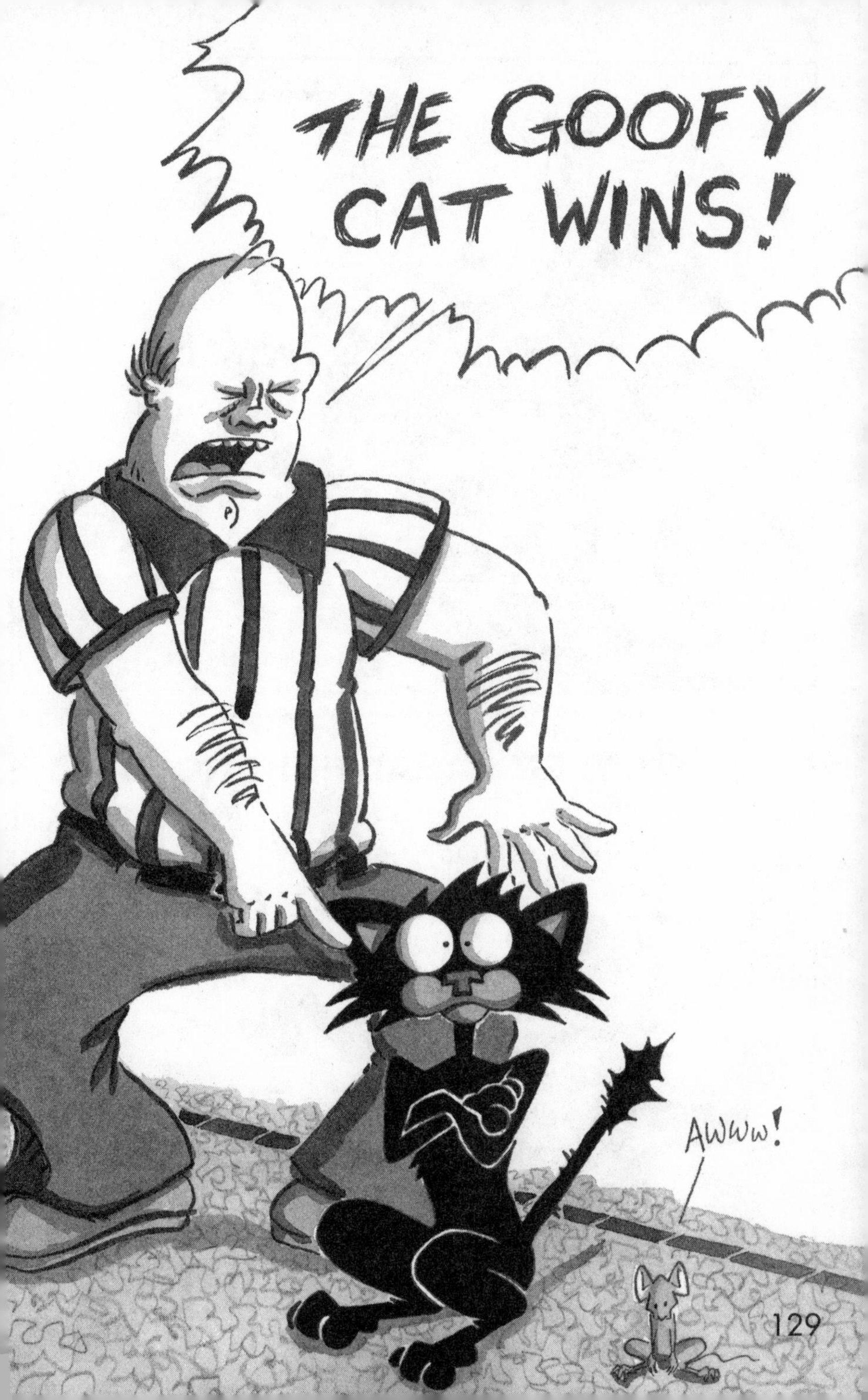
THE GOOFY CAT WINS!
AWWW!

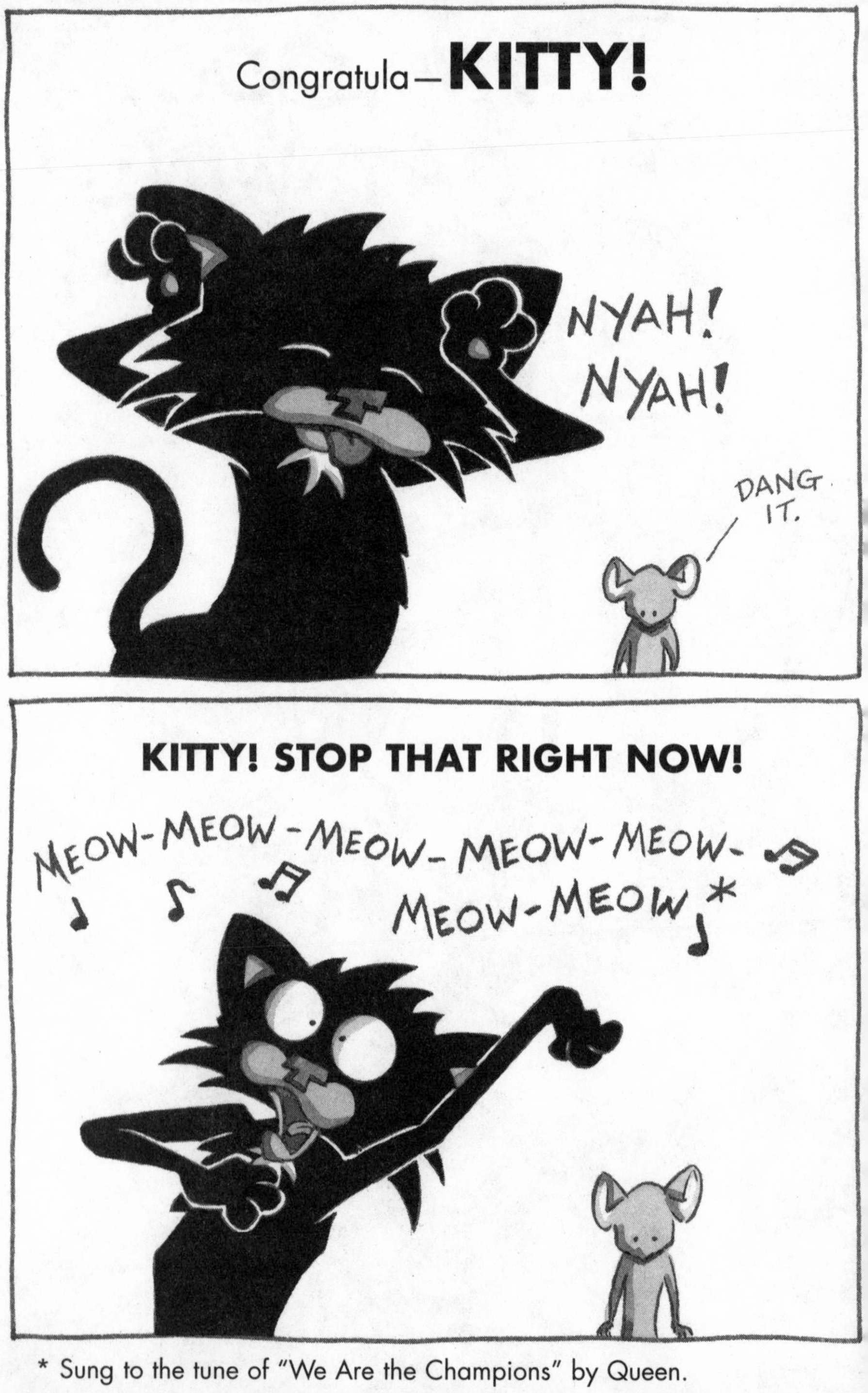
Congratula—KITTY!
NYAH! NYAH!
DANG IT.
KITTY! STOP THAT RIGHT NOW!
MEOW-MEOW-MEOW-MEOW-MEOW-MEOW-MEOW*

* Sung to the tune of "We Are the Champions" by Queen.

The only thing as bad as a sore loser is a bad winner. I'm happy that you won, but showing off because you won only hurts the feelings of the other side. I need you to apologize right now!

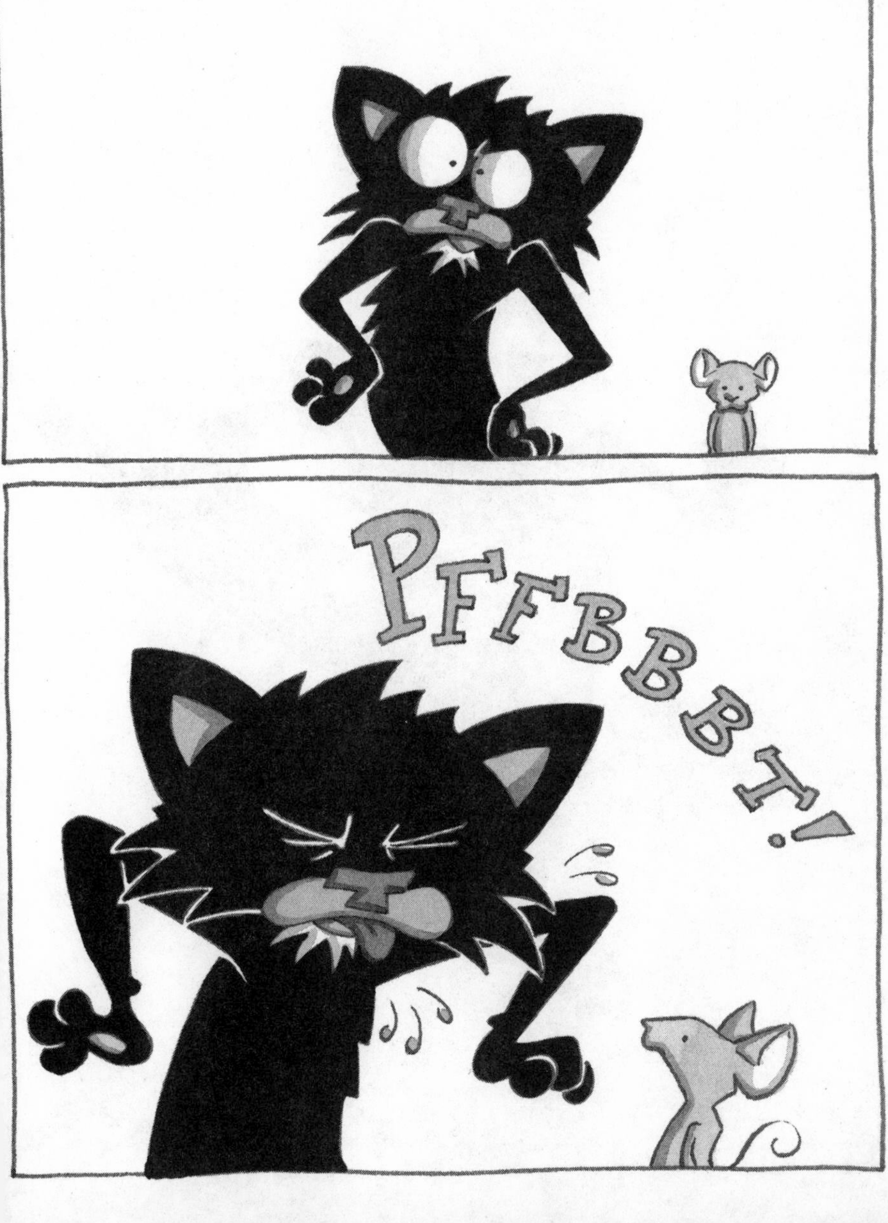
PFFBBBT!

THAT DOES IT!

Kitty, you're in a time-out, young lady, and you'll stay in time-out until you figure out what it means to be a good sport!

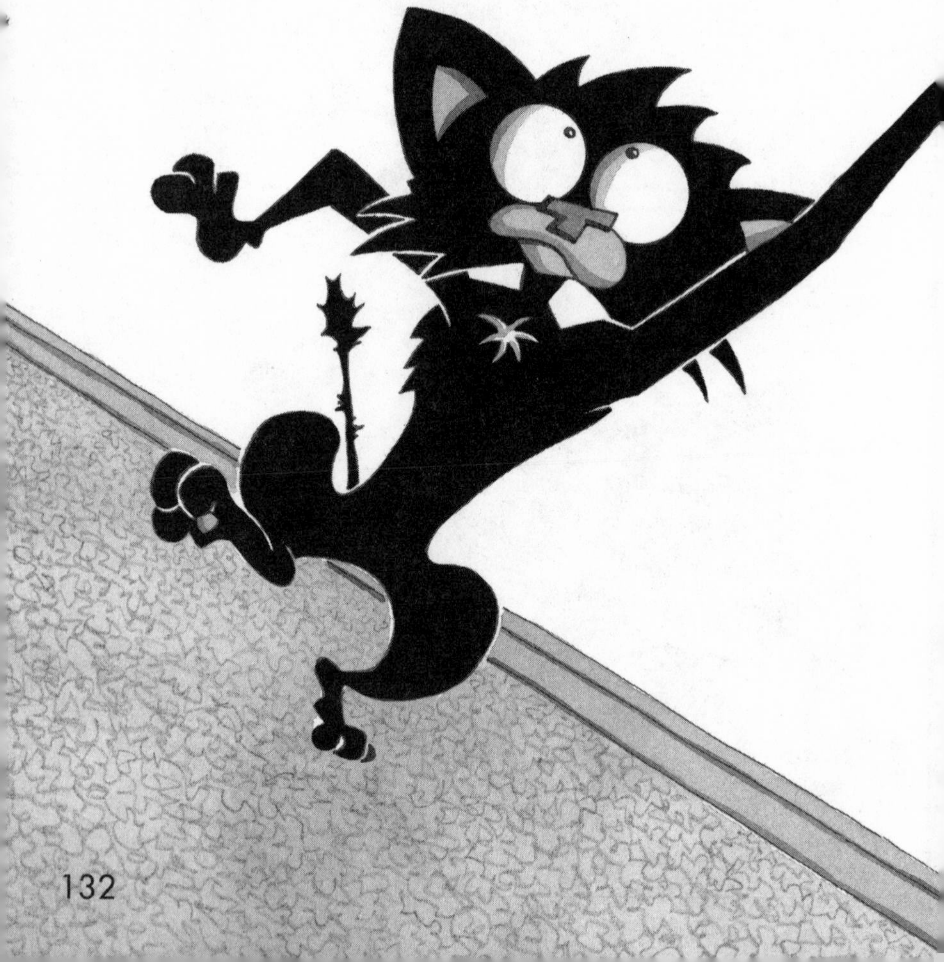

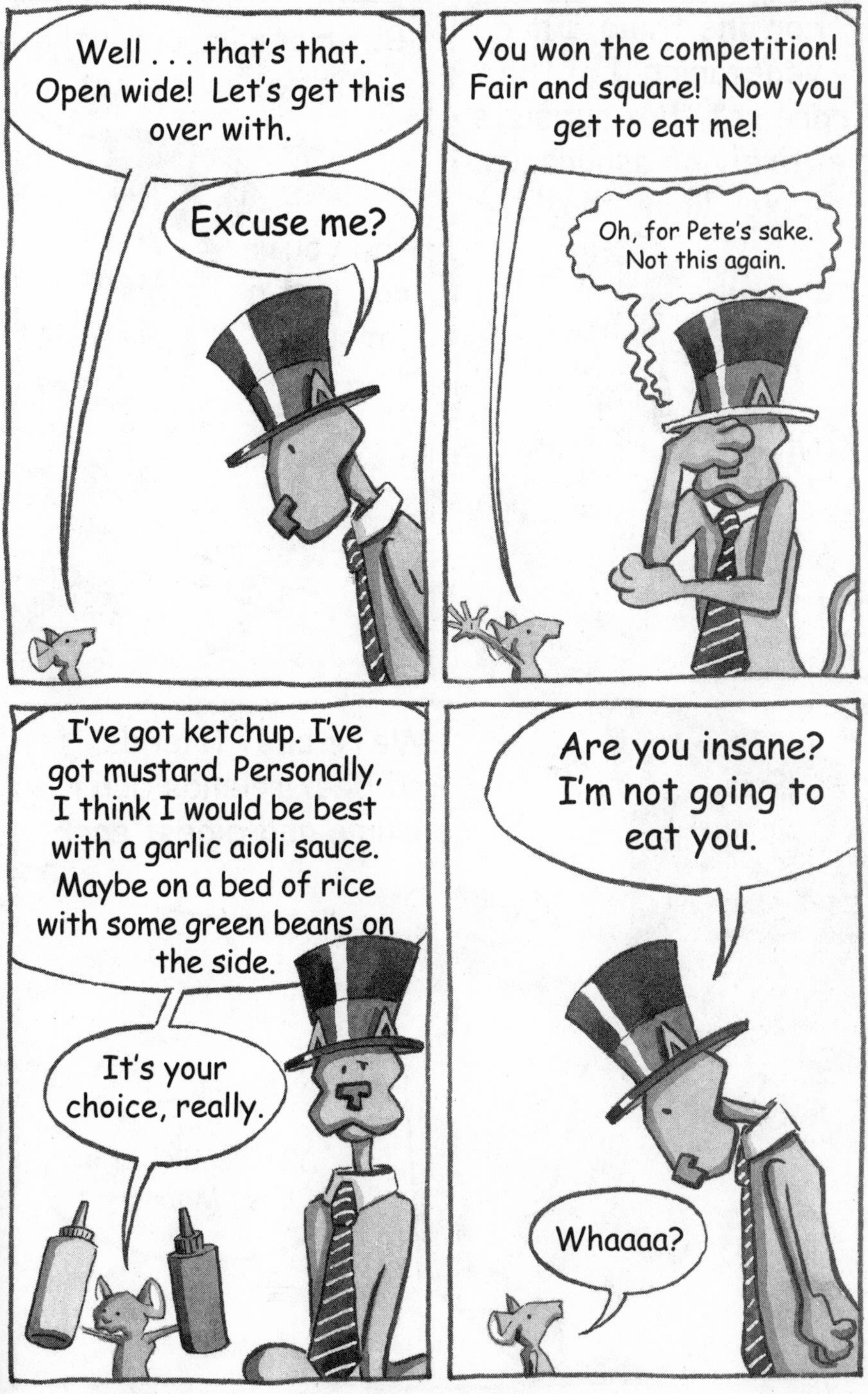
Well . . . that's that. Open wide! Let's get this over with.
Excuse me?
You won the competition! Fair and square! Now you get to eat me!
Oh, for Pete's sake. Not this again.
I've got ketchup. I've got mustard. Personally, I think I would be best with a garlic aioli sauce. Maybe on a bed of rice with some green beans on the side.
It's your choice, really.
Are you insane? I'm not going to eat you.
Whaaaa?

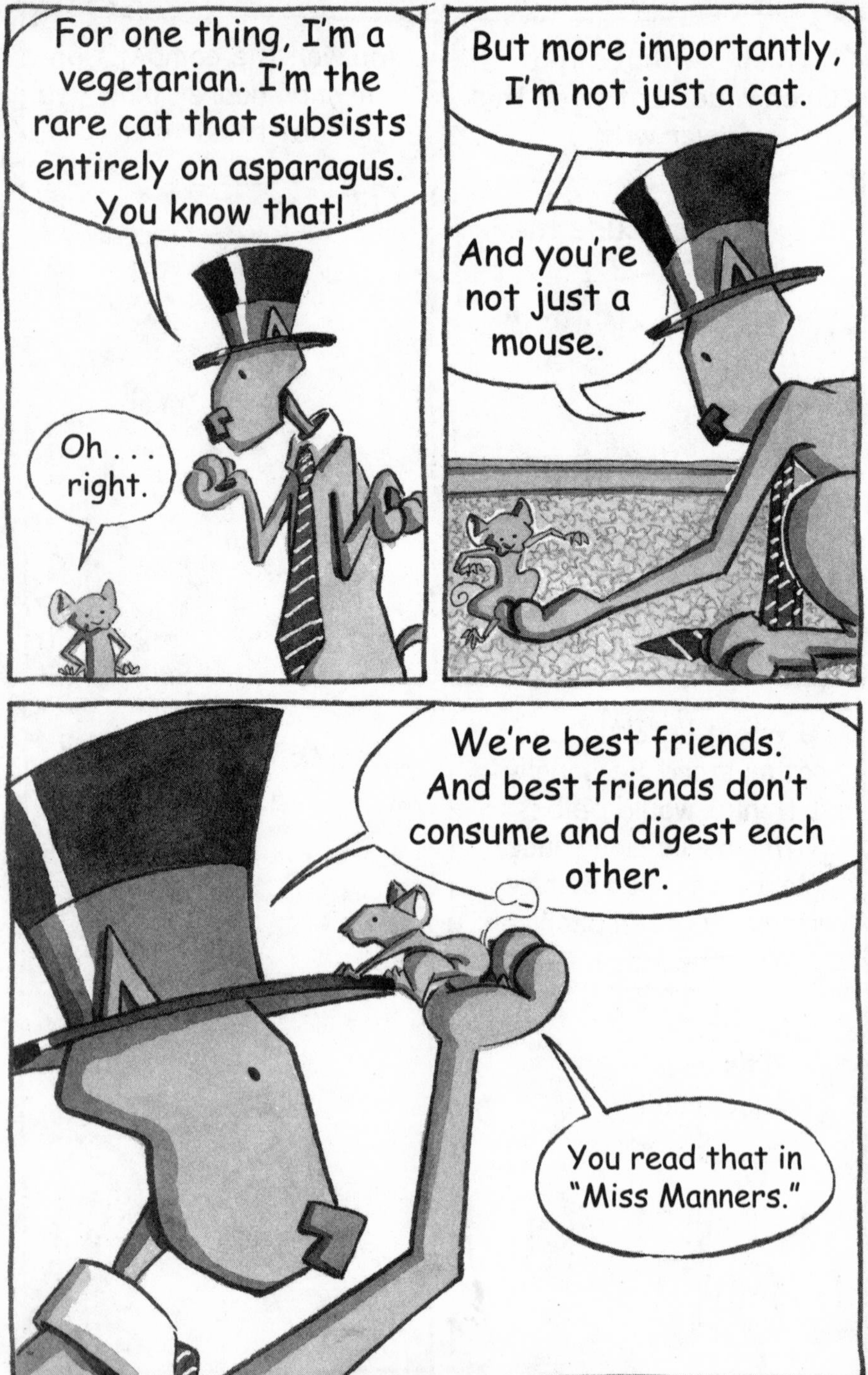
For one thing, I'm a vegetarian. I'm the rare cat that subsists entirely on asparagus. You know that!
Oh . . . right.
But more importantly, I'm not just a cat.
And you're not just a mouse.
We're best friends. And best friends don't consume and digest each other.
You read that in "Miss Manners."

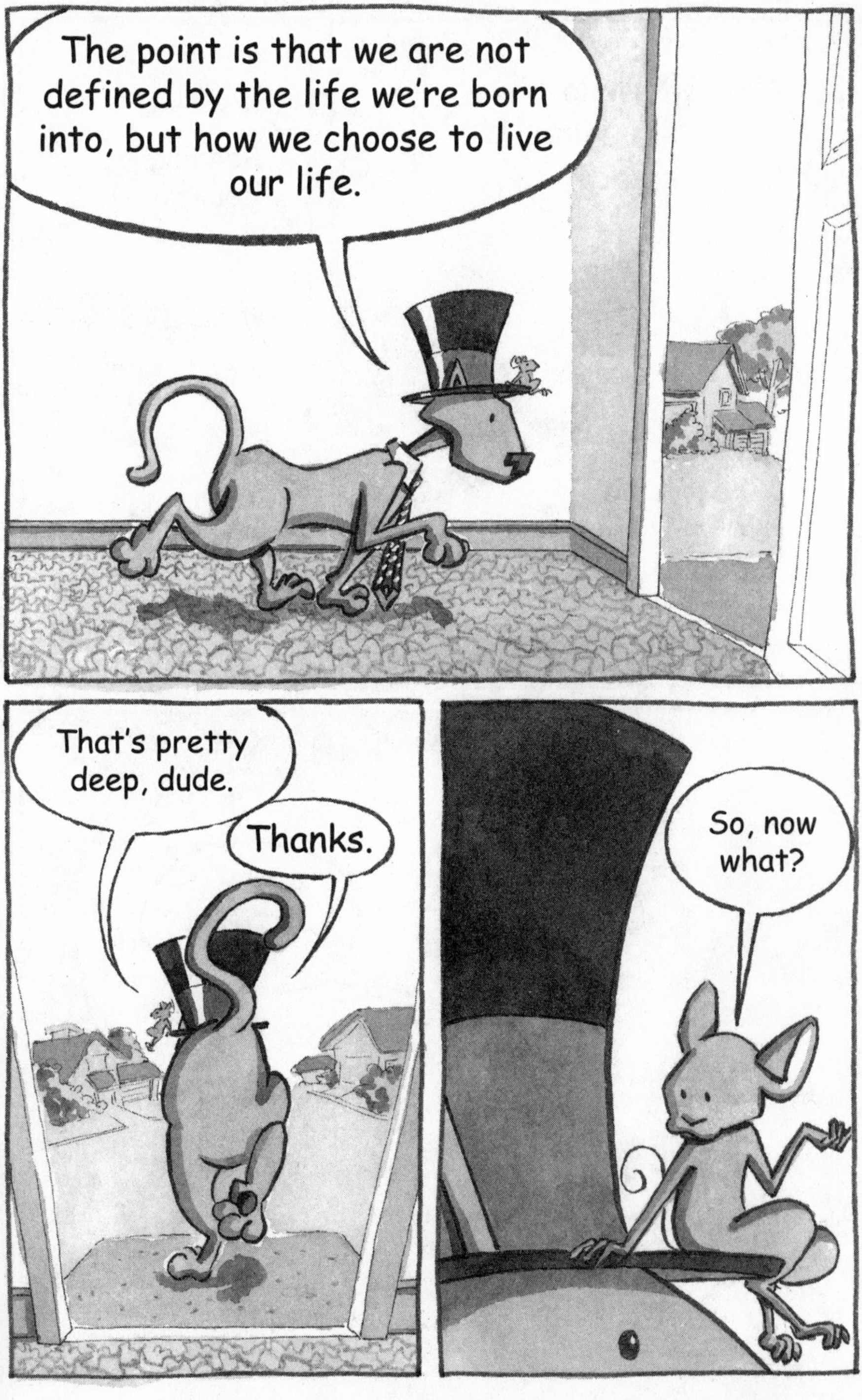
The point is that we are not defined by the life we're born into, but how we choose to live our life.
That's pretty deep, dude.
Thanks.
So, now what?

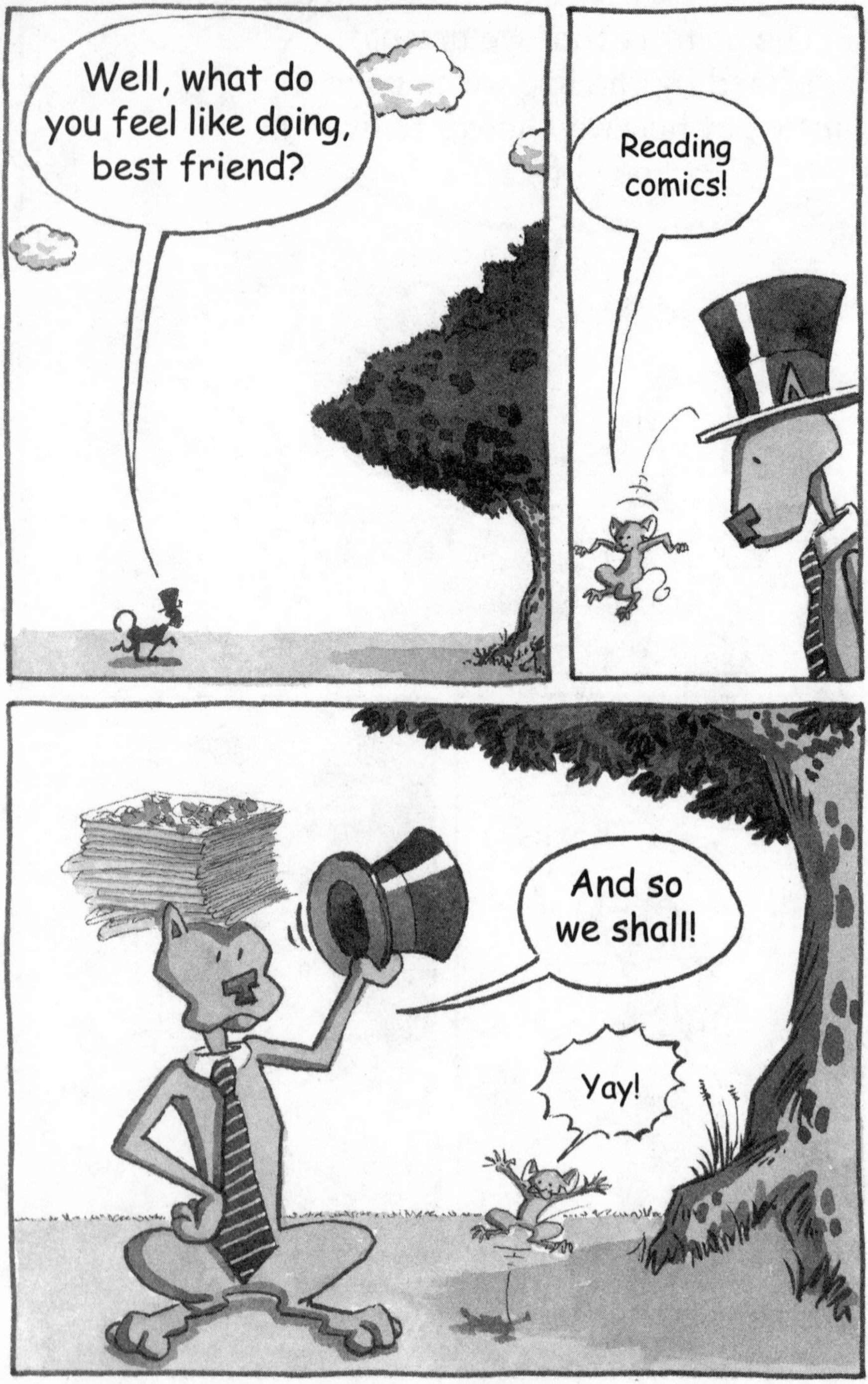
Well, what do you feel like doing, best friend?
Reading comics!
And so we shall!
Yay!

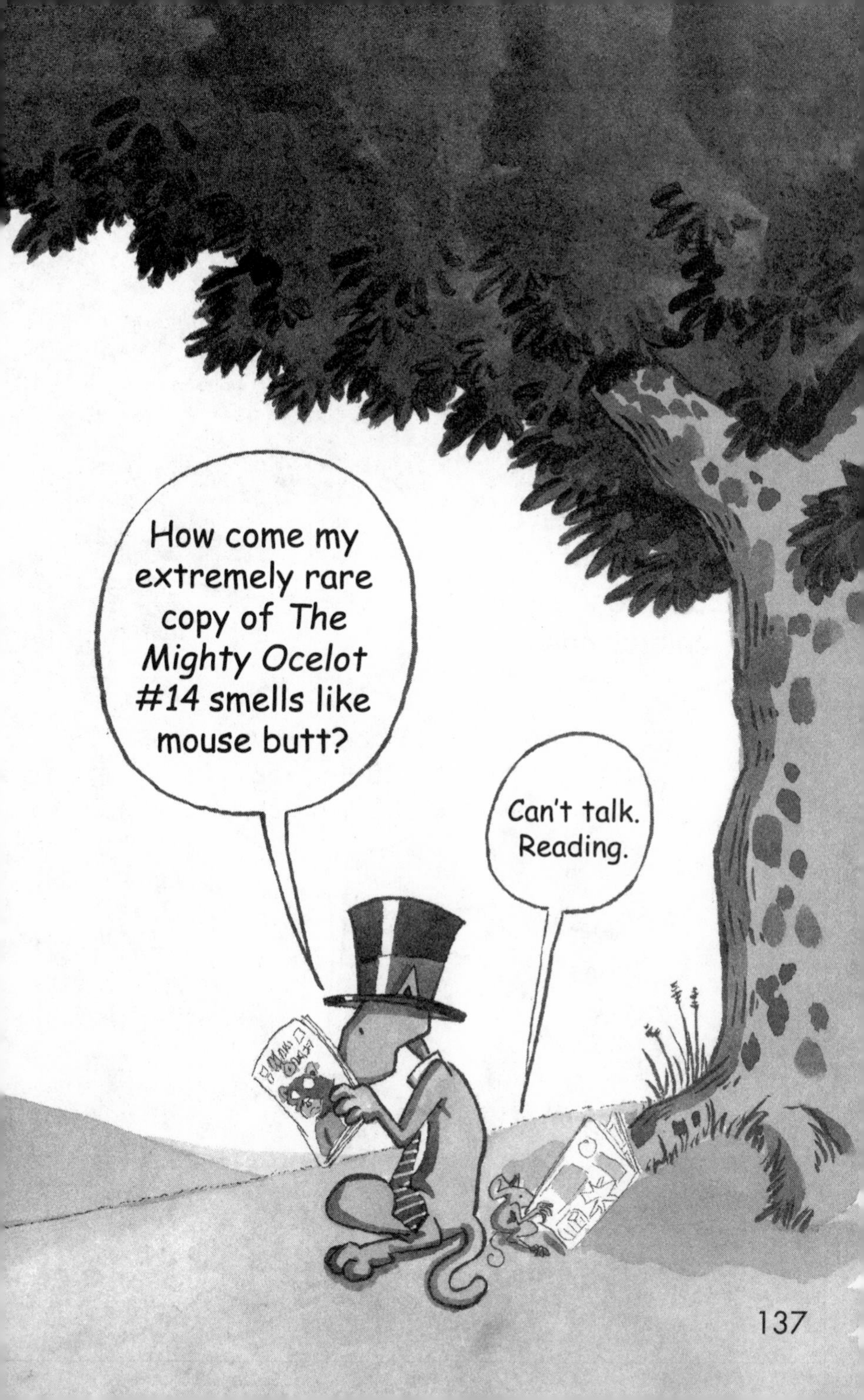
How come my extremely rare copy of *The Mighty Ocelot #14* smells like mouse butt?
Can't talk. Reading.

• CHAPTER NINE •

FOUR AND A HALF HOURS LATER

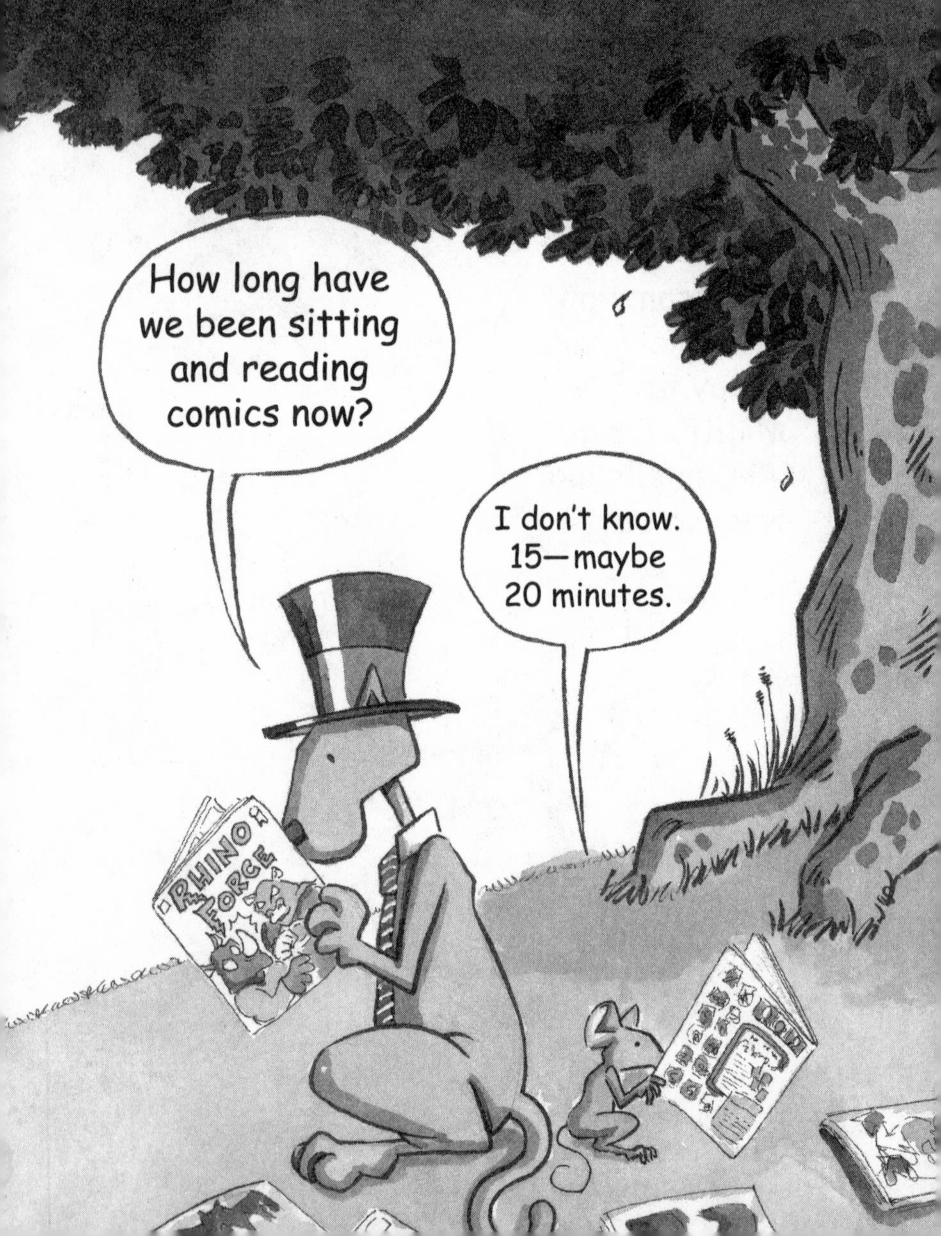
How long have we been sitting and reading comics now?
I don't know. 15—maybe 20 minutes.
RHINO FORCE

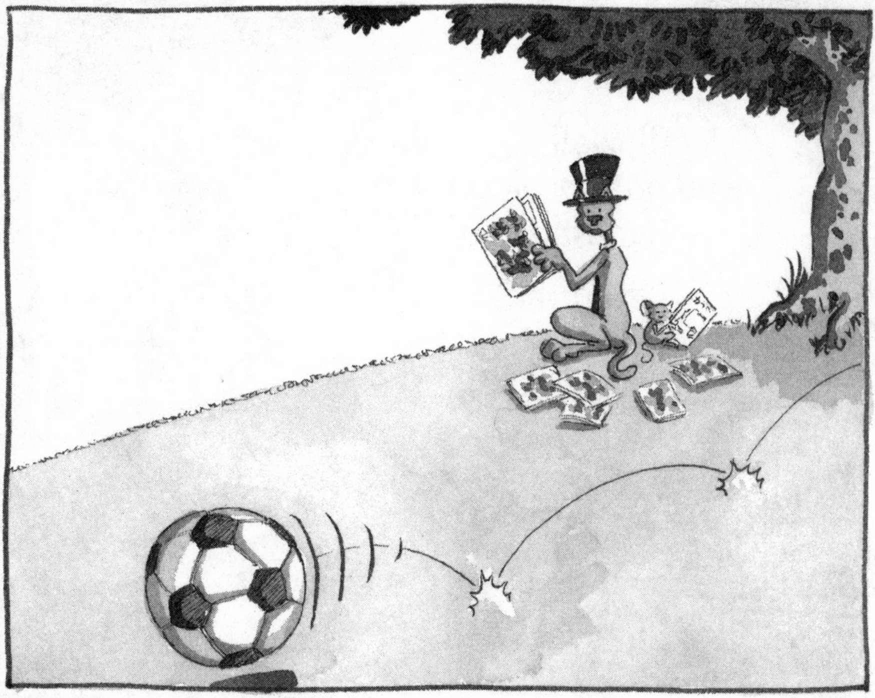

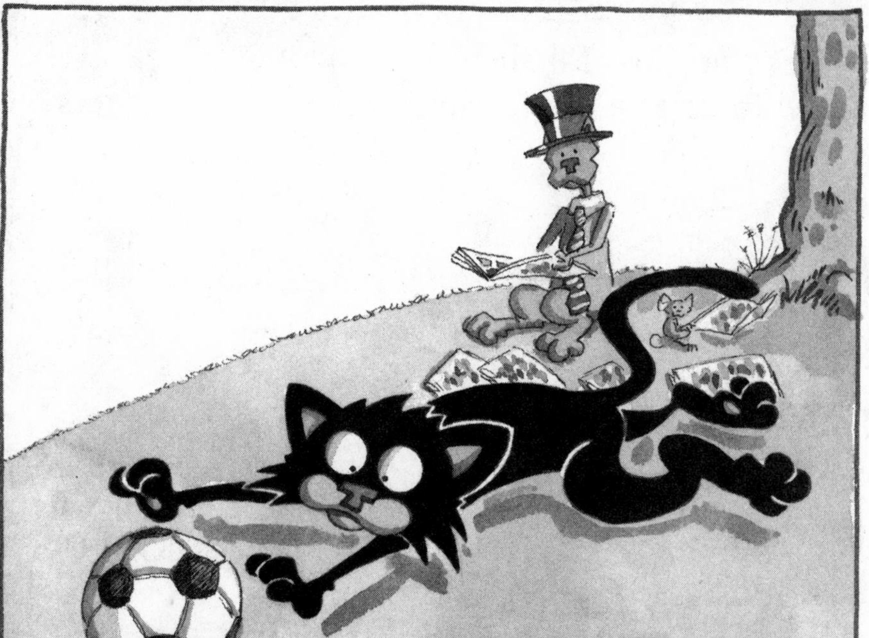

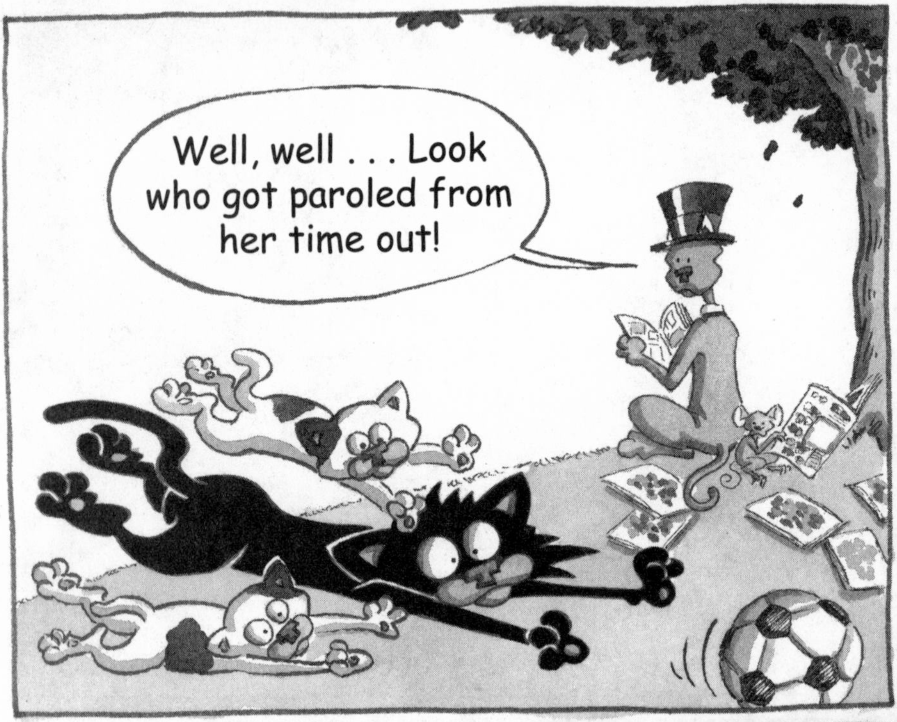
Well, well . . . Look who got paroled from her time out!

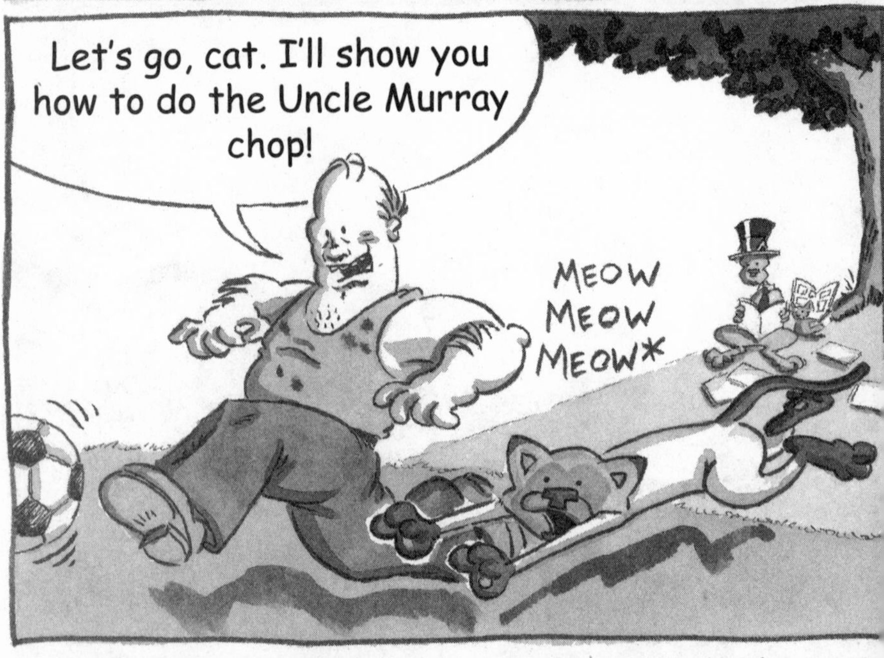
Let's go, cat. I'll show you how to do the Uncle Murray chop!
MEOW
MEOW
MEOW*

* In England, soccer is called "football." In Italy, it's "calcio." And in Slovenia, it's "nogomet."

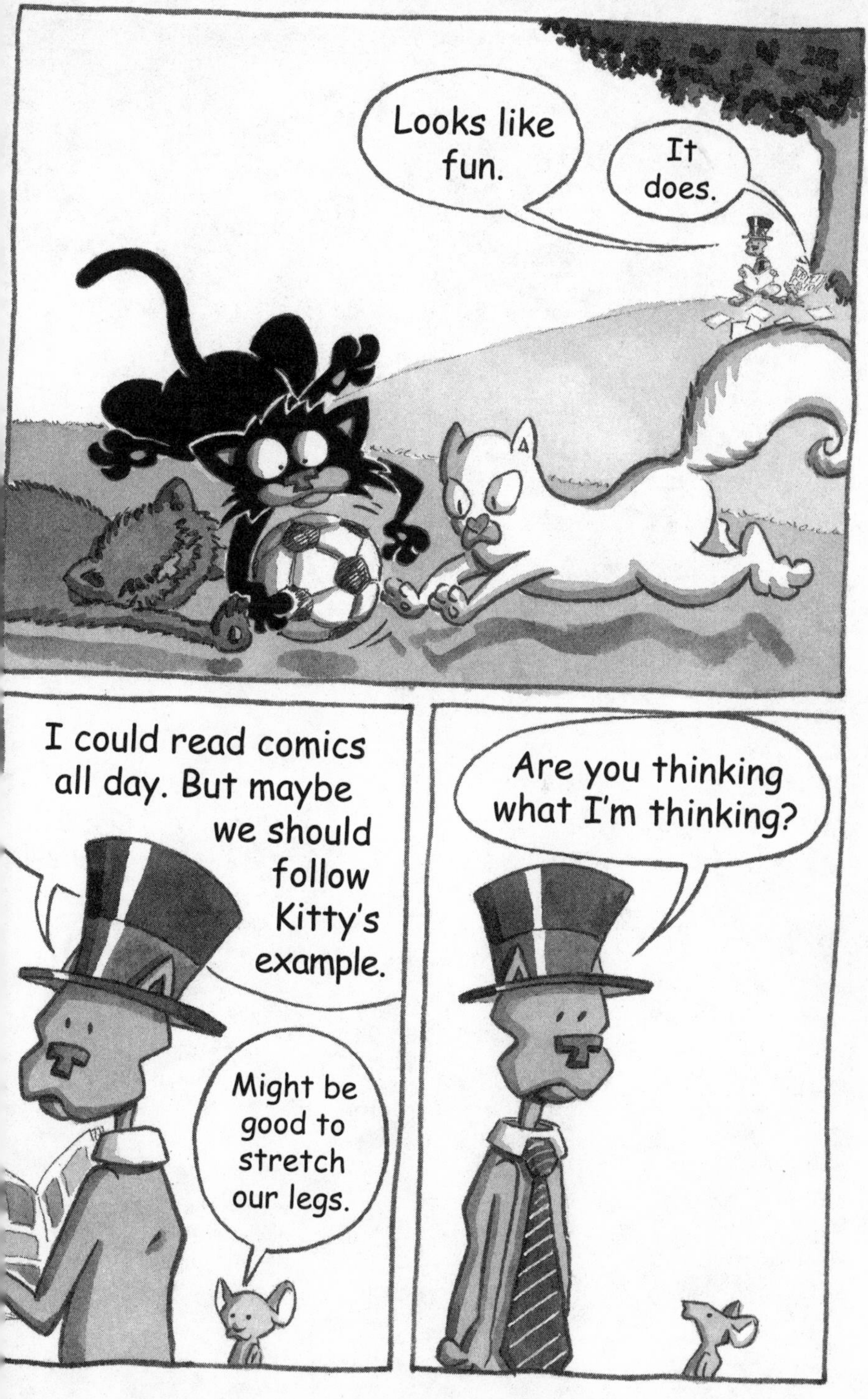
Looks like fun.
It does.
I could read comics all day. But maybe we should follow Kitty's example.
Might be good to stretch our legs.
Are you thinking what I'm thinking?

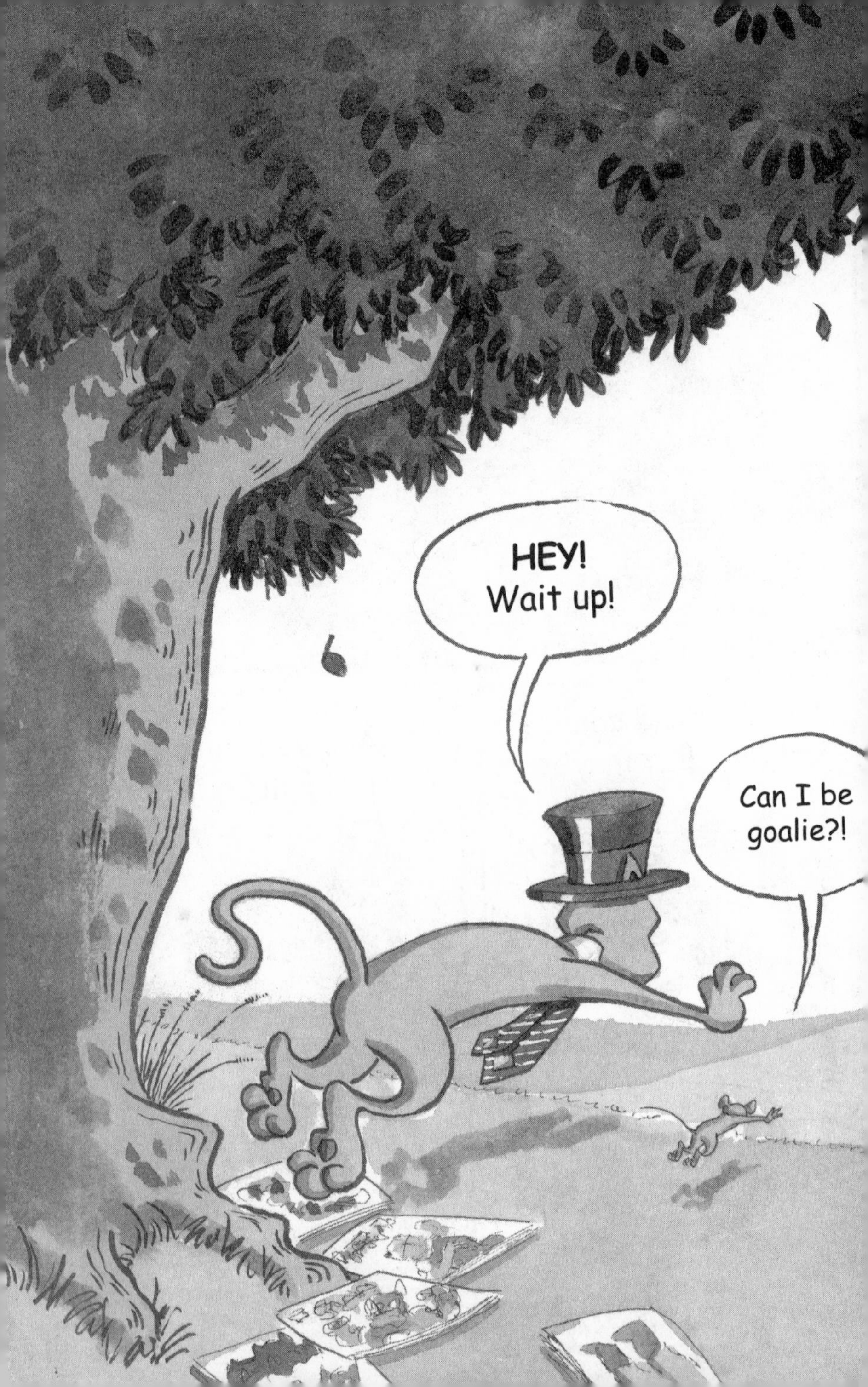
HEY! Wait up!
Can I be goalie?!

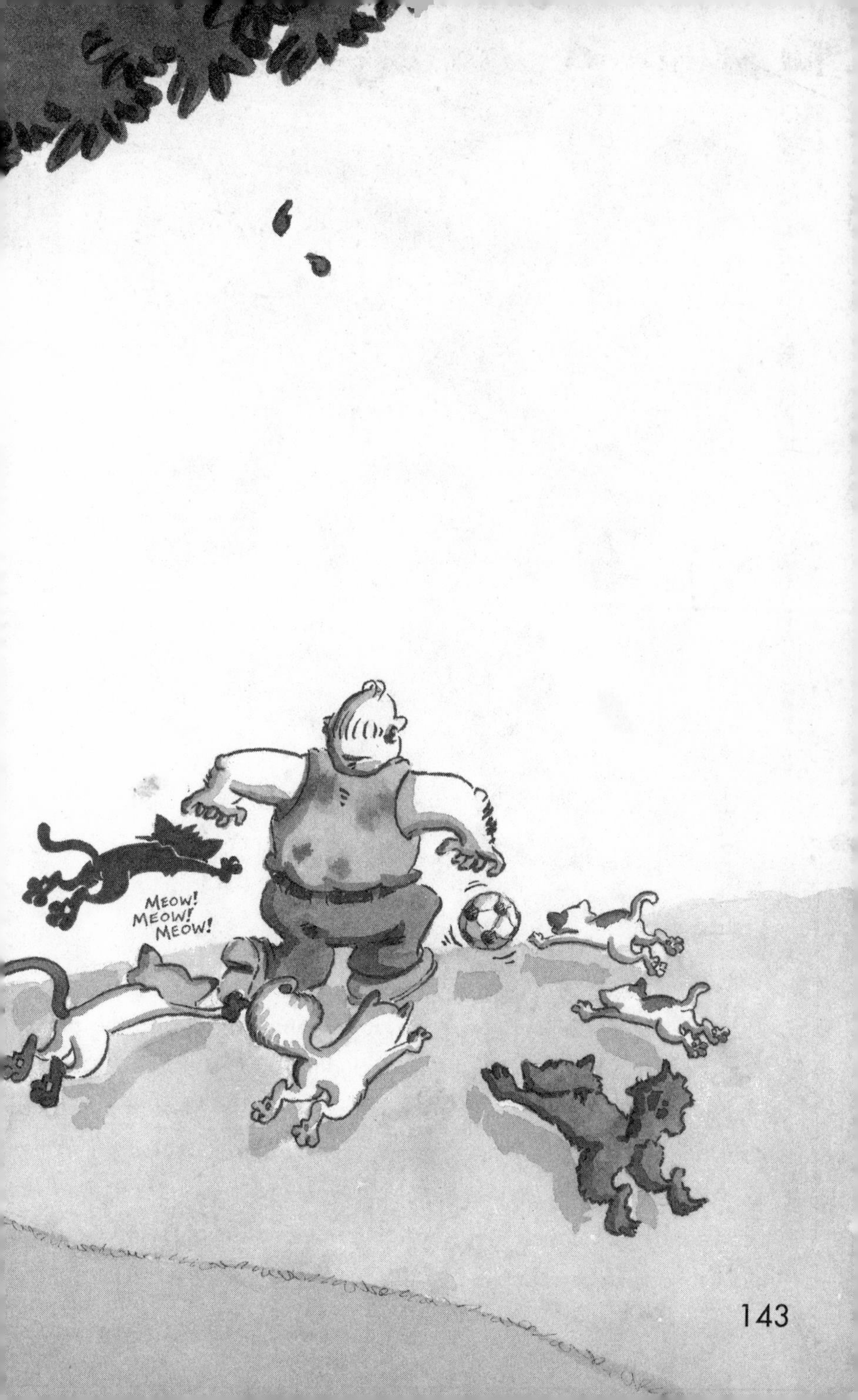
MEOW!
MEOW!
MEOW!

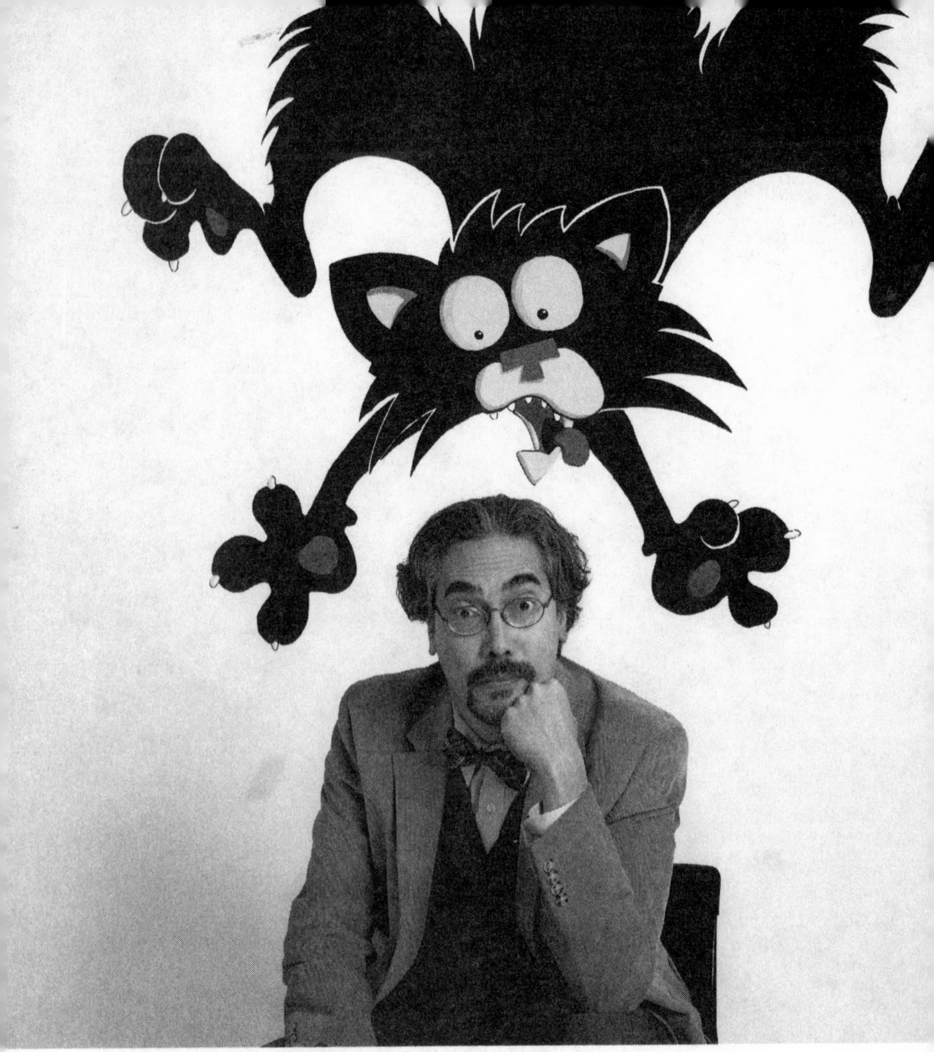

NICK BRUEL is the author and illustrator of the phenom-enally successful Bad Kitty series, including the 2012 and 2013 CB Children's Choice Book Award winners *Bad Kitty Meets the Baby* an *Bad Kitty for President*. Nick has also written and illustrated popular pi ture books including *A Wonderful Year* and his most recent, *Bad Kitt Searching for Santa*. Nick lives with his wife and daughter in Westcheste New York. **nickbruel.com**